# EMPRESS OF ROME

a novel

by

# Robert DeMaria

The Vineyard Press
Port Jefferson, NY

Copyright by Robert DeMaria, 2001
Originally published by
Jove/HBJ 1978

Vineyard Press Edition
Vineyard Press, Ltd.
106 Vineyard Place
Port Jefferson, NY 11777
ISBN: 1-930067-05-4
Library of Congress Catalog
Card Number: 2001 126340

# THE

# EMPRESS

*to Amanda*

# PART ONE

# I

Baiae. Pleasure resort for the Roman aristocracy on the Campanian coast, that lush sweep of land that cupped the Bay of Naples. From Misenum in the north to the island of Capreae in the south the shore was an almost unbroken series of maritime villas. Beyond these villas the volcanic plains produced rich crops of vegetables, fruits, olives, and roses. Vesuvius breathed quietly, a sleeping giant between Herculaneum and Pompeii.

In her villa by Lake Lucrine, Agrippina emerged from the outdoor pool, a nude, statuesque figure of a woman with sqaure shoulders and abundant bosom. She moved with the grace of an athlete and the confidence inspired by her noble breeding. Water trickled from her white skin. An autumn breeze raised a chill of gooseflesh on her arms and combined with the cool water to make the nipples of her breasts erect. Her slave Myia stood by to receive her into her saffron robe. She was taller than Myia, taller, in fact, than most women. Her body was a perfect blend of beauty and strength. And her face was all gorgeous arrogance: strong chin; delicate, symmetrical bone struc-

7

ture; passionate mouth, revealing discipline and appetite; elegant nose, and large, intelligent eyes, combining the weapons of Mars and Venus. She was not a woman to be trifled with either in love or war.

Waiting for her in the portico beyond the fluted columns was Cleon, her benign eunuch, and Europa, her intimate handmaiden, a dark-haired mature woman full of affectionate obedience. Agrippina stood for a moment beside the marble table and looked back toward the sea. A narrow strip of land separated the sea and the lake. The three-sided portico enclosed the pool, which was the centerpiece of a meticulous garden, an embroidery of flowers and shrubs, soothing fountains, and small statues in the Greek fashion. The fourth side was open to the bay and looked out across an expanse of blue water toward the port of Puteoli. The gray rocks were decorated with patient cypress trees and pines that meditated in the Mediterranean sun. It was a view that never ceased to fascinate her. Summer lingered here into the fall and early winter, extending the dreams of pleasure and peace.

Potted plants and birdcages adorned the interior of the portico. In his blue-fringed tunic the soft-skinned Cleon waited to massage her body with olive oil and perfumes from the exotic East. She allowed Myia to remove her robe, and she touched her tightly curled and braided blonde hair before stretching herself out on the marble slab with a feline sigh of exhilaration.

Europa rubbed Agrippina's body dry. Then she took up the copper pitcher of oil and poured some along the spine of her mistress. Then Cleon's large pale hands worked the oil into her skin and muscles. He was practiced in this art and could release the tension in even the most hysterically contracted body. He was tall and fleshy, with a round, effeminate face, a man of forty or so, who looked like an overgrown boy. In his earlier years he had been the slave of Agrippina's mother, before she died a political exile on the island of Pandateria in the Tyrrhenian Sea.

"Fetch the boy Alfius and his lute," said Agrippina. She was looking at Myia through eyes half closed with satisfaction. "And Alexis and Myron."

8

Myia went into the house—more mansion than house, befitting a direct descendent of the Divine Augustus and the daughter of Germanicus. Agrippina closed her eyes and felt the long fingers of the eunuch sliding up her back and over her shoulders, then down again along her sides to her narrow waist and the roundness of her hips. She remembered the hands of a young lover she once had at Antium, where she had another villa, considerably more lavish than this one. He was lean and strong, but with poet's eyes, pale blue, like deep pools of water, in which shimmered the mysteries of the bottom of the sea.

She opened her eyes to the sound of music. The pretty boy Alfius was seated on the steps, leaning against a column. His delicate fingers caressed the strings of the lute, and after a few minutes, he began to sing with a wistful whisper of a voice that might have been wafted across the world from the shores of the Aegean Sea.

The arrival of Alexis and Myron was an intrusion of business into a dream of passion. The former was a wiry, aging secretary, diminutive and quick, with the blinking eyes of a nervous bird and the lisping speech of a homosexual. Long and faithful service had earned him his freedman status. And an outright gift from Agrippina of 100,000 sesterces had guaranteed him a comfortable old age, complete with the little entourage of boys that all his life he had dreamed of.

Myron, still a slave, was the portly commander of the kitchens. The immensity of his belly was sufficient evidence that he loved his work. He hesitated when he saw his mistress stretched out nude in the shaded porch, but she motioned him toward her. "Come on, come on, Myron, you fat fool. Have you never seen a naked woman before?"

He came forward, reasonably composed. His vast white apron was a map of blood. His small eyes kept drifting away from Agrippina's body to the group of triremes that had just appeared on the horizon—naval ships from Misenum. He assumed a permanent semibow and awaited instructions.

Agrippina lifted herself slightly and leaned her chin against her folded hands. Cleon and Europa concentrated

9

on her legs. "Tell me what you are planning for my guests tonight. Something a little special, I hope."

"I think the menu will be very suitable," said Myron. "First the *gustatio*: Hors d'oeuvres and salad and—very special—Lucrine oysters with fish sauce and honeyed wine. Compliments of old Valusius. He sent them over this morning."

"Of course," said Agrippina. "In a day or two he'll be looking for a favor. You wait and see."

"Then the *fercula*: lampreys and turbot. Peacock, pheasant, and partridge. And my favorite—roast boar. And, just for a little excitement, wild hare with an excellent new recipe that I have from a good friend of mine, whom I met the other day, by sheer chance, on the Via Antiniana, on my way to Naples."

"Never mind the digressions," she said. "Get on with the menu."

"Sorry!" he said. "So much for the *fercula*. Then we have the *mensae secundae*: the usual pastry, sweetmeats, and dried fruit. And, of course, the wines. The very best: Setine, Caecuban, Falernian, and Alban."

"Very good!" she said. She waved him away and turned her attention to Alexis.

The perfume that Europa poured, drop by drop, into the cupped hands of the eunuch was carried on the gentle breeze onto the porch. Agrippina paused to breathe it in. Alexis waited impatiently, arranging papers on a small wooden table and dipping his reed pen into the inkpot to check its point. "Now," she said, "Where did we leave off before all those interruptions this morning?"

"You were about to send a message to Tiro, your caretaker at Antium," said Alexis. Familiarity and his own sexual predilections made him oblivious to her nudity and the sensual attentions of Cleon and Europa.

"Oh, yes. Tell him that I expect to be bored with this place within a fortnight and that he should have the house in good repair and ready for an indefinite stay. Tell him to make room in the north garden for a rather large statue of Aeneas and Anchises. Tell him to choose an inconspicuous place. It's a poor piece of work, but a gift that must be diplomatically displayed."

Alexis nodded. "Speaking of gifts, did you want to send something to the wife of Cornelius Scipio for her birthday?"

"Of course," she said. "A very sympathetic senator. He will be useful when the time comes. My freedman Mestor will take care of it, but he must be reminded. Tell him the lady likes silverware or Chinese silk, if it can be had."

He scratched rapidly with his pen and then paused. "We have this unfinished letter to your uncle. Did you want to reconsider it?"

"Yes. I've been thinking about it. One must be cautious with him these days. His wife Messalina is involved in everything. She has made our old intimacy impossible. And she will do anything to protect their son's claim to the principate. An outrageously predatory and willful young thing she is. And she winds old Claudius around her little finger. He must be almost sixty by now. He should know better than to have a wife who is only twenty-five. But one day she will go too far. And when she does, we must be ready to—" She stopped herself.

"Shall I destroy the letter, then?"

She hesitated. "No! Just recast it. Leave out everything except the part about the horses. Address him with a term of endearment. Tell him that I have seen Tigellinus at Naples, where he has received a fine shipment of race horses from Sicily—an excellent mixture of the Sicilian and Libyan, very graceful and very fast. Tell him that Tigellinus has agreed to send to him the best team for his chariot races, and that he expects nothing in return but the good will of the emperor."

She let her head relax onto her forearm and sank back into the pleasures of her massage. "Is that all?" asked Alexis.

She made an affirmative murmur, and he quickly picked up his papers and implements and walked down the long gallery and then into the house.

Europa wrung out a large cloth in hot water and then held it ready beside Agrippina. Cleon urged her gently, and

11

she turned, revealing the fullness of her breasts. Europa dropped the cloth across Agrippina's upper thighs, covering her pubic hair and the base of her white belly. "Mmm," sighed Agrippina. "What a lovely sensation." She spread her legs and allowed herself to be washed thoroughly. She made no effort to conceal her enjoyment of this intimate part of the massage. In fact, she had made it clear in the past that she wanted the most meticulous attention paid to this part of her body, especially when she was in the mood for making love.

Cleon oiled her shoulders and breasts, which grew firm at his touch. She opened her eyes a fraction and looked up at the eunuch. "Ah, what a pity you're not a real man," she said, her whisper echoing the dreamy stretch of sea.

"If I were, would I be here?" he said with a girlish smile.

"I mean, to feel the things that men feel when they touch a woman's body."

"I have feelings of my own, madam," he said. "I envy no one."

"Ah, but you would, if only you knew. That marvelous surge of blood. That animal desire. That driving and thrusting." She heaved her hips and brought a blush to Cleon's soft, round face. She laughed and sat up. "Oh, you poor thing. Have I embarrassed you?" Europa and Myia joined in the laughter. They were a little league of women in their humor, and the joke was on Cleon. He said nothing. "If I could, I would give you back your manhood for just one wild night, so that, at least, you would not die wondering. But in lieu of that I will give you fifty sesterces and a day of freedom to find your kind of pleasures in the markets of Puteoli or Naples."

Cleon's face broke into a broad smile. "Thank you! Thank you, madam. It's more than I deserve."

She waved him away and he scurried off in slippered feet, as graceful as a Syrian dancer.

"And you, Europa, what shall I give you for all your years of love and loyalty? Would you like a husband? You really should have a man, you know."

Europa blushed. She was sturdy and plain. "No, thank

you, madam," she said. "I'm done with all that. I'm quite happy with things as they are."

"Ah, sweet Europa, how I wish I could say that. But things as they are have not been very happy for me. How much easier it is to be a slave than the daughter of kings."

"But things will change," said Europa. "They always do."

"Only if you make them change," said Agrippina. "And when that wretched girl who calls herself the emperor's wife over reaches herself, as she will—well, then we'll see. I'll make a destiny for my son and me that will outfox an ordinary fate."

"Shall we do your hair?" asked Myia.

"No," she said. "Send for Tigellinus. And leave us alone in the garden a while. She stood up and waited for her saffron robe.

When Tigellinus arrived, she was seated in the sun in a small alcove formed by high hedges. The tiled terrace overlooked the pool. And the stone balustrade was decorated with the spouting statuettes of naked nymphs.

"Ah, there you are," he said, striding toward her. He was a tall and handsome man, but not pretty. Very dark and masculine. The shadow of his beard gave a boney angularity to his face and made his perfect teeth seem startlingly white between his full, expressive lips. He was a notorious Sicilian horsebreeder of questionable birth who, through sheer bravado, had intruded himself into some of the best circles in Rome, only to be exiled for his adulterous relationship with Agrippina some ten years earlier. Gossip-mongers at the time attributed his exile to the jealousy of Caligula. The mad emperor, they said, had an unnatural attachment to all three of his sisters—Drusilla, Julia Livilla, and Agrippina.

"Look at you," Agrippina said. "You're filthy. What have you been up to?"

He looked down at his soiled cloak and linen tunic. Marks of perspiration streaked his bronze face. And splattered mud had dried to dust from his sandals to his knees. "I've been up to Cumae to look at a brood mare."

13

"You look like the unsuccessful stud."

He flashed his brilliant teeth. "You know me better than that."

"You arrogant bandit. What was it this time?"

"Well, I ran into Lucius Varius. It was his brood mare, in fact, that I was looking at. Good blood. Very good blood. But a bit over the hill at twelve. I had my Invictus in mind for her. In any case, we had a bit of wine, and before I knew it, he was boasting about a horse of his that could take mine over the short course. You know how I am about such things."

"All too well," she said.

"So there and then we made the wager and ran the race. Two out of three sprints." He paused.

"And?"

"And what?"

"And who won?" she asked impatiently.

"Need you ask? I beat him flat out, the first two heats. To the tune of ten thousand sesterces. Not a bad day's work."

"You would have been better off losing."

"What do you mean?"

"If I've told you once, I've told you a thousand times, you brainless animal. You have been restored to a degree of respectability through the good offices of my uncle Claudius, on the condition that you live an ordinary and inconspicuous life. You cannot afford to attract any attention. Do you understand? Lucius Varius is a hot-tempered man, corrupt to the eyes. He's also an ex-consul, a senator, and still influential. He could ruin you."

Smiling, he shared the marble bench with her. "It's nice to know you care."

"I care about you the way you care about your horse Invictus. You're a good stud. Now go and bathe yourself and sweeten your mouth."

He stood at attention in a mockery of submission and then dropped to one knee before her. "Your wish, my goddess, is my command," he said. And then he ran like a maniac toward the placid pool and plunged in, fully

14

clothed. He stripped away his clothes as he swam, and then floated, naked, on his back and spouted like a whale. Agrippina was forced to smile. Her flesh was still alive with the stimulation of her massage, and her anger melted in the furnace of her desire for this undisciplined brute.

She walked to the edge of the pool and watched him swim. "Come in, my love," he shouted. "I dare you!"

"I'll give you a dare," she said. "For that ten thousand sesterces you won, I'll race you the length of the pool and back." She undid her saffron robe and let it fall. She stood there gleaming and naked in the sharp sunlight.

"Not my favorite form of combat," he said, "but you know I can't resist a challenge." He was below her at the edge of the pool, his face illuminated by his savage smile. With a swift motion he splashed her and made her shriek like a girl. And then she was arching over him in a perfect dive and did not emerge until she had gone the whole length of the pool under water.

When he saw where she was, he pursued her, churning up the water with reckless strokes. He arrived gasping and laughing.

"All right," she said, "two lengths of the pool for ten thousand sesterces. Are you ready?"

"I'm always ready," he said, trying to pin her amorously against the side of the pool.

"Good!" she said, slipping away. "Then go!" And she was off, leaving him several yards behind at the very start.

"Hey!" he spluttered in her wake, and took off after her with powerful but undisciplined strokes.

As she moved gracefully through the water, she could feel him gaining on her. She wasted no motion. Her strong shoulders pulled her forward, and the quick and perfect rhythm of her legs was an athletic ballet. When they touched the rim of the pool for the first time, he had nearly closed the gap, and she caught a glimpse of his face and his look of fierce determination. He could not let her win, but she could see in that instant that he was already beaten. She drew away, breathing easily, feeling the water rush past her face. As he grew weaker, she grew stronger, and the

15

thrill of her victory was a wild sensation like slow lightning from her thighs to her breast.

When they returned to the alcove, dripping wet and laughing, she allowed him to take her, there and then, without a word, on the cool Arabian tiles.

## II

In Baiae, at the imperial villa, the emperor's daughter Antonia stared out to sea and along the coast toward Lake Lucrine. Beautiful Antonia, the dark-haired, dark-eyed light of her father's life. If old Claudius loved anyone at all in this world, the gossipers said, he loved this daughter of his, the wife of Faustus Cornelius Sulla, a young man handsome and noble enough to deserve her. They were a splendid couple, an imperial couple, universally admired, and sometimes even discussed as heirs to the empire, though the emperor had a son to consider, a lad of nine named Britannicus. His mother was Messalina, the emperor's third wife. Antonia's mother was Aelia Paetina, Claudius's second wife.

On the main terrace of the imperial villa, Antonia and her husband Sulla watched the sky deepen into a silken blue over a sea as seductive as the Siren songs that called to the sailors of Odysseus. There was magic in this bay and mystery in the vast sea beyond. And there was danger in the brooding volcano of Vesuvius. According to an old legend, the Sirens who failed to lure Odysseus and his men

17

to destruction drowned themselves. The body of one of them washed up on these shores. Her name was Parthenope, from whence derived the ancient name of the Bay of Naples, a name still used in poetry and the old songs sung by the local fishermen.

"It's such a calm night," said Antonia, "that you can hear voices from all the villas from Bauli to Puteoli."

"It's a festive evening," said Sulla. "The last of the season. We'll all be back in Rome before long."

"Yes," said Antonia, "the days are getting shorter."

"Perhaps we should have accepted Agrippina's invitation," he said. "She has a reputation for giving interesting dinner parties."

Antonia stood up and walked to the stone balustrade, her arms folded firmly across her breasts. "No!" she said. "We cannot play that treacherous woman's game. We cannot allow ourselves to be used by her."

"But you need not fear her," he said. "She has spent time in exile. She has many enemies. Messalina hates her. And she has no husband. All she has is her wealth. But that, I must admit, is substantial."

"She has a son," said Antonia. "Nero!"

"He's only twelve years old."

"But in that boy's veins flows the purest blend of Julian and Claudian blood of anyone alive, including my father. Do you think for a moment that a woman like Agrippina will rest until she's made an emperor of that boy?"

"Impossible!" said Sulla. "What about Britannicus? What about you and me?"

"Our claims would not seem so impressive as Nero's, if my father were not the emperor."

"Ah, but he is."

"Yes, but he's getting old. And he refuses to name a successor. He doesn't want to talk about death. And his thoughts are a bit distracted."

Sulla came up to her and put his arms around her waist. "You're making too much of all this," he said. "It was only a dinner invitation."

She turned in his arms and faced him, drawing away to look into his eyes. "You loveable man! Don't you under-

18

stand what she wants? She wants to insinuate herself into our family. Claudius is her uncle. I am her cousin. She will take her support wherever she can find it. She lurks here at Baiae, biding her time, buying influence, seducing men who might fit into her plans. Well, I for one do not want to fit into her plans."

A woman appeared in the doorway, catching in her face the deep glow of the dying light. She was poised and neatly proportioned, an attractive middle-aged woman. She was Aelia Paetina, the emperor's former wife and the mother of Antonia. "Well," she said, "what's this all about? A little domestic argument?"

"No, Mother," said Antonia. "We were talking about Agrippina."

"I should have guessed. Why does no one ever talk about that woman in a normal tone of voice?"

"Because she provokes people," said Antonia. "And she seduces them. And she lies to them. And she stabs them in the back. She is a fantastic animal, a tigress, a wolverine."

"Now, now, Antonia, don't get carried away," said her mother. "We all know the lady is ambitious and her past has been questionable, but she is, after all, only a woman. She has her desires and limitations. And she is vulnerable. She can be contained."

"Don't underestimate her, mother. I sometimes even wonder if she *is* a woman. She may well be some kind of monstrous visitation on the world."

Aelia Paetina laughed. "You're so dramatic, my dear. If you were a man, you would have made a marvelous orator."

"If I were a man, I would be the next emperor of Rome. And my first official act would be to banish that woman to the bleakest corner of the empire."

There was a commotion inside the house. They looked through the archway and the double doors to see a man in riding clothes talking rapidly with two attendants. In another moment they were on the terrace, and they could see that the sweating messenger was a trusted slave of Claudius. He was a lean man of thirty with a determined face. The dust of his hard ride clung to his damp arms and legs.

19

"What is it? What's happened?" asked Antonia. Her hands gripped her husband's arm.

"I've been sent by Narcissus. He says you must go at once to your father, who is at Ostia."

"Why? What's happened to him?"

"Nothing, madam. I mean, he has suffered no illness or accident. But there has been some trouble in Rome. And there will be difficult days ahead. Narcissus, too, is going to Ostia to confer with the emperor."

"But what is it?" asked Antonia. "What could have happened?"

"I'm afraid I am not well informed, madam. But it seems that Messalina has done something. Something political. The city is full of rumors. There may be a conspiracy. Assassinations. Narcissus says that she must be brought to trial and that her punishment must be extreme."

"Is she in custody?" asked Antonia.

"No, she remains at large in Rome, but in what condition I do not know. I was sent away in such haste that all my news is confusion. But if you will come back to Ostia in the morning, you will find out what is happening."

"No," she said. "Not in the morning." The messenger looked puzzled. "I want to go immediately." She marched across the terrace. "There will be a sufficient moon tonight, and the sky is clear. It's a long trip, amd my father needs me."

"I will go with you," said Sulla.

She came to him and took his hand. "I too will ride back with you," said the slave.

"But you need food and rest," said Antonia.

He smiled. "I've been a soldier, madam, and have ridden many more miles than this on an empty stomach."

"Take some guardsmen with you," said Aelia Paetina. "The roads are dangerous at night."

20

# III

In the middle of the spacious dining room there was a square wooden table, decoratively carved around its outer rim with a sequence of scenes from a wedding celebration. On each of three sides of the table, there was a broad couch. Each couch accommodated three people in a comfortably reclining position. Half a dozen slaves in blue tunics waited on the guests. A group of five musicians provided subdued music. It was largely ignored in favor of some rather intense conversation.

Petronius had arrived from Rome only a few hours earlier, carrying with him on his swift ride the startling news about the emperor's wife. His account set every tongue at the table in motion simultaneously. At least as loud as anyone else's was the voice of Lollia Paulina. How pleased she seems to be by this disturbing news, thought Agrippina, eyeing the competition of her ex-sister-in-law. Lollia was a very fashionable lady, a season or two past thirty. She could easily afford to keep herself in the best of everything. Like Agrippina, she came from an excellent family. And like her hostess she was twice married, once to Caligula,

21

Agrippina's brother. She lost her husbands by divorce. Agrippina lost hers by death, a more profitable way of resolving things. Lollia had adopted the latest fad in hair styles—a great, complex, swept-up structure made of real and borrowed hair and decorated with small jewels. She chose to tint her hair blonde, which did not quite suit her. She was heavily painted—again, in the new style. Her eyebrows were plucked thin. Her heavy lids were shadowed. Her skin whitened and then rouged. Her lips, full and blood-red.

When Lollia had first arrived, Agrippina felt a small pang of jealousy at her theatrical appearance, but, on closer inspection, she decided that the poor woman had overdone it. In her desperation to be in the vanguard of fashion, she had overreached herself and come down on the side of vulgarity. Nevertheless, to many she would appear elegant and attractive, even if her weakness for food was beginning to show in her bosom and the hint of a second chin.

The news that Petronius brought from Rome excited Lollia because, having once been married to an emperor, she saw no reason in the world why she should not be considered a match for Claudius—that is, if anything unfortunate should happen to young Messalina. Lollia had already thought it through. She could even put up with his age, his vile habits, and his bad health.

Young Petronius, poet and hedonist, loved to talk. With his golden voice, his sharp wit, and perfect timing, he shared with the others at the table the incredible account of Messalina's ultimate outrage to common decency, morality, and religion. "I don't have to tell you what sort of a reputation Messalina has earned for herself." He affected the tone of a female gossip and drew a ripple of laughter from the guests and a hard smile from Agrippina. "And it's not just the old story of a young, beautiful wife bound to a doting, senile husband. There's more to it than that. She never had any trouble deceiving the old goat. Intelligent as he is, you know, the man is very absent-minded. We lost count of her lovers years ago. A very passionate lady. The great-grandaughter, after all, of Mark Antony. And there are those of us who would not condemn her for the simple amusements of the flesh, especially with an old husband who loses himself in the writing of ponderous histories. Nature herself propels us in these directions. And who are we to defy the laws of Nature? Her excesses were, in fact, rather charming—even a little bizarre. If I were not sworn to secrecy, I would tell you how, one spring, she took part in the rites of Cybele. And anybody who is anybody in Rome has heard that delicious tale of how she cavorted on the beaches of Bauli with the young officers of the Praetorian Guard. She's always been fond of the naked exercises. All that fine muscle and firm flesh. They say she spices her wine with aphrodisiacs. But I say she hardly needs them. Oh, a little poppy wine, from time to time, perhaps, to induce a dream or two.

"In any case, old Claudius apparently knew nothing about her adulterous games. As you know, he lives in a strange world all his own. Poor fellow! Stammering and stuttering and slobbering. No wonder he drinks himself into oblivion every night. Some say he turned his back, gave her license, so to speak. That would have been an act of high generosity on his part—and wisdom. I personally think dotage is a better explanation. And, besides, who would have had the courage to accuse his wife to his face, especially if the emperor did not want to hear those accusations. The lady, after all, gave him two rather attractive children, one of them a son and heir. It was more than he had a right to hope for, given his age and ugliness.

"Her current lover, as you may know, is Gaius Silius, a consul-elect. A handsome fellow and fashionably insane. He is about as discreet as a thunderstorm. He has talked openly about his love for Messalina and about his desire to marry her. And he has laughed at the blindness of Claudius, growing bolder and bolder in his rendezvous with his precious lady, to the delight and amazement of her whole circle. I must confess that we encouraged him in his amorous acrobatics—a cruel but exciting amusement. It gave us something to talk about, something to laugh about. And it made him feel like something of a hero. He would make love to her in the palace itself, in the corridors, the gardens, the baths. And once, it is rumored, in the emperor's bedroom, while the old man was snoring away his wine. What incredible bravado!

"Still, that wasn't enough for either of them. Driven by criminal recklessness they devised a scheme that, for sheer audacity, will never be matched. They waited until Claudius went off to Ostia to perform a routine sacrifice. While he was gone, they arranged a full-scale wedding ceremony. What in the world they hoped to accomplish by this is difficult to say. One speculation is that it really was part of a political conspiracy. Not only would Claudius be embarrassed, but he would be driven out of power. Perhaps the conspirators—quite a few in number—hoped to rally round them the popular support of the people and possibly the Senate and the Praetorian Guard. If so, it was an odd way to go about it. It was an immense ceremony, witnessed by hundreds of people, complete with gifts and all the rituals, and followed by a riotous celebration at the luxurious estate of Silius, into which Messalina moved, as though she were, indeed, a new bride. They organized a bacchanal. They pressed the grapes and overflowed the vats. Frenzied women in animal skins danced as in the ancient rituals. Silius roared drunkenly, crowned with ivy and wearing the buskin. The army of guests splashed in the fountains, climbed trees, only to fall out of them, and made random love all over the place.

"When I left, exhausted by pleasure, but no longer amused, the orgy was still going on. But any moment news from Ostia was expected. Fearing a storm, I welcomed this legitimate excuse to flee the scene. I don't know what will happen, but if Claudius is persuaded by his freedmen that all this was, in fact, an attempt upon his power and his life, then there will be a heavy price to pay, not only for Messalina and Silius, but for a lot of other people. If, on the other hand, Claudius is convinced that it was only wild playfulness on the part of his wife, he might actually forgive her. In his own crippled way I think he loves her."

"Nonsense," said Lollia. "He doesn't know anything about love. He spends all his time roaring like a commoner at the arena and sqandering his money on dice and chariot races."

"I understand that he has an extraordinary fondness for his wives," said Asconius Labeo, who had just recently been appointed the official guardian of Agrippina's only child, Nero.

Beryllus nodded to confirm that observation. "He was certainly that way with his first wife. And even more so with Aelia Paetina." Beryllus was a bald-headed man with a kindly round face and the benign smile of a man willing to give all the world the benefit of the doubt. He was one of young Nero's tutors.

"They say he has a totally irrational urge to please them," said Annaeus Serenus, another of Nero's tutors. He was lean and dark-eyed, with a bad combination of a long nose and a receding chin. "They say, in fact, that he is afraid of them and lets them have their way in practically everything, including things political.".

"How else could little Messalina have committed all those official murders?" said Agrippina, a dagger in her voice. "They might have been ordered by Claudius, but it is not likely that he cared about what he was doing half the time. And then there are those about which he knew nothing at all. Private arrangements of his petite wife. But it looks as though our queen has pushed her luck a bit too far. If good advice holds the day with my uncle, he'll have the little bitch strangled."

The face of Poppaea Sabina turned to polite stone at this vicious remark. But her green eyes, flashing across the table, could not conceal her distaste for Agrippina. Poppaea was young, pampered, and demanding. At nineteen she already had a reputation for debauchery that threatened eventually to eclipse Messalina's. She was also, in the minds of many people, the most beautiful woman in Rome. She was married to Rufius Crispinus, one of the two commanders of the Praetorian Guard. For Rufius the marriage was a mixed blessing. His friends envied him to his face and pitied him behind his back. Nobody believed for a moment that the marriage would last.

Poppaea had been invited to dinner because she was a

25

house guest of one of Agrippina's closest friends, Junia Silana. Junia had an attractive little villa less than a mile up the coast. Arriving with them also was Aemilia, another matronly and wealthy widow.

In spite of her reputation, Poppaea still had the appearance of an innocent girl. Her face was delicate, her eyes set wide apart, and her mouth sensous with a perpetual hint of a smile. The small bones of her graceful and feminine body echoed the delicacy of her face. And, as though an affront to Lollia and all those women of fashion, she wore her hair in the simple old Republican fashion, parted in the middle and gathered into a chignon. It gave her a look of Hellenic purity. One would never have guessed that she insisted on a small fortune's worth of milk in which to bathe her precious body.

"On the other hand," said Poppaea, "one has to admit that Messalina has never been boring. She provides more than her share of scandal and gossip, without which Roman society would collapse, just as surely as if it was cut off from wine and oil."

Agrippina gathered up her fifteen years of seniority, her royal blood, and her superior physical presence and scolded young Poppaea across the luxuriously laden table. "My dear, you seem to have forogtten the oldest lesson of all in your upbringing. The ideal of womanhood is to not be spoken of at all, either for good or for evil. Ancient wisdom!" Petronius devoured an oyster with fish sauce and appreciated the little drama.

Poppaea smiled. "As usual I've got it all mixed up, but then I lack your years of learning."

Petronius reached for another oyster. A slave made the rounds of the couches, offering a bowl of water and small towels. Beryllus burped his appreciation of the hors d'oeuvres and then raised his voice good-naturedly to smother the little fire that was flaring up between these two women. "Speaking of gossip," he said, "is there any news of our friend Seneca? It's so awful to imagine that great man languishing there in Corsica."

"I had letters from him on the occasion of his fifty-third birthday," said Annaeus Serenus, an intimate associate of

26

the Stoic philosopher. "He is still extremely bitter. He consoles himself with his philosophy of cool indifference, but it is clear that his noble heart is almost crushed. He talks about the starkness of the cliffs, the wind, the isolation. His health has suffered in spite of his ascetic discipline. Exile is worse than death, he says, and I fear that he has more than once contemplated suicide."

"Of all the cruelties and crimes of Messalina," said Agrippina, "this is by far the worst. It is more unforgiveable than any of her personal debaucheries."

"Why in the world was she so determined to have him out of the way?" asked Petronius, offering his cup to the slave who poured the honeyed wine.

"You're so disgustingly young that you don't remember that ridiculous scandal," said Agrippina.

"I've heard it talked about," said Petronius. "There was a charge of adultery, wasn't there? Involving your sister Julia Livilla, in fact."

"Nonsense! There was never anything of any importance between them. It was a trumped-up charge. Messalina hated Seneca because Claudius would drink with him for hours and talk about rhetoric and philosophy. She could never tolerate that sort of intimacy. What's more, he was a good friend of mine."

"Surely, she wasn't jealous of *you*," said Poppaea. And the smothered fire burst into flames again.

"It was not a question of jealousy," said Agrippina. "It was a question of influence. But I don't expect you to understand political refinements."

"I'm not interested in politics," said Poppaea.

"I thought all Romans were interested in politics," said Beryllus, his fat eyes focused on the platters of fish and fowl that were now being served up.

"Man is a political animal," said Asconius Labeo. "His chief business in life is to function in relation to other human beings."

"And, therefore," said Beryllus, "the main preoccupation of the ruling class is statecraft."

"Which is to say *power*," added Agrippina. "Without power you cannot rule. All the philosophical wisdom in the world is as nothing confronted with a sharp sword. What's more, philosophy diverts mental energy, stirs up doubts, and weakens the will. That's why, as these gentlemen know, there will be none in my son's education."

"Then why, dear lady, have you for years praised the talents of Seneca?" asked Petronius. There was a hint of decadence in his melodious poise, as if he never quite believed in anything he said.

"Philosophy may be a toy," said Agrippina, "but oratory is a weapon. Seneca is an extremely persuasive man. He has the secret of manipulation. And he does it all with his wits. He's also quite rich, you know. And not at all the Stoic he pretends to be. Besides, he is the most entertaining man in the world. I'm very fond of him."

"Obviously," said Poppaea, who was too young to have ever sat at the same table with Seneca. "You make him sound fascinating. I look forward to meeting him, should he ever escape from that island—what is it?"

"Corsica!" said Agrippina with a certain sharpness in her voice that intervened between Asconius Labeo's gaping mouth and the peacock meat he held between his fingers. He looked up, as did the other guests. Petronius could barely stifle his amusement. "But I don't think he's your type. To appreciate his intellectual gifts you need a few of your own."

Poppaea acknowledged the cut with raised eyebrows and a pleasant nod. "But," she said, "he's old. And I don't much like old men."

"I resent that," said Beryllus, who was, himself, past fifty, and launched into an amusing defense of the capacities of older men.

The crisis passed. The dinner party was settling into serious eating and drinking. Before the evening was over there would be music, and Syrian dancing girls, and who knows what else.

# IV

Less than a week later the news of Messalina's death was carried from Rome in all directions on galloping hooves and billowing sails. Rumor outraced the speediest messenger, distorting the tale, adding riots in the streets, assassinations, and suicides.

Agrippina wandered the beaches of Baiae like an uncaged animal. The brief message from Pallas left everything unclear: "Messalina is dead. Departing instantly from Ostia on the *Poseidon*." Pallas was her lover. He was also the Emperor Claudius's financial secretary, a man of enormous influence in the current regime. Though only a freedman, he was rumored to be one of the wealthiest men in Rome, worth possibly as much as 500,000,000 sesterces. His hand was in a hundred enterprises. He dealt in real estate, slaves, shipping, precious stones, and money-lending.

In the waning afternoon Agrippina paced the length of the stone landing, her white robe fluttering dramatically in the vigorous breeze. It blew from the northwest, curling the sea into whitecaps and sending a chill through her feverish body—feverish with excitement and impatience. Three slaves lingered at the end of the dock, stationed there indefinitely to secure the *Poseidon* the minute it put in. From the terraces of the villa other figures watched, members of the household staff, their faces glowing with curiosity and the last rays of the setting sun. Dogs barked in the distance. The wheels of a cart made a clattering sound on the cobbled road.

So intent was she on scanning the horizon that she did not see or hear Tigellinus come up behind her. She gasped at the sound of his voice and whirled around to unleash on him a furious series of curses. "Stay out of sight!" she shouted. "Disappear. Go to Naples and drink yourself to death."

As Tigellinus stalked away, muttering curses under his breath, a ram's horn moaned unmusically from the promontory above the stone landing. A sail had been sighted. Agrippina strained her eyes across the gray-blue, unsettled waters. The *Poseidon* was a small silhouette against the blazing orange of the setting sun. But it *was* the *Poseidon*. She knew it well. Pallas's private boat, as sleek as a trireme, though somewhat smaller. Its enormous red sails billowed with the following wind. Before the wind it was faster than anything afloat. "Make ready!" she shouted to the loitering slaves on the dock, and they sprang into aimless action, as if it were the ghost of her father Germanicus who bellowed at them from the battlefields of the Rhine.

Aboard his luxurious and speedy vessel, Pallas walked the deck in silence. His boots stomping the boards was all the threat of violence his crew needed. The captain called out his commands. His first mate echoed them. And sailors scurried to haul and furl. The boat pitched and rolled and rode the wind-driven waves shoreward, pursued by a darkening sky, in which there began to gather gray billowing clouds that seemed to grow out of the horizon. "We'll make port just in time," said the captain to the wealthy owner.

Pallas, who preferred action to talk, listened and said nothing. His eyes were fixed on the shore. He imagined he could see Agrippina on the landing, but the light was growing dim. He was a tall, substantial man in his mid-forties. His curled black hair mixed with gray. His face was hard and uncompromising, but illuminated with a secret wisdom and appreciation of life. When he spoke, his voice was soft yet he was concise, as if there were a tax on language. He was several generations removed from Greece, but only half a lifetime removed from the slavery that bound his ancestors. He was a young man when Antonia, the emperor's mother, had given him his freedom in recognition of his talents and impressive service to her family. That sturdy old Roman matron had died more than ten years earlier, but she lived in Pallas's mind as the kind of woman the empire needed. Claudius was not her fault. One had to keep in mind that she was also the mother of Germanicus. In Agrippina, oddly enough, Pallas saw some of Antonia's qualities. The forceful personality, the determination, the sense of history. Even the selfishness, unfortunately. But there the comparison ended. Antonia had been committed to the old virtues. When her husband died, she was only twenty-seven years old, but she took a vow never to marry again. She honored the vow for forty-five years. Not exactly the sort of thing that would appeal to Agrippina. No, she was neither innocent nor modest nor virtuous. Pallas knew that. And perhaps it even mattered to him, but not enough to keep him from loving her. If something as calculated as his passion for her could be called love.

The sea heaved. The planking groaned. Night stalked the sunless sky, attacking the streaks of orange and blue. Pallas steadied himself on a rope that, in turn, steadied the mast. The giant red belly of the sail captured the wind and swept along the hull with its ram's head and painted eyes.

By the time the *Poseidon* was fastened to the dock, the last light had faded in the west and a stiffening breeze had brought in an overcast sky that blotted out the stars. Agrippina never left the stone landing, but Europa had to bring her down a woolen cloak to keep out the chill and dampness of the evening. Pallas came down the gangplank looking more like a general than a financial secretary. There was no dramatic embrace, no public display of affection. He nodded. She smiled. They walked side by side up to the villa, like a pair of merchants eager to get down to business.

31

Refreshed by wine and settled in the small room Agrippina called her study, Pallas described the events of the past week. Agrippina sat forward tensely in her chair to listen. Nude figures in the brilliant wallpaintings eavesdropped on the account. The oil lamps flickered.

"We understand now," he said, "that the marriage with Silius was, in fact, part of a conspiracy. But it wasn't Messalina's conspiracy. She was persuaded to join forces with it. She was led to believe that Claudius was doomed, and she imagined that she and Silius would find enough support to succeed her husband. It was insane, of course. I think she realized that as soon as the mock ceremony was over. She abandoned herself to reckless celebration, fatalistically, drunkenly accepting her doom. But when the danger became a reality, it sobered her and frightened her. Messengers arrived from Ostia with the news that Claudius was returning to Rome, bent on vengeance. The party was over. The wedding crowd scattered. Silius tried to bury his fear by going about his business at the Forum. And Messalina, in a panic, decided to throw herself at the feet of her husband, accompanied, of course, by her crying children. Such tactics had always worked for her in the past; there was a chance they would work for her now.

"The centurions appeared on the scene and tracked down the chief participants in the whole fiasco. They slapped them immediately into irons wherever they found them. Some were in hiding, some were wandering in the streets or at the Forum. Most of them confessed freely. Some, like Silius himself, made no excuses for themselves and asked only for a swift execution. How many escaped we still don't know.

"Meanwhile, Messalina was trying to arrange a way of seeing Claudius in person as he returned from Ostia. She was convinced that this was the only way to save her life. Narcissus, however, was well aware of the emperor's weakness for this lady. And he was determined that they should not meet face to face. The situation at Ostia was tricky. Lucius Geta, co-commander of the Guard, was not altogether trustworthy, though an old friend of Claudius. Should he get the impression that the conspiracy had a chance of success, he might very well go over to the other side. Narcissus and I persuaded Claudius to relieve him of his command for just one day, so that one of us freedmen and close associates could take over officially. He agreed and put Narcissus in charge of the Praetorian Guard. It was really Narcissus who carried the whole thing off. You see, we had to keep Messalina from seeing Claudius. But how were we going to do that? She planned to meet him on the road. She had gone to Vibidia, the eldest of the Vestal Virgins, and she had begged her to intercede on her behalf. Vibidia could not be arrested, nor could she be prevented from approaching the emperor. She rushed ahead to intercept him.

"In the emperor's carriage there was a curious drama going on. Some hangers-on were riding with him, who would agree with anything Claudius did or said. They might even encourage him to forgive his wife, knowing that he had a secret inclination in that direction. When Narcissus got word that Messalina planned to intercept the carriage on the road from Ostia to Rome, he insisted on seating himself beside Claudius, in order to prevent any weakening of his resolve. All his stakes were down against Messalina. If somehow she escaped this time, he was finished. As they rode along discussing the situation, Narcissus presented strong arguments and evidence that Messalina and her accomplices no doubt intended to destroy her husband.

"Well, you know what a victim of terror your uncle can be. He has such a fear of personal harm that it overrides everything. Stuttering and moaning, he reaffirmed his vow to execute every last conspirator and adulterer. When Vibidia arrived to plead for a hearing for Messalina, Claudius said nothing. And when Messalina, herself, arrived, accompanied only by a couple of slaves, Narcissus leaned out of the carriage and roared the accusations at her, filling, at the same time, Claudiu's ears. What's more, he handed Claudius a document to read that contained a list of all his wife's debaucheries, including the names of many of her lovers. In a rage Claudius ordered the carriage to move on. Fortunately, Messalina's children, Octavia and Britannicus, had been prevented from making an appearance at that crucial moment. Otherwise, who knows what might have happened. Still, he yielded to the final cries of Vibidia that he should, at least, hear the explanations of his wife, the mother of his children. He relented. He sent back word that a hearing would be arranged.

"Messalina, deserted now by everyone, fled to the gardens of Lucullus. There she was joined by her mother Lepida, who, for years, has barely spoken to her daughter, such an embarrassment to the family has she been. Driven by an old instinct and mother's compassion, she comforted the girl and urged her to end her life with dignity and courage before the tribune and his men arrived. But she still believed that she could have her hearing and that she could move her husband of ten years to pity and forgiveness.

"Meanwhile, Narcissus could not be sure of Claudius. As they entered Rome the emperor fell into a strange silence. Narcissus was afraid of those mental lapses that Claudius had, his peculiar forgetfulness. It was as if he only remembered what suited him. Clearly now he longed to forget this whole business. He yawned. His eyes drooped. He was actually falling asleep. In the midst of this great crisis he was escaping into sleep. A stroke of genius saved the day. Narcissus ordered the carriage to the house of Silius. He forced Claudius to look at the place where Messalina's outrage and adultery had taken place. Narcissus showed him the statue of Silius's father, which the Senate had ordered destroyed. He showed him also certain gifts that Messalina had given to her paramour. They were the emperor's heirlooms. When Claudius recognized them, his anger was genuinely aroused for the first time. And when, at last, he was shown the very bed in which no doubt his wife proved him the cuckold, he began to howl and foam at the mouth. Then, at the peak of his anger he was swept away by Narcissus to the Praetorian Camp. A written speech was shoved into his trembling hands. He read it to the cohorts without stammering. It was brief and to the point. The soldiers roared their agreement with him and demanded punishment for the offenders.

"The very same day the accused were brought, one by

34

one, before the tribunal. Neither confessions, nor excuses, nor pleas for mercy did any good. They were all condemned to death, save two, whose crimes were more sins of the flesh than acts of political intrigue. Even poor Mnester the actor was doomed, though he showed the bloody wounds where he had been beaten into collaboration and virtually raped by Messalina. Perhaps we were too harsh, but we meant to be. Any sign of softness at that point might have been an invitation to renewed upheavals. The city was uneasy, as you can imagine."

"And during these trials where was Messalina?" asked Agrippina.

"She stayed in the gardens of Lucullus with her mother, waiting for word from Claudius. Any moment she expected him to grant her the hearing he had promised her. This encounter, we felt, had to be avoided at all cost, in spite of the promise. We stayed with Claudius that evening. A banquet had been arranged for his return from Ostia. A small affair, but with an abundance of food and wine, as though his household staff understood that he had sorrows to drown. Under the influence of wine he began to talk more freely about the whole horrible incident. And he began to speak more kindly and nostalgically about Messalina. He called her *poor creature*. The dam we had so carefully constructed was beginning to crack. We tried to stop him from drinking, but it was no good. He insisted now on seeing her—first thing in the morning. His anger was gone. His face was all flabby and sentimental. There were actually tears in his sad, old eyes. I must confess I felt sorry for him. But Narcissus was near hysteria. It was he who would lose his life if Messalina slipped out of his hands. The rest of us seemed more noncommittal in the matter. A reserve for which I will probably be criticized.

"Narcissus had no choice. He had to gamble. As soon as Claudius was incoherently drunk, he rushed out of the banquet room and, in a very businesslike way, informed the attending tribune that the emperor had ordered the instant execution of Messalina. He said that he was to go immediately with the necessary centurions and witnesses to the

35

gardens of Lucullus and do the deed. A freedman was sent along to assist in the execution.

"Later, we heard from her few remaining slaves and friends that Messalina was rapidly informed of what was transpiring. A messenger reached her before either Narcissus or the tribune. Lepida pleaded once more with her daughter to kill herself. She even provided the dagger. But Messalina, still a girl, really, was unable to puncture her own precious skin. She fumbled at her wrists and throat, but could not do the necessary and honorable thing. Her mother wailed. She wailed. Her slaves ran about in confusion and then finally fled as the tribune approached. First Narcissus entered the garden, breathless and perspiring. He found Messalina lying on the ground in a panic. It was all over for her. She grasped at his sandaled feet and the hem of his long tunic. He pulled away and assailed her cruelly. 'The tribune is coming,' he said. 'The order has been given. Spare yourself the pain and humiliation.' Her mother took her in her arms and raised her into a sitting position. Once more she put the dagger in her hand. But at this point they heard the tribune and centurions approaching. And in another moment they were all in the gardens, standing about the fallen woman as stony-faced as fate. 'Death is here!' she shouted, and held the dagger pointed at her heart. But hesitation and fear froze her arm. It was the tribune who drove it home with a quick blow of his large hand. She gasped with wide eyes, as if she saw something that she could not believe, and then pitched forward onto the ground."

"Good!" Agrippina exclaimed, unmoved by compassion or any squeamishness about blood. "She deserved it. After all the horrible things she's done, she deserved all that and more. But, tell me, how did Claudius take the news? He had not, after all, ordered the execution."

"By the next day he didn't know what he had ordered," said Pallas. "He was convinced that he had, in effect, condemned her to death. But it really didn't matter because, by the end of the day, he apparently had put the whole affair, wife and all, completely out of his mind. He went to his dinner that night as though nothing unusual had happened. He overate, as usual. And, as usual, was drunk by the time he rose to go to bed, and had to be assisted by two muscular slaves. In short, he showed neither joy nor grief nor anger nor hatred. He showed no emotions whatever—toward the victim, the accusers, or even the bereft children. A strange old man, impossible to love. Impossible to hate!"

"But not impossible to marry," she said, getting up and sweeping gracefully across the room. She stood with her back against a life-size wall painting, as though she were joining the bare-breasted women and the murdered bull.

Pallas gazed at her without saying anything. He ran his long fingers through his generous hair. His fatigue showed in the hard lines of his face and the shadows under his eyes. But his thin lips, damp with wine, betrayed a hint of a smile. "Precisely why I am here," he said. "I did not come all this way to describe to you the blood on the ivy in the gardens of Lucullus. As soon as it was clear that Messalina was doomed, rumors began to fly about who might succeed her."

"I know," said Agrippina. "We heard the beginning of the story from Petronius. Lollia Paulina happened to be here that night. She's obviously interested."

"What's more, she has the support of Callistus. And certain other things to recommend her."

"What do you mean?"

"I mean, she's not an unattractive woman."

"She's fat."

He smiled. "Your point of view is somewhat biased."

"She's a vicious woman."

"She has a reasonably good reputation."

"Are you suggesting that *I* don't?"

"I don't have to be that subtle. I love you dearly, but you have a rotten reputation."

"I don't know what you're talking about." She marched across the room and then turned to confront him, her arms folded across her breasts.

"Come, come! Don't look so offended. You're talking to the only person in the world with whom you can be absolutely honest. To begin with, during your marriage to

Ahenobarbus you were banished to the island of Pontia for adultery. That in itself might not have been so bad. The real scandal behind the banishment was that you were incestuously connected with Caligula."

"I'm not responsible for malicious lies about me or my brother."

"They can't all be lies. For years your sister-in-law Domita has been complaining quite publically that you not only stole her husband away, but that, after you married poor Crispus Passienus, you, rather obviously, arranged for his timely death so that you would inherit his extensive fortune."

"That's never been proven. Domitia has always been jealous of me. It's not my fault that she was too ugly to hold on to her husband. The choice was his not mine."

"I'm not asking you to defend yourself. Your guilt is not the issue, but your reputation *is*, including the current gossip about you and Tigellinus. I understand, incidently, that he's been staying here with you."

"I meant to explain that to you when I came to Rome."

"You owe me no explanations. You remember the pact we made at Antium. No explanations, either way. We're not slaves. We don't belong to one another. Neither one of us can put up with that sort of romantic nonsense."

"All right, then, what are you trying to tell me?"

"I am trying to tell you that there are several major obstacles in the way of a marriage between you and Claudius. There is, as I say, your reputation. But there are more important things. To begin with, Claudius has decided never to marry again."

"Do you believe him?"

"We'll know better in a few months. Perhaps even in a few weeks. He is, after all, fifty-nine years old. And he has an heir. My guess, however, is that he can probably be persuaded—for both political and personal reasons."

"What other obstacles are there?"

"One rather obvious one."

"What's that?"

"My dear girl, the man is your uncle—your father's

38

brother. Such a marriage will be construed as incestuous and perhaps illegal."

"There are ways to get around that," she said.

"Yes, with the cooperation of the Senate, perhaps. But you are not on the best of terms with them."

"I'll have the help of Vitellius, I'm sure."

Pallas shrugged philosophically. "We can deal with that later, if we come to it. There's another, even greater, difficulty."

She frowned, unable to imagine what he was talking about.

"Narcissus!"

She smiled nervously. "Surely, he doesn't plan to marry my uncle."

"No, but after this latest disaster, he may be in a position of considerable influence. And he's not likely to support your candidacy."

"I find him somewhat unapproachable."

"I'm not surprised. The fact is he doesn't like you. What's more, he's got a scheme of his own that has considerable merit. He's going to propose that Claudius remarry his second wife, Aelia Paetina."

Her face tightened and paled. "I'd forgotten about her. She must be in her forties."

"He's an old man. She's familiar territory. And quite well preserved. Good family. Good reputation. And, above all, the mother of his daughter Antonia, of whom he is very fond. It would be the most sensible thing for him to do at his time in life. She will have considerable support. She would be a good stepmother to Britannicus, without a son of her own to rival him."

"Do you think he will see my Nero as a rival to his own son?"

"He would have to be even blinder than he is not to. Your boy is more closely descended from the combined Julio-Claudian famlies than his own Britannicus."

"None of that will matter, unless he can be eventually persuaded to adopt him."

"Now, now, don't leap so far ahead. You haven't even

39

found your way to the altar yet. How can you talk about adoption or succession?" .

She clenched and unclenched her fists in a desperate grasping motion. "Because that's what I want!" she shouted. "And that's what I will have."

He grew calmer as she grew more tempestuous. He refilled his cup, allowing the wine to trickle slowly from the pitcher. It made the sound of a tiny waterfall, a suitable symbol of his steadiness and patience. "Between the desire and the fulfillment, my precious one, there often falls a shadow. I, too, would like to see you satisy this dream of yours. It would, for one thing, guarantee my own position. I am not quite sure where I would stand in any other succession."

"Mine is the only true succession. You know that. Everyone knows that. Germanicus should have been the emperor after Tiberius, but my father was poisoned. And, after him, my husband should have been emperor by adoption, since all my brothers are dead. And all my sisters too. We come down directly from Augustus—by the female line. And there was only the female line, since Julia was his only child. From Augustus to Julia to my mother to me and to my Nero. Nothing intervenes. Nothing else matters. If I were a man, I would be ruling the empire this very minute, and doing a better job than Claudius. What's more, there is no law that says a woman cannot rule—only tradition. And I don't see why that can't be changed. Why shouldn't a woman rule? What makes a madman like my brother or a cripple like my uncle Claudius better than I would be? I'm stronger, saner, and smarter. I understand politics, administration, and the military life. I was practically born in battle in the German campaign. What more can a country want in a leader?"

He shook his head slowly and looked at her with tired fox's eyes. "Agrippina," he said, "you are wasting your time with these idle speculations. You will never be the sovereign ruler of this empire and you know it. Tradition may be hard to explain, but it is almost impossible to change. The concept of the emperor, with its suggestions of divinity and paternity, requires that that person be a man. It is deeply ingrained. It is a mystique. Logic has nothing to do with it."

She sighed and threw up her arms. Then she came to him, despair replacing frustration. "I know, I know!" she said. And, on the brink of tears, she fell on her knees before him and allowed her head to rest in his lap.

It was a request for reassurance and comforting, and he did not deny it to her. He touched her hair gently, stroking her, patting her shoulder. "Our ambitions must be within reason," he said quietly. "And it is not unreasonable to assume that one day your Nero will be the ruler of this sprawling collection of nations we call the empire. But none of this will be achieved without work. We have a great deal to do."

She raised her head and looked at him. He had not felt her crying, yet tears stained her cheeks, cutting through the whiteness of her makeup and soiling her painted eyes. As she looked at him, she seemed to be reading a piece of ancient history in his blue eyes. "You know," she said, "Nero's father despised me. When he saw the baby, he said nothing could be born of him and me that would not be an abomination and a public danger. And what's more, my Nero was born feet first. That's bad luck.

"Mere superstition. You musn't worry about that sort of thing."

"One can't help but wonder."

"You were never one to tolerate such weak-mindedness." he held her chin cupped in his hand as though to restore her confidence."

"You're right," she said, standing up suddenly and pulling herself together. "I hate frailties. I'll put it out of my mind."

"Good!" he said, also rising. "Let's have a toast then." He lifted his cup and handed her the other. "To you. To your son. To the future." They drank and laughed.

"I wish he were here," she said. "I'd ask him to join us."

"You mean you don't have him with you?" said Pallas, slowly lowering his cup and looking very concerned.

"He was visiting his aunt when all this happened."

"Not Lepida! Not Messalina's mother?"

"I couldn't help it," she said. "He's quite attached to her, you know. And he was getting restless here."

Pallas turned away from her, displaying a controlled temper. "You must be mad. The woman hates you."

"But she loves Nero. No harm can come to him in her house. Besides, she's been at odds with her daughter for years. I thought—"

"Don't think about it another moment. I want you to go to Rome in the morning and take him to your own house. With all this trouble, who knows what's liable to happen. She'll subvert him. She'll rob his affections and turn him against you."

"It was only meant to be a brief visit, but I will, of course, end it. Take me with you on the *Poseidon*"

"And do not be deceived by any overtures she makes to you. Remember that her very own grandson, Britannicus, is the emperor's heir."

"I promise you he'll never see her again."

"Good! Now let's put all this troublesome business out of our minds and find a place to rest. These arms have been without you much too long."

They embraced and sealed with a long kiss the future regency of the empire. For neither of them was there any other avenue to power: she was born a woman, and he was born a slave. They would never rule. They would never marry. But between them they could create an emperor. And through him they could consummate their lust.

# V

Rome. The center of the world. Wolf-mother to millions.
Blazing with wealth. Stinking with poverty. Temples and
palaces. Arenas and theaters. Marketplaces with open
shops. Tenements for the poor. What a clanging and
shouting and grinding of cartwheels. What commerce and
traffic from dawn until dusk. Rome. The throbbing heart of
the Mediterranean, linked by arteries to all the outposts
from Britain to Asia. Administrative capital. Seat of the
emperor. Residence of the aristocracy. Its monstrous appetites were fed from far and near. Metals, grain, wine, fish,
marble, timber, wool, wild animals, slaves, and horses.
Goods poured into the city from Spain, Gaul, Greece,
Asia, and Africa. Wherever a Roman soldier set his foot,
traders and merchants followed. And what an influx of
races. What a babble of languages and riot of costumes.
The most thrilling and dangerous city in the world. There
was nothing in Rome that could not be bought, from a
slave to a senator; from a whore to a pearl. Gleaming
white in the stifling day. Dark and damp in the cobbled

night. A city of walls within walls, searching for society, retreating into privacy.

But it was only the rich who could afford a fortress of privacy in the jammed precincts of this noisy metropolis. And the very rich found it on Palatine Hill near the Forum and the Circus Maximus. Here they built their elaborate mansions, their fishponds and gardens and baths. Here they crowded luxuriously together to form the ruling families, the ruling class. For all of the hundreds of thousands of swarming citizens and slaves, only a few belonged to that inner circle that owned the wealth, the power, and the blood. They were a city within the city. They cavorted together. Conspired together. Feasted on gossip and rumor. And made politics their daily bread. Many of them were related, a handful of noble families having intermarried themselves into impossible genealogies.

One of the houses on the Palatine, a house of ordinary magnificence, belonged to Domitia Lepida, mother of Messalina, grandaughter of Octavia and Mark Antony, and sister of Agrippina's first husband, Ahenobarbus. And not far from it was Agrippina's own house, somewhat neglected in recent years because of her diplomatic preference for Baiae and Antium.

So intertwined were the families of the aristocracy that almost everybody was, at least, everybody else's cousin, perhaps slightly removed. Even these two rivals for the affections of young Nero were related, and not so distantly. Lepida, was, in fact, a first cousin to the emperor Claudius. She was also, therefore, a first cousin to Germanicus, Agrippina's father. However, Lepida had also been Claudius's mother-in-law. And now Agrippina was determined to make a husband of her uncle. It was the subject of a brilliant piece of spontaneous satire by Petronius one drunken evening. And no one seemed to mind being made fun of. Marriage was, after all, political. And love—well, that was something else entirely, and much less important.

Lepida's house was an inconsistent blend of the lavish and the simple, depending on the gifts that had been foisted upon her over the years. The walls were high, the gardens meticulously manicured. The atrium was large, the bedrooms small. The dining room was one of the most congenial on the hill, the scene of memorable feasts of food and sophistication. Lepida was not without her cultural refinements, and was known to devour a lover or two in her time, though certainly no competition for Agrippina in this respect, nor for her own daughter either. Nature, unfortunately, had not equipped her for great amorous achievements. Her wealth and social position could not entirely compensate for a poor complexion and a straight, small-breasted figure. She was, nevertheless, a likable woman with a sense of humor, even about herself.

Her modicum of learning and sharpness of wit made her popular in a way that more beautiful women would never understand. These qualities also invited envy and suspicion, both of which Agrippina had in abundance. In short, though thrown together by breeding and history, they did not like one another.

Agrippina came to Lepida's house in the middle of the morning, accompanied by Europa and her freedman Mestor. It was a beautiful fall morning, and they came on foot, with all the appearance of paying a social call or a visit of condolence after the tragic events of the past few weeks. Lepida greeted her former sister-in-law with exaggerated politeness and no sign whatsoever of grief.

The two women exchanged pleasantries as they moved through the coolness of the house and then out into one of the walled gardens. The seclusion of the Palatine house kept out the sights of a busy city, but not the sounds, which rose like a distant hum or the rush of the surf up the shingle of the shore.

When they were alone and seated among a riot of roses and other flowers beside the circular fishpond, Agrippina brushed a loose strand of hair across her forehead and tried to look compassionate. "I can't tell you how shocked we all were to hear about your daughter," she said.

Lepida arranged the folds of her blue gown and refused to change the expression on her fifty-year-old face, which remained remarkably unlined, though somewhat marred by a childhood disease. "Now, now, dear Agrippina," she said. "Let's have no hypocrisy on such a lovely morning. The girl is dead. She brought it on herself. Nobody's really sorry."

"But how awful for you to have been right there."

"I was there because it was my final duty as a mother. There was, as you know, very little affection between us. Quite the contrary. It's all over now and I'm rather glad. Is that too brutal a thing to say?"

"There's not much else that one can do, is there?" said Agrippina.

"There's nothing at all that one can do," said Lepida. "Life goes on—and on."

"I admire your courage."

"I'm not being courageous; just sensible."

"Of course! But, tell me, have there been any repercussions? I hope no one has suggested that you had a hand in all this."

Lepida's thin lips contained a smile. "Why should they? Everybody in Rome knows how things stood between me and Messalina. And my personal politics are simple. Law and order. Legitimate succession."

"By which you mean your grandson Britannicus?"

"Naturally! Need you ask?"

"I only meant to suggest that the succession to power in our family has rarely followed a *natural* course. So many *unnatural* things seem to happen to us. But that's neither here nor there. How is my darling son Nero?"

"He's just fine. He's been sheltered somewhat from this upheaval, though he knows now what's happened."

"You told him?"

"Yes. He had to know, sooner or later. But I simplified it for him. He is, after all, only twelve."

"I think I would have preferred to tell him myself."

"Why? Do you think that your version could possibly be better informed than mine?"

"Hardy! But he is *my* son and I don't want him to get the wrong impression—about this or anything else."

"You will forgive me for sounding possessive, but I sometimes feel he is as much my son as he is yours. Because he's my dead brother's son, and because he spent his infant years with me, while you were—how shall I put it—doing penance on the island of Pontia."

Agrippina stood up suddenly but controlled her anger. "Put it how you please, but let's not discuss that unfortunate incident. I think I have thanked you sufficiently for all your generosity and solicitude over the years. Now, if you don't mind, I would like to take my son home. I am back in my house, and I will be staying here indefinitely."

"Closer to the heart of things, so to speak?"

"You know as well as I do why I was forced to stay away. But the reason has been removed. I hate to say this, under the circumstances, but your daughter was a dangerous woman."

"I'd be the first to agree with you," said Lepida. "On the other hand, she thought of *you* as a dangerous woman. I can't imagine why. If he were alive, we could ask my sister's ex-husband Crispus Passienus." Her eyes were narrow and cold under the arches of her eyebrows.

Agrippina marched away from her in the narrow distance between the benches and the pool. Her fists were clenched. When she turned at last to confront Lepida she seemed not to have heard the remark. "Where's my son?" she said.

"He's having riding lessons. He should be back any moment."

"He doesn't need riding lessons. He's got a perfectly good instructor."

"Not Tigellinus, by any chance?" said Lepida with a little thrust of her dagger.

"Save your sarcasm for your salon. You will only provoke me to pity. I'm afraid that recent events have scrambled your wits and made you bitter."

"All right, then, we'll put aside the banter. I'll tell you straight out what's on my mind. I don't think you're a fit mother for Nero. I think you'll use him, abuse him, and ruin him. I want to keep him here where he is safe and happy."

Agrippina was speechless with rage. Her face turned red under the powdered whiteness of her cheeks. Her widened eyes grew murderously dark. "You incredible bitch! You

47

hypocritical whore, posing as the guardian of virtue, accusing me of the very things that you yourself are guilty of. Shall we talk about you? Shall we talk about your fitness as a mother? About how you once shared a lover with your daughter, only to have him stolen away from you by her, because he was fifteen years younger than you? Shall we talk about how you *used* your daughter, how you made a child bride of her for that incoherent old monster Claudius? No, no, my dear woman, you are in no position to accuse anybody of anything. I'm taking my son home. And I hope you've enjoyed the visit because, believe me, it's his last. You'll never lay eyes on him again, as long as I'm alive to prevent it."

"That will be hard to manage in a city like Rome," said Lepida. "But it hardly matters. In a few years he'll be a young man. He'll be able to do what he pleases."

"He'll do what I tell him to do," said Agrippina.

"And what will you have me do, mother?"

The two women were startled. Standing in the archway of greenery was a pretty boy with a cheerful round face and blonde hair. He wore riding boots that crisscrossed halfway up his slender legs and a leather belt that gathered in his simple brown tunic. Dust defined the streaks of perspiration. He looked physically exhilarated but otherwise puzzled.

"Ah, there you are, my sweetheart," said Agrippina, recovering her poise and rushing to him in the archway.

Nero allowed himself to be roughly embraced and was just tall enough to see his aunt over his mother's shoulder. They exchanged a glance. Lepida's smile was tender. Nero's was tinged with confusion and fear.

"What were you talking about?" asked Nero, trying to withdraw from his mother's arms.

"We were talking about you," said Lepida, with forced cheerfulness, "but what we were saying is none of your business."

"Was it good or bad? Tell me that, at least."

"Oh, bad. Very bad! I was telling your mother what an awful boy you've been while she was away at Baiae." She laughed. He studied her face and then also laughed, but hesitantly.

"Well," said Agrippina, "aren't you glad to see me?"

"Oh, yes, of course," he said.

"Then show me with a kiss."

She offered her mouth. He kissed her cheek. "Your mother says you've got to go home now," said Lepida.

"That's right," said Agrippina. "The holiday is over. Yours and mine. We'll be staying in Rome now—for a long time."

He brightened. "That's good," he said. "Then I'll be able to come here any time I want to."

Agrippina caught Lepida's eye and registered her look of triumph. "We'll talk about that another time. Come, I've got great surprises for you."

"I'll have your things put together," Lepida said and went off along another path and through another archway into the house. Nero followed her with his eyes and, for a moment, failed to hear what his mother was saying.

". . . and the biggest surprise of all is something you've been wanting for months."

His attention returned. "You mean a new horse?"

"Yes. A beauty! All white. Fast as the wind."

His confusion disappeared. He smiled broadly and wheeled around in a complete circle. "Oh, I can't wait to see him."

"It's a a gift from Tigellinus."

"From Tigellinus?"

A shadow crossed his face but was quickly swept away by boyish excitement. Hand in hand they went back through the hedges toward the house.

49

# VI

The mountains of Corsica rise nine thousand feet on the western side of the island and plunge straight into the sea. Its interior is rugged and, in many places, remote from civilization.

Not far from the port of Aleria, on the tamer eastern shore, the exiled philosopher Seneca had a modest house with a crude garden and two slaves to look after his needs. His view of the sea was, at times, a consolation in the tediously quiet hours of the afternoon. At other times it was a cruel reminder of the distance that had been put between him and Rome, which he thought of as his home, though he had been born in Spain. He had been reared in Rome. He had studied there. And he had achieved his fame there as philosopher, teacher, rhetorician, and close friend of aristocrats from senators to emperors. Now, in his late middle years, he longed to return to the excitement of the intellectual and political arena. Before Messalina's death this had been impossible. But now the vixen had been snared and his hopes were fired anew.

It was Annaeus Serenus who brought the good news. He

had agreed to make the crossing, in spite of his terror of the sea. Still pale from the journey, he made his way from the white cluster of houses at Aleria to the small villa up the hillside, guided by a minor official from the village who babbled all the way about the progress that was being made on the island in the improvement of the roads, as if this boast might win him an assignment in Rome or, at least, on the mainland.

The old friends embraced and wept, leaving the local official standing there shifting from foot to foot until Seneca dismissed him.

The two retired to the Spartan simplicity of Seneca's study. The stone floor was bare, but the walls were lined with books. "You've gathered quite a library in the past eight years," said Serenus.

"You have no idea how difficult and expensive it's been," said Seneca. "Nobody on this rotten island has the slightest interest in literature—or anything else, except pigs, and roads, and timber for export. What a pack of fat provincials and Italian malcontents. But, come, tell me. Tell me. What's the good news? What's happened since the death of Messalina?"

"The good news is that Agrippina has prevailed upon her uncle Claudius to allow you to return to Rome, using as her reason her desire to enlist you as a tutor for her son."

Seneca sighed. A slow smile of appreciation spread across his square, lean face. He passed a bony hand over the baldness of his head. "It's more than I hoped for," he said. "Tutor to Nero? What could be better? Between you and me we ought to be able to make somthing of him, eh?"

"His mother is determined to prepare him for greatness," said Serenus.

"An ambitious woman."

"Much too ambitious."

"What exactly does she have in mind?"

"The rumor is that she intends to marry Claudius."

"And what does Claudius have to say about *that*?"

"Oh, he doesn't know yet, of course. She and Pallas haven't informed him."

They laughed. Seneca touched his friend's hand. "By

God, it's good to see you, Serenus. And so good to hear the language spoken as it should be. Now, tell me everything. And tell me how all my friends are. And is Felix still in Judea? And Asconius Labeo? Is it true that he's been made Nero's guardian?"

"Yes, it's true. Yes, everyone is fine. They ask for you constantly. How delighted they will be to see you once more."

He rubbed his face, as if to wipe away the lines. "They won't recognize me. I've turned into an old man. You see how thin I am, how my hair has turned gray—what there is of it."

"Nonsense, my friend. You're as youthful as ever. And the filthy air of Rome will soon restore your health."

Once again they laughed. And once again Seneca prodded his visitor for news. The hours slipped away. The sun disappeared prematurely behind the rim of the mountains in the west. A chill crept into the air. Seneca called in an old man who built them a fire. And they sat before it into the night, reminiscing, planning, exchanging ideas and philosophical observations. "It is the will that links conviction and practice," said Seneca. "Without it we are nothing but stones rolling down the side of a hill."

When their dinner was brought into them, Seneca had to apologize for his vegetarian diet and the absence of wine. "How thoughtless of me," he said. "How Pythagorian! I do this not out of conviction, mind you, but only because it keeps my mind clear. I hate the dullness, the torpor induced by wine and meat."

"You should lecture Claudius on that subject. He's grown quite disgusting."

"Ah, poor Claudius. There's no changing him now. Such a strange combination of man and beast. So wise. So ignorant. So desperate and alone. If only someone in his life had loved him. But that would have been asking a great deal."

52

# VII

Tiberius Claudius Drusus Nero Germanicus, the emperor Claudius, sat in the *pulvinar*, the royal enclosure at the Circus Maximus, chattering and trembling with excitement. The morning session of the games was about to begin: chariot races, preceded this time by the sacrifice of the October horse, this ancient ritual moved this year from its traditional place in the Forum by a special edict of the emperor.

The holiday mob continued to file into the enormous hippodrome that stretched out luxuriously between the Palatine and Aventine hills. The crowd would number over a hundred thousand before the races were under way. Under the marbled arcades of the exterior of the stadium, vendors hawked their wares, adding to the noise and excitement: wine merchants, caterers, pastrycooks, astrologers, prostitutes, moneylenders.

In the imperial enclosure with the emperor were a dozen personal friends, guests, and family members. On one side of him was Narcissus; on the other side Pallas. Directly behind him were Xenophon, his personal physician, Callistus,

Turranius, the superintendent of the corn market, Lusius Geta, one of the co-commanders of the Praetorian Guard, and the very influential Lusius Bitellius. In front of him were his daughter Antonia and her husband Faustus Cornelius Sulla, his former wife Aelia Paetina, and his two children by Messalina, Britannicus and Octavia.

The fifty-nine-year-old Claudius was like a child at the games. He lost himself in them completely and was sometimes carried away into unseemly shouting and stomping, in spite of his stuttering and poor coordination. He knew the names of all the horses and the records of all the charioteers thoroughly. And he wagered with wild abandon, sending his slave Theon scurrying to announce his stakes. "Fifty thousand on the green! A hundred thousand on Scorpus!"

He moved constantly in his seat, shifting his weight, turning to those around him, nudging them, pushing them, roaring his appreciation, assuming inconsiderately that everyone in the world loved a thundering good race. His full head of white hair tossed in the breeze, adding to the wildness of his general appearance. Such a head of hair would have enhanced the looks of most men, but on him it was an ironic contrast to his hopeless unattractiveness. What's more, it grew too low on his forehead and too far down the back of his thick neck. Protruding from it laterally were his excessively large ears. His low forehead was deeply lined horizontally and split by a chronic frown. He had a tortured, worried look, in spite of his spastic outbursts of enthusiasm. His shadowy blue eyes were set deep under fleshy brows. He squinted and blinked nervously. Furrows of age ran down his lean face to the corners of his mouth, which was a broad, damp, hungry aperture that he was forced to dab at constantly with a white handkerchief. His unfinished, receding chin was so ill defined it almost joined in an unbroken line with his disproportionately thick neck, the unfortunate result of years of exertion because of a tremor and wobble that made him such an easy mark for the satirist. He was tall, but narrow-shouldered, and his chest was unathletically shallow. He was a noisy breather, who repeatedly cleared his throat and nose of the mucus that had plagued him from birth. Nothing was more ludicrous or appalling than this awkward specimen caught up in the feverish excitement of the race, struggling to his feet on weak, uncertain legs, slobbering incoherent encouragements to his favorites, his nose running, his head wobbling. But his absolute sincerity and complete involvement endeared him to the mob, who felt that, at least in this respect, he was one of them. But, for that same reason, his friends and relatives were often embarrassed for him, convinced that he was making a vulgar spectacle of himself.

The seats were almost filled. The day was bright, but for the wisps of clouds they called the hair of Zeus. The race course, perfectly tended, was a long oblong almost six hundred meters around, with a pole at each end marking the turn. It could easily accommodate four chariots, each drawn by four horses. The straightaways were flanked by stone grandstands, with the emperor's *pulvinar* on the Palatine side. A temporary altar had been set up in the infield for the *flamen* of Mars, the sacrificing priest. He waited with his assistants in flaming red robes. They held the vessels in which the blood would be collected.

"Theon!" shouted Claudius, fussing with his richly embroidered toga. "F-f-ind out what the d-d-delay is. Let's get on with it, eh." He leaned forward to intrude himself between his daughter Antonia and her handsome husband. "We're going to ha-ha-have the October horse now. Two g-g-great horses. And to the victor the honor of a public sacrifice. By God, how they f-f-fought for the head last year. Remember that, Sulla? Remember that? How that S-S-Subura crowd outshouted that mob from the Sacra Via. Almost killed each other to g-g-get that head. Should let them fight for it, eh. Should let them tear each other to p-p-pieces." His laughter exploded between them. Their faces were turned. Antonia smiled patiently, her face illuminated by kindness. She had black hair and olive skin and large brown eyes. Having grown up with her father around, she had an affectionate tolerance for his eccentricities.

"Who will you give it to this year?" asked Sulla. His dark hair matched Antonia's. He had the tall, elegant grace of a Greek athlete and the inherited good looks of his family, fine eyes, full lips, lean face and strong chin, pleasantly dimpled to give a slightly pretty edge to his masculinity.

"I don't know," said Claudius. He nudged Narcissus, who sat stoically watching the preparations below. "Who got the horse's head l-l-last year?"

"I think it was hung in the Subura," said Narcissus.

"As a matter of fact," said Pallas from the other side of the emperor, "I think it was exhibited on a wall in the Sacra Via."

"I could be mistaken," said Narcissus. "We have so many festivals."

"Ah, but only one October horse," said Claudius. He waved his hand recklessly. "And what's the difference who got it last year. We'll award it to the mob that raises the loudest clamor this year." He sucked in saliva and wiped his nose.

Trumpets sounded. The crowd let loose a roar that welled like the sea and then subsided into silence. The ceremony was about to begin. The two horses were presented, one gray, one startling white. "From the stables of Fuscus and Crescens," said Claudius, this time nudging Pallas. "I w-w-wish it were not a religious ritual, I'd w-w-wager on the gray. What do you think, Pallas? What do you think? The gray, eh. The gray will take it. I think the gray."

In the row behind the emperor, Vitellius and Callistus conversed freely, protected by the noise of the crowd and by Claudius's partial deafness, though there was some question about how real that deafness was. Some said it was merely political, that he heard only what he wanted to hear.

"I didn't know that Aelia Paetina was to be included here today," said Callistus.

"Well, she *is* Antonia's mother, after all," said Vitellius.

"Yes, but you know as well as I do that there's talk of a remarriage."

Vitellius looked at the back of Narcissus's head and lowered his voice. "Believe me, my friend, if I could have prevented it, I would have. You know who's got his ear. But there will be other occasions. Though, I must say, it makes a pleasant enough family group, doesn't it?" He was a spare old man with poise and dignity, the very epitome of the senator. His gray hair was receding, but a certain youthfulness lingered in his sharp, noncommital face. "You have to admit that she's not a bad-looking woman, considering her age."

"She's a good twelve years older than Lollia Paulina," said Callistus, "and probably past childbearing.

Vitellius smiled. "That may not be a serious consideration."

Callistus hesitated, pretending to look at the ceremony. Then he leaned closer to Vitellius and whispered, "Is it true you've thrown your supoprt to Agrippina?"

"My dear fellow," said the old senator. "How can you ask such a question? I'll just pretend I didn't hear it. Besides, don't you think it's a bit premature to tip your hand?"

"We've all got to gamble, don't we?"

"In that case, I suggest you gamble on the races. There you can only lose your money, not your life."

The trumpets sounded again. The crowd stirred as the horses were led to the starting line. They would be ridden bareback, in the old way, their riders in abbreviated tunics and buskins. Once around the great oval and back to the starting point, a dash to victory and death, at stake the honor of the stable and the good will of the gods.

Antonia moved closer to her husband and slipped her hand in his. Behind her she could hear the shuffling perpetual motion of her father's wasted legs. Her heart went out to the white stallion, who reared at the starting line, as though he caught the meaning of the race and ritual. She was afraid he would win. He was so beautiful, so alive, so strong.

The president of the games stood on a high wooden platform. Over his scarlet tunic he wore an elaborate Tyrian toga and on his head a wreath of golden leaves. In one hand he held an ivory baton topped by an eagle in flight; in the other he held the white flag that he would drop to start the race.

Up to this point Narcissus was preoccupied, staring at the attractive Aelia Paetina and wondering whether or nor Claudius even noticed that she was there. But as the critical moment approached even he was drawn into the excitement, though he had often enough expressed his personal feelings about these senseless old ceremonies.

And then they were off. Head to head they raced down the first straightaway to the far turn, leaving behind them puffs of dust that drifted away toward the infield and the colorful group of assassins, who waited with their traditional equipment to receive the winner.

At the first turn the white horse took the lead and stretched it out to three lengths. The rider gave him his head, and he galloped like a god, sending a thrill through the gasping spectators. His muscles strained. Saliva foamed around the bit. His gorgeous tail sailed behind him. He was wind. He was flying clouds in a storm.

But down the back stretch the sturdy gray horse began to build momentum. He was thicker, more powerful in the thighs, but infinitely less dramatic. Nevertheless, he gained on the white hero of the deafening crowd. He was duty and determination, his steady eyes fixed on his wild rival.

By the final turn the gray horse moved alongside and made a powerful bid for the lead. His head was low and bobbed rhythmically forward. Claudius, struggling to his feet, echoed the bobbing determination of the gray horse, and let out a gutteral scream that sent the blood rushing to his face.

The gray horse took the lead in the last furlong. But suddenly the white horse, who seemed for a moment to be tiring, found new energy. Fired by the challenge, galloping more with his noble heart than his legs, he surged back. The rider's whip lashed at his flanks, sending a sting of pain through Antonia's womb. And she buried her face in her husband's arm to avoid seeing the beautiful beast plunge across the finish line, the winner by half a length.

Claudius sank down into his seat, trembling from head to toe and gasping for air. Pallas turned to him with friendly nonchalance and said, "Are you all right?" The emperor nodded his unsteady head and spit elaborately on the ground in front of him. Narcissus said nothing. His attention drifted back to Aelia Paetina, who was reaching out a hand to quiet the boy Britannicus. He was leaping up and down uncontrollably.

Claudius looked up at the sound of his son's name. "Leave the boy alone!" he coughed, his eyes lost in a dream. "Aelia! L-l-let him be." It was the tone he used with her when she was his wife. And it was as if nothing had changed in over a dozen years. And, indeed, for him, nothing had, such distortions of time was he susceptible to. "He wants to see the October horse. Let him see the horse. There's a good lad. Watch the flamen cut off his head."

The nine-year-old Britannicus smiled back at his father and jerked his arm away from Aelia. In his face one could see Messalina's. And his hair was as thick as his father's but black and curly. "Is he going to kill him now?" he said, scrambling over the seats to find a place between his father and Pallas.

Pallas inched away with a look of quiet contempt. Claudius, still red in the face, pulled the boy to his side with a trembling hand. "Yes, yes. Watch now. They'll rope him to the altar and cut his throat. Noble horse. Great horse. I'll buy the gray for you and we'll race him to victory next year, eh. What do you s-s-say to that?"

And then a great hush fell over the throng. The snorting, sweating beast was flung to the ground and bound into helplessness. Then a board was slipped under his middle and he was raised to what seemed, from a distance, a standing position. More ropes were fixed to him as the priests recited the verses of their hymn to a background of trumpets and drums. The horse's head was drawn back to expose his throat. The sacred blade was raised. The vessels were ready beside the wide silver basin. The exhausted and terrified animal barely struggled. The hush became an absolute silence. Sun glinted from the blade. A tenth of a million people were drawn into the magic of the moment. A dead religion came to life. Mystery filled the air. Even the horse was hypnotized until the swift, clean cut opened his artery and the deep red blood spurted out, staining the assistants and splashing into the silver basin. Then all his insticts exploded into a cry of anguish that rose from the Circus Maximus to the flanking hills to the very skies. And

59

the tension was broken with a shudder that became a universal sigh that became a roar of animal exhilaration. The blood poured out of the horse, streaking his white coat. His terror seeped slowly from his dying body. And his mournful sounds were lost in the thundering ovation.

"I'm glad to see that some of the old forms survive," said Vitellius.

"But is it quite right to move this ritual from the Forum and combine it with the games?" asked Callistus. "It turns it into mere spectacle."

"Which is precisely what these dirty beggars want," said Vitellius. "Even the games were religion once. But the meaning is gone, of course. All we can hope for is the form. It's form that holds things together. Don't you agree, Xenophon?"

The emperor's physician looked calmly at the old senator. He was a middle-aged man with round, fatalistic eyes. "I'm sure you're right, Lucius," he said. "This is the sort of passion that riots are made of. It must be drawn off, just as the priests are drawing off that horse's blood."

And then the ghastly work of butchering the animal began. Claudius leaned forward for a better view. The augur examined the entrails and pronounced the time auspicious. And, at last, the highly prized head was cut and hacked from the white corpse. It was raised on a staff held by two men in scarlet robes. The crowd greeted the presentation with lusty cries that resolved themselves into the rhythmic chanting of two factions: Subura! Subura! Subura! Sacra Via! Sacra Via! Sacra Via! The tempo increased. The noise expanded. Fists and flags and flowers were waved about and then tossed into the oval. Fights broke out and were contained by the Praetorian Guard.

Claudius rose unsteadily to his feet, one hand on the shoulder of Narcissus, the other on the slender shoulder of his son Britannicus, who looked frightened under the burden. There was a mad gleam of satisfaction in the emperor's eye. He waved to his subjects, and they roared all the louder. "Which shall it be?" he shouted. "Which shall it be?" He prolonged the shouting duel by his indecision. Then he looked down to catch the sweet but troubled face

60

of his daughter Antonia. She was silently pleading for him to make up his mind. He appealed suddenly to her, confusion in his old face. "Which shall it be, Antonia? You decide. C-c-come now. Tell me. Tell them. Which shall it be?"

She was paralyzed with embarrassment. All eyes in the enclosure were on her. It was her husband who rescued her by whispering, arbitrarily, the word *Subura* in her ear. "Subura," she blurted out. And the emperor threw up both hands to command silence so that he could announce his decision.

When order was restored, the regular races began. In a full day there were normally twenty-four races, but because of the added ceremony today there would only be twelve, six of them prior to the midday recess for food and rest.

The races went well for Claudius. By the intermission he had won a total of 85,000 sesterces. But, happy as he was with his luck, his appetite gradually won a commanding position in his mind, and all the way back to the palace in his litter, accompanied by Narcissus, all he could talk about was food. Narcissus, on the other hand, had other things on his mind. "Your fortunes are rising in more ways than one," he said.

"What do you mean?" said Claudius, his wet mouth moving as if he was already tasting his food.

"I mean, you seem very high in the affections of the people."

"Do I? Mmmm! You think so, eh? M-m-more than usual?"

"Oh yes. Much more than usual. I think they were pleased with the gathering of your family in the imperial enclosure. It was very domestic, very charming. One could tell they approved. They have not forgotten Aelia, you know. She's very popular. She'd be a fitting stepmother for your children. And, of course, you know her well. A good woman. All the old virtues."

"Yes, yes, a good woman. I always rather liked her. Quiet. A man should have a quiet wife for his old age."

"Precisely! You know her. She knows you. As I've told

61

you before, you must consider her. It would be very wise politically. Especially after your recent misfortunes."

He grew silent, his heavy brow furrowed, as if he were trying to avoid remembering something. "Marriage? You think I should marry again, eh?" Then he shook his head. "No, no. Not again. I'm too old. It's too d-d-dangerous."

"But this is hardly like marrying," said Narcissus. "It's like revisiting an old friend, someone you can trust."

He thought again for a long time. The motion of the litter exaggerated the tremor of his head on his thick neck. "Perhaps you're right," he said. "Yes, you're probably right." And then he broke into a lecherous smile. "And, what's more, she's still got her looks, eh?" He exploded into a gurgling cough. When it subsided, he said, "I could eat a whole pig. Do you think we have pig for lunch? I hope we have pig. And some of that Greek wine. What is it? You know, that L-l-l-lemnian. Yes, that's it. Pig and Lemnian wine. Ah, there's something to f-f-fix your mind on."

And they lumbered up the hill to the imperial palace, all further conversation cut off by the emperor's enormous appetite.

# VIII

After the midday meal, a modest affair of a dozen or so
courses, and after a nap, they all returned to the Circus
Maximus for the afternoon session of the games. With only
six races remaining, it was an abbreviated affair, much to
the relief of almost everyone, except Claudius, who could
lose himself forever in an endless sequence of such events.

After the exertions of the games came the relaxation of
the baths, for men and women, for rich and poor, private
and public. Some of the spectators, their blood high from
the violence of the races, would combine their bath with a
sexual adventure. The prostitutes who worked the Circus
Maximus did very well on such gala occasions as this.

Refreshed, perfumed, and purged, Claudius flung himself
into the evening meal with high spirits and gusto. His
friends were still with him, as were the members of his
family, including his children. He plunged into the food as
though years had passed instead of hours since he last ate.
He stuffed himself with mullet and sturgeon, peacock and
pork, babbling all the time, somewhat incoherently, about
the chariot races. He fell into an argument with Turranius

63

over the comparative skills of two of the leading charioteers, Chilon and Scorpus. Pallas watched him with cold
detachment, wondering if, after all, he should deliver
Agrippina into the arms of this glutton. He was himself
profoundly fond of her, in spite of his personal determination to remain safely detached from emotional involve-
ments. "Our feelings are hostages to fate," was one of his
favorite observations.

"Nobody handles the *funales*, the outside horses, like
Chilon," said Turranius. "Did you see him today? Did you
see him take those turns? Only once have I see him cut
himself loose from the reins bound round his body. Only
once, and that was not his fault."

"S-S-Scorpus can make a horse do anything," said Claudius. "With a team of four he cuts those c-c-corners closer
than anybody else. Much closer. And he knows how to rate
those beasts, holding them in with tremendous power.
What arms! What m-m-muscles in those legs of his. What a
hero! C-c-can't run them out in the first three laps. Lay off
the pace through the fifth. And then—then s-s-see him
move. Eh, Vitellius. Am I not right. S-s-sometimes, he
takes it down to the sixth, even the seventh and final lap.
But that's where he's s-s-supreme. Nobody takes Scorpus in
the stretch!"

The wine flowed. The courses kept arriving. Musicians
played. A troupe of jugglers was ushered in, but was met
with indifference. Claudius tucked in his already invisible
chin and let out a series of gustatory compliments to the
cooks. He grunted and nodded to Xenophon. His physician
helped him to his feet and led him into the small room
adjacent to the dining hall. There, as everyone knew, he
would have his throat tickled with a feather until he gave
up the half-digested food that bloated his stomach.

When he came back, he looked much better. What's
more, some of the racing had gone out of his mind, and he
addressed himself to other subjects, among them the corn
supply, the Alexandrian Jews, and a fine point in Etruscan
history, about which he had once written a book, with considerable help from his literary secretary Polybius—the late
Polybius. At moments like this Claudius could be some-

thing of a scholar—the result of his having been hidden from public life for fifty years by a family that found him an embarrassment.

As the evening wore on, the drinking became more serious and the laughter became louder. Pallas looked concerned. He had been trying for hours to whisper something in the emperor's ear, but the opportunity never presented itself. Narcissus was by his side constantly, maneuvering him, hour by hour, toward a remarriage with Aelia Paetina.

It was only when Claudius left the room to relieve himself that Pallas could get to him. Pretending to be as pleasantly inebriated as the emperor, he put his arm around Claudius and they went, laughing like schoolboys, into the garden to urinate.

Claudius swayed uncertainly on the terrace and filled his narrow chest with fresh air. Then he pulled aside his toga and bared himself to the night to rid himself of some of the wine he had been gulping.

"A beautiful evening!" said Pallas, turning away slightly for a little privacy and going through the motions.

Claudius grunted, glanced up at the stars, and then shuffled a few steps further toward a decorative balustrade. There he amused himself by urinating all over a statue of Cupid and Psyche, chuckling to himself through a slight grimace.

Pallas waited until he was done and then approached him. "I have something very important to tell you," he said, "before we go back in."

"Eh? What's that?" asked Claudius, as though he hadn't quite heard his wealthy freedman-secretary.

In the faint light Pallas held out his hand. In his palm was a pair of lady's earrings. They were extravagant jewels in a gold setting. At the center of each cluster was a huge ruby. "Do you remember these?"

Claudius squinted. His nearsightedness added to his confusion, "What is it? What have you got there?" His head wobbled. He took hold of Pallas's hand. "What are they? Jewels? Why are you showing me jewels here in the dark in the garden?"

"Shh!" said Pallas, putting a finger across his lips. "The

owner of these precious earrings is waiting for you. You know her. You gave her these as a gift. I thought you might remember."

"I gave her these?" He picked them up and held them close to his face. They caught the moonlight and glistened. "I must have been very fond of her. Who is she?"

"Ah, that's a surprise," said Pallas. "And this is the only clue I am allowed to give you. She assures me that she is prepared to make you the happiest man in the world tonight."

"Tonight, eh?" He shuffled from foot to foot. "I think I catch your meaning." He laughed confidentially and somewhat lecherously. "A rendezvous, eh? I love a rendezvous. Where is she? What am I supposed to do?"

"Go back into the dining room, pretend that you are sleepy, and excuse yourself for the evening. You'll find her in your bedroom."

"B-b-but what about Calpurnia?"

"We've taken care of that," said Pallas. "Besides, she's only a slave. She knows when to speak and when to remain silent."

"She may be jealous."

"Nonsense! Jealousy is a luxury that slaves can ill afford. Take my word for it, all is arranged." His voice fell to a heavy whisper, adding fuel to the fire that was kindled in Claudius.

They went back into the house arm-in-arm, the emperor mumbling happily to himself and nudging his friend.

Back in the dining room, he took his place on his couch and asked for more wine. "The ordinary Falernian," he said. "That damn Th-Th-Thasian Greek wine burns your urine. D-d-don't you agree, Narcissus? Delicious but d-d-deadly. Just like a woman!" And he burst into uncontrollable laughter. Aelia looked across the table at him and frowned. She knew instantly what was going through his mind, having lived with him for some years. He contemplated women much the same way he contemplated food. She could tell when he was sexually distracted. The only thing she could not know was who the unfortunate woman was this time.

66

When he made his clumsy exit, yawning unconvincingly, her suspicions were confirmed. Everyone rose to wish him goodnight. Only his ten-year-old daughter Octavia had the courage to kiss him. He hugged her suddenly with a jerky motion that literally lifted her off her feet. And then he was gone, dragging his right foot in that awkward gait of his.

As soon as he was out of the room Aelia approached Narcissus and said, "What do you suppose he's up to?"

"I supppose he's going to bed," said Narcissus.

"Yes, but with whom?"

"Calpurnia?"

"I don't know," she said. "I doubt it. He's got that look in his eye."

"A new slave perhaps."

She thought about it for a moment. "Perhaps." And then her daughter Antonia was at her side suggesting that it was probably time to leave.

Meanwhile, Claudius was lurching, as fast as his weak legs would take him, down the corridor to his bedroom. He was pleased to see that the two Praetorian Guards who were stationed outside his door had vanished. In his mind he thanked Pallas for his part in this amorous adventure. He stood for a moment before the door and listened. Then he went in. The room was dimly lighted by a single oil lamp. He closed the door behind him and bolted it. As his eyes became accustomed to the light he could see that there was someone lying on his oversized bed. His heart pounded. There was a stirring in his groin. Saliva accumulated in his mouth and trickled past his lower lip. He used the back of his hand to wipe it away.

"I've been waiting for you," said a sultry voice from the bed.

He approached slowly, his eyes gradually accustoming themselves to the light. "Who is it?" he said deep in his throat. His breathing could be heard in the quiet room.

The form that came into focus was a nude woman, her loose blonde hair arranged on the bolster, her long body lying on its side, emphasizing the shapeliness of her hips. He was puzzled. "Who is it?" he said. "Who are you?"

67

"When I was just a girl," said the deep feminine voice, "you used to call me your daughter. Remember? My sisters and I played a game with you called *monster*. Now do you remember?"

He stood by the bed, trembling and swaying. "I remember." he said. "You were all my daughters. And I would c-c-catch you. And we would fall on the bed and—and—and we would play monster. Yes, monster. I remember." Then he was standing directly over her and staring down at her. Suddenly he sucked in air mixed with saliva. "Agrippina!" His heart thumped in his throat.

"That's right, uncle. Dear uncle!"

His speech dissolved into a series of incoherencies. She held out a long white arm to him. He took her hand and allowed himself to be led into a sitting position beside her. "It's been a long time since those happy days."

He sat beside her and absorbed her nakedness. His hand reached for her and ran along her hip and thigh. Then her hand drew him closer. "Come," she said. "Let's play as we did in those happy days. Take off those silly clothes."

He stood up and struggled out of his toga and his underclothes. She watched him. In the inadequate light he could not see the look on her face. She was a mask of seductiveness over secret eyes of contempt as she stared at the tall, aging, trembling, disproportionate creature.

"Don't ask me why I'm here," she said. "Don't ask me anything. Lie beside me. Let's dream of childhood, of all the pleasures we have known. The bodies. The moments of ecstasy."

Her voice embraced him. He crawled onto the bed on all fours and eased himself into a reclining position. Perspiration beaded on his forehead. His breath was almost visible. She faced him. Then she urged him to lie down on his back, knowing full well the weakness of his arms. He sighed as she ran her fingers through his hair. Then she kissed him, first on his cheek, then on his mouth, thrusting her tongue like a serpent until it found his. He moaned and sucked at her mouth. She moved away and down, toying with the hair on his chest, licking at his nipples. And then down, down, down, until she found the half-erect center of his desire. Her full breasts rubbed against him. He fondled them with wooden hands. She gathered his loose scrotum in her long fingers and excited him into firmness. Then she took him in her mouth and performed with all the agility of a practiced whore. He would have wasted himself in that simple act had she not played him as though she were a musician, curbing him near the climax. And then mounting him and teasing him at the damp aperture of her deepest secret. His hips rose. His head thrashed from side to side. Her whisper was a musical accompaniment, a recital of earlier joys, some real, some invented. "How we played in the palace when I was a girl. And Drusilla and Julia. Remember how they giggled. Remember how you played the monster and ate them up, holding their little thighs and putting your tongue there between their legs. How new we were! How eager for fun! We were all your daughters. That's what you called us. And we loved you. We loved you. Our old monster. Always grabbing at us. Always coming into our rooms at night. Sucking our little breasts with wine on your breath. Do you remember? Do you remember our little hands on you, making that big worm spit on our white bellies? How we laughed and squirmed and whispered dirty things to each other. Do you remember? Wrestling and tossing and kissing and itching. Our fires turning us into little Sapphos, so that we kissed each other and played boys, pressing our thighs into each other until we died for the thrust of a man, a bull. How we teased you! How we avoided you, girlishly afraid of that throbbing weapon of yours. Until, at last, you pushed it into one of us—Drusilla, Julia, me. Oh, yes, more than once into me. Deep into me, like hot stone, like fire, like a god descending to make us one with the earth."

She moved her hips on him, her breasts moving with their own weight before his heavy-lidded eyes. She straddled him. She swallowed him between her thighs. She stroked him with the predatory motion of her hips until he cried out, without his stammer, "Oh, my daughter, my daughter, little Agrippina. All my little girls. Sweet womb of Venus. Kill me now. Oh, kill me now. Now, now, now!" Each word a rising thrust until the little death when she drew him forth and emptied him.

When he eventually opened his eyes again, he was alone in bed. Agrippina was standing like a visitation in the middle of the room, draped in a yellow robe. "Am I d-d-dreaming," he said.

"We are all dreaming," she said.

"My god, how almost d-d-dead we are."

"The gift of life consumes us."

"Why are you here?"

"It's where I belong."

"Will you go away again?"

"That, dear uncle, lover, monster, husband, is up to you."

"How can I keep you?"

She laughed. "Need I tell you?"

"Can I do that? Can I?"

"You can do anything you want. Make me your slave, your wife, and I will make you immortal—for a while. What more can an old man want?"

"Nothing," he said. "Nothing, nothing, nothing." And he subsided, once again, into sleep.

# IX

Several weeks later, besieged by the agents and champions of a dozen eligible women, Claudius agreed to confront the marriage question in an open and official fashion. He wanted to make a choice without offending anybody. So he called together a conference, at which, he said, the representatives of the three contenders could present their arguments. His whole circle of close friends, secretaries, and advisors would be present to help him decide. The women themselves would *not* be present.

Narcissus would speak on behalf of Aelia Paetina. Callistus would sing the praises of Lollia Paulina. And Pallas would make the case for Agrippina.

The setting for the conference was an atrium in the Palatine palace that was permanently arranged for receptions. It was here that Claudius received petitions and ambassadors. It was here that he conferred with the senators and generals and conducted the affairs of state. This impending marriage, too, was a state affair, a political matter. About that there was no question at all in anyone's mind, though the emperor's flesh was still alive with the memory of his rendezvous with Agrippina.

Claudius presided on a slightly raised platform, flanked by Pallas, Narcissus, and Callistus on one side, and by Turranius, Vitellius, and Burrus on the other. These flanks extended into a double row of seats on each side of the room, forming a small arena in the center for the principal speakers.

The seats accommodated some of the most important men in Rome. There were the co-commanders of the Praetorian Guard, Geta and Crispinus. There were senators and officials, advisors and relatives. Men with power. Men with money. Men with vested interests of one sort or another.

Claudius sat silently for a long time as the speakers made their points. There were shadows under his eyes. He tugged meditatively at the skin of his neck. His tremor was less noticeable, as if deep thought steadied him. But what thoughts he might be entertaining nobody knew for sure. He might have been thinking about the proceedings. On the other hand, he might have been thinking about one of his pet projects—the new port at Ostia, the tunnel at Fucinus. He might even have been thinking about what food would be served for lunch. Suddenly, he yawned elaborately and rubbed his eyes. He suffered from insomnia and often fell asleep at public functions.

Callistus made his presentation first. He was a good speaker, well-versed in the old rhetoric, complete with its formal gestures. He paused frequently to pose like an appealing statue before his attentive audience. "I need not remind you of the patrician family from which Lollia Paulina comes, nor of their accomplishments and wealth. Many of you knew her illustrious father, the former consul Marcus Lollius. There is no question at all that she has the high breeding required for an exalted marriage of this kind. In her youth, she was, in fact, the choice of our previous emperor Caligula, the nephew of Claudius and the son of Germanicus. Though she is still in her prime, she has not been blessed with children of her own. This may now prove to be a blessing of another sort. Without children of her own to distract her, she can serve the emperor as a loving and

72

devoted stepmother for his now motherless children. We all know how difficult it is for a woman to place another woman's children before her own." He allowed his gaze to wander to Pallas as he said this. And then he paused for emphasis.

"I don't mean to imply that the other ladies are less beautiful or less qualified, but we must consider the specific circumstances. Aelia Paetina was divorced from the emperor some years ago for reasons that were at the time acceptable but are now forgivable. Time changes everything. Nevertheless, a woman taken back by a husband who once put her aside is liable to feel a certain haughtiness, a certain superciliousness. The relationship is, in a way, soiled, and may never recover its original innocence. I strongly advise an entirely new relationship, untainted by past bitterness or the complication of competing children."

Claudius nodded his head slowly, as if he was moved by these arguments, but he said nothing.

When Narcissus rose to speak, it was clear that he had considerable support in the room. He was, after all, the recent hero of the Messalina affair. He was a man with courage and principles, a man devoted to the well-being of Claudius and Rome.

"I'm suggesting a conservative and sensible course of action," he said. He spoke in a simple, forthright fashion, without the elaborate rhetoric of Callistus. His bluntness and honesty were refreshing. "With all due respect to our beloved emperor, he must surely realize that he is no longer a young man. He is mature in years and set in his ways. He has children to consider and other weighty responsibilities. What he needs at this time in his life is a good woman to help him raise and protect those children and a companion with whom to share his thoughts and his private life. He has already had three marriages. The first was an unhappy misalliance. The third, as you all know, was a disaster. It was only with his second wife that he enjoyed the quiet domesticity that we all eventually long for. In the case of Aelia Paetina, it was not the marriage, but the divorce that was a mistake. She has been, in these intervening years, a woman of unimpeachable reputation, a

73

woman with quiet dignity and grace. She has never remarried. And she has been a devoted mother to the daughter whom both she and Claudius love, the beautiful Antonia. The family of the Tuberones has a right to be proud of this remarkable lady. There is no question at all, in my mind, that she would be an excellent stepmother to Britannicus and Octavia. Indeed, she has already served in that capacity because of the closeness of her relationship to the imperial family. But above all other considerations is the fact that Aelia Paetina is a known quanitity, which eliminates the sort of risk that comes with a new alliance. And, finally, a delicate matter. How shall I put it? The selection of Agrippina is liable to stir up a storm of criticism and protest on the grounds of close kinship. Not a happy way to begin a new marriage."

As he spoke, Claudius moved uneasily in his chair. His frown grew deeper. His expression slipped from weariness to brooding. He seemed, in fact, on the brink of tears, as if he were about to be deprived of something he thought he could have. Perhaps he was scolding himself for being a foolish old man.

In any case, when Pallas rose to commend Agrippina, the veil of sadness fell from the emperor's face, and he pulled himself out of his slouch to pay particular attention to every word. He obviously wanted to be convinced that she was the proper choice.

Pallas was not popular with most of the people in the room, but they respected his wealth and his power. He was too arrogant for their taste, too sure of himself. He did not like asking for things. He preferred to command. And he expected to be obeyed. In the world of commerce he was something of an emperor himself. And in the imperial household he was the real power behind the throne, in spite of the recent popularity and influence of Narcissus.

He began dramatically: "If Agrippina does not find favor in the eyes of the emperor, she will marry someone else. That is the key to this whole situation. You will forgive me for this political bluntness. She and her son Nero are the closest living descendents of the Claudian-Julian line. She is the great-grandaughter of Augustus on one side, and the great-grandaughter of Tiberius on the other side. The union of these two great houses is precisely what determined the marriage of her mother Agrippina to her father Germanicus. What could be more politically sound than to repeat that union and once again solidify the imperial family? We can not afford factionalism, intrigue, or conspiracy. We've had enough of that. We want the harmony of a happy household. Agrippina is a woman in her child-bearing prime. She is beautiful and intelligent. What's more, she has the forcefulness and conviction of her famous mother. She would be more to the emperor than just a wife. And more to his children than just a stepmother. She would be a source of strength, inspiration, vast wealth, and political stability. To choose her would be the wise and courageous thing to do. Not to choose her would be—" he hesitated and looked slowly around at his grim, attentive audience—*"dangerous!"*

The word descended in a cloud of ambiguity, which he chose not to resolve. He had made his point.

# X

By the next morning a rumor was running rampant through the city that the emperor Claudius had decided to marry his thirty-four-year-old niece, Agrippina. It greeted yawning senators at their breakfast. It swept through the market places and the Forum and monopolized conversation. Arguments lasted deep into the night and were sometimes violently resolved. *How could he? How could he not? The fool! The fortunate old bastard!*

But it was over a month before the rumor became official. The marriage was stalled awkwardly before the tricky hurdle of incest. It was Vitellius who provided Claudius with a solution. "What if the Senate passed a resolution urging you to remarry for the good of the state?" he said. "And what if they passed another resolution sanctioning the marriages of uncles and nieces?"

"Well, as a citizen and a s-s-servant, I would have to acquiesce to their demands, wouldn't I?" said Claudius with a wet smile.

And so it was done, as professionally as a theatrical production. The senators were rehearsed. A throng was hired to clamor outside the Senate building, demanding the remarriage of the emperor for the safety of the state.

When the situation had been brought to an adequate boil, Vitellius himself went before the Senate and begged to be heard. The old pirate, having seen which way the wind was blowing, lifted his sail to catch a bit of its benefit. "My dear colleagues of the Senate," he said, "our emperor is in despair. His domestic misfortunes have made him unfit to carry the burdens of his high office. While he languishes in loneliness, the business of government is neglected. Decisions are delayed. Appointments are unsigned. And our prosperity and security are threatened. We must urge him toward a solution that will benefit us all. And what better solution is there than a happy marriage? What a sweet comfort a happy family life is! Especially in the waning years of a man's life. And especially for a man too virtuous to find satisfaction outside the marriage bond. We must urge him to remarry, however reluctant he may be . . ."

He went on for an hour this way, weaving into his appeal "the woman with the highest possible qualifications," none other than his niece Agrippina. "Alien as this may seem to our sense of propriety, it is quite common in other countries. We must pave the way with our approval. We must rescue the nation from almost certain disaster . . ."

The impotent herd bellowed its approval. Outside, the throng kept up its incessant noise. Before long, even the engineers of the scheme began to believe what they were saying.

Both resolutions passed unanimously. And the news was greeted with sighs of relief and celebrations, as if the empire had, indeed, been rescued from some imminent danger of collapse.

# XI

"We are all doomed!" said Aelia Paetina. The impending marriage of Claudius and Agrippina was old news, but Aelia was still announcing ruin from the seclusion of her house on the Palatine. She was pale and thin. Her disappointment and embarrassment were profound. But worse than her personal defeat was her conviction that Agrippina would prove to be even more ruthless than her predecessor. "We might have been better off with Messalina, erratic as she was. She was more interested in pleasure than power. But to Agrippina there is no greater pleasure than power."

She was in the garden talking with her daughter Antonia, her son-in-law Faustus Cornelius Sulla, and her unsuccessful champion Narcissus. Young Octavia, accompanied by a slave was paying a visit to her half-sister. She was less interested in the adult conversation than in the flashing silver fish in the pond. In a pretty pink tunic, short in front, long in back, she skipped along the pond, tossing pebbles in the water to make the fish jump and flash. And then she would let out a girlish squeak of satisfaction.

"Octavia!" said Aelia. "Must you do that? Surely you can find something else to amuse you."

Octavia stopped instantly and looked embarrassed as everyone's eyes suddenly focused on her. She was a delicate girl, with blonde hair and sad eyes. She had the helpless look of a living toy. She was, in fact, already being used in the political game. Her father Claudius, had betrothed her at the age of ten to the handsome and popular Lucius Silanus, a young man of twenty-five, well on his way to great achievements and distinctions.

Antonia touched her mother's arm to keep her from saying anything further. Then she went to Octavia and put her arm around her affectionately. "Why don't you gather some roses for Father," she said. "You know how much he likes roses. There are hundreds of them in the other garden. But mind the thorns." She kissed her half-sister and sent her off with a smile.

"I'm sorry," said Aelia. "I didn't mean to snap at her."

"She meant no harm," said Narcissus. "She's a lovely little girl."

"I tremble to think how awful her life will be under Agrippina," said Aelia. "That witch will make those children wretched."

"She will have my father to contend with," said Antonia.

"I'm afraid she's equal to the task," said Narcissus.

"What do you think she will do?" asked Antonia.

Aelia fingered her gold necklace and looked meditatively toward the high, ivy-covered wall in the distance that marked the boundary between the grounds of her house and the lesser establishment of her daughter. In the bright sunlight of the late morning, one could see the few gray hairs that had insinuated themselves among the black. She was a mature, compact woman in whom the last traces of youth still lingered. As she spoke, her thin lips trembled. She was not the sort of woman who would ever allow herself to cry. "She will do whatever is necessary to gain absolute control of things. I know her. She's ruthless."

"She's got money," said Narcissus. "And she's got friends in key positions. What's more, she's got the support

79

of all those people who loved her mother and father. Was there ever a more popular hero than Germanicus? She'll make good use of that."

"But what exactly will she do?" asked Antonia. She sat close to Sulla and with him made the couple that all of Rome envied for their beauty and devotion. Theirs was the rare political marriage that blossomed into love. And they had much more to live for than conspiracy and power, if only the world would leave them alone.

"For one thing," said Narcissus, "she will try to destroy your husband. You mark my words. He has the heritage, the name, the popularity to become the rallying point of opposition."

"But I want nothing to do with politics," said Sulla. "I've made that clear to everybody." His sensitivity and modesty were reflected in the softness of his voice. But he spoke with manly precision. He was forthright and honest, and, therefore, not to be trusted in this twisted world.

"You are a descendent of the legendary Sulla," said Narcissus. "You don't have much choice. You will be used, whether you like it or not."

"All we want to do is to live in peace," he replied, taking his wife by the shoulders and drawing her to him.

Narcissus laughed. "That's a dream. And this is a nightmare. We are all trapped in it. And there's no running away, except into self-imposed exile. And what sort of life is that? Ask Seneca how he fared in Corsica."

"Is it true that he's coming back?" asked Aelia.

"Oh, yes! Definitely! He's going to play a major part in Agrippina's plans."

"And just what *are* her plans?" asked Sulla.

"We can only speculate at this point. There are a thousand rumors. She will surround her son Nero with hand-picked tutors and guardians and groom him for the role he is destined to play. She will undoubtedly try to persuade Claudius to adopt him. She may even attempt to marry him to Octavia."

"But her eventual marriage to Silanus has already been arranged," said Antonia.

"She's not going to let that stand in her way."

80

"He was Claudius's own choice."

"So was Agrippina. Or so he imagines. I hate to say this about your father, Antonia, but he can be managed. He can be manipulated, especially by women. It's his chief weakness. And Agrippina is no ordinary woman."

"What else have you heard?" asked Sulla.

"They say she's got a list of personal enemies and that she is already conspiring to bring them down."

"And are you on that list?" asked Sulla.

"Of course! I opposed her marriage to Claudius."

"Who else?"

"You. Aelia. Lollia Paulina. All of us here, in fact. Callistus. Silanus. Lepida. Lucius Geta. Crispinus. And who knows who else. It all depends on how things fall out. Rome is full of cowards who will do almost anything to survive. They can be bought. They can be threatened." He paused and sighed. "It's a perilous situation." He studied the palms of his hands and then rubbed them together.

"Isn't there any way to stop her?" asked Antonia.

He shrugged. "There's only one way. We've got to maintain whatever influence we have with Claudius. But we are at a distinct disadvantage. We can only talk to him in his study. She can talk to him in his bedroom." He raised his eyebrows and looked around at his friends, settling, at last, on Aelia.

"The old fool!" she said. "She'll have him eating out of her hand in no time at all."

And then, as if to illustrate her point, there was a commotion in the archway leading to the house. The man trying to reach them was Demetrios, a close friend and associate of Narcissus. His face was damp with perspiration. He had run all the way from the Forum, and he was neither young nor slim. "Let him in," shouted Narcissus, and he came into the garden, gasping for air and, for a moment or two, unable to speak.

"What is it?" asked Narcissus impatiently.

"Silanus!" he said. "He's just been—he's been expelled from the Senate."

"But that's impossible," said Narcissus. "The roll has been reviewed and the lustrum closed."

81

"He was expelled by a special edict. Vitellius has brought charges of incest against him—at Agrippina's bidding, they say."

"What? Incest? How incredible! Couldn't they think of something more believable?"

"Silanus and his sister," continued Demetrios. "Junia Calvina."

"But that's Vitellius's own daughter-in-law," said Antonia, her face a torment of abused innocence. "How could he charge that?"

"The case will be brought personally before Claudius," said Demetrios. "They are predicting that he will break off the engagement between Silanus and Octavia."

"And so it begins," said Narcissus, his grimness verging on fatalism.

And then, at that moment, Octavia came running into the garden, followed by her slave. They were both laughing and both of them had arms full of roses. Everyone fell silent and all heads turned toward the pretty girl.

# XII

When Antonia decided to visit Agrippina, she told no one, not even her husband. She called on her cousin unexpectedly in the middle of the morning. Agrippina's house, unfortunately, was the scene of considerable confusion, as preparations for her wedding were in full swing. What's more, the weather had turned bad. Heavy clouds hung over the city, and there was a chill in the air. Winter was coming. The days were getting shorter.

Antonia arrived alone and on foot. One of the guards posted outside the house took the message in. She was asked to step into the vestibule to wait. Some men were unloading a cart at another entrance to the house, and there were voices behind the garden wall. Women were laughing. As she waited, a merchant arrived, followed by two of his assistants carrying bolts of fabric. They went right past her and into the atrium. She waited. Outside, she could hear rain beginning.

After a long time, the guard returned. Antonia was wondering whether she had been forgotten in the confusion. The guard was accompanied by Europa. Antonia remembered her from years ago. She used to come to this house as a very small child, even before Agrippina's mother died. The house was owned for a while by her cousin Caligula. But, after his death it went to his sister Agrippina.

"She can see you now," said Europa with a smile. "You're Antonia, aren't you?"

"Yes," she said, as she followed the sturdy woman through a corridor into the atrium, and then from there into a small sitting room or study. There were lots of people in the house. Some workmen were repairing cracks in the wall. Women were sewing. Everything was being made ready for what promised to be a gaudy and colossal wedding.

"My, how you've changed," said Europa. "I haven't seen you in years. But then the mistress has been away so much. And things are never the same, are they? How old are you now? Eighteen? Twenty?"

"Twenty-two," said Antonia.

"My, my, my! And very pretty, too!"

They stopped before a door. "You may go in," said Europa. "Mestor is with her. They're writing letters or something."

When Antonia came into the room, Agrippina got up from her elaborately carved chair and rushed over to her with her arms outstretched. "My dear Antonia. How good of you to come. You've been such a stranger to this house these past weeks.

"I knew you were busy," said Antonia. "And I hope I'm not disturbing you."

"Nonsense. I've been meaning to have a talk with you. There never seems to be time enough to do the things we really want to do." She turned to Mestor. "Leave us for a while, but be available." Her tone was businesslike. "Come, Antonia, sit down. Make yourself comfortable. May I get you something?"

"No, thank you," said Antonia. "What I have to say won't take long." She took a deep breath. "I want to ask you about Lucius Silanus."

"Lucius Silanus? My dear, you've come to the wrong person. What do I know about him? All I know is what the

84

rest of Rome knows. He's apparently been having a naughty relationship with his sister."

"You and his mother are first cousins."

"Yes, but we've seen very little of one another—except on public occasions. I always thought he was a rather nice young man. I had no idea—I mean, I didn't think he would risk this sort of scandal. I'm afraid he's in rather serious trouble."

Antonia's dark eyes registered her disgust and impatience. "Do you know that people are suggesting that you have instigated these charges in order to break off the engagement between him and my sister Octavia? Is that true?"

Agrippina's unconvincing sweetness dissolved into a solemn smile. "These are serious accusations, Antonia. Be careful what you say."

"I thought we were alone."

"We are."

"Then we can say what we want, can't we?"

"Yes, and deny it later, if necessary," said Agrippina, looking at her cousin with new insight and respect.

"In that case, we can be honest with one another."

Agrippina hesitated. She got up and walked slowly across the floor. "Honesty, my dear, comes in all colors and is, in any case, highly overrated. But what precisesly would you like to know?"

"I would like to know what truth there is to the rumor that you have deliberately ruined the reputation of Lucius Silanus in order to persuade my father to break off his engagement to Octavia. Is my language plain enough?"

"Your language is not only plain, my dear, but a little coarse. Before long we will all be part of the same immediate family. I am hoping that we will find a way to get along."

"It seems to me that we are already closely enough related," said Antonia. "In any case, you haven't answered my question."

"But my dear cousin, you are asking me to admit that I committed a crime. How naive can you be?"

"Then you don't deny it?"

"Am I on trial, then? And are you the prosecutor?"

"A serious wrong has been done to my sister and to Lucius Silanus. If I am in a position to help them, I will. I will not hesitate to talk to my father, as soon as I have sufficient information."

"And what exactly will you tell your father?"

"I will tell him that you urged Vitellius to bring these ridiculous charges against Silanus in order to break Octavia's engagement."

"And why would I want to do that?"

"To marry her to someone else, of course."

"Very clever! And in this fantasy of yours, who is the lucky young man who will inherit the frail charms of your half-sister?"

"The news in the marketplace, *cousin*, is that you'd like to marry Nero to Octavia." Her tone was sharp. She had emphasized the word *cousin*. Somehow that made them equals, in spite of Agrippina's impending marriage and her dozen years of seniority.

"I am not responsible for rumors. And surely you don't believe everything you hear in the marketplace. But even assuming that all this is true, why would you come here like this? What would you expect me to do?"

"Whether you are guilty or not of this outrage to human decency, I would expect you to help set it right. If it is your doing, then undo it. Make amends. Have a little compassion for Lucius and my sister. If it is not your doing, accept my apologies and join in my efforts to see that justice is done."

"That is a very nice speech, Antonia, and I admire your integrity, but let me give you a valuable piece of advice. There is little room in this world for compassion or pity or what you call decency. The whole world's an arena, and we are all gladiators. The weak die. The strong live. There are only winners and losers. There are only victors and victims. And the secret to survival is power. Does that sound hard? Well, then, I'm hard. But it is also true. People are governed by self-interest, not principles. Everybody. Including you. If you want to live long enough to see the wisdom of this philosophy, follow a simple rule. Once you've brought your enemy to his knees, ignore his pleas for mercy—and *cut his throat."*

Antonia stared at her. The younger woman's lips moved, but she could find no words with which to express her horror.

"Do I frighten you?" Agrippina enquired.

"No!" said Antonia. "You fill me with pity. I feel sorry for you. You must be miserable."

"On the contrary. I am about to marry the emperor of Rome. Even you would be thrilled by such a prospect. But now you must excuse me. I have a great deal to do. It was good of you to call on me. Come again."

Without another word, Antonia walked out of the room and closed the door behind her. As she made her way through the atrium, Europa came shuffling after her in her sandaled feet. "What! Leaving so soon? I was hoping you'd spend the morning. I wanted to ask you about your family. How's that lovely little sister of yours? How terrible about her mother!"

Antonia let her babble on until they were at the front door. When she turned to offer her a farewell smile, Europa could see that there were tears in her eyes. She went silent and pale, but she extended her plump hand to touch Antonia's cheek. Her sympathic expression was all that Antonia needed.

# XIII

Agrippina was determined to have a traditional wedding, as though she were appearing at the altar for the first time, to be delivered as a fresh and innocent virgin into the hands and house of her new husband. The gossip that day was laced with a good deal of obscene humor. On the other hand, she had her admirers, people who knew and adored her mother, people who believed she was keeping alive the ancient rituals. To them she was more a name than a real person. And the name was impressive.

She woke early, her hair bound in the traditional crimson net. Half a dozen slaves spent hours dressing her and preparing her face and hair. First she put on the tunic, which had to be woven in the old way. This was tied around the waist with a knotted belt made of wool. Then came the *palla* or cloak—a bright saffron. Also saffron-colored were her sandals. And around her neck she wore a metal collar, a stunning decoration. Her own hair was carefully covered with six patches of artificial hair, separated with bands, in the manner of the Vestal Virgins. They wore it that way all the time. Agrippina would imitate them for only a day

—and only in this way, according to one of the widely circulated jokes. Finally, over her elaborate hair structure, she wore a flaming orange veil called the *flammeum,* which covered the upper part of her face. This was supposed to suggest her modesty, but it also provoked laughter. And then, to top off everything, came a wreath of verbena and sweet marjoram.

"Everything is ready," said Mestor.

Agrippina was standing in the center of a large group of people in the atrium of her Palatine house. She was tall and splendid looking. Custom required that she be surrounded, thus, by her family and friends. In this case, there were more friends than family—the family having been decimated by disease and violence.

To swell her entourage, she had to add some miscellaneous names to her list, among them Petronius and his young friend Claudius Senecia. Scanning the room, Petronius said, "It's amazing how few of her relatives have survived. She's practically the only one left."

"I thought she had a million cousins," said Senecia.

"Yes, but they seem to have eaten each other up," said Petronius. "Only her aunt Julia's line has survived, but for how long remains to be seen. They've already got poor Lucius Silanus under house arrest. But his parents are here, I see. And his brothers. How nice of them to come."

"Did they have any choice?"

"Of course! They could have either come here or gone into exile." They stood to one side by themselves, more observers than participants.

"The emperor is on his way!" announced one of Agrippina's attendants. The crowd was stirred by the announcement and gathered round the bride.

"A pity to make the old man come all this way," said Petronius, "just to kill a pig and marry a fox. I understand that after the ceremony they are all going directly back to the palace for the festivities. Actually, they should be held here, and after the wining and dining, they should carry her off in a drunken procession to her husband's bed. But that part was altered to accommodate the emperor. After wining and dining, he's not likely to be able to take part in a procession."

"Or anything else," said Senecia. The young men laughed at their own remarks and watched the procedings with amused detachment. After all, they believed in nothing but style and wit. Why shouldn't they laugh at this cynical mockery of the old stupidities.

Agrippina stood in the center of the grouping of "relatives," tall and blonde and arrogant. She was determined to put on a good show. Europa made last minute adjustments to the bride's cloak and veil. The room was full of flowers. And at the far end the colorful sacrificial altar was flanked with five witnesses on each side. The *auspex* waited to slaughter the pig and examine the entrails. Smoke from the torches curled to the high ceiling. The Pontifex Maximus, before whom they would exchange their vows, was elegant in his colorful robes.

"He's here! He's here!" shouted an attendant. And a hush fell over the vast room. In another moment the family and friends of the emperor began to file in and to mingle with the bride's people. There were cheerful greetings. The noise increased again.

Antonia had considered staying away, but she was urged by her husband to avoid an out-and-out provocation. She arrived with Sulla and her mother and the two children, Octavia and Britannicus.

Claudius was carried in on a gilded chair. His freedmen helped him descend not far from the altar so that he would only have a few feet to go on foot. He could have walked the length of the hall with his bride, but both Pallas and Narcissus wanted to spare him the embarrassment of his awkward gait. He tended to drag his right foot, and his body lurched from side to side. He was, otherwise, quite presentable in his purple-hemmed toga and myrtle wreath. His robes concealed the odd proportions of his body, and as he stood before the Pontifex at the altar, he seemed tall and confident.

The crowd grew quiet. The *auspex* held up his hands and pronounced the ancient introductions to the sacrifice. Agrippina stood beside her emperor, radiating satisfaction and passion. The witnesses stood with hands folded in front of them like statues.

"They should have chosen a ewe instead of a pig," said Petronius, whispering behind his hand to his companion. "But they say the pig's his favorite animal."

"I'm not at all surprised," said Senecia. He nudged his friend and pointed out where young Nero was standing between his new tutors, Burrus and Seneca.

"Poor lad," said Petronius. "What do you suppose is going through his little head?"

Before the frozen pageant of dignitaries, the pig was slaughtered as discreetly as possible and then disemboweled so that his innards might be investigated as a sign from the heavens that all was well. "What if they find a putrefaction in the pig?" whispered Senecia.

"Why, then, they'll charge him with incest, of course, and place him under house arrest," said Petronius. And his friend had to cover his mouth with his hand to keep from laughing aloud.

The *auspex* announced that the gods approved of the union of this man and woman and that their vows could now be exchanged before the Pontifex. The couple faced each other, their eyes cast down. Though the room was silent, the words they spoke were barely audible. And, suddenly, it was done.

The audience broke into a restrained cheer, and the frozen crowd thawed into movement, glad, for the most part, that it was all over, except for the festivities. These would take place at the palace. And they all moved out of the house to form the great procession. Musicians played, people lined the streets. The bride and groom rode in a carriage drawn by mules—a Greek touch. A chorus of maidens sang, "Hymen, O Hymenaee, Hymen." And a toothless butcher coughed into his wife's ear, "If she's a virgin, I'm the king of Parthia." Torchlights illuminated the night. Spectators waved and shouted congratulations. Nuts and sesame cakes were showered among them. Children scurried and wrestled to gather them up.

The procession did not have far to go, and soon they were at the door of Claudius's house. Here a final ceremony was required. Agrippina anointed the door with oil and placed woolen fillets on the doorposts. She was then supposed to be carried across the threshold into the house. This ritual was performed by Pallas on behalf of the emperor, to the scandalous delight of those who knew that he was her lover. "Oh, marvelous! Marvelous!" said Petronius, clapping his hands.

"I wonder what other duties Pallas will perform for him tonight," said Senecia.

And then they were all inside among fluteplayers and dancers and tables loaded with food and wine. The bride and groom presided on a raised platform on chairs placed side by side, the symbolic sheepskin across their knees.

"G-g-get me some wine!" said Claudius.

"You were magnificient!" said Pallas to the emperor.

"I f-f-felt like a bloody f-f-fool," he said. "All that f-f-fuss and bother."

"It was for the people," said Agrippina. "It was what they expected. It will increase your popularity."

"Mmm!" he said. "D-d-do you think so?"

"Oh, definitely," said Pallas.

"G-g-good," he said, his face still a shadow of irritation. "Now bring me some wine. Lots of wine."

"Now he'll get drunk," said Senecia to Burrus, "to drive from his memory all those years when they hid him in the palace to keep the mob from laughing at him."

"I'm starving," Claudius announced. "Prepare a table for us. The smell of that roast pig is driving me crazy."

Serenus joined his friend Seneca. "Well," he said, "how does it feel to be back in the thick of things?"

He smiled philosophically. "The spectacle goes on."

"How long do we have to put up with this obscene ceremony?" Antonia asked Sulla.

"In a little while our absence will not be noticed," he said, "but now you must go and kiss your father."

"What if she, too, expects to be kissed?"

"Then do it. What harm can it do?"

"None that is visible," she said, "but you should see the gashes in my heart."

He quickly silenced her with a finger over his lips and

urged her toward the platform. "Come, get it over with so that we may leave."

She went to her father, who was now surrounded by well-wishers. They stepped aside for her. With one hand he clutched his wine cup; with the other he reached out for her. "Ah, Antonia, sweet Antonia!" he said, and she felt the arrow of Agrippina's glance.

Antonia was leaning forward to kiss her father when a terrifying scream came from the center of the room. It was multiplied by others and by the shouts of men. "Watch out! Seize him!" the crowd fell back from the center, as if a huge boulder had fallen into the sea. And, there, revealed alone on the stage was none other than Lucius Silanus, having materialized out of nowhere. He flung aside his cloak and yelled, "Agrippina! Agrippina!" His hair and eyes were wild. He held a dagger in his hand. For a few moments the guards were confused. And even when they realized what was happening, they had to force their way through a ring of people to reach the intruder.

Claudius dropped his cup of wine and grabbed his daughter. He cried out like a child. "Murder! Murder!" though he didn't know what was happening.

Agrippina stood up, as if to meet the challenge. But everything happened in an instant. Lucius Silanus was pointing at her and holding out his dagger. Before the guards reached him, he had just time enough to scream, "Agrippina! I have a wedding present for you. You wanted my life. Here it is! Here! Here! Here!" And, with that, plunged the dagger into his own chest and staggered forward. A great gasp went up from the crowd. Panic threatened, then was suddenly arrested. The guards were on him even before he hit the floor. His blood assaulted their uniforms and streaked across the marble surface.

Antonia clutched her father, whose head was burried in her bosom and whose body shook uncontrollably with fear. It was Agrippina who took command. "Silence!" she roared, and was heard above the noise of the guests. Every face was suddenly turned toward her, and an absolute silence fell over the room. "Our apologies for this ugly scene and for this young man's atrocious manners. Now take that garbage out of here and let us get on with the celebration. Music!" she shouted. "Music!" And the stunned musicians began to play.

# XIV

Outside the city walls, in a flat field embraced by a large bend in the Tiber, was the Campus Martius. It was used as an exercise ground, both for the military and for the ordinary citizen. Decorating the borders of the immense field were the temples of foreign cults, and at the south end there rose impressive public works, including the Theatrum Pompei with its huge portico.

The new empress insisted that her son Nero and her stepson Britannicus be brought here regularly, not only for their own physical training, but so that they could observe the military exercises. She would often accompany them and drag with her some of Nero's tutors.

On this occasion she had with her Seneca, Serenus and Burrus. Petronius, too, came along, but only out of curiosity and because he had nothing better to do. Besides, he was amused by naked athletes.

They sat on portable chairs under a colorful orange and blue striped canopy, and they were waited on by three slaves, who offered them wine, water, and fresh fruit. In the distance, clouds of dust were raised by a marching unit of uniformed men carrying shields and swords. The bellowing voice of the commander drifted back to them and mingled with the other sounds of the active field. Two nude runners on the track passed near the canopy. Agrippina followed them with her eyes. The others looked up to see where she was looking. Petronius smiled.

"Horsemanship is extremely important," said Agrippina. "Don't you agree?" She was talking to all of them indiscriminately, and her eyes shifted from the naked runners to the three horses that approached them. It was early spring. The sun was brilliant and the air was charged with life.

"A harmony of body and mind is what one hopes for," said Serenus.

"He seems to like horses," said Burrus, a stocky and attractive man of forty-five with the disciplined face of a soldier. His dark eyebrows were a small echo of his black hair. His closeness to the empress was the subject of some recent gossip.

When they came closer, one could see that the riders were a man and two boys. The man was Tigellinus, who had been cautiously reintroduced into Roman society. The boys were Nero and Britannicus, twelve and nine years old respectively. They wore tunics and leather breastplates that made them move a bit stiffly. Tigellinus waved a greeting to Agrippina with his whip as his sweating roan stallion pranced to a halt in front of the canopy. His smile was a flash of white teeth against his dark skin. He seemed to be exulting in his physical skills and flaunting them before the more sedentary tutors, who sat quietly in the shade discussing education. He paused only briefly and then led his charges away at a gallop.

"Nero's quite the little man," said Burrus. "A natural horseman. I remember his performance in the game of Troy. He was clearly the favorite of the crowd. Fairly remarkable considering his interest in the arts."

"I have no objection to his interest in poetry and music," said Agrippina, "but we'll have no philosophy."

"But surely some fundamentals will do him no harm," said Seneca. "He's got to learn to use his mind."

"Let him use it for mathematics and rhetoric," she said.

96

"And history, of course. He should have a strong sense of his heritage. And I am confident that you will make him an excellent orator. But philosophy? Speculations about the meaning of life? No! I don't approve of that sort of nonsense. It has a crippling effect on the will."

"Would you turn him into a parrot of dogma?" said Seneca. "Would you keep him from thinking for himself?"

"Precisely," she said. "He may one day have to rule the empire. We can't afford a brooding prince. Brooders are dangerous and ineffectual. I want him to learn loyalty, respect, courage, and physical grace. I want him to be the most beautiful little emperor who ever lived. In his leisure time give him good literature to read. Teach him Greek. And if he wants to dance, let him dance."

Burrus frowned. "Do you think all this dancing and singing is seemly for the lad? Personally, I would emphasize the martial arts. Horsemanship. Weaponry. The javelin and the bow. He should be capable of command—in the military sense. The people will expect it. Any display of effeminancy might be harmful to his reputation."

"I don't foresee his involvement in military campaigns," said Agrippina. "It's much too dangerous."

"But tradition demands it," said Burrus.

"Oh, tradition be damned! We'll make it up as we go. We'll cull from history what suits us and throw the rest away. There's a new age dawning for Rome, a golden age. The world will be brought to heel. The city will sparkle with monuments. Unification of power and a thousand years of prosperity is the dream we must all keep in mind. And we will be the architects of that dream. That boy there with the golden hair is only the principal piece of furniture in that dream. We will fashion him to suit our vision, and the public will worship him as a god."

"And who will *he* worship?" asked Seneca.

"Why, himself, of course!" she said. "And me! I am, after all, his mother, his creator."

"I think we all follow your meaning," said Seneca, "and admire your high ambitions. There is nothing we would like more than to see this product of our collective skills achieve that office for which he is being so carefully groomed. But there remains the problem of Britannicus. He, too, has much to commend him and will not be lightly put aside by Claudius."

"What's more," said Burrus, "he has a certain amount of support—popular and aristocratic. And the Praetorian Guard is firmly in the hands of Claudius."

Agrippina nodded as her attention once again drifted toward the exercises not far off. "We have time for all that," she said. "As some of you know, the way is already being paved. Nero will shortly be engaged to Octavia. Claudius will eventually adopt him. When it comes to naming a successor, my husband will have to contend with my son's popularity and heritage. I think Claudius can be persuaded to see the wisdom of the choice."

"And if he can't?" enquired Seneca.

"How can you doubt it?" she asked. "You, of all people! The great artist of persuasion!" She looked at him with satirically innocent eyes and waited for him to return her smile. He did, and the amusement was contagious under the striped canopy.

A slave came around with an amphora of wine and filled their cups. He was followed by another slave, bearing the immense bowl of fruit. They watched silently as Tigellinus and the boys returned. They dismounted in a cloud of dust and approached the elegant little gathering. Nero was beaming and damp with perspiration. "We had a race to the obelisk and I won," he said.

"But he bumped me on purpose and knocked my horse off stride," said Britannicus. His boyish, complaining expression was a combination of anger and tears.

"It's not my fault if you can't control your horse," said Nero.

"You were showing off for Tigellinus," said Britannicus.

"So were you!"

"He should have called a foul."

"Miserable little crybaby!"

"Bully!"

Nero shoved the smaller boy, who staggered back from the weight of his equipment and fell down. Tigellinus helped him to his feet and put an end to the dispute. "Now,

98

now, boys, that'll be enough of that. Good soldiers don't squabble—or cry. Come, say hello to your mother and then be off to the baths."

Agrippina held out her hands and took her son, dust and all, into her arms. "A victory kiss," she said, and pressed her mouth to his. On her breath he could taste the blend of wine and fruit, and the fragrance of her body was like flowers.

# XV

Her mother and husband pleaded with Antonia not to visit Lollia Paulina, but she went anyway—out of compassion. The woman was ruined. People shunned her. "It's like walking into a house that is being visited by the plague," said Aelia. "You mustn't provoke Agrippina," said Sulla. To these arguments Antonia replied angrily, "She is an innocent woman, and she is being destroyed in the name of my father. The least I can do is to comfort her in her last bleak hours."

So she went to the lavish Palatine house of the former wife of Caligula. And there she found Lollia Paulina, completely deserted, but for one loyal slave named Sibylla.

In the few short weeks since the assault on Lollia everything had changed. She had gone from one of the wealthiest and most attractive women in Rome to a neglected recluse, stripped of her fortune, and about to be exiled. Even the gardens of the house reflected the decline. Formerly so meticulously cared for, they now seemed slightly overgrown, a bit ragged and wild. And a green scum was beginning to form on the fishpond.

Antonia had to pound on the door with the heavy knocker for a long time before Sibylla called out from the other side. She greeted Antonia with tears of gratitude, hoping perhaps that something could still be done. The visitor, after all, was the emperor's daughter.

The interior of the house was chaos. It might have been looted by barbarians. Closets were emptied. Clothes were strewn about. Curtains were torn. Wine and food were spilled on the floor. "She told the slaves to take whatever they wanted and to flee," said Sibylla. "And then the other night a gang of hoodlums came and forced their way in. The guards had left. What they didn't steal, they smashed."

"Did they harm Lollia and you?" asked Antonia.

She looked down at the soiled floor of the atrium, her face damp with tears. She nodded.

"Both of you?"

"Yes!"

And, at that point, Lollia came into the room. Her gown was spotted and torn, revealing one breast. Her hair, once such a careful construction, was a disheveled tangle of tinted straw. And the cosmetics with which she painted her face were smeared into a grotesque expression. She walked unsteadily and carried in her hand a cup of wine. On her face there was a dreamy smile. "She's been drinking since—since all this happened," said Sibylla quietly. "And she's been putting certain potions and herbs in the wine, something she carried in a gold locket."

"Oh, Antonia, Antonia," said Lollia, floating across the room as though she were chasing clouds or visions. When the visitor proved to be living flesh she almost recoiled. She looked stunned. "Antonia!" she said again. "It's really you. Have you really come?"

"Yes, Lollia. I've come to tell you how sorry I am and to offer you whatever help I can. I had no idea that this—all this was happening. And you and my mother once were good friends."

"Is she here? Is your mother here? Good Aelia Paetina."

"No," said Antonia.

"Is she afraid to come? Like all the others? Afraid of Medusa Agrippina? But, ah, she should be. The rumor is out that I am dangerous. Tainted. I've consulted oracles to destroy the emperor. Did you know that? And anyone who associates with me is guilty by association. So you see you're risking your life. Except, of course, that you are the emperor's daughter. But, beware! She'll find a way around that immunity of yours."

"My father and I have an understanding," said Antonia.

"My father and I!" she echoed in her dream. Then she wandered away across the room. Antonia followed after her.

"Lollia! Is there anything I can do for you?"

She didn't seem to hear Antonia. "My father and I were very close. We went to meet him once in Brundisium. Have you ever been to Brundisium? That's where all the ships come in from the East. He had been to Bithynia." She laughed. "I was a little girl. I didn't even know where it was. And I mispronounced it. I called it *Bithia*. And my brother laughed."

Antonia came up to her and took her by the arms. "Lollia, I want you to tell me what happened. Exactly what happened. Perhaps there is still time to do something."

"Time? Oh no, there's not much time left. Not for me, anyhow. Not for any of us, really." She sipped at her cup.

Antonia tried to take it away from her, but she clutched it to her chest, spilling some of the wine on her torn dress and on the naked skin of her white bosom. Then, fascinated, she watched the red liquid seep down her body. "I'm sorry!" said Antonia.

"You can't take my cup away. It's all I have left. It was a gift from Caligula—her brother. I was married to him, you know. Did you know that? Of course, you did. How silly of me. And he taught me all about the poppy and the mushroom and how to make love like dogs, from behind, and a lot of other interesting things. You would have hated him."

"I did," said Antonia.

"You were only a child."

"I was fourteen when he was killed. I remember it very well. They carried my father to the Praetorian Camp and made him emperor. Everybody said Caligula was mad. We

102

all knew it. Some sickness had affected his brains. He was completely unpredictable, and cruel."

"Don't tell me about cruelty, dear girl. It is the worm in the apple of my world. O lacerations and blood!" She raised her voice to a kind of sighing howl. "Cruelty! Your family's famous for it on both sides. Claudian cruelty! Julian cruelty! You'll eat us all up like wolves and then devour yourselves." She laughed, quietly at first and then more loudly, almost hysterically.

Antonia put her arm around her waist and led her toward the door. "Come, let's go out into the garden. The air will clear your head. I want to know what happened."

She allowed herself to be led but paused along the way to pick up an empty birdcage. "I had a nightingale named Catullus once. What a sweet voice he had. A gift from a lover." She carried the open cage along with her. It dangled limply at her side. Antonia tried to steady her. "You know, I don't even remember his name. I had a lot of lovers. Too many. But I was always very discreet. When he divorced me, Caligula said that I was never to make love again for the rest of my life. It was an imperial order." She laughed again. "Imagine that! An imperial order! As if that could hold your thighs together when a man's hot flesh was on you. Oh, how I wish one of my lovers were here now. Not those dirty little rapists, those scavengers of the night."

"Did they hurt you?" asked Antonia.

"They insulted me. They killed me. If I were a man I would have cut them to pieces. How I would have loved to disembowel them. Castrate them. Stuff their mean little genitals in their filthy mouths."

"Did she send them?"

"I don't know where they came from. I don't know who they were. But first the tribune came and quietly advised me to commit suicide. When I refused, he went away. But he's coming back. And next time, he said, I would have no choice. They're sending me away, you know. They're taking all my property and sending me into exile. Perhaps I can go to Tarraco and be a whore in one of those narrow streets and live above a butcher shop and hear the murdered pigs scream. Ah, Tarraco! Tarraco! I was just a girl

103

when we first went there—Memmius and I. We had only been married a year, and he was sent to Spain. How romantic, I thought. My first trip overseas. My first glimpse of the world." They came through a door into the garden. Some of the statuary had been knocked from their pedestals. "We were happy. He loved me very much. We never imagined that it would end so suddenly. A message from Caligula. He had heard of the legendary beauty of my grandmother, and he wanted to marry me. As simple as that. It wasn't a request, it was an order. It was divorce or death. I went back to Rome. He lavished gifts on me. He married me. He plundered me. And then, less than a year later, he tossed me aside with that imperial command: 'You will never have intercourse again with any other man!' "

"Come, sit here," said Antonia.

She sat down wearily and touched her uncombed hair. On the other side of the neglected fishpond a peacock suddenly opened its magnificent tail. Lollia stared at it, hypnotized.

"Forget the past," said Antonia. "Tell me how this happened."

She shook her head slowly back and forth. "Don't you know about Quado?"

"I've heard rumors, that's all. And the statement my father made to the Senate."

"Quado is one of Agrippina's German slaves. They hired him to inform on me. His reward was his freedom and fifty thousand sesterces. He said he had personally seen me at Claros, consulting the prophet about her marriage to Claudius. He said he had followed me there, and he gave out very convincing details, complete with the cryptic message from that magician. He went into the grotto. He drank from the sacred spring. And he said: 'The gods will bless with an arrow/The union of the hawk and the sparrow.' Pretty poetry, don't you think? But a terrible prophecy. How I wish it were true. But I was nowhere near Claros. I had gone north to Verona with some of my uncle's friends."

"Doesn't you uncle know that?" said Antonia.

"Of course he does."

"Then why doesn't he speak up?"

104

She laughed again. "Because, old as he is, he wants to go on living. He was sitting in the Senate when Claudius made his accusations. He, the famous, the noble, Lucius Volusius. We were all so proud of him when we were children."

"Weren't you given a chance to defend yourself?"

"No! They went to Claudius with this Quado. She and her lover Pallas. They spoke to him in private. They frightened him with this lie. They said that, out of jealousy and rage, I had consulted astrologers and magicians about the marriage. They said I planned to murder them both, that I had planned to have a spell of some kind cast on them. Lies, lies, lies! They fed all these lies to your gullible father. Your sick old father. They said he refused to see me. They wrote a speech for him and stood him in front of the Senate like a shuffling puppet. And those sheep nodded, and I was doomed. Not one spoke up for me. Not one! Gutless cowards! Deserters! And the very next day my house was empty—my house that was always such a gathering place of petitioners and senators and literary gentlemen. You remember, Antonia. You remember how it used to be. And now look at it. It's a mausoleum. My tomb!" She pushed her hair back from her forehead. "Where are my friends? Where is Callistus? Yes, where is my dear friend Callistus now? Had I married your father, as he hoped, he would surely be here, reaping his reward. Oh, Antonia, Antonia, why couldn't it have been I instead of Agrippina? I'd be your stepmother now. I always wanted children—a daughter. But I was never blessed. I don't know why. Perhaps it was the men. I wanted a baby, a child of my own. Even if it spoiled my looks. And now I'm going to die and leave nothing behind. Nothing, nothing, nothing!" She began to cry. Her hand drooped. The wine spilled.

Sibylla came into the garden carrying a large basket with a cover on it. Her face was grim. She said nothing. She simply sat down across from them on another stone bench and waited.

"You're not going to die," said Antonia. "You may have to go away for a while. But there is always the chance that you will be recalled. It's happened before. Look at Seneca.

Nine years in Corsica. He's back again. In favor once more. Unfortunately, her favor."

"No, no, no!" said Lollia. "The tribune was right. I should do the honorable thing. All I need is a little courage. A lot of courage. I don't want to live. I really don't want to live. But I am afraid to die. Oh, Antonia, what shall I do?" She let her wine cup drop to the ground and leaned forward to bury her head in her hands. Antonia put her arm around her shoulders and then stroked her heaving back.

After a few minutes her sobbing stopped and she looked up. She stared across the mosaic tiles toward Sibylla, who seemed to be waiting patiently with her basket. She smiled. "Sweet Sibylla. So loyal. So true."

"What does she have in the basket?" asked Antonia.

"She has the golden vessel on which I will sail to freedom," said Lollia.

Antonia went to Sibylla and paused before the basket. "What do you have in there?" she asked.

Sibylla looked up at her with her sad eyes. And Antonia saw in her face the unpainted ancient beauty of the simple slave, a girl from Greece, a wasted woman, aware of her own small tragedy and the larger tragedy of her mistress. She said nothing, but she lifted the woven lid and allowed Antonia to look in. She recoiled at the sight of the twisting deadly adders.

"I have always wanted to die like Cleopatra," said Lollia. "But I am such a coward. Too beautiful. Too pampered. Too barren. Too nothing. Come, Sibylla, be my courage! Make a heroine of me. Come!"

And Sibylla rose and carried the basket of death to her mistress. Antonia watched, but said nothing. There was nothing more to say. Horror welled in her like the sudden surge of a wave in the sea. Her heart pounded. The blood rushed to her face. She wanted to scream. She wanted to run—out of the garden, out of the house. Out of Rome. Out of the world.

"They say there is nothing worse than the smell of dead lilies," said Lollia.

Sibylla paid no attention to her words. She sat down beside her and took the lid off the basket.

"Little darlings of death!" said Lollia, looking into the basket, apparently unafraid. She cupped her naked breast with one hand. "I could have nursed a child. But I would have left a daughter to this tattered world. And she would have been raped by fate. So come little babies of death. Do your natural work. O innocent executioners. What do you know of politics or rhetoric? What do you know of love? But love me, love me, love me!"

And she plunged her hand into the basket and grabbed the snakes and pressed them to her bosom, while Antonia gasped and Sibylla looked on with all the quiet wisdom of a woman who knew that there was nothing to be done, except to help her mistress toward this final consummation—a wedding of beauty and death.

The litter of vipers did their work. There was a pause that lasted a thousand years. And then the childless woman looked up and smiled once more before she collapsed and slipped to the ground.

Antonia closed her eyes and, for a moment, blotted out the nightmare. When she opened them, Lollia was asleep in the zodiac of mosaic tiles.

# XVI

The week-long festivities at Lake Fucinus had been planned for over two years. The actual work on the project itself had been going on for eleven years. The idea, orginally Julius Caesar's, was to tunnel three miles through Mount Salviano in order to connect the huge lake with the Liris River. Controlling the flow of water into the Liris would make that river more navigable. But more important was the draining of the lake itself in order to be rid of the periodic flooding and in order to provide a vast new fertile plain suitable for grain. And all this not far to the east of Rome. Those who were critical of Rome's dependence upon grain shipments from overseas applauded the project. But there were many critics who felt, over the years, that it simply could not be done. After all, even the great Augustus had shied away from the monumental project. But Claudius plowed ahead, encouraged by Narcissus, to whom the Fucinus Fiasco, as some called it, was assigned.

For days people had been pouring into the valley and into the hills around the lake. They came from all over for what promised to be the most extravagant celebration in many years, and perhaps the greatest spectacle ever. The main attraction would be a full-scale naval battle on the lake, involving two fleets and almost twenty thousand men. There would be other maneuvers and games. And there would be a huge feast for the public, provided by the emperor himself. A gift to his people on this auspicious occasion.

The hills and plains were dotted with tents and camping grounds. A stretch of shoreline was a continuous series of shipyards. Beyond them were the symmetrical rows of brick-and-mortar houses for the workmen. In other areas there were similar little villages for the men who worked on the tunnel and the dam. Thirty thousand of them, all told. For all those eleven years. A colossal challenge. And colossally expensive. There were contracts and subcontracts. There were bribes and frauds and scandals. There were outbreaks of fever, shortages of food, threats of riot and violence. But the work went forward, propelled by the emperor's plodding conviction that it could be done.

The lake was twelve miles long and almost seven miles wide. An inland sea to the mountain people who lived in the interior, some fifty miles from Rome. For generations they had argued over the advantages and disadvantages of the great project. Romantic old men in their waning years protested that it was a violation of tradition and nature. They remembered the long reflection of the moon over the waters of the lake, the low-flying birds, the boats they built, the fish they caught. And they remembered the women to whom they had made love in the gentle arms of their little sea. More aggressive souls schemed for the land beneath the lake, dreaming of fortunes in grain. And merchants and contractors milked the imperial treasury for their profits, providing everything from shovels to slaves.

In her two years of marriage to Claudius, the empress had done everything she could to discourage the project, but she was too late. There was too much invested. Not that she was afraid the project would fail. Quite the opposite, in fact. She was afraid it might succeed and that all the credit would go to Narcissus.

The whole area around the lake was alive with activity,

109

but especially in the immediate vicinity of the great dam, a structure designed to hold back the water until completion of the three-mile tunnel. Here the grandstands were built. Here the emperor's viewing deck was constructed, complete with canopies and kitchens and enclosures for privacy. It followed the steep terrain like a series of enormous wooden steps on a forest of pilings. From this imperial center the whole stage was visible. From here one could see the whole length of the lake on a clear day. The shipyards, the triremes in formation, the barges along the shore, the dam with its complicated gates, the tunnel entrance, the deep ditch between, into which the water would first fall, the work camps, the roads, the clearings in the slopes of the hills where whole forrests had been cut down, the Praetorian encampment with its colorful striped tents, and the swarms of people, who crawled like ants all over the place in search of a good vantage point from which to watch this once-in-a-lifetime event.

The atmosphere had been festive for days before the official festival began. Cooks and bakers and prostitutes displayed their wares. Wine dealers set up their huge barrels and their spigots and awnings. There was music and dancing far into the night. A thousand campfires turned the landscape into another sky. Young hearts were won and broken. Lovers disappeared into the hills to lie naked between the skins of sheep and goats. And the gods applauded from the heavens, providing a blazing blue umbrella for the days and a dome of stars for the nights.

Claudius and his entourage were lavishly provided for on the central platform of the imperial stands. And, at night, they were even more lavishly provided for by young Rubellius Plautus, the son of the emperor's niece Julia. Julia was the daughter of Livia, Claudius's sister, who had died some twenty years earlier. Rubellius happened to have a large villa less than a mile from the base of Mount Salviano. He was barely twenty—a tall, somewhat dissapated young man with a haunted face, as though he were the storehouse of a hundred family ghosts. In spite of his distracted expression, he was quite attractive, with deep brown eyes and a full head of hair, much like his great uncle's. His wife had recently died in childbirth, taking with her a strangled infant son. But for all of his natural and immediate sadness, he was a good host and put his entire estate and staff at the disposal of the emperor.

On the first day there were opening ceremonies and incidental demonstrations of seamanship on the lake. Claudius sat with his old friend Julius Pelignus, procurator of Cappadocia, a man renowned for his grotesque appearance and feebleness of mind, but a man with whom Claudius had cavorted in his youth in the taverns and brothels of Rome. Beside this ugly specimen of humankind, the emperor almost looked handsome. Pelignus had a slightly hunched back and an oversized head. His large nose had been badly broken once, and his teeth were brown with decay. He had a habit of sucking on his own fat lips, as if he wanted to devour himself. When he laughed he coughed and lifted his right knee, as if he had a pain in his groin.

"The ships of the blue f-f-faction" said Claudius, "will p-p-put out from the port at the farthest end, about eight miles down. The r-r-red will intercept from the south port about three miles from here. The object will be to cut off the blue before they reach the dam. It should be very exciting, don't you think?"

"Are they going to draw blood or fight a mock battle?" asked Pelignus.

"I haven't decided yet," said Claudius. "What do y-y-you think?"

"Oh, blood, of course! What's a battle without blood?"

"Narcissus says all those bodies might clog up the floodgates." He pointed to the dam. "You see, we'll be opening the dam in a couple of days or so. The water will cascade into the broad moat and then into the tunnel opening. We really shouldn't befoul the waterfall with the corpses of a lot of condemned criminals. But most of the men themselves want a real fight—a chance to earn their freedom. Perhaps we'll compromise. A preliminary engagement between one of the red and one of the blue. Let them hack each other to death and burn the defeated ship." He laughed loudly, his head wobbling more wildly than ever. Pelignus joined him, coughing and slapping his knee.

111

Smoke rose from a bank of charcoal fires at the rear of the platform. Pigs and birds were turned on spits, a special luncheon for the imperial family. Slaves in brown tunics kept the wine cups full and offered around a wide variety of delicacies on silver platters. Banners and flags fluttered lazily in the gentle breeze.

"I think your father is very pleased," said Narcissus to Antonia. They were seated on the same platform, but somewhat removed from Claudius and his friend. With them were Aelia and Sulla. "This has been a long-time dream of his. It will be talked about for a thousand years."

"I don't know how you ever managed it," said Antonia. "On top of everything else, you had Agrippina to contend with. It's a wonder she didn't wreck it for you."

"She tried!" he said with a sly smile. "But there are limits even to her power. What's more, she's overreached herself a bit. She can't kill everybody. She may have cried *wolf* once too often to the old man. He's beginning to ignore some of her insane accusations."

"Too late, unfortunately, for those she's already had killed," said Aelia. "They won't come back."

"She certainly had enough influence to protect Vitellius," said Antonia. "When he was recently accused, it was the accuser who was banished, not the old fox. That was her doing."

"Of course!" said Narcissus. "She owes him that and more."

Sulla looked up and down the shore and across to the half-denuded mountains, his expression a combination of sadness and stoicism. "And what will Claudius owe to you for all this?" he said, waving his hand in a broad arc.

"A great deal, I hope," said Narcissus. "Oh, not in money, but in confidence—in faith. I hope in the future he will listen to me—to us!"

"I hope so," said Aelia. "But do you think he will?"

"He already trusts me. That's imporant."

"She won't put up with it, you know," said Antonia.

"Will she have any choice?" he said.

Antonia hesitated. "You know as well as I do what choice she has."

"Yes," he said. "It's been on all our minds. But I don't think she can manage it. Not yet, anyway. The risk is too great. If she tries and fails, it will mean the end of her—and her son. And all her dreams."

"Don't underestimate her recklessness," said Sulla. "Now that she has persuaded Claudius to appoint Burrus as the sole commander of the Praetorian Guard almost anything is possible. If her personal power over Claudius wanes, she may very well resort to murder. And she may get away with it."

"Not so long as I draw breath," said Narcissus.

Sulla glanced at him and caught his eye. His comment was unspoken.

Julius Pelignus sipped at his wine. A few drops escaped from his lips and dripped onto his toga, but he didn't notice. His eyes were fixed on a group of ships with red sails out on the lake. They seemed to be searching aimlessly for a formation.

"So t-t-tell me, my friend," Claudius said, during a pause in the ceremonies. "How do you find things in Cappadocia?"

"Boring out there in the provinces," said Pelignus. "Hot sun. Desert. Bunch of screaming beggars in all the market places. Barbarians with all the trouble they've caused. Bells and horns and camels and dung and flies. I don't know how many men we lost with the fever. But the palace at Tyana is grand. And the women are exotic, if you give them a bath first. Crusty with dirt they are."

"The w-w-women?" said Claudius.

Pelignus chuckled lecherously. "Oh yes! Dark and mysterious. Full of tricks in bed. They know how to treat a man like a king." He leaned closer and fell into a hoarse whisper. "I have these two young sisters. About sixteen and seventeen. Breasts like hard pears. And hips like young athletes. We bathe together and they will do anything. Anything!"

Claudius's deep eyes widened. His open mouth was wet. "Anything?"

"We play two-on-the-horse sometimes. A little game I

113

invented." He nudged his friend. "You can imagine, eh! Two-on-the-horse! One up here near my mouth, succulent as figs. The other in the saddle, squirming like a Syrian dancer."

"Enough to make an old n-n-nag feel like a young stud again. I'd ask you to send me a brace of those young things, but I've got a new wife to contend with. And she's about all I can handle."

"That Agrippina's quite a woman, I hear. Beautiful and ambitious."

"Oh yes, very beautiful. And—and—" He couldn't find the words. A surge of noise from the crowd below distracted him. On the terraced platform one step higher, Pallas and Agrippina talked with Felix, Pallas's brother, returned recently from Judea for these festivities. Agrippina caught her name and looked down toward the old men. Pallas and Felix were lost in conversation.

Pelignus raised his voice. "They say she's forceful—that she likes to have her way. Is that so, my friend?"

"Mmmm! Yes, I suppose so."

"Well, then, you must watch that she doesn't get the upper hand, eh?"

"No, no, you mustn't worry about my wives, Julius. They like to think they own me, but I know better. I play the fool, but I keep my wits about me. The same way I foxed Caligula. He thought I was an idiot. Otherwise, he would have k-k-killed me. No, I let them have their way, as long as it doesn't harm me, but, in the long run, I always have the option, eh!" And he made a gesture to complete his point. He drew his forefinger slowly across his throat and then exploded into laughter before slopping down the rest of his wine.

Agrippina went pale. A chill ran through her, and she drew her cloak around her. "What's the trouble, my dear?" asked Pallas.

"Nothing," she said. "A breeze off the water."

Felix looked at her with soft, suggestive eyes. She returned his glance and then motioned to one of the slaves for some wine.

114

Trumpets sounded and drums rolled. Seneca appeared beside Claudius and handed him a scroll on which was written a short, formal speech. He helped the emperor to his feet, and the crowd greeted their ruler with wild applause. Everyone else on the platform stood up. It was time for the emperor's speech. The emperor, unfortunately, was a little drunk.

The crowd grew quiet. Only those immediately below the imperial platform would be able to hear him, but all along the shores of the lake and aboard all the ships everyone stopped for a few moments to look in the direction of the emperor. It didn't matter what he was saying. All that mattered was that he was the emperor, the symbol of the empire. An idea. An abstraction. And there was not a single person present who was not moved in some way.

"Friends and f-f-fellow Romans, I want to welcome you officially to these magnificent proceedings." Seneca stayed beside him as he spoke, ready to support him should he do more than sway or wobble. His voice grew rough. He cleared his throat and spat on the platform. "What you are w-w-witnessing here is the triumph of human ingenuity and perseverance. It is a heroic accomplishment against enorm——enormous odds. And the result will change the course of history. It will move us closer to s-s-self-sufficiency. If we can f-f-feed ourselves at home, we will be less exposed on the high seas. We will save the cost of shipping and bring down the cost of grain." A great cheer went up from the crowd.

Claudius cleared his throat again and glanced at Julius Pelignus, who sat nearby. They exchanged drunken smiles. "You're doing fine," whispered Seneca.

"Yes, but I don't know what I'm saying. Where was I?" Seneca pointed to the proper place. Claudius began again.

In the stillness of the starry night Antonia stood by the window of their bedroom at the villa of Rubellius Plautus. Through the open shutters she could see the silhouetted hills, dark against the light of a moon rounding to fullness. The breeze had died to nothing, and a ghostly mist was beginning to rise from the marshes. With it came the night

115

sounds of small creatures and occasionally the squawk of an invisible bird. These sounds mingled with the more distant sounds of the dying celebration at the lake. It was odd how they carried almost a mile along the unpaved road that skirted the marshes and then climbed the hillside, where the sprawling villa looked back toward the south.

She took a deep breath. It was almost a sigh. The air was damp, and she could feel it in her chest. Or was it something else she felt—a heavy hand pressing against her ribs. An oppressive weight. She sighed again and looked up at the stars. How vast the world was, she thought. Mountains and seas and deserts. A babble of languages. Lands beyond the rim of the horizon. Reality beyond the stars. The cold indifference of the night. No gods to guard the innocent or guide the weak. Nothing! Her faith was dead. The fairytale faith of her childhood. Time had made pygmies of the giants of her youth. The mysterious world of grown-ups. If she ever believed in anything it was they. How they paraded in their gorgeous clothes. How they talked about enormous things. How they ordered people about. They were the structure, the organization, the very dome of life. They were the gods, until—until they gradually became ordinary people. Frail, confused, drunk, and insane. Where, then, was she to look for truth? Not in the temples. Not in the smoke of the burnt offering. These empty rituals meant nothing to her. There was only the mystique of the family and the state. And these had been reduced in recent years to murder and mockery.

She glanced back into the dark room at her sleeping husband. He was on his side facing away from her and breathing quietly. The room was white and simple. The bed was large. What a good man he was, she thought. Firm in duty. Loyal in his affections. Recently a consul, in spite of Agrippina, and respected by the people. But what ambitions did he dare have in a world of vultures and vampires? How sad for him. How sad for Rome. He would be the best of all possible emperors. Benign. Intelligent. His friends knew it. His friends urged him. But he put aside their talk gently and lost himself in books. Perhaps the best thing they could do, he often told her, was to leave Rome altogether—retire to the country or to some other place, far away. Athens, maybe, or Crete. Even Spain was a possibility.

She fixed her eyes on the distance as if she were trying to visualize Spain or actually see it, a thousand miles away. Yes, she thought, that was the thing to do. Escape from this luxurious dungeon. Defy tradition, her father, the gods, everything. Convert all they owned into gold. And flee aboard a ship with a handful of slaves. Explore all the shores of the civilized world, until they found a white city gleaming in the sun, overlooking the sea. A city of beautiful people, free of intrigue and the stench of death.

Her hand wandered down her body, feeling the warm nakedness under the simple gown. It paused on her belly and then moved back and forth. A caressing motion over the beginnings of life. She was pregnant, and it was still her secret. Somehow she knew it would be a son. A beautiful boy. The grandson of an emperor, and perhaps one day— She stopped herself. The blazing eyes of Agrippina intruded from among the constellations in the moonlit sky. Her heart skipped a beat, then raced. She shook her head. There would be no place to hide him, no way to protect him from that malicious force. For what if Agrippina should succeed in her schemes? What if she should rule the world through the medium of her son? Then none of them would be safe. Her husband, her brother, her son.

And what of her poor father? How old he was. Pushed this way and that by his freedmen, by his wife, by senators and tribunes. Lost in the interior compartments of his complex mind and grinding appetites. Weeping to her about age and death. Surrounded by guards and slaves and tasters. Suspicious of everyone, even her perhaps. How could she love him? How could she not? Was there, perhaps, a handsome warrior lost inside that old crippled body of his?

Sulla stirred and then turned over. She stood very still by the window, almost holding her breath. But then he stirred again and then sat up. He looked toward her for a moment, emerging from the cave of sleep. "What's wrong?" he asked. "Can't you sleep?"

"I'm all right," she said. "The air is heavy here in the mountains."

He got up and came to the window. He was wearing a short white tunic, wrinkled from dampness and sleep. He ran his fingers through his confused hair and looked out into the darkness. "Have they finally all gone to bed?" he asked.

"I think so," she said. "I haven't heard anything for a while."

"Your father must have been exhausted. I don't know how he can carry on that way at his age—eating and drinking, staying up until all hours."

"When he gets together with old friends—" she shrugged.

He shook his head. "That Julius Pelignus is absolutely revolting. Ugly inside and out."

"My father enjoys him."

"Perhaps they've wallowed in the same mud."

She looked at him as though she had been touched with the cold point of a knife.

"I'm sorry," he said. "I didn't mean to—"

"It's all right. I understand. He *is* that way. We all know it."

They stared out the window in silence together. "You can see the reflection of the fires from the lake. See, there?"

"Yes," she said. "Some of them will be awake to see the dawn."

He said nothing for a while. Then he put his hand on her shoulder and let it wander down her slender arm. "Antonia!"

"Yes."

"Are you sure everything is all right? You seem so sad lately."

"I am sad," she said. "Very sad. I could weep for all of us—for all of them."

"You mustn't let yourself become obsessed."

"With what?"

"With her—with Agrippina."

"Oh, it's not just that. It's—it's—*everything!* This deep, awful feeling of emptiness. It's as if nothing really mattered and no one really cared."

118

He put his arm around her and said in a cajoling voice, "If you were a good Stoic, you wouldn't care either."

She tried to smile for his sake. "Is that your way of getting even with the universe?"

"Philosophy is not a matter of vengeance," he said. "In any case, it's the middle of the night and hardly the time for metaphysical discourse." He tightened his embrace. "Come to bed. We'll make love and you will feel better in the morning. And then tomorrow we can loose ourselves in the spectacle of the ships on the lake."

She drew back. "I don't want to lose myself. I want to find myself. Everybody in Rome seems bent on spiritual self-destruction. I hate it! All this empty noise. All this distraction."

He laughed, but somewhat seriously. "You begin to sound like your sister Claudia, the castoff from your father's first marriage. She goes about saying that she has found comfort and salvation in a new religion. A certain sect of Jews."

"Yes, I know. They call themselves Christians, followers of a carpenter's son who was crucified in Judea. I was asking Felix about them today."

"And what did he say?"

"He said it was an ugly and dangerous superstition."

"He's probably right."

"Who knows! The promise of eternal life and justice in heaven is very appealing."

"Especially for the wretched beggars of this world who have nothing else to live for."

She turned to him and stared up into his eyes. "But I, too, am a wretched beggar. I, too, have nothing to live for, except—"

"Except what?" he asked, comforting her in his arms.

She was thinking of her unborn child, but she said, "You!" And then she leaned her head against his chest, and he kissed her dark hair.

Sulla held her close, and she could feel in his tenderness the quiet passion of his love. And then he whispered it to her, his lips close to her ear. "I love you, Antonia! I love you more than anything in this world, more than life, more than

119

myself." And the warmth of his words filled her emptiness and protected her from the vastness of the sky.

They were about to close the shutters and go back to bed when they heard whispering voices in the garden below. They looked out but saw nothing at first, only the stone balustrade, the fountain, and the assemblage of heads on their pedestals, the illustrious dead. Moonlight played through a row of poplars, casting shadows across the stone terrace. Then something moved. They held each other and stood very still, just inside the window and out of sight. Someone was coming along a narrow path, through an archway of roses. There were two people, walking close together, walking unevenly, then pausing to embrace. Then laughing and whispering. "Sshh! You'll wake the house." It was a woman's voice. And then a man's: "It's my house. I'll do what I please." They kissed in an alley of moonlight. A long, passionate kiss. And then they melted down, down, down, into the shadows and grass beside the balustrade. One couldn't see them if one didn't already know they were there.

"Who is it?" inquired Cornelius.

"Agrippina, I think," said Antonia.

"And Rubellius?"

"Yes."

"A neat trick," he said, "to deceive a husband and a lover all at once and in the same house."

"She's incredible!"

"She's a whore to her own ambitions."

"Insatiable!"

"No, my sweet! That's not passion you see there. That's politics. A little insurance against the scrambling of her plans. I'm not the only one who has dissident support. Rubellius is descended from Tiberius." His hushed voice grew even quieter. "She'll do anything."

The shadows shifted slowly as they watched in silence. There was nothing to see until moonlight fell on a long, naked leg, then another. Then the back of a man moving rhythmically. Then his buttocks and the familiar thrust of sex. Antonia and Sulla were disgusted and aroused all at

120

once. She could feel the stiffening of her husband through his light tunic. He did not try to conceal it.

"Does that excite you?" she asked. It was not an accusation.

"Yes," he said, "in spite of myself."

"It's all right," she whispered. "I understand."

He drew her closer to him, their bodies separated only by their flimsy garments. And it was she who raised those garments to allow their bodies to meet flesh to flesh.

Recklessly unaware of the creeping moonlight, the couple below was soon exposed. Drunk and naked they wrestled toward their union, their movements more and more urgent. And, face to face, Sulla and Antonia, too, were joined and sliding into the pit of animal pleasure. Unable to reject a thousand years of inherited debauchery, Antonia heard herself moaning into her husband's face as he held her soft, white flesh in his large hands. "Oh, do it. Do it to me. To all of us. To her."

He was too swept away to be astounded. And as the couple in the garden gasped their satisfaction to the fires of the night, he and Antonia, too, felt the madness of the general excitement, as if all the world were contracted into a general orgasm to drive out the demons of despair.

When it was over, he carried her limp body back to the bed. And there they lay awake like two corpses, until the first light of dawn. Only then did they turn to each other. And she cried in his arms until they both fell asleep.

The next day, Claudius was with Pelignus again on the imperial platform. Pallas was a statue of arrogance and patience. The empress conversed with Felix. Narcissus and Aelia exchanged polite intimaces. And Antonia wondered whether they had been sleeping together. And the children, Octavia, Britannicus, and Nero, wandered from level to level, relieving their restlessness in mysterious little games.

The grand spectacle of the full-scale naval engagement was an enormous success with the thousands upon thousands who lined the shores and scabbed the hills to watch. The preliminary slaughter was as convincing as the real thing because it *was* the real thing. The ramming, the boarding, the burning, the killing. All as real as war. And

121

how the crowd roared with excitement and genuine joy when a man was cut to pieces on the slippery deck and tossed overboard to stain the sea. The ferocious bellows of the condemned mingled with the clash of metal and the groaning of oars. Flaming arrows set fire to the blue ship and scorched slaves plunged into the water. When the vessel was rammed and sinking, when its fighting men were dead and its sails and decks ablaze, when the victorious red forces withdrew to count their casualities, a great roar of satisfaction went up for miles around and resolved itself into a chant of freedom for the victors. The emperor rose, his unsteadiness visible for half a mile. And then with a wild, sweeping emancipation, he announced their graduation from the ranks of condemned criminals and slaves. The crowd could barely control itself. Waves of approval swept along the shores and up into the hills. The entire landscape was alive with little screaming people. Pallas's thin mouth twitched in contempt. He glanced at Agrippina, who met his gaze with cold bravado. She knew how he felt about the common herd. But she knew also that there was more in his look than mere contempt for the mob. In that instant she knew that he knew what had happened during the night.

The main battle followed, a masterpiece of rehearsed maneuvers. The wind cooperated, billowing out the blue and red sails. The full-scale triremes of the blue faction came into view far off in the center of the lake. Each was the standard 120 feet long by 20 feet wide. They would sail into the battle area and then lower their sails in favor of oars. Each ship carried about two hundred men. And its most deadly weapon was its bronze and wooden ram, which protruded forward between two large eyes, painted to ward off evil. As the ships drew closer, one could see the rows of shields behind which men made ready for battle. Though the clash would be bloodless, against the wishes of the combatants, other prizes had been promised by the emperor to spur the men on to a convincing performance.

Through his morning-after haze, Claudius lectured Julius Pelignus, whose face was a thousand broken capillaries. The two wrecked old men drank mineral water and punctuated their speech with dyspeptic noises. "The r-r-ram is the m-m-main weapon. And f-f-fire," said Claudius. His right hand trembled visibly as he shielded his eyes from the sun to look down the lake at the approaching blue fleet. "The blue will form a kind of flying wedge, much as an army m-m-might on land. They will try· to p-p-penetrate the red as they come out from the south port to intercept. The b-b-blue will have the momentum. They will be hard to stop. They also have the following wind."

"But I hear the captain of the red is a military genius," said Julius Pelignus.

"Ah, that's what we're all counting on. Imagine that this were a r-r-real attack and that the enemy were trying to l-l-land its troops on our shores—raid our p-p-port, destroy this dam, r-r-rape the women, k-k-kill the children. Imagine that!"

Pelignus held his aching head. "It's a bit early in the morning for that sort of thing, isn't it?"

Claudius charged ahead into his fantasy. "How to t-t-turn them back. How to save the city. What will our captain use? A d-d-diversionary move from the rear? Fire ships? Or should he m-m-meet them head on with a w-w-wedge of his own? Now take the ancient battle at Amorgos, where the Athenian fleet of 170 galleys was destroyed by a Macedonian fleet of 240 ships. Now th-th-that was a classical s-s-struggle. S-s-someday I will write a book about it. You s-s-see—"

It was hard for Pelignus to keep up the pretense of interest. His eyes wandered away from the slow-moving blue fleet, and away from the wobbling face of Claudius. He surveyed the people about him. There was that very domestic group, that Antonia and her family. Why, he wondered, did Agrippina tolerate the emperor's exwife Aelia? An odd arrangement. Perhaps she preferred to keep her in sight rather than to drive her into secret conspiracies. And there was Agrippina herself, talking intimately with Pallas. He squinted his baggy eyes. No, they were not just talking, he decided. They were quarreling.

And, indeed, on the far side of the platform, farthest from the water, Pallas and Agrippina were discussing the

123

events of the previous night. They sat side by side in wooden armchairs and leaned their heads close together but kept their eyes on the lake. Pallas was, above all, discreet. He did not like discussing personal matters in public. "I thought we had an understanding," she said. "I thought there was to be no jealousy between us."

"I'm not talking about jealousy, you fool. I'm talking about jeopardy. You were seen last night."

She actually blushed. "By whom?"

"I'd rather not say."

"I want to know."

"A member of the guard, for one."

"Who else?"

He hesitated. "I understand that Narcissus was out walking."

"Oh, no! Not him! Do you think that he will talk to Claudius?"

"I don't know, but you're a damn fool for taking chances like that."

"I was drunk."

"I don't believe it."

"Then what do you believe?"

He looked at her. "I believe you're interested in Rubellius Plautus."

She smiled. "You think I'm in love with him?"

"Of course not."

"Then what are you talking about?"

He leaned even closer and whispered rapidly between tight lips. "I think you are cultivating him as a potential husband in case Claudius should die. I think you are trying to expand your options. You will never be able to marry me. And you might not be able to control your son, should he come to power one day. You can't do things like that without antagonizing people."

"What people?"

"Me, for one! We have had an arrangement, political and personal. Or have you forgotten?"

"Why, I do believe you're jealous, after all. How quaint!"

Felix returned to the platform and interrupted them. "I just heard a rumor that the red commander is planning an ingenious new strategy." He was genuinely excited as he sat down again with them.

"How nice!" said Agrippina, glancing at Pallas. "I like new things."

The next day, everyone was talking about the marvelous victory of the red fleet over the blue and arguing over what should and should not have been done. Every man was a captain. Money changed hands. The ordinary man shared in the glories of the empire and had an immediate sense of its might.

But as the day wore on their attention shifted to the chief business of the whole festival—the opening of the floodgates that would mark the culmination of eleven years of massive effort. Two giant wheels turned by fifty slaves each would lift the gate and allow the waters of Lake Fucinus to pour into the sluice that led to the three-mile long tunnel through Mount Salviano.

The imperial party returned to their viewing platform after the midday break for food and rest. Claudius fidgeted nervously. He was like a child waiting impatiently to play with a new toy. He talked endlessly, calling out to people around him. He jabbed at Pelignus with his elbow. He stamped his feet. He guzzled wine.

Narcissus, too, was nervous. On his shoulders rested the weight of responsibility. He wasn't sure that the scheme would work. Nobody was. In theory it seemed fine, but the moment of truth would come with the opening of the gate. Would the machinery work properly? Was there too much pressure from the dammed-up waters of the lake? Would the tunnel supports hold against the first great surge?

He was on a barge with his engineers and with Anicetus, the commander of the fleet at Misenum. They were consulting a sheet of plans. They huddled together, then looked up, first this way, then that, pointing to something. The troops of slaves appeared at either end of the dam and moved, four abreast, toward the huge wheels. The crowd grew tense.

Antonia looked at the sky. Clouds were beginning to

gather along the rim of the hills. "I hope nothing goes wrong," said Sulla. "A lot depends on this project.".

"It'll be all right," she said. Her eyes wandered down to the large ditch between the dam and the sluice. It would accommodate the overflow, should anything go wrong. "But why was this platform built so close to the ditch?"

"Your father insisted. He doesn't want to miss anything."

Trumpets sounded. Banners waved. "Are we about to b-b-begin?" asked Claudius to Burrus and Seneca, who were standing directly behind him. Eh? Are they going to open the dam? C-c-can you see? What's Narcissus d-d-doing? Why are they standing there? Is anything wrong?"

"The slaves are in position," said Seneca. "Everything seems ready."

On the barge, Narcissus stepped to one side. One of the engineers signaled to a man on the dam. He signaled back with a white flag. Anicetus handed Narcissus a red flag. He went to the raised portion of the deck and held up the flag. The trumpets sounded again. A hush fell over the crowd. Then, for a moment, everything was dead silence, and one could hear the cawing of a flight of crows as they passed in front of the gathering clouds.

All eyes were on Narcissus. He held the flag aloft for what seemed ages. And then he let it fall. The crowd responded with a cheer. And the slaves instantly started to push their wheels around. The hawsers groaned. The greased wood creaked. And the gate was visibly rising. When the first sound of water was heard, an even greater roar went up from the crowd.

Claudius was on his feet. A waterfall tumbled into the ditch and into the sluice just beneath him, sending a haze high into the air. He applauded and shouted. "Wonderful! Marvelous! Oh my! Oh my!" Every part of his body was in motion.

Then, suddenly, there was a cracking, awful sound, almost like slow lightning. The slaves at one of the huge wheels lurched forward and then went sprawling as something gave way. The crowd was confused. The lake seemed to heave and then sink, as though it had taken a deep breath. And then there was the thundering of tons of water, bursting through the broken gate and rushing into the ditch and sluice, a tidal wave that pounded against the tunnel opening, destroying the supports and bringing down rock and earth. The water welled backward and upward, sending a huge spray up beside the platform and washing under it around the pilings.

Claudius turned ghostly white and stumbled backward. Seneca took him by the arm and tried to lead him away to safety. Burrus came up quickly and took his other arm. But he seemed frozen, paralyzed by fear. Antonia leaped to her feet and rushed to her father. She tried to calm him, talking gently but swiftly. "Come, father! It's all right! Come away from the water." He seemed to be trembling in every part of his body.

"Wha-wha-wha-what?" He couldn't speak. They dragged him across the platform between a file of Praetorian Guards. They had come up to hold back the crowds who had spilled over the hillside. There was confusion and near-panic. Some of the pilings gave way, and the edge of the platform sagged, then broke away and fell into the churning water.

On the barge, Narcissus was running up and down shouting orders. The slaves recovered and manned the wheel. The engineers made a quick repair. It was not so bad as it seemed—just a sudden surge of water. The gate was not broken through, just awkwardly dislodged. The hawsers groaned again. The wood creaked. And the gates were drawn almost shut.

Within a few minutes the imperial party was reassembled on higher ground, a kind of dining patio with wooden couches and chairs. Claudius rested on one of the couches, surrounded by his solicitous family and friends. It did not take him long to recover. "Is it over?" he asked, sitting up. Agrippina was beside him, holding his hand.

"Yes, darling, it's over," she said. And Antonia winced at the falseness of her tone.

"Wh-wh-what was it?"

"Something gave way," said Seneca, "but it's all right now. Nothing to worry about. The water has been stopped."

"You m-m-mean it didn't work?" His fear was turning into anger and frustration. "D-d-don't tell me it didn't work."

"A slight malfunction," said Burrus. "We've sent for Narcissus. He's coming across the lake now. He should be here any moment."

The empress stood up and addressed herself to the group and the guards. "All right, now, let's have a little order here. Make yourselves comfortable. Have some refreshments. We'll soon find out what went wrong."

Sulla took Antonia aside. "We've got to watch her. She'll try to make something of this. Just you wait and see."

"It was only an accident. Nothing serious," said Antonia.

"She's liable to play on his paranoia. She's liable to blame it on Narcissus. After all the ground we've gained . . ."

Claudius was sipping wine and catching his breath. "I c-c-could have been killed," he said.

"We'll find out who's responsible," said Agrippina.

Narcissus and Anicetus arrived. The supervisor of the project was wet with perspiration and breathing hard. "Is everything all right?" he said.

"Yes, but no thanks to you," said Agrippina.

"What happened?" inquired Seneca.

"One of the gates buckled," said Narcissus. "But it held. It was not so serious as it appeared. And the tunnel needs widening. We'll have it all repaired by tomorrow. I'm sorry for the delay and the—the inconvenience."

"Inconveience!" shouted Agrippina. "You call this near-tragedy an *inconvenience?* You should have thought of this when you were taking bribes from your contractors."

Pallas came up to her and tried to calm her by putting his hand on her shoulder. She shrugged it off. "Corruption and faulty construction, that's what it is."

"Wh-wh-what? What are you saying?"

"I'm saying your beloved Narcissus has been robbing you blind. We've all heard the rumors. Now we know how true they are."

Anicetus stared at her with hatred and started to speak, but he was cut off by Narcissus, whose temper was flaring.

128

"Malicious lies! You're lying. You're trying to discredit me." He turned to Claudius. "Don't listen to her!"

Claudius looked confused. "N-n-now, now," he said. "Enough of this. Enough! We'll look into it later. The main thing is that we're all still alive."

Pallas took Agrippina aside by the arm. The group dispersed. Refreshments were brought in. Down below they could see that the waters had subsided and the crowd milled about calmly. It was almost as if nothing had happened.

"Go easy!" whispered Pallas. "Go easy!"

Pelignus rejoined his old friend. "That's more excitement than one gets in a year in Cappadocia." He coughed and laughed and patted Claudius on the back. The emperor responded, remembering, perhaps, ancient adventures they had together. His fear receded, and a wet, slobbering smile took over, a smile that rescued him from the brink of tears.

"He'll pay for that mistake," said Agrippina to Pallas. "And for his insults."

"All in good time," said Pallas. "All in good time!"

# XVII

As soon as Agrippina heard that Octavia had come of
age, in the physical sense, she insisted that a date be set for
the wedding. Messalina's delicate young daughter was
barely thirteen. Nero was sixteen. Europa had been in-
structed by Agrippina to examine the girl's bedsheets and
to report any signs of blood. But the aging Europa tem-
pered her absolute devotion to her mistress with compassion for the young Octavia. She withheld the vital information for several months, convinced in her own heart that
the poor young thing wasn't ready for marriage. Europa
had, in fact, grown rather fond of Octavia in a grandmoth-
erly way. And she tried to allay her fears by guiding her
gently into the mysteries of womanhood. She would take
her sewing into the garden, and Octavia would sit with her
and listen to the gradually revealed facts of life.

"But why would a man want to put himself inside of a
woman like that?" she once asked, her wide eyes betraying
her innocence.

"Because it gives him a great deal of pleasure," said Europa, her eyes fixed on her sewing. "That part of his body

that we sometimes call his weapon is made of special flesh. Very sensitive and capable of great excitement. When it is rubbed or caressed it gets larger and larger, until it is as stiff as bone. Have you never seen a boy in that condition?"

"Only my brother. We both thought it was very funny. He showed it to me once and asked to see how I looked between my legs."

"Did you show him?"

"Yes," she said, looking down at her hands and blushing. "But there's nothing much there, is there? I mean, he, at least, has something to show. And then he said I was a bad boy."

"A bad *boy*?"

"Yes, he said bad boys had their things cut off by demons and Jews."

Europa laughed and put her sewing down on her lap. "Nonsense, my dear. Rot and nonsense! Girls must be open there in order to have children. How else can babies be born? You see, the juice of life is contained in the man. And when he rubs himself inside of you like that, the juice spills out, provoking in your womb a new growth. How exactly we don't really know. It's a miracle of sorts, requiring also the blessing of the gods. From that first beginning of new life the child grows and grows, until the poor woman looks enormously fat around the belly. You know, like your sister Antonia, when she gave birth last year to her son. In about nine months or so, the child is ripe and must be delivered, or else it will die. You see, it must have room to grow. If all goes well and the birth is natural, why the baby simply comes out. All one has to do is to cut the cord, or even bite it off."

"The cord?"

"Yes! Come here, I'll show you." She held out her hands and then drew Octavia to her. She lifted her tunic and then her undergarment. "You see this?" Octavia giggled at her touch. "Well, when you were first born you had a kind of cord of flesh that went from here into your mother. You probably got your nourishment through it. I mean, you couldn't very well sit up and eat in there, could you?"

They both laughed. Europa adjusted her clothes and then hugged her to her old bosom and kissed her lavishly on her smooth pale cheeks. "Oh, my poor baby, my poor darling!"

"Why am I your poor baby?" asked Octavia, pulling back to look at Europa's face.

"Because, simple as it is, marriage is very difficult."

"Do you think it will hurt?"

"Oh no, my sweet, I wasn't thinking of that. I was thinking of the whole thing. You will have to find ways to keep your husband happy. He may grow tired of you. He may break your heart. And I can't quite see how you and young Nero will get along. But that's the way it's meant to be, and it's not for the likes of me to make any fuss about it. Nor you either, since it's your father's command."

"I wish I didn't have to do it," she said in her childish way, as if she were only talking about a chore or a day trip to the country.

"Ah, but you must, so put it out of your mind and try your best. Besides, you'll make a lovely little bride."

Claudius, too, was concerned about his daughter's early marriage. "But it's not unusual," argued Agrippina. "I mean, I've known of any number of girls who married at thirteen."

"She's just b-b-barely thirteen," said Claudius. "And a f-f-frail little thing. Such a ch-ch-child. Are you sure she—uh—are you sure she—"

"I'm sure! Europa tells me that the girl now bleeds as regularly as any woman. What's more, my son is impatient to have his future settled."

"You mean, you're impatient to have his future settled," said Claudius.

She glared at him. "What are you suggesting?"

"N-n-nothing! Nothing at all! I can't see why he's in such a hurry to marry. He's only sixteen."

"All right, then, I want him to marry. I want the proper alliance. And we've been all over this before. It's the logical thing to do to solidify our position. Unity and peace are what we want."

He sighed. "I guess so."

"I don't dare place him in the hands of another family. You wouldn't want that either, would you?"

He hesitated and looked wearily into his wine. "I sh-sh-should talk to my advisors—to Narcissus and Pallas."

"I've already talked to Pallas. He favors an early wedding."

"And Narcissus?"

"It doesn't matter to me what *he* thinks."

"But it matters to me."

"I don't trust him."

"Well, I do. He's a good man."

"You seem to forget that he advised you against marrying me."

"He was entitled to his opinion."

"And I suppose now, after four years of marriage, you think more highly of his opinion."

"I didn't say that."

"You implied it."

"I didn't. I-I-I didn't imply anything."

She marched back and forth in front of him, her arms folded over her chest. "All right, then, give your consent. We will soon be into December, a most appropriate time for a wedding."

He seemed to be thinking. His eyelids drooped. His head wobbled on his thick neck. He took a long drink from his wine cup and then wiped his mouth with the back of his hand.

She waited a few moments. And then, afraid that his mind might wander from the point, she flung herself at his knees and said, "Say yes and make me a happy woman. Oh, please say yes, and I will love you for the rest of your life and cherish your memory forever after. Say yes, Claudius. Say yes!"

"All right, then, have your w-w-wedding." He felt her breasts against his knees and looked down into her hard, theatrical eyes, with which she played the devoted wife.

"Thank you!" she said, and promptly stood up. She

133

kissed him with businesslike brusqueness and disappeared from the room before he could say another word.

Something he wanted to say was rising slowly from his dull heart, but it wasn't until he was completely alone in the room that he muttered, "Love me!" And then he stamped his foot and called out roughly for more wine.

Having dedicated her toys to Artemis a few days earlier, Octavia prepared herself for the ritual that would bind her, body and soul, to the man she would call her husband. More boy than man, clean-shaven, because there wasn't much to shave; blonde and well-shaped, handsome enough but for the closeness of his eyes and the excessive fullness of his lips. He looked, in fact, as though he had only recently been weaned from his mother's breast, such was the shape of his sensuous mouth. He had grown to more than average height in the past few years, and exercise, especially wrestling and horseback riding, had filled out his frame.

Agrippina was determined to make the wedding celebration a memorable occasion. She remembered how her own last wedding had been marred by the stupidity of Lucius Silanus. This time everything would be perfect. The wedding would be fit for an emperor.

At the rising of the star Hesperus the festivities began. The procession was grand, but it ended where it began, because both bride and groom lived in the same house— the palace, in fact. There were flute players and singers, a choir of maidens, and matrons of honor. Octavia was lovely, all in white, with saffron-colored veil and shoes. Three curls hung down on each side of her face, part of the hairdo of the Vestal Virgins. Her grandmother Lepida beamed. Her father Claudius looked distracted. He was very fond of her in his eccentric way.

Everyone complimented Octavia on her beauty and grace and poise. Nero, too, played his part well, having been thoroughly rehearsed by his mother. But he could not entirely hide his impatience or smother his contempt for this girl who was becoming his wife. He found it hard to have thought of her one day as sort of a bothersome younger sister and then to think of her suddenly as his wife. It was all so strange—almost as if they were playing a game that would surely end after the tossing of the nuts and sweets and after the banquet and general celebration.

But it did not end there. After the raucous feast, after the compliments and gifts and bawdy songs, after all the traditions had been satisfied, there still remained one, final tradition: the bride was conducted to the nuptial couch, where her laughing or tearful relatives left her to face the mystery of sexual initiation. There she was joined by Nero. As the house was slowly emptied of guests, amused attendants prepared the young couple for their first night together. And then they withdrew discreetly to enjoy a private laugh in the corridors and kitchens of the gradually retiring house.

Beautifully but scantily attired for their domestic adventure, Octavia and Nero sat at opposite ends of the room staring at the matrimonial bed, but saying nothing to one another. Nero noticed a crown of myrtle on the floor. Slouching in his chair, he reached it with his foot. He picked it up and played with it, making it circle round his toes. Octavia watched him, afraid to say anything whatsoever, though she was secretly impressed by his agility. She had come to think of him as a big brother. And though she "hated" him, as all girls her age hate boys, she admired him for his accomplishments, his horseback riding, his singing, his amateur attempts at juggling.

The bridal crown slipped from his foot and flew halfway across the room. Octavia suppressed a giggle. He glared at her but said nothing. She stared down at her ring, an arrow of terror lodged in her heart. She turned the golden symbol of their union on her finger, then slipped it on and off, on and off.

"Will you stop playing with your ring," he finally blurted out.

"Why?" she said automatically.

"Because!"

"That's no reason."

"It's reason enough," he said.

She stopped toying with the ring and folded her hands in her lap. She sat that way for a long time, looking up surreptitiously now and then to see what he was doing. He stayed slouched in his chair, his face sandwiched between his fists, as though sulking.

After a long while the house became absolutely quiet. "I guess everyone has gone," she said.

"I guess so," he said.

She waited. "Well," she said.

"Well what?"

"Well, are we just going to sit here all night?"

"Shut up!" he said, his face still between his hands.

She sank lower into her chair and started playing with her ring again. It was so quiet now that they could hear the wind blowing outside the closed shutters on the December night. At last she said, "I have an idea."

"What?" he said, the edge of his anger somewhat blunted by the impasse at which they found themselves.

"Why don't we just tell them we did it."

"You mean and not really do it?"

"Yes. Who would ever know?"

"We can't do that."

"Why not?"

"My mother said it was important."

"What's so important about it?"

"I don't know, but if we don't do it, she's liable to get angry."

"How will she know?"

"She'll know."

"How?"

"I don't know," he said impatiently, "but she will."

"Well, then, do you want to do it?"

"I don't know. Do you?"

"Not really. It sounds sort of stupid."

"It is stupid."

"Have you ever done it before?"

"That's none of your business," he said. Then he raised his head and looked at her. "Have you?"

"No, of course not, you ninny."

"I just wondered. Some girls do."

She sighed. "I'm tired."

"Why don't you go to sleep then?"

136

"How are you going to do it if I'm asleep?"

He shrugged. "I don't know. It might be better that way. I don't want you looking at me when I do it."

"I won't look. I'll close my eyes."

"I thought you were scared."

"I am, but if we don't do it, I'll never get to sleep."

He tapped nervously on the arm of his chair. "I don't know," he said. "It's all so dumb. I don't know if I can."

"You mean you can't?"

"I didn't say I can't. That's not what I meant."

"Then what did you mean?"

"I didn't mean anything. Now just shut up and let me think."

"What's there to think about? Either you do it or you don't do it."

"Maybe we can do it in the morning."

"Are we allowed to do it in the morning?"

"I don't know. Maybe."

"Perhaps we should ask your mother."

"Don't be funny."

"I'm serious."

"Then you ask her."

"No."

"Why not?"

"Because I'm afraid of her."

He looked at her for the first time without hostility. "So am I," he said.

She stood up and ambled about the room. She circled the bed and then tested its softness. Then she sat down on it. "It's certainly big enough, isn't it?"

"Mmmm!" he said.

She stretched out and put her head down on the bolster. "I think weddings are horrible, don't you?"

"Mmmm!" he said.

She closed her eyes and waited, wondering whether or not he would join her on the bed. He didn't. In a few minutes she was overwhelmed by sleepiness. But just as she was about to succumb to that feeling, there was a gentle knocking on their door. She opened her eyes and saw Nero standing by the door. A voice on the other side said, "It's your mother. Is everything all right?" She saw Nero open the door and let his mother in. A chill went through her. She lay very still and pretended to be sleeping.

"What's wrong?" said Agrippina.

"Nothing," said Nero. "She fell asleep."

"She what?"

"She fell asleep."

"Did you do what you were supposed to do?"

"How could I? She fell asleep. It's not my fault."

"Nonsense," she said. "Now go to her and do your duty. After tonight, it won't matter."

"Why is it so important?"

"It's part of the ritual, that's all. Now get it over with."

"But, are you supposed to be here?"

"What's the difference. Now, come here." She led him to the bed where Octavia seemed to be sleeping. She drew back the girl's gown and revealed her almost hairless body. "It's all very simple. Just part her legs and do it."

"What if she wakes up?"

"It doesn't matter. Do it quickly. Consummate the marriage." She sat down on the edge of the bed and drew her son to her. She kissed him on the mouth. "Do it for me."

He felt the warmth of her body and the wetness of her kiss. She lifted his tunic and looked at him. "You're quite a man," she said. "You should have no trouble."

He clung to his mother. She kissed him again and then slipped her gown from her shoulder to bare her generous breast to him. He buried his face in her and took her nipple in his mouth. She could feel his excitement against her. "Now," she whispered. The three of them were on the large bed. "Do it now!" And she urged him toward the terrified Octavia.

He mounted the frail girl's body and parted her legs. "Yes," said Agrippina. "Yes!"

And he found his way between Octavia's thin legs, knowing that she was only pretending to sleep, and knowing also that his mother knew. A general conspiracy of silence.

"That's right! That's right!" she whispered hoarsely, her own excitement now uncontrollable.

138

In her pretense of sleep, Octavia winced and almost cried. But in a few moments it was all over, and Nero stood up and walked away from the bed. Agrippina lingered. She laid a comforting hand on the girl's head and leaned close to her. "Not a word about my being here!" she said. "Not a word, if you want to live to be a mother."

And then she gathered herself together and went to her son. He was standing, stunned, in the middle of the room. She took him in her arms. He did not resist. She kissed him. "There now,". she said. "Everything will be all right, now!" And then she left, closing the door quietly behind her.

He looked at his assaulted wife. The sleep that was a pretense had become read. He dared not approach her. He slumped into a chair and, in a few moments, was sound asleep.

# XVIII

After Octavia's marriage, Britannicus seemed dull and depressed. He had lost a sister and a playmate. It was not proper for her to cavort like a child. Other things were expected of her. She had duties to perform—at temples and festivals, at weddings and funerals. He was twelve, the only real child left in the palace. The place was always heavily guarded. He was not allowed to go anywhere unattended. Sometimes another boy would be brought in for a visit, but there was no one he liked especially. He spent most of his time either with his tutor Sosibius or wandering alone in the garden.

When Sosibius first reported to Claudius that his son seemed unhappy, the emperor responded by asking him how old the boy was. "Twelve, sir," said the tutor.

"Mmm!" said Claudius. "And why should he be unhappy?"

"Perhaps he's lonely, sir," said Sosibius.

"Well, well, there are always books. I was lonely, too, as a child. Not much wanted, you know. I-I-I found much pleasure in books. Does he read?"

140

"Yes, a great deal, in fact."

"Mmmm! Perhaps he reads too much. It c-c-can make you dull, you know. One has to strike a happy b-b-balance between the physical and the mental. He's athletic. He's strong. Does he take part in the exercises?"

"Oh yes. He's quite good. And an excellent little horseman."

"Then what is it, Sosibius?" With his sad, almost helpless gaze, Claudius appealed to him. "Have I done something wrong? Do you think he still misses his mother?"

"That's difficult to say."

Claudius shook his head and pounded the arm of his chair with his fist. "How terrible it all is, Sosibius! How terrible! How can I expect him to love me when I killed his mother?" He seemed about to cry.

"It wasn't your fault, sir."

His voice faded into a dream. "She was so beautiful, so lovely! I can see her in my son's face." Then he shook off the mood and said roughly, "Ah, but that's all dead and done! What can we do for the lad? How can we cheer him up? Has he been to the arena lately?"

"I'm not sure he likes that sort of thing, sir."

"Nonsense, all children like animals and games. Boys like violence. It'll keep him from brooding. Have him up early in he morning. We want to be there by dawn when those creatures condemned *ad bestias* are dragged into the arena. It's the most interesting part."

And so Britannicus went with his father to the amphitheater in the early hours of the morning. He arrived, sleepy-eyed and a little confused. Only attendants and guards accompanied them. No other relatives or friends were interested in getting up that early. But few of the seats in the huge place went begging. By the time the first ragged, pathetic criminals were hauled into the arena, the crowd was immense and awake.

The first group consisted of half a dozen men and two women. No one could be sure what their crimes were. The assumption was that they were especially villanous, and deserved, therefore, an especially brutal form of execution.

141

And that's all that these morning spectacles were. Later there would be contests. These were not.

Claudius, as usual, was excited. Each day it was as if he had never been there before. "Ah," he said, "it's beginning."

Britannicus leaned forward with curiosity and said nothing. His face was tense. It was a handsome face, much stronger than his father's.

The lions came out and circled around the panic-stricken victims. For a while nothing much happened. The two women screamed. The men made no attempt to protect them. Additional beasts were let into the arena. A fight broke out between a lioness and a black panther. The fighting stirred the other animals. They became more agitated. The criminals fled to one side of the open circle and grouped together. Disappointed, the crowd began to chant for action. And in a few minutes they were satisfied. The animals closed in. The group scattered. A woman was attacked by a lion and killed almost instantly. He had his teeth in her throat. Her simple tunic was torn away to a rag. Her arms and legs twisted grotesquely as the lion shook and nudged the corpse. Then he fell to the business of tearing it apart.

"Why have these people been thrown to the beasts?" asked Britannicus.

"Oh, they've been very bad. Very bad, indeed!" said Claudius, his attention fixed on the mauling of another victim, but one who fought back, thrashing and punching. "Murderers! Rapists! Thieves! Perverts! No good at all to themselves or to the world. Got to get rid of them. C-c-can't have that sort of thing. Ah, see, there. He's got him now."

"I suppose my mother was bad, too!" said Britannicus. But, fortunately, his father was a little hard of hearing. He merely turned to him for a moment with raised eyebrows over tragic eyes. And then he returned almost instantly to the action and let out a desperate bellow demanding *blood!*

Britannicus had been to the arena before, but never to these morning massacres. There was something about them that bothered him. Was it the viciousness of the crowd? The frailty of the human body? The immediacy of death? He frowned and sighed. How difficult it was to come to terms with all this: his dead mother, his old father, his stepmother, Nero, conspiracies, and corpses. There was a lot of whispering and a lot of blood. And he missed his sister Octavia terribly. It was his age, Sosibius tried to tell him—that time of life between boyhood and manhood when one is besieged by new feelings. He would be thirteen soon. And, yes, he felt these things. He was restless. He was angry. Sometimes he wanted to kill something, but he never knew what.

At the first intermission Claudius turned to his son and said, "They tell me that the main attraction today will be a contest between a tiger and an elephant. That ought to be something, eh?"

He smiled and a little well of joy tried to burst through his sadness. "Yes, Father," he said. "And I'll bet fifty sesterces on the elephant."

He made a gesture that imitated his father, and Claudius laughed and coughed and said, "Done!" He beamed affectionately at his boy. "But beware of tigers."

They both laughed, and he put his arm around Britannicus and drew him closer. "You're getting to be qu-qu-quite a young man," he said. "Look at these shoulders. And what's that I see? Is that a little sh-shadow of hair on your lip?"

Embarrassed, Britannicus drew away. "Not a boy anymore, eh. You'll be running after g-g-girls soon."

"I prefer horses," he said.

"D-d-don't blame you. Much less trouble. Still taking lessons from Tigellinus, eh?"

"Yes, except when he's away on business."

Claudius cleared his throat elaborately. "Well, now, what's this Sosibius tells me? He s-s-says that you're unhappy about s-s-something. What is it? Tell me."

Britannicus hesitated. He looked into his father's deepset blue eyes, surprised but pleased to know that he was aware of things. "It's nothing, really."

"Now, now, it must be something."

143

"Well, actually, it *is* something, but I'm not sure it would be right for me to tell you."

Claudius tightened his grip on the boy's shoulders and cajoled him. "Come now, you can tell me. I *am* your father, after all."

"You're also the emperor," said Britannicus. "I suppose you could order me to tell you."

They both smiled. "All right, then, let me guess. You're lonely. Not enough companionship in the palace. Is that it?"

"Not exactly."

"But what about Nero? Hasn't he been company for you. Or is he too old?

"Nero and I will never be friends. He's cruel."

"C-c-cruel?"

"He taunts me."

"He t-t-taunts you?"

"He says you adopted him in order to make him your successor."

"Well, well, well, well! N-n-now that's news to me. Where did he get that idea?"

"From his mother probably."

"Is that so? V-v-very interesting. But just between you and me, she doesn't know as much as she thinks she does."

"Then why *did* you adopt him?"

"That's complicated. She wanted it, and, frankly, I was tired of listening to her. Besides, there is this tradition of adoption in our family. I m-m-mean, Tiberius adopted Germanicus and s-s-so forth. I don't know. I just gave in. But I never had any intention of—I never promised her—I mean, you are my real son, after all. I fully expect to name you as my successor. Don't you worry about that." He suddenly squeezed him with greater feeling. "You'll be the next emperor of Rome." His head wobbled uncontrollably. "I'll put it in my will. I'll make it p-p-public. That ought to put her in her place, eh?" He dabbed at his wet mouth with his toga and called for his slave Theon. Even in the midst of this emotional speech, a part of his mind was thinking about food.

Behind them a member of the Praetorian Guard, standing

144

as still as a statue, overheard every word of the conversation. He knew it was important and reported it immediately to Burrus, who then carried the information to Agrippina.

# XIX

Narcissus was physically and mentally exhausted. Pressure from the empress kept him in constant jeopardy, and there had recently been an attempt on his life. An intruder had slipped past the guards at his house and had actually made his way halfway to the bedroom where he was taking a midday nap. The would-be assassin had been captured after he startled a young slave girl, who screamed and brought the guards running. Narcissus was a wealthy man. His house was large and well protected. Unfortunately, the intruder was killed before he could be made to talk. Pallas dismissed the incident as the bravado of a common thief looking for valuables in a rich man's house. It was never even mentioned to Claudius, lest it disturb his already agitated mind. But to his friends Narcissus said that he had reason to believe that the man was a hired assassin.

At Aelia's house he said he had to get away from Rome for a while. "I want to go to my villa at Sinuessa and to recover my health." He held out his hands, palms down, "You see how my hands shake. I'll be as palsied as Claudius before long." And, indeed, he did look unsteady and suddenly older than his forty-eight years.

"But if what you tell us is true, this is the worst possible time for you to leave Rome," said Antonia.

"Are you sure that Claudius plans to make his will public?" asked Sulla.

"I am trying to persuade him not to," said Narcissus. "But the man grows more and more difficult each day. He's so hard to predict. He makes one decision during the day and another during the night."

"Agrippina gets to him at night," said Lepida.

"If he names Britannicus as his heir, Agrippina will almost certainly try to kill the boy," said Antonia. "Don't you agree?"

"She will certainly be furious. How far she will be willing to go is hard to say. She is, as we all know, capable of murder. I have advised Claudius to keep his successor a secret for a while. It strengthens his position. My personal feelings are mixed. I hope he chooses Britannicus over Nero, of course. On the other hand, it makes me somewhat uneasy to think that I might have to serve the young man whose mother I helped to kill. Messalina's faction is still alive, if not very vociferous right now."

"I disagree," said Lepida. "I think my grandson should be named at once, and publicly. If anything should happen to Claudius before a successor is named, Agrippina will see to it that Nero is the next emperor. She might do anything: use the Praetorian Guard, forge a will, kill Britannicus. Anything! The boy should be named and then thoroughly protected, day and night."

Narcissus sat down heavily in an armchair. He looked around the room at the others. Sunlight streamed through the open shutters and admitted garden sounds and a patch of clear blue sky. He shook his head wearily. "That it should come to this! What a pack of wolves we've all become. Murder in our hearts. An army of guards to see us through the day. Assassins in our bedrooms. Poison in our food. How can we enjoy even the simplest pleasure? A walk in the country. The sound of birds. I don't dare to do anything alone these days. Claudius barely leaves the pal-

147

ace. Agrippina watches everybody like a hawk. It's enough to drive one insane." He covered his face with his hands, as if to block out the world.

Aelia went to him and put her hand on his shoulder. "Perhaps you should go to Sinuessa, after all," she said.

"No!" said Antonia sharply. "No, you mustn't. If you leave him now, my father will be killed. I'm sure of it. I have a terrible premonition. Agrippina will take advantage of your absence. She will prevent him from naming Britannicus. She already knows what he has in mind."

"Are you sure?" asked Lepida.

"Yes," said Antonia. "I have good sources. Something was overheard at the arena. And my father has indiscreetly hinted to friends that it was his destiny to endure the infamy of his wives and to be forced to punish them."

"I know all that," said Narcissus. "But will he do it? Does he have any will left?"

"Yes," said Antonia. "I know he does. You musn't be fooled by his apparent absent-mindedness. He knows what's going on."

"Then talk to him, Antonia," urged Lepida. "Persuade him. Persuade him to name my grandson and to rid himself of that woman, that succubus."

"I will do my best, but I can't promise anything," said Antonia. "Narcissius, I need your help. Don't leave us now."

He sighed. "I will talk to my physicians. If my health fails, I will be good to none of us—including myself."

Lepida got up and paced nervously back and forth, twisting a yellow handkerchief in her hands. Her face was tight with determination, but it did not diminish her poise or mar her beauty. Her claims to nobility were, after all, almost as great as Agrippina's. And her wealth was at least appropriate to her station in life. It was, in fact, considerable. Though not malicious, she was not the sort of woman who liked to lose.

She paused suddenly in the center of the room and looked around at the others. It was clear that what she was about to say was already in their minds. "There is, of course, another way," she said, her voice dark and precise.

148

They all looked at her for a long moment. Silence trembled in the room. It was Antonia who shattered it. "No!" she said passionately. "No, no, no! We cannot allow ourselves to consider such things. We must not be dragged down to her level."

"But it is she who is dragging us down," Lepida said.

"We may have no choice."

"We always have a choice," said Antonia.

"What choice?"

"To die with dignity. With honor. I cannot—I will not—"

Sulla went to her and put his arm around her shoulders. "Violence only leads to more violence," he said. "There's already been too much slaughter and fear in this family."

Lepida waited for Narcissus to speak. He rubbed his tired eyes and looked at her. "They're right," he said quietly. "There must be an end to it somewhere. We can't go on like this forever."

Aelia nodded her approval of what he said, and Lepida seemed suddenly alone in her fierce determination. She walked slowly back to her chair and sat down. "All right, then," she said, "what do you suggest we do?"

"Let me talk to my father once more," said Antonia.

"And then what?" asked Lepida.

Antonia hestitated. "I don't know."

Narcissus stood up. "We can only wait and see," he said. "Things change. Sometimes unexpectedly."

# XX

The suicide of Lepida came as a surprise to no one after the first accusations of treason and conspiracy. It all happened swiftly. Lepida was visited in the early morning hours by a tribune and placed under house arrest. A few hours later she was brought to the palace, where she heard the charges against her. It was a preliminary hearing before the emperor, not an official trial. Burrus presided. Witnesses were produced. They were absolute strangers. They swore that they had come upon Lepida in the act of casting spells and using incantations to destroy Agrippina. It was outside the Porto Pincian, at the crossroads with the Via Salaria Vetus. In the ruins of the old temple of Hecate, they said, they saw her kneeling before a fire and muttering magical words in a strange language. In these incantations the name Agrippina was repeated over and over again.

The whole thing was a fantastic fabrication. Lepida was hauled away screaming curses at her accusers and warnings at the emperor: "She will kill us all! She will kill you! Listen to me, Claudius." But it was useless.

Within twenty-four hours Lepida was dead, persuaded to

150

suicide, much in the manner of Lollia Paulina. Narcissus carried the news to his friends at Aelia Paetina's house. Antonia and Sulla were there, as was a knight of the equestrian order who was a strong supporter of Britannicus.

Narcissus was extremely weary and shaken. He had slept in his clothes and had not seen his barber. He had managed once to confer with the emperor, but Claudius had been deep in his cups and beyond everything but his chronic fear. He actually fell asleep during the conference, muttering to himself, "Scold me but don't hurt me." It was a childhood memory of the torments to which he was subjected by the sadistic tutor assigned to him by his mother, who was convinced that punishment could cure anything.

"There was nothing further I could do," said Narcissus. "They had gotten him to sign the order immediately after the preliminary hearing. In desperation, I thought we might be able to engineer a last-minute escape by force, but I could not afford to commit myself that far. I am in serious enough trouble as it is, having been Lepida's chief defender. Besides, I don't think she would have wanted to escape. When the tribune came to suggest that she end her life with honor in the old Roman way, I understand she accepted the option and carried it out with all the dignity of a true noblewoman, unlike her sniveling daughter. She calmly prepared herself, reviewed the household accounts, and put her will in order. She chose her favorite gown, had her hair redone to remove what was artificial, and arranged herself on her bed. There she asked the gods to protect her grandson Britannicus from the viciousness of Agrippina, upon whom she called down a powerful curse, using an ancient Macedonian incantation given to her years ago by the old woman of the grotto. And finally, she drank a poison prepared for her by Locusta, a poison that was swift and painless, inducing almost immediately a kind of deep sleep. Her breathing grew slower and slower, and within ten minutes she was no more. Her body was taken immediately to a hastily arranged funeral pyre that was already ablaze when the tribune pounded on her gate to announce the emperor's decision. With no relatives present and only a handful of witnesses, her body was committed to the flames, to be resolved into the elements from which it came."

His voice fell away. He slumped in his chair. Sulla reached for Antonia's hand and held it tightly. Aelia Paetina brought Narcissus a cup of wine, at which he stared for a long moment before recognizing what it was. He accepted with a nod. She let her hand fall lightly on his shoulder. "You must go to Sinuessa," she said. "You must go to your villa and rest. The country air will be good for you. It will drive out the stench of these terrible events."

# XXI

For a full week after the death of Lepida, Claudius was a terrified recluse, hiding out in his bedroom or study, eating alone, persuaded by those around him that his life was in danger. He trusted only Pallas and Burrus. He wasn't altogether sure what to think about Agrippina. Her display of concern and affection after the Lepida affair was elaborate, but was it real? He wished that Narcissus had not gone to Sinuessa. He needed his soothing, level-headed advice.

Day after day went by and nothing further happened, though the group that surrounded him and controlled him could have done almost anything in his name for a whole week. Agrippina pressed for further purges, but Pallas and Burrus restrained her. "You have a way of provoking people to violence," said Pallas. "You must go easy or you will lose your advantage."

"Had I gone easy with her she might have found a way to destroy me," said Agrippina.

"Nevertheless, it will not do to stir up this sort of thing again. The city is tense. The emperor must make a public

153

appearance to put the people at ease. There are even rumors that he's been killed."

"Where could such a rumor have started?"

"Rumors are like flies. They appear spontaneously out of the dung."

"Perhaps it was Antonia. She has been wanting to see her father all week."

"We must be careful about Antonia. She and her husband are popular."

"She's weak."

"Not weak," said Pallas. "Idealistic!"

"It's the same thing," said Agrippina.

"Nevertheless, watch out for her. She strengthens the Britannicus faction."

"Which, I understand, is becoming quite a fashionable movement."

"Yes! The lingering supporters of Messalina, the substantial following of Domitia Lepida, the admirers of Antonia and Sulla."

"And the emperor's promise of succession?"

"Neither announced nor in his will," said Pallas.

They looked at one another, their eyes completing a forbidden conversation. Her voice fell to a whisper. "Come to my room tonight. We must talk some more." And then in her normal voice, but honey-sweet: "Ah, here's our little Antonia again, come to see her father."

Antonia came into the atrium. "Is he any better?" she inquired.

"Yes, he is," said Agrippina. "And I'm sure he would be happy yo see you."

"You mean I may go to him now?" asked Antonia.

"Yes, by all means, child," said Agrippina. "He's in his study reading. I'm sure he won't mind being disturbed by *you*."

Antonia did not like being called *child* by her stepmother, who was only twelve years her senior. She forced a smile for the two of them and walked toward the corridor. "Oh, incidentally," called Agrippina after her, "how is your little boy?"

The sinister note did not escape Antonia. "He's fine,

thank you," she said, and went on down the corridor to her father's study.

Claudius looked up when she came in. He was seated behind a large desk, piled with scrolls and manuscripts and maps. "Ah, Antonia," he said, obviously glad to see her. "Come in, come in. How good of you to come. I was hoping you would. I'm f-f-feeling much better now, after that nasty b-b-business."

She went to him and kissed him on the cheek. He stroked her back with his trembling hand. "What are you reading?" she said, looking over his shoulder at the book in front of him.

"Oh, I was j-j-just looking at my own b-b-book on the Etruscans. R-r-remember that? Eh? Remember how hard I worked on that? It's not a bad piece of work. Perhaps I'll give a r-r-reading from it. Agrippina says I've g-g-got to make a public appearance. Is it true? Are the p-p-people worried?"

"Of course they are," she said, still standing beside him. She fussed with his thick white hair. "I mean they're concerned about your health."

"Oh, well, yes!" He laughed. "And assassination is bad for one's health, isn't it?"

She glanced toward the door, on the other side of which were two members of the Praetorian Guard. The room was quiet. Their voices carried. "Father," she said, "do you think we could have some music?"

He frowned. "M-m-music? Here? At this hour?"

"Yes, I'm in the mood for music. And perhaps a little something to eat. A bowl of fruit? Some cheese?"

"Ah yes, ah yes, I understand. A little f-f-food. A little m-m-music. Cheer us up, eh?" He rubbed his hands together and called out, "Theon!" The slave appeared from the next room. "Tell Cleobis to come and play for us. And bring us some fruit and cheese and a little wine."

"So, father! How have you been? You look well. We heard you were ill."

"Well, all that ugly business with L-L-Lepida and incanta-

155

tions. I-I-I didn't know where it would stop. I-I was afraid that someone had cast a spell on *me*."

"Now why would anyone do a thing like that? The people love you."

Theon, Cleobis, and another slave came in. Theon directed his underling to put the food and wine on the corner of the table reserved by Claudius for such things. And Cleobis arranged himself on a cushion in the corner and asked if any special kind of music were required. "No, no," said Claudius. "Play what you like."

"But something lively," said Antonia. "Something pleasant."

When Theon and the other slave were gone and Cleobis was plucking out a tune on his instrument, Antonia poured them each some wine and drew up a chair close to her father's. "Now I must talk to you very seriously," she said.

"Of c-c-course, my dear," he said, but he was preoccupied with the cheese. "Here, you must taste this. It's s-s-superb! Excellent with the Falernian." He stuffed his mouth and chewed without closing it all the way. Crumbs of cheese stuck to his lips and collected in the corners of his mouth.

"Father!" she said. "I did not come here on a social visit."

"Wh-what? But you asked for music and—"

"The music is for privacy. I don't want to be overheard."

"Oh!" He looked at her, his face somewhat blank, his mouth full of cheese.

"Father, I must know what's going on. Are you planning to name Britannicus as your successor? Are you planning to make your will public?"

"D-d-difficult questions! T-t-too difficult!"

"I have to tell you that if you name Britannicus publicly, you may place his life in jeopardy."

"Y-y-yes, I know that."

She was pleased at this moment of lucidity. His eyes looked clear. His head almost stopped wobbling.

"And if I d-d-don't name him? What then?"

"Perhaps if you keep everyone wondering, you will be in a stronger position."

Suddenly his clear eyes went a little wild. "I-I-I don't understand. Is someone trying to kill me?"

She hesitated, then took his hand in hers. "If they think you plan to make Britannicus your successor, your life may be in danger."

"Who?" he asked, his eyes wide, but his comprehension incomplete. "B-B-Britannicus is my son."

"Nero is your adopted son."

"I don't much like Nero."

"Perhaps you should pretend to like him. Perhaps you should give the impression that you are considering naming him your successor."

"But why?"

"Father, don't you understand? It's your wife."

"M-m-my wife? Agrippina?"

"Yes! You must be careful of her. She's not to be trusted."

He shook his head. "N-n-no, no. I have to trust some-one."

"Trust me! Trust Narcissus!"

"He's gone to Sinuessa."

"All the more reason to be careful."

He poured himself another cup of wine. "Y-y-you musn't talk this way. You're making me upset. I don't want to think about it. Wh-what if I should die without naming a successor? But, oh, Antonia, I don't want to die. I don't want to d-d-die. Death is an awful thing. N-n-nothing else matters."

"Then get rid of her."

"Who?"

"Agrippina. She's only using you. She doesn't love you. She has lovers."

"I-I know that. It's a small price to pay. Let her have her lovers."

"She wants more than that. She wants power. Absolute power."

"D-d-don't say anymore. Don't say these things. I don't want to hear them. Let's listen to the music. L-l-let's have some more wine."

157

"Father! Face up to her. Put her aside."

"I c-c-can't! Don't you understand? I can't. If I provoke her she will kill me. She's like my mother, strong-willed and c-c-cruel. B-b-but I need her. I'm old. I'm afraid." He clutched at his daughter, as if he were drowning. She allowed him to embrace her but felt, uncontrollably, a certain repulsion. She felt his wet mouth against her smooth cheek. She heard his heavy, unhealthy breathing in her ear. It was a growling sea. She wanted to pull away. She wanted to run out of the house—out of the city. She wanted to be alone with her baby and her husband in the simplicity of the country, under a clear sky, beside a stream. She wanted to wash away all the filth and confusion.

Instead, she comforted him. She felt him sobbing against her, and her tears mingled with his. Impassively, the musician played on, trained to ignore the people for whom he played.

Suddenly the door opened and Agrippina came in, still wearing her smiling mask, still talking in that artificial tone. "My, my, what a touching scene. Father and daughter! How happy you both must be to see one another. But what's this? Music and wine so early in the day. No, no, that will never do. Xenophon has forbidden wine before the evening meal. What a naughty old emperor you are, allowing yourself to be seduced into these debaucheries by your daughter."

Cladius gathered himself sheepishly together and cleared his throat. "J-j-just a trivial refreshment," he said. "J-j-just normal hospitality. I was happy to see my daughter."

"You've both been weeping for joy, I see. But I think you've had enough excitement for one day. You must get some rest. There's considerable business to attend to this afternoon."

Antonia got up and prepared to leave. Claudius looked up at her. "C-c-come again tomorrow," he said. "Bring your s-s-son." She smiled at him affectionately.

"Yes," said Agrippina, "by all means, bring your son. He may, after all, be the emperor of Rome someday, just like his grandfather."

158

The look that they exchanged was so charged with hatred that it was almost audible. She did not reply. She kissed her father good-bye and walked quickly out of the room.

# *XXII*

In the days that followed, Antonia spent a great deal of time with Britannicus, almost neglecting her own son in order to be with her young half-brother. She was haunted by the premonition that something dire would happen to him, and she did not know how best to protect him. They read aloud to each other for hours on end. They took walks. And she got her father's permission to share his lesson in Greek. Sosibius was delighted. He too was deeply anxious about Britannicus. Like Antonia, he had grown very attached to the boy.

"He's got an excellent mind," she said one day to her brother's tutor.

"He does, indeed," said Sosibius. "And, as you can see from our recent lessons, he's remarkably advanced in Greek. In another year or two there will be nothing he can't read."

And then he led them through the intricacies and passions of Sophocles and Euripides, explaining the difficult passages, weeping over the lines that had wrenched his heart for thirty years. He believed in art and philosophy and the philosopher-king and saw in Britannicus an opportunity to make a reality of Plato's dream. Here was a lad with all the talents and with an innate goodness. With proper training he could lift the veil of corruption and despair from Rome and change the course of history.

Antonia knew this too and prayed that nothing would interfere with his succession to power. But within the deep recesses of her being she felt the snarling serpent of her cousin's ambition. Even as she and Britannicus walked in the dazzling sunlight of the garden and marveled at the ancient wisdom of the Greeks, she could hear imaginary thunder and see the billowing of ominous clouds.

They had lunch by the fishpond and digested the morning sessions with Sosibius. "Why didn't Socrates escape when he was condemned to death?" asked Britannicus in his innocence. "He had every opportunity. He was not heavily guarded. I would have tried."

"But you're young," she said. "And he was seventy years old. He was not afraid of death. And do you remember what he says in the *Apology*. He could have earned his acquittal by saying what they wanted to hear. But he preferred his integrity to life. He would not be forced to live in a fashion that compromised his principles. He knew he was going to die soon anyway. So why fawn or beg or lie. Why run away, as though you were a common criminal, when by accusing you your persecutors themselves become the accused. But in a higher sense. You see, he valued truth more than he valued life."

Britannicus stared into the green-clear pool, torn between Roman realities and Greek ideals. "Yes, but as long as he was alive, he could preach his principles and hope that they would spread. And, besides, he would be alive. Which is better than being dead."

"But no one lives forever, and he was old," said Antonia. "Don't you see? One must believe in something beside himself."

"And what do you believe in, Antonia?" he asked.

"I believe much as Plato did. That the world is a universal harmony, from which there is no escape. It is governed by order and beauty and truth—the eternal verities. You can no more violate them in your personal life than you can in the physical world. You cannot force water to run upstream. You cannot alter the course of the heavenly bodies. You must be true to the real nature of things. Otherwise, you will be at war with the world. And you will be at war with yourself. Evil people are never really happy. They are almost always cowards, buying a little extra life with dreadful compromises and conspiracies. And all for what? There is no immortality on this earth. If there is any immortality at all, it is part of that universal harmony."

"But what if there are no gods, as some people say? What if we die and are merely eaten by worms?"

"Why, then, that's all the more reason for living a good life. Why gamble away your peace of mind and earthly virtues for a few more days on earth, if, like everyone else, you are only destined to feed maggots and worms?"

He thought about that for a while and tossed a pebble into the pond that scattered the fish. "If I am ever emperor of Rome," he said, "I will put an end to all that slaughter in the arena." And then he looked up at her with boyish uncertainty. "Would I be allowed to do that?"

She smiled down at him. "Of course you would, my dear. Of course you would."

# XXIII

The tone of Nero's education was quite different. Having been warned about speculative philosophy, Seneca concentrated on the pragmatics of power. Both he and his pupil assumed that one day he, Nero, would rule the Roman empire. They did not discuss the matter directly, but the tacit assumption was often in the background of their conversations.

One day, accompanied by two guardsmen, they rode out to the villa of Publius Anteius to wish him well on his birthday. Halfway there they were caught in a downpour and were forced to find shelter in a large abandoned stable. From the crude structure they could see the whole slope of the mountain, the grazing sheep, the tortured olive trees. The guardsmen provided them with a simple lunch of bread and cheese and olives. And Nero shared their wine.

Squatting on two blocks of stone like peasants, the adopted son of the emperor and the foremost philosopher of Rome talked about the simple life. "The Greeks romanticized it," said Seneca. "It's not so marvelous and innocent as it seems."

"But it's all so beautiful to look at," said Nero. "And I remember a collection of bronze figurines that someone sent to my mother. From Arcadia, I think. All shepherds and maidens. Lovely work."

"Oh yes," said Seneca. "Very lovely, indeed. But idealized. Real life in ancient Arcadia was an entirely different matter. You can see it in their myths and cults. It was rude and savage. They practised human sacrifice. They were probably poor, filthy, and ignorant."

"Well, then, how can they have inspired all the attention that's been given to them?" asked Nero. "I mean, we talk about beautiful shepherds all the time."

"I think it is a dream of innocence that people long for when their lives have become too complex," said Seneca. "They imagine that there is a beautiful place somewhere, beside a babbling brook, where they can recline forever with a lovely lady and make love to the sound of magic music under a sky eternally clear. Fruit falls in their mouths. The sheep go baa! And all's right with the world. But it really doesn't work that way. The wench gets pregnant. The sheep die of mysterious diseases. The wolf comes in the night. Flies buzz around the flawed fruit. And there are no books to read."

Nero laughed. "You're right. I don't want to be a shepherd, not even one of those prancing idiots on a Grecian urn. I want to have riches and glory."

It was Seneca's turn to laugh. But in a moment he grew serious again. "On the other hand," he said, "the common man is a serious problem."

"In what way?" asked Nero. He was looking at the horses. They stood patiently in the rain, water dripping from their faces and saddles.

"First, because there are so many of them. They are the source of one's power. They perform the work. They fill the ranks of the military. They grow the food. Slaves or freedmen, they must be dealt with cautiously."

"But if they are slaves, we can always kill them," said Nero. "I mean, if they misbehave."

"Yes, but you can't kill them all."

"Why not?"

"First of all, who will do the killing? And what if the slaves organize themselves and fight back? As you know, there have been slave rebellions in the past. The possibility still remains. Sparticus, you remember, raised an army of ninety thousand and devastated southern Italy. He might, in fact, have conquered all of Rome, if his intentions had been clearer in his own mind."

"All right, then," said Nero, "we won't kill the slaves. We'll bribe them. If they're happy, they won't rebel."

"Precisely," said Seneca. "You have just discovered the basic principle of how to maintain authority and power."

"By bribery?" Nero looked puzzled.

"In a sense, yes! The ordinary man, citizen or slave, is not concerned with principles, with religion or politics or art or philosophy. He is only concerned with his belly and his bed. If he has enough to eat and somewhere to lie down when he is tired, he will be reasonably content. The imperial policy has always been to keep the mob content. Hence, our concern with the grain supply. And, of course, the distractions of the circus and the arena virtually guarantee a populace incapable of revolt. In Rome we go even further. We not only feed them well and distract them, but we let them bathe. We do not do these things out of sheer goodness. It is politically wise."

"But what you are saying, then, is that the people have the power. I never thought of it that way. I thought the emperor had the power."

"Whoever controls the raw strength of the masses has the power. A mob without a leader can only create chaos. And since order is a universal principle, to rule is divine. When the troops hail our emperor, they are not only acclaiming him commander in chief, but they are saluting, in his person, the power that brings victory. There is no greater honor or glory or destiny in this world than to be a leader of men and, thereby, participate in the eternal harmony of things."

"But what about war? There's no harmony in war."

"We only go to war to put an end to discord and to restore peace and unity. There is often beauty in battle and heroism in death. What else is the *Iliad* of Homer all

165

about? Perhaps we should reread it. It is a great work of art."

"Yes, I thought it was fine. So much better than all those weeping women in the plays of Euripides. Must we read much more of that sort of thing?"

"Your mother likes *Medea*."

"Then let her read it," he said. He stood up and pointed toward the hills. "Look, there's a rainbow." He strutted like a mock emperor. "Send some slaves to fetch it." And his tutor laughed.

# XXIV

Claudius did nothing to resolve the question of the succession, paralyzed as he was by real and imaginary fears. However, he had completely forgotten about a special issue of coins that he had secretly ordered minted for his son's birthday. They showed him and Britannicus together in profile. He had intended the coins as a surprise—for everyone. And they were. Agrippina was not only surprised, she was shocked and horrified, seeing in the incident a subtle political move on the part of the emperor. Too subtle, in fact, for him. It was more the kind of thing that Narcissus would dream up. A clear indication of which way the wind was blowing.

Clenching a half dozen of the newly minted silver coins in her damp palm, she stormed down the hall to the financial secretary's private office. There she found Pallas sitting calmly behind his desk. "Do you know what I've got here?" she shouted, waving her fist at him.

"I heard about it this morning," he said.

"Well?"

"Well what?" he said, his voice calm, his eyebrows raised.

"Well, what are you going to do about it? How can you just sit there as if nothing has happened? Don't you see what this means?"

"I don't think it means anything."

"It means he's made up his mind to name Britannicus his successor. This is only the first step. A traditional move. You know that as well as I do."

"I think it was an impulsive and sentimental act, something he thought up on the spur of the moment some months ago. My guess is that he's completely forgotten about it. You know how he is."

"He doesn't need to remember things; he's got Narcissus."

"Narcissus is a sick man. He may never come back from Sinuessa."

"I hope he rots in Sinuessa."

"Now, watch that temper of yours."

"Don't tell me what to do!" she screamed. "I will not put up with this sort of thing. I don't care how it happened. The coins are in circulation. All Rome will be talking. Damn him!" And she flung the coins across the room. They bounced off the books that lined the wall and rang metallically on the marble floor.

"There's not much you can do about it," Pallas remarked, trying to temper her fury with cold logic.

"That's what you think. There's a great deal I can do. And the time to do it is now. Send for Locusta."

"The prisoner?"

"Yes."

He hesitated, his mind was making fast calculations, but his voice betrayed nothing. "She's in the custody of Julius Pollio, the tribune."

"I don't care! Have him bring her to me in disguise. Tonight!"

"What you are contemplating, Agrippina, is very, very risky. And you know how cautious I am."

"To hell with your caution. I want Locusta. And I want

168

the eunuch Halotus, the one who tastes Claudius's food."
Pallas stood up and paced slowly back and forth.
"What's the matter, my hero? No stomach for violence?"

"I like my life. I'd prefer not to bungle it away."

"Don't worry. When it comes to murder, I'm no bungler. And, oh yes, send for Xenophon, too. I've sounded him out already. I'm inclined to think he'll go along with us."

"Us? How us? I didn't hear myself agree to this scheme." Her eyes narrowed. Her voice lowered. "You wouldn't dare abandon me now."

"I might," he said, standing up to her.

"For what? To cling to the cloak of a dying old man whose power is gone? Think about it. Don't be a fool. We control everything: the Praetorian Guard, the treasury, the tribunes, the Senate. I have been laying the groundwork for this for five years."

"And what if we fail?"

"If we stay together in this, we won't fail. We'll work it out. We'll do it right. And afterward we'll own the world."

He looked at her for a long time without saying anything. She allowed him the luxury of a few moments to savor the delicious prospect of absolute power. Then with a nod he agreed. She went to him and whispered, "Good!" and sealed their contract with her lips. His kiss was cold, but his blood was racing.

Later that night they met secretly with Locusta, Xenophon, Haltous, Julius Pollio, Burrus, and Seneca. Though they all had guessed accurately why they were there, Agrippina explained the situation in her own language. "The emperor has lost his mind," she said. "To avoid chaos and destruction, we must make a swift transition of power. He is having hallucinations about us all. None of us is safe. Rome is not safe. We are on the brink of civil disaster. Think of what we are about to do as an act of kindness to him and as an act of heroism for Rome."

None of them needed her moral justification. They had believed for a long time that, sooner or later, she would kill her husband, and that perhaps he had even married her to

169

consummate a lifelong flirtation with self-destruction. Almost immediately they got down to the harder business of how to do it.

Locusta was a wiry, dark-haired woman with a bony face and gaunt eyes. She looked like a woman who never had a youth and would never get any older. She dealt in poisons and potions, aphrodisiacs and incantations. She was too useful to be killed, but too dangerous to be set free. After certain indiscretions, she was kept in a limbo of perpetual custody, the unofficial apothecary for aristocratic assassins.

The eunuch Halotus was a moon-faced man in his middle years. His bleached hair was tightly curled, and he wore a necklace of black pearls, a gift from the emperor for years of service. It was worth nothing compared to the fortune promised to him by Agrippina. A fortune and freedom for his part in the conspiracy.

"We must not be obvious," said Agrippina. "A poison that works instantaneously may give us away. We want him to die at a small banquet, in front of witnesses, and in such a way that it will seem he took ill from something he ate or from some other natural cause. On the other hand, if he lingers too long and retains any clarity of mind, he is liable to name Britannicus his successor in front of these very same witnesses. What we want, Locusta, is a poison that will, at first, derange his mind and then gradually weaken him. His death must be gradual and without dramatic symptoms."

"I can make you a compound as convincing as any disease," said Locusta. "But it will be most effective if he has consumed a certain quanity of wine."

"That should be the easiest part," said Seneca. "He always consumes a quantity of wine. In fact, it is fairly amazing that the wine has not, in turn, consumed him."

"I sometimes suspect that it's damaged his brain," said Burrus.

"Wine is itself a small poison," Locusta added, smiling to reveal her broken teeth, and then rememebereing to cover her mouth with her hand. She had been kicked by a horse in her youth, she claimed, but the more reliable rumor

170

was that she was nearly beaten to death by a husband she had betrayed and tried to kill.

"Now, how shall we taint his food and not have the poison either tasted or detected?" asked Agrippina.

"The compound I have in mind is tasteless," said Locusta.

"I am required to taste everything that passes the emperor's lips," said Halotus.

"An unwholesome job!" said Seneca.

Agrippina glared at him. "You seem in unusually good spirits for a man about to kill a king," she said.

He made her a silent apology with a nod of his head.

"May I suggest a food that involves a certain natural risk," said Locusta. "Such as mushrooms."

"Ah, very good!" said Agrippina. "He's fond of mushrooms. We can have them gathered in the morning and reviewed for the evening meal. They will have to be sampled early to make sure they are not a harmful variety. Isn't that so, Halotus?"

"Yes, madam!" He looked puzzled. "But if they are sampled then and tasted later, how shall they do the job?"

"The question is, how will *you* do the job? Between the final tasting and the first serving, you must somehow infuse the poison into some of them."

"A few drops will do," said Locusta. "As much as might be contained in a false fingernail molded from wax."

"Excellent!" said Agrippina. "And I assume you can split it open with the touch of another fingernail on the same hand."

"Precisely!" said Locusta, smiling again and covering her mouth.

"The ingenuity of you evil magicians amazes me," said Seneca.

"Now, what if the poison fails to work or only works halfway?" asked Burrus. "And what if he is not in the mood for mushrooms on that particular evening?"

"First," Agrippina replied, "I have *never* seen him refuse mushrooms. Neither joy nor sorrow, neither sickness nor health has ever stood in the way of his monstrous appetite. If ever a man could dine after death, that man is Claudius.

171

Believe me, Burrus, he will eat the mushrooms. But whether or not the mushrooms will kill him, that we cannot know for sure. And that is where our friend Xenophon comes in. What we cannot cure with doctored food, he may have to cure with his magic feather. In other words, should Claudius merely fall ill from his delicacy, he is to be placed in your charge on the grounds that he has eaten something disagreeable and must be made to vomit. Locusta will provide you with a rapid poison that will dispatch him instantly. But this can be done in the privacy of another room, from which he can be spirited away, presumably to his sick bed. You do have such a supplementary compound, do you not, Locusta?"

"I do indeed. A venon from snakes, as swift as cobras, but as expensive as gold."

"Never mind the cost. We are dealing with a thousand years of history, not with a lover's quarrel."

If ever a sorceress had met her match, it was in that instant when their eyes met. Like a dazzled cat, Locusta squinted, blinked, then turned away.

Three days later, on the twelfth of October, all was arranged. The small gathering for dinner included the usual members of the emperor's family: his daughters and their husbands. It included, also as usual, Pallas, Burrus, and Seneca. On this particular occasion Vitellius was invited. And there were two special guests: Alexander Lipinachus, the Jewish alabarch of Alexandria, invited at the last minute by Claudius; and Marcus Salvius Otho, invited by Nero, who was unaware of what was planned.

In the quiet atmosphere, enhanced by music, Claudius renewed his acquaintance with his old friend Alexander, who was on a brief visit to Rome in connection with the continuing disturbances in the Jewish community in Alexandria. Claudius listened sympathetically and offered his cooperation and help. "I have n-n-nothing against the Jews," he said. "They have a v-v-very long and interesting history." They were offered oysters, and Claudius washed his down with a generous swallow of wine.

The empress addressed her attention to Nero and his

friend Otho, a handsome young man some five years older than her now seventeen-year-old son. "I knew your father," she said. "An admirable man."

"Your husband," said Otho, "was responsible for his patrician rank. They were great friends."

"Were they really?" she said. There was a light in this fellow's eye that she found both attractive and yet made her wary. She realized how her son might be drawn to Otho, and she wasn't at all sure he was the kind of company Nero should keep. But she could pursue the observation no further. She had other things on her mind. Out of the corner of her eye she watched Antonia. And, in turn, Antonia watched her father, sensing a slight strangeness in the atmosphere. She couldn't define it or find a word to describe it, but she knew that something was not quite right. She watched the food being served course by course. She listened to the music and the hum of conversation. There was Halotus. There was Xenophon. Everything on the face of it seemed so ordinary, and yet—what was it? A certain stiffness. A certain tension. She caught Agrippina dabbing at the perspiration on her upper lip. How odd on a cool October evening.

Sulla joined in the conversation with Otho, who proved to be a clever lad. "Nobody goes to the theater anymore," he said. "I mean, why weep over imaginary murders in the theater when you can laugh over real murders in the arena."

Nero laughed aloud, his eyes alive with admiration for his fashionable friend. Antonia noticed that Nero's hair was done in the new style and clearly in imitation of Otho's. Nero had recently been initiated into certain artistic circles, and it was beginning to show in adopted mannerisms: an air of worldly indifference, an affected lisp, and a peculiar rolling of the eyes to express contempt.

Octavia chatted with her half-sister, avoiding the intimate details of her personal nightmare. "We had a gift of silver dragons from somebody in Cappadocia. I'm terrible about names. But they are lovely dragons. All the way from China, I'm told. I don't know what they were intended for, but they're almost as good as dolls for company. I mean, they're very fierce looking and all that, but they're also rather lovable, like that ivory elephant that I used to have in my room."

Pallas was as composed as a sphinx. Only his busy eyes betrayed his agitated mind. He listened politely to Vitellius, who could be counted on to fill all the intersticies in any dinner-table conversation. "And how is our friend Narcissus?" he asked. "I understand he's gone to bask in the balmy sunshine of Sinuessa."

Pallas was distracted for a moment by the sight of Halotus. He was approaching the emperor with a platter of mushrooms. Xenophon's hand trembled as he lifted his cup of wine.

Vitellius plowed on. He needed no answer to keep the conversation going. "He ought to be well in no time at all. A touch of liver, I imagine, judging frm his color. A bit of sun and pure water should fix him up all right, don't you think?"

"Uh, yes, yes," said Pallas. "I'm sure he's doing fine."

Halotus placed the platter in front of Claudius, who stopped in midsentence at the sight of the mushrooms. "Ah!" he said. "What a sweet surprise." He impaled one of the largest ones with his his knife and held it up for Halotus to taste. The eunuch took it in his mouth, chewed it and swallowed, then swallowed again as it almost refused to go down. Then he took the platter and offered it around to the other guests. Just before he returned it to Claudius, he did the deed. But not even Agrippina had seen him crack open the waxen nail that covered his thumb. He kept it carefully out of sight.

"N-n-nothing better than mushrooms," said Claudius, and plunged in with his usual appetite. "Are you s-s-sure you won't have some?" he said, with his mouth full, to Alexander.

"No, thank you," said the bearded Jew, somewhat appalled at the emperor's display of gluttony. .

The conspirators all held their breath. There was a sudden lull in the conversation. Then Agrippina raised her cup and said in an unnaturally shrill voice, "Don't you think

174

it's about time we offered a toast to our honored guest from Alexandria?"

"Oh, b-b-by all means," Claudius. He took his cup in his hand. The others followed suit. He drank. His head wobbled a bit more than usual. He looked unsteady, as though he were suddenly very drunk. He put his cup down and dug his finger in his ear, as though something in there was bothering him. "I f-f-feel odd," he said. He swayed forward and then backward. He swallowed repeatedly. His speech was slurred. "Shuddenly f-f-feel—" He shook his head to clear it, but only increased his dizziness.

"Are you all right?" asked Alexander, reaching a helping hand toward him.

"He hasn't been feeling at all well lately," Agrippina remarked.

"What is it, father?" asked Antonia. She was alarmed. She stood up.

He waved a hand drunkenly in her direction. He drooled and wiped his mouth with the back of his hand. "Perhaps he's had too much wine," said Burrus.

"Xenophon," said Antonia. "Can't you do something for him?"

Claudius let out an enormous burp and struggled into a sitting position. Xenophon was at his side. "Perhaps it was the mushrooms," said Alexander.

Claudius reached for his cup but knocked it over, sending a stream of wine across the table. His lips kept moving, but he seemed unable to speak. And yet his eyes moved around the table as though he were still aware of what was going on. He pointed to his stomach and to his throat. And then he actually smiled—a ghastly, insane smile.

"He needs purging," said Xenophon. "Nothing serious. He's had these attacks before. Poor digestion."

The poison was working, but not quite as they expected. They had hoped he would merely fall asleep.

Xenophon helped him to his feet and took him into the little room adjoining the dining room. He walked with difficulty.

"I better go to him," said Antonia.

"No, no," said Agrippina. "He's just going to have his

175

throat tickled. He'll give up whatever it is that's bothering him and be all right in a few minutes. You wait and see.

"He never did have the gift of moderation," said Alexander. "And at his age—well, one must be careful."

Vitellius played his expected role and talked the table around to feeling that nothing was really wrong.

"Perhaps he's been poisoned," said Otho with a playful smile.

Nero was the only one who laughed. "Wouldn't that be amusing," he said. And then he glanced at his mother, whose face was as grim as granite.

After a short while Xenophon returned. "I am happy to report," he said, "that the emperor is feeling better, only somewhat fatigued. He asks that you all forgive him for his early retirement, but he has gone to bed."

Antonia stood up again. "I insist on seeing him," she said.

Xenophon tried to smile. "I'm afraid he doesn't want to see anyone. In any case, he'll be sound asleep in a few moments. Believe me, madam, in his condition it is the best possible thing he can do."

"Well, then, promise me that if he takes a turn for the worse, you will notify me immediately."

"Certainly, madam. You will be one of the first to know if this proves to be a serious illness."

"My apologies on behalf of my husband," said Agrippina. "But this is not the first time we've had to finish dinner without him. The night is still young, the company interesting. Let us carry on."

Two hours later the guests began to leave. As they rose from the table Agrippina said, "Antonia! Octavia! May I have a word with you?"

They lingered while the others said good night, except for the emperor's staff. "We think it will be wise," said Agrippina, "for all of us to spend the night in the palace." Her tone was firm. "We will all want to be on hand in case anything happens."

"What makes you think anything will happen?" asked Antonia.

"Your father is not well."

"I can see that," said Antonia. "But I think we'd rather go to our own house, if you don't mind. We're not far off. You can reach us there if his condition worsens."

Agrippina looked at Burrus and then nodded to the two guards standing inside the doorway. They approached at her silent command. "No," she said to Antonia. "I think it would be much better if you stayed here with us tonight. We'll send word to your house."

"I don't understand," said Antonia. "What's this all about?"

"I hope nothing. But to please me, go to your rooms and do not try to leave."

Antonia started to protest, but Sulla took her by the arm. "It's no use," he whispered, "they're all in on it." The two of them looked around the room at the stony faces of Pallas and Burrus and Seneca and Xenophon. Without another word the young couple preceded the guardsmen out of the dining room and down the long corridor.

Within minutes the palace was sealed off from the outside world by a force of handpicked guards. Messengers were sent to certain key men in the city with the news that the emperor had suffered a serious illness, but that he was resting comfortably and there was every hope that he would recover. Troops were alerted. Vigils were held through the night. Visitors were turned away at the gates.

The conspirators conferred throughout the night on how next to proceed. In his chamber, Claudius was already dead.

The next day dawned in a near-panic. Rumors swept the Forum. Hourly bulletins promising hope and improvement were issued from the palace in guarded language. The Senate convened in an emergency session. The Praetorian cohort was poised for action but uncertain about what might be demanded of them.

When Britannicus awoke in the morning, Agrippina was in his room. She embraced him and cried and told him that his father was very ill and might not live. The boy looked confused, but he did not weep. He asked to see his father.

177

He was told it was impossible, and he was detained as gently as possible by his tutor.

"We must make no public announcement until we are sure that Nero will be accepted by the Praetorian Guard. That part is up to you, Burrus. When can you give us this assurance?"

"I can give it to you now. I do not believe there will be any opposition. If there is, we may have difficulties. But only with Antonia and Sulla, and they are here in the palace. Narcissus, fortunately, is away. The other supporters of Britannicus are not likely to make a public protest without these strong centers of support. Lepida, thank the gods, is out of the way."

"We are secretly sounding out the Senate," said Pallas, "but I don't think we'll have any trouble there."

"Are we agreed, then," said Agrippina, "that the emperor died without a will and that on his deathbed he named Nero his successor?"

They nodded.

"Seneca, will you rehearse Nero?" she said. "Tell him what he ought to know, nothing more. Write him a speech that he can read when he is carried to the Praetorian camp, and another that he can read to the Senate. Make them brief—and generous."

"I understand," he said.

She went to Pallas and took his cold hand. "We've done it," she said. "I hope you have no regrets."

He looked into her eyes. His own showed the strain and fatigue of the long night. "It's done," he said. "If we look back now, we may stumble."

"I suggest we make an appearance no later than noon," said Burrus. "I will assemble the palace guard and appear before them with Nero at my side. See that he's properly attired. I will tell them briefly what happened. They will escort us to the encampment. There I will address the cohorts. If all goes well, we will proceed to the Senate."

"Very well," said Agrippina. "That gives us an hour to prepare ourselves and to review the situation once again. In the meantime, let us send one last announcement to the public telling them to pray for the recovery of their beloved emperor."

At precisely high noon, the main doors of the palace opened and three people appeared. They were Nero, flanked by Burrus and Seneca. Along a cobbled path they approached a wide lawn bordered in the distance by popular trees. On this lawn, below a stone wall, the guardsmen assigned to the palace were assembled. There were about sixty of them. They waited patiently, talking among themselves, speculating about what might be happening inside. At the sight of their commander they straightened their ranks. When he and the others reached the break in the wall where four steps descended to the grass, the troops automatically came to attention.

Burrus addressed them from the top of the steps. Nero and Seneca stood beside him. Nero was dressed in a clean white toga with a purple border. His hair was carefully arranged. In one hand he carried a small scroll. He had grown in recent years and was now as tall as Seneca, who was a man of average height. Young as Nero was, he did not seem frightened or embarrassed. If anything, he seemed pleasantly excited, almost like an actor about to go on stage. For the past hour he had been committing to memory the speech written for him by Seneca.

"My friends of the Praetorian Guard," said Burrus. "It is my sad duty to announce to you the death of our emperor, Tiberius Claudius Drusus Nero Germanicus. He succumbed less than an hour ago from natural causes. In the face of certain chronic disorders, his heart failed. May this day, the thirteenth of October, in the consulship of Asinius Marcellus and Acilius Aviola, be declared a day of mourning throughout the empire. Our beloved leader has left us in the sixty-fourth year of his age and the fourteenth year of his reign. May his spirit rest with the gods for all of eternity.

"He died, unfortunately, without a will, but, before sufficient witnesses, named as his successor Nero Claudius Caesar Drusus Germanicus, his adopted son, who shall, henceforth, be known as the Emperor Nero. It is your duty now

179

to escort your new emperor to the Praetorian camp, so that he can be hailed and approved by the cohorts."

Burrus stepped aside, stood at attention and saluted Nero. His troops imitated the gesture. "Hail imperator Caesar! Hail Nero!"

A litter was produced, and, falling into a marching formation, the troops carried Nero to the Praetorian camp. Burrus and Seneca marched along on foot.

In the central Praetorian encampment there were twelve cohorts, each consisting of five hundred men. If they were all present at once they would number about six thousand. But on any given day a number of these men was out on assignment, some of them even overseas. It was the greatest single force in Rome, made up of selected men, whose pay was three times that of an ordinary soldier. It was a force that had to be contended with, especially in times of crises. It was the force that had selected Claudius to succeed Caligula. And it was the force that now had to ratify the somewhat mysterious selection of Nero to succeed Claudius. The Praetorians were not without their politics. The tribunes and centurions had their political leanings and sympathies.

The procession made its way from the Palatine to the Porto Viminalis along the Via Tiburtina, which skirted the cluttered tenements of the Subura. Midday crowds stopped solemnly to watch them go by. The news was already spreading through the city like fire. In his litter Nero smiled to himself and looked out at *his* empire. If only Otho could see him now, he thought.

Close to half of the six thousand men were assembled at the camp just outside the walls of the city. Expecting something to happen at any moment, the troops were in their ranks and in uniform. They were called to order smartly by their commanders, and then allowed by Burrus to stand at ease. He made to them the same announcement that he had made earlier to the palace guard. He concluded with the presentation of Nero as the newly designated emperor. "And this worthy young man, the dying choice of his great father, has come before you now on this grim occasion to

180

ask for your approval and suppport. I give you the new Emperor of Rome, Nero Claudius Caesar Drusus Germanicus!"

The announcement was greeted with a momentary silence. Standards flapped in the freshening breeze. A sudden burst of sunlight, escaping between clouds, illuminated the upturned faces of the troops. A wave of whispering swept through the ranks. Some of the faces turned toward the two cohorts known to be commanded by supporters of Britannicus. In that tense moment, Burrus and Seneca exchanged glances. A break in the dam could result in a flood of resistance. But no one spoke up. No one challenged the presentation. And then came the shout of "Hail Imperator Caesar! Hail Nero!" And the day was carried.

When the troops were quiet again, Nero stood forward to address them, his theatrical confidence unshaken. "My gratitude for your support is more than mere words can express. My first official act as your new emperor will be to sign an order for a special donative of five hundred sesterces for each and every one of you." This announcement was greeted by a roaring cheer, considerably louder than the tentative salute by which he had just been hailed.

"Money is the universal language," whispered Seneca to Burrus, unable to conceal a certain note of contempt in his voice.

"You have served us all well, and I trust you will continue to do so in the years ahead. Great and sudden changes in the government cannot take place without anxiety for the future of the state. I hope by my personal behavior to put the minds of the citizens at ease. Though I am young, I have the advantage of mature advice and the assistance of experienced secretaries. I will make no major changes for the moment, in the hope that we may proceed with the business of the nation with stability and justice. With the help of the gods, this day will mark not the end of a great period in our history, but the beginning of an even greater one."

Once again he was hailed, and this time more enthusiastically. Seneca beamed with pride at his protégé as the

181

troops shouted, "Hail Caesar! Hail Nero! Long live the Emperor!"

And then began the march to the Capitol, where ratification by the Senate was now as certain as death or the motions of the stars.

# PART TWO

# XXV

As soon as the news returned from the Senate that her
son had been confirmed as the new emperor, Agrippina
personally ordered the arrest of Narcissus, the man she
hated more than any other man in Rome. He was still at
his villa in Sinuessa, that pleasant seaside town north of
Baiae with its sunshine and warm mineral springs. A tribune and two guards were ordered to bring him back to
Rome as quickly as possible and to place him under house
arrest. She did not think he would offer any resistance. But
she was not at all sure that he would not try to flee when
the news of events in Rome reached him.

Later, Antonia asked him why he did not make an effort
to escape. She had bribed her way in to see him during his
last hours. "Because," he said, "the news of Claudius's
death only reached me a few hours before the tribune and
his men arrived."

"But you could have predicted what was going to happen."

"You forget, my dear, that I went to Sinuessa because I
was physically and mentally exhausted. Besides, where can

185

one run to? The empire is so extensive. The administrative structure is so efficient. I should know. I helped to create it. Wherever I went I could be found, unless I left the Roman world altogether. And what sort of a reception would I get in an enemy camp? Or should I disguise myself as a peasant and hide out in a mountain village in Macedonia? No, no, Antonia, it's all so impossible. All so futile. I should have ended it at Sinuessa. But life is so odd. We keep hoping for one more year, one more month, one more week, one more day—even one more hour. Lying in the sun at Sinuessa I told myself that nothing mattered but the moment and that I would live out my life moment by moment, enjoying the simple physical sensation of being alive. I tried to put everything out of my mind, and for a while, I succeeded. The Epicurean approach. Peace of mind. Nothing is either good or bad but thinking makes it so. And the world is going nowhere." He took a deep breath and sighed. His smile was more wistful than sad. "And so I have danced around a while. And now it is all coming to an end, and it really doesn't matter. It's either this or coughing out my lungs at eighty. What's the difference?"

"I hate to see you like this," said Antonia. "You were so good to my father. So good to the country."

He laughed. "I got rich off your father and the country. I have not been altogether altruistic. I have lived up to my name. You know the story of Narcissus, who loved no one until he saw his own reflection in a pool of water. He pined away and died and was turned into a flower."

"You may turn into a flower, but don't try to tell me that you have never loved anyone but yourself. It's not true. You loved my mother."

He looked down at his hands and did not deny it.

"And perhaps you even loved my father, strange, unlovable man that he was."

"I understood his feeling of desperation. I sometimes shared it. He was so terrified of life—of death."

"Inside of that ugly body he was like a child," she said. "His desires and appetites were very simple and very simply expressed."

186

"Yes," he said, "food and sex, the arena and his writing." His smile was benign.

"There was also love," she said.

"Yes, there was love." The pebble of that thought made widening circles in the pool of his mind. Then he stood up suddenly and walked away from her as if he were walking away from all his memories. He went to the window and looked out on the beautiful gardens of the house they called the Athenian villa. Then he turned back to her and said, "But enough of this idle talk. What about you and Sulla? What about your other friends? Will anyone survive in this new regime?"

"Callistus has been dismissed."

"I'm not surprised."

"Junius Silanus has been placed under arrest."

"My God, what for?"

"For daring to be descended from the divine Augustus."

"But he's so harmless, so unpolitical. Caligula called him the golden sheep."

"You forget his brother's death at Agrippina's wedding. And there are some who felt that Silanus should have been chosen emperor over Nero."

"He would have died with embarrassment," Narcissus said.

"And now I suppose he's going to die anyway."

"Poor Silanus. He should have had a more ordinary birth; he might have had a more ordinary death."

"My mother will ask about you," said Antonia. "What shall I tell her?"

"Tell her she has the most beautiful eyes in Rome and that it was in the pools of those eyes that I first saw my own reflection."

Antonia's chin quivered. The tears welled up in her eyes and spilled over. They streaked the whiteness of her cheeks. "Oh, Narcissus," she said, in a sudden flood of feeling. "What shall we all do without you?"

He came to comfort her, and she threw her arms around him and cried into his shoulder. He patted her back and silently allowed her to purge herself of all her pent-up sadness. The sobbing shook her delicate body. Her voice was

187

the eternal wailing of women down all the corridors of time. She cried from her heart. From her womb. She cried for her father and mother, for herself and her son, and for the whole confused, tormented race of mankind.

When the storm of her passion was spent, she drew herself shyly away from this man who had been like another father to her. She apologized for her weakness. "I came here to comfort *you*."

"You have, Antonia," he said, his own eyes heavy with the tears he could not shed. "Believe me, my child, you have!"

A few hours later, in the dying light of the afternoon, Narcissus ordered his steward Demetrios to prepare a warm bath. He calmly descended the tile steps into the soothing water, and then offered his wrists to a loyal and obedient slave, who opened the veins to let out the life. And while it ebbed away Narcissus had Demetrios read in Greek a favorite passage from Plato's account of the *Apology* of Socrates.

Holding back his own tears, Demetrios read: "Let us reflect in another way, and we shall see that there is great reason to hope that death is a good; for one of two things— either death is a state of nothingness and utter unconsciousness, or, as men say, there is a change and migration of the soul from this world to another. Now if you suppose that there is no consciousness, but sleep like the sleep of him who is undisturbed even by dreams, death will be an unspeakable gain. For if a person were to select the night in which his sleep was undisturbed even by dreams, and were to compare with this the other days and nights of his life, and then were to tell us how many days and nights he had passed in the course of his life better and more pleasantly than this one, I think that any man, I will not say a private man, but even the great king will not find many such days or nights, when compared with the others. Now if death be of such a nature, I say that to die is gain; for eternity is then only a single night. But if death is the journey to another place, and there, as men say, all the dead abide, what good, O my friends and judges, can be greater than this? If indeed when the pilgrim arrives in the world below, he is delivered from the professors of justice in this world, and finds the true judges who are said to give judgment there, Minos and Rhadamanthus and Aeacus and Triptolemus, and other sons of God who were righteous in their own life, that pilgrimage will be worth making . . ."

When he looked up from his reading, the steward could see that Narcissus was dead. And on his face there was a look of wistfulness and serenity, as though he had, indeed, merely escaped from the cares of this world.

# XXVI

In the days that followed, Agrippina seemed to swell with power, like a sponge nourished by the sea. She rode to the Capitol in a chariot. She presided with her son at state affairs. She sat next to him to receive visiting ambassadors. And at night, in the privacy of the palace, she rehearsed him for the business of the following day.

Seneca wrote all his speeches, and Burrus provided him with the appearance of soldierly manners and discipline. The influence of Pallas was felt more indirectly. The man was his mother's lover and her chief advisor. His arrogance and high-handedness provoked the boy emperor to sulkiness and irritation.

In the streets and taverns and barber shops of Rome, the ordinary citizen weighed his new leader in the hard scales of his gossip and judgement. "They say he's fond of painting and singing and things of that sort. They say he writes poetry. Do you think he's a little queer?"

"You wouldn't say that if you saw him on horseback in the Campus Martius or at the Circus. He rides as well as any man I've seen. And he's only seventeen."

"Of course, his mother's got the little bastard by the throat."

"By the balls, you mean. He takes his orders from her, and that's the truth."

"Maybe he'll grow up one day and put her in her place."

"Some say it's really Burrus and Seneca who run the boy. For sure it's Seneca who writes his speeches. They say the boy's not good with words."

"That funeral oration was a joke, wasn't it? I mean, all that praise heaped on old Claudius. His graceful accomplishments! His foresight and wisdom! I could hardly keep myself from laughing."

"But I liked what he said later. I liked his promises, if he sticks to them. About how he will not be the judge in all cases. About how he would not let the power of a few favorites get out of hand. About how the Senate would retain its ancient powers. And all that business about keeping his private life and public life seperate."

"But he's taking personal command of the armies."

"I don't blame him. Wouldn't you, if you were emperor?"

Agrippina did not seem to mind being talked of as the power behind the throne. But Nero was sometimes taunted by his friends for being nothing but mama's little puppet. "Who dared to talk to you that way?" said Agrippina, when he told her this.

- "I'd rather not say."

"What do you mean you'd rather not say? I'm your mother. I gave birth to you. I made you emperor of Rome. Don't you ever forget that."

"Sometimes I wish you hadn't bothered," he said.

The color in her face deepened under the white cosmetics, and her eyes blazed. "How can you say that? How can you mouth such idiotic, childish nonsense?"

"I'm sorry," he said quietly, reading her expression and mood the way sailors read a threatening sky. His heart quickened. He was frightened.

"Now tell me whom you've been talking to. Tell me who's been insulting my little emperor."

191

"I don't remember," he said. "It wasn't Otho. One of his friends, perhaps. But it wasn't an insult."

"What was it then?"

He wanted to say, *It was the truth*, but he said, "It was probably the wine that made him talk that way."

"And how did you answer this charming fellow, whoever he was?"

"I told him that I had to rely on your advice until I became a little more experienced in these things. I defended you."

"You defended me. How kind of you!" Her anger subsided into irritation. "I would have done more than that."

"It was only an idle conversation."

"I would have broken off with whoever he was. You don't need friends like that. You've got plenty of others. Aren't there enough to amuse you in our own circles?"

"Sometimes I get bored," he said. They were sitting in the old library where Claudius had spent so much time. The walls were lined with books, and the shelves were interspersed with painted panels. Agrippina was behind the desk instead of Nero. He sat to one side like a petitioner.

"My dear boy, everybody gets bored sometimes. You can't expect your life to be filled with sensational events every day of the week. I think you will discover that many of your responsibilities are mundane. You still have a lot to learn."

"I'm tired of hearing about the Armenian question and the Parthians and the problem of collecting taxes in Bithynia."

She leaned back in her chair and studied him. Her expression changed. She smiled and tapped her long fingers nervously on the table. With aggressive eyes she gathered him in and cataloged his feelings. She saw a sensitive, athletic boy, caught between childhood and manhood. She sensed both his dependency on her and his need to assert himself. Of course! That's all it was. The constant dilemma of the awkward years, as she called them. But that's not what she said to him. What she said was, "I understand. Believe me, Nero, I understand. These are difficult days for you. Not only are you still being tutored in the usual

192

things, but you are being initiated into the drudgeries of government administration. Legislative subtleties may excite the hearts of old men who have been going to the Forum for thirty years, but they may strike you as dreary and inconsequential. That's understandable. What you want is a little fun. A little diversion from time to time. I thought the games and dinner parties might be enough for you, but I see they are not." She hesitated, her eyes never leaving him. He, in turn, avoided her gaze. Slouched in his chair, he stared down at the floor like a scolded schoolboy.

"I don't quite know how to ask this, but how are things with you and Octavia?"

He looked up with a frown of annoyance and confusion. "What does she have to do with it?"

"Darling, she's your *wife!*"

"You don't have to remind me."

"What I am trying to say is that she owes you certain duties. Surely you know what I'm talking about."

"Yes, but must we? It was you who insisted that I marry her. I'm still not sure why."

"It was politically wise. We didn't want her to marry anyone else, did we?"

"Personally, I wish she had. She's skinny and boring. And she cries all the time."

"What has she got to cry about?"

"I don't know and I don't care."

"Nevertheless, she is your wife, and—well, there are certain things she must do for you. In bed, I mean. You're a young man, now, and men must—you know! They must have satisfaction. In bed! Am I embarrassing you?"

"Yes! Do we have to talk about it?"

She got up from behind the desk and went to him. She put her arm around his shoulders. "Of course not, darling. But I begin to understand now why you've been so restless. Just keep one thing in mind: it's not a matter of love; it's a matter of necessity. You really should make use of her."

"Please, mother, I've told you that I don't like her. How can you expect me to—" He interrupted himself and blushed. Then he stood up and walked away from his mother.

193

She followed him and took him in her arms. She looked pleased for some reason. "Well, I suppose at her age she's not much of a woman, is she."

He allowed himself to be embraced. He inhaled his mother's perfume. He felt the abundance of her bosom and the shape of her body as she stood next to him. Much as he had grown, she was still an inch taller.

"Oh, mother," he said. "I'm sorry if I made you angry. I can't stand it when you're angry with me."

"Sweetheart, I wasn't angry with *you.*"

"Good!" he said, offering his face up for a kiss.

She smiled at him with predatory affection and then kissed him gently but passionately on the mouth. It was a lingering kiss from which he did not try to retreat. It was she who finally stepped away. "I tell you what," she said. "Let's be naughty today and skip our lessons. Pallas will listen to the petitions, and Seneca can go somewhere and read philosophy. We'll go to my rooms and have a little private lunch."

His face blossomed into a smile. "All right," he said. "And music too?"

"Yes, my dear, and music too"

She called for Alexis, her secretary. "Cancel all our appointments," she said. "The emperor and I are having a very important luncheon conference." She caught Nero's eye, and they both smiled. How amusing she could be, he thought. And how young and attractive when she smiled. She was thirty-nine.

Agrippina's private apartment consisted of three rooms: a bedroom, a dressing room, and a study, where she often received guests or conferred with officials. It was a large room, with a set of doors that opened onto a garden. It was filled with personal memorabilia. The walls were covered with paintings and bookshelves. The floors were plush with Eastern carpets over smooth marble. And a collection of busts reviewed her private descent from the divine Augustus, among them the notorious Julia, her grandfather Agrippa, and, of course, her parents Agrippina and Germanicus. It was a busy, cheerful room, full of things to provoke conversation.

194

Europa brought in some mullet and wine and set them down on a low round table. "Shall I bring in some fruit?" she said.

"No, thank you," said Agrippina, dismissing the old slave with her eyes.

Europa shuffled out, but looked back with a dark frown before closing the door.

Nero was staring at a sword and scabbard on the wall. "Is this really your father's sword?" he said.

"That's right! He carried it into battle on the Rhine. My mother rescued it and passed it on to me."

Nero fingered the dry leather and the metal studs, his fair face lost in a dream. Suddenly, he turned around and said, "Tell me about *my* father. What was he like?"

"Your real father? Why are you suddenly interested in him?" She picked up two cups of wine and handed one to Nero. Sunlight patched the room, enriching the brightness of the rugs.

"I don't know. I just am. Nobody ever talks about him. And now that I'm emperor, I suppose I should know where I come from. And I should bestow certain honors on him, just as I have already done for you."

"Well, it's not really necessary."

"But it *is* traditional, isn't it?"

She equivocated. "Not really!"

"Anyhow, I want to know. Was he tall and handsome? Was he brave? Was he a good lover?"

"Nero!" she said laughing. "You naughty boy! What do you know about such things?"

He deepened his voice comically. "Madam, I am a married man."

She allowed her body to recline, catlike, on the couch. The soft material of her gown was draped about her limbs and breasts, revealing the fullness of her hips and the curve of her belly. Her gown was cut very low and wide. The white flesh of her bosom formed a little valley, into which a gold chain disappeared. Leaning on her left elbow, she sipped her wine. She touched her braided blonde hair and the normal hardness of her face subsided into a girlish look as she reached back in her mind over the years. "Your father!" she said, and then paused again.

Nero sat opposite her on an identical couch, the round table between them. Birds argued in the greenery of the garden. A gentle breeze brought in the scent of roses.

"Ahenobarbus was a bit of a devil! His grandfather was Mark Antony. What can I tell you that will not give you the wrong impression? Some people found your father charming. Some found him cruel. He had good breeding, no accomplishments, and he died young. But I rather liked him, red beard and all. He was hardly what you would call intellectual. An athletic man. Well built. Fond of chariot racing. In fact, he insisted on driving himself. He loved horses. Just like you. And he loved the wild of life— food and wine and women. Oh yes, women too. I knew all about it. I didn't mind. Jealousy is a silly thing. A man will make love to women. And why shouldn't he? It does no harm, so long as he treats it as a simple pleasure. Besides, he never neglected me. We had some marvelous times. We built the villa at Baiae. We knew all the best people. But unfortunately he had no discipline. And he had a fierce temper. He was a man who had to have his own way about everything. And when he could not get it by ordinary means, he stooped to other means—violence! Fraud! He did considerable harm to his own reputation. Perhaps that's why you knew so little about him. We all tried to spare you."

"I wish I could remember him," said Nero. "And I sometimes think I can."

"You were only three when he died. It's not likely."

Nero sipped at his wine. "Do you think he was unhappy? I mean, sometimes people do desperate things because they're unhappy."

"If he was, it wasn't my fault," she said. "I certainly did my best to keep him happy."

"How?" he said. His eyes were playful.

"You little devil," she said. "I think you're more of a man than you let on. Come here and give me a kiss. I don't want to talk about your father anymore."

He emptied his cup and then sat down beside his mother. Still reclining, she pulled him toward her and kissed him. Her mouth was cool and moist with wine. Her breath was warm. He drew back. "I don't care what sort of a man he was, I still want to honor him. I want to have a huge statue made of him—and—and some sort of ritual."

"We'll talk about it another time," she said.

"Why do we have to talk about it? I'm the emperor. I can do whatever I want."

"You're a spoiled little boy with lessons to learn." She held out her cup, and she filled hers and his. Somewhere from the garden there came the sound of music, a stringed instrument. Its sweetness mingled with the chorus of the birds, and the sheer curtains at the window bellied into the room like pregnant ghosts.

He felt the warmth of her body through his white tunic. The wine had made his eyelids heavy. He slipped off his sandals and stretched out beside her, resting his head on her bolster. She was on her side, still leaning on her elbow. She looked down at him and fussed with his blond hair. "But it's only natural, isn't it?" he said after a long pause.

"What is only natural?" she said, having drifted away from the conversation into the dreamy unreality of the afternoon.

"For a son to honor his father."

"And how will you honor your mother?"

He looked up into her eyes, a fever of passion blooming in his cheeks. "I will make you a statue of solid gold. We will mint new coins with both our images on them. I will give a new password to the palace guard—*optima mater,* the best of mothers. For you are, indeed, the best of mothers."

"How sweet of you! What lovely trinkets from a loving son. But soon I will have a birthday, and there is something special that I want."

"Then you shall have it, mother, whether it be rubies or pearls or a new villa at Baiae."

"It's none of those things. Something much less expensive, but a token of our partnership."

"What is it?"

"I want to share with you the allegiance that is sworn by the Praetorian Guard. Fidelity to me as well as to you."

197

"But why?"

"So that nothing will ever come between us, my precious boy."

He thought about it, blinking his eyes toward the white ceiling, listening to the distant music. "But of course! I mean, if that's the thing you want, it shall be yours. I would have chosen the rubies myself. Such a thrilling color. Like frozen blood."

She smiled. "I think you have a streak of wildness in you—like your father. You like exotic things." Her hand moved from his hair to his cheek. It was no longer as smooth as it once was. "I feel the roughness of your beard. If you let it grow, I imagine it will be the color of bronze." She sighed. "How swiftly time passes. Less and less the boy. More and more the man." He let his eyes close and gave himself to her seductive carasses. "When you were a child, you often came to my bed and lay with me like this. Your hands were so tiny. You put your mouth to my bosom, as though you wanted to be nursed again. Do you remember?"

He nodded without opening his eyes and moved closer to her until his face was against her half-naked breast. She held him there and ran her hand over his shoulders and down his back. She stroked him as if he were, indeed, a little child. A boy's voice from the garden was wafted into the perfumed air of the room. The song was about Arcadia and love and Mount Erimanthus. It was a familiar song and she hummed it to her son as he seemed to be falling asleep against her.

But he was not asleep, only dreamy with wine and the magic of the moment. His mouth sucked at her breast through the thinness of her gown. Her nipples were erect. With a delicate motion of her fingers she pulled away the blue material and lifted her heavy breast toward him. He took it in his mouth, his lips and tongue suddenly alive and his body stirring with animal urgency. Against her thigh she felt his excitement and soothed him with her song and with the reassuring caresses of her hand. She touched his legs, his hips, and under the tunic, the firmness of his young manhood. How well she knew that desire in men

198

that would not be denied. And how little she cared about the barriers of blood. "We are all merely men and women," she had once said. And the prohibition against this sort of passion only heightened it and made it more delicious. Besides, what harm could it possibly do, especially if no one ever knew. The gods themselves, if there were such things as gods, were easy victims of the same delights. These arguments and more she gave herself and urged her son to find satisfaction where so many lovers before had found theirs. She reassured him with whispers. She kissed his hair. She drew him onto her now fully reclining body and freed him from the brief undergarment that contained him. She herself wore none. He moaned with desire and confusion and buried himself in his mother's arms. She embraced him, possessed him, devoured him. And at the peak of their peculiar pleasure she felt sure that he would never belong to another woman.

# XXVII

Sextus Afranius Burrus, the dark-haired ex-soldier from Gaul, went regularly to the public baths. He went not only for physical refreshment but for social amusement. In lavish surroundings he could visit the shops in the portico, he could exercise his body in a variety of games, he could be bathed, steamed, massaged, and generally groomed. He could relax in the library or walk in the enclosed gardens and promenades of the quad. There he would often meet friends or associates, with whom he could exchange news or gossip or even ideas of a more philosophical sort. He saw the baths as a brilliant achievement, an essential part of the Roman concept of civilization. His daily visit, after a difficult day, cleansed him physically and mentally and prepared him for the rituals of the evening, usually the imperial banquet, with all its entertainments, its steady stream of dignitaries, its exotic foods, and sometimes marathon drinking sessions.

The baths, admitted Seneca, were seductive. They were marvels of engineering and repositories for some of the best art and architecture in Rome. But they were also places where one could waste an enormous amount of time. He preferred to avoid them as a regular habit, but ocassionally accompanied his colleague Burrus. He did not go, he claimed, to pamper his body but to sound out public opinion. For he was convinced that a wise ruler must take into account the public will.

His colleague was amused by Seneca's austerity, but his teasing was friendly, even affectionate. "Aren't you afraid," he would ask, "that your image will be tarnished when you are seen at the baths? The people think of you as the philosopher of stoic simplicity. A vegetarian. A nondrinker. Hard-working and suspicious of the pleasures of the flesh."

"To have an image of one's self," the philosopher replied, "one has to spend a great deal of time in front of a mirror. And I'm too busy for that."

"Your purity is admirable, but a glance in the mirror will show you that your body is not. All your scholarly efforts are making you flabby and thick."

"Ah, but my mind is an Olympian athlete," he said with a smile.

It was late in December under a gloomy sky when they went off to the baths together. Agrippina's ugly mood that day had been enough to persuade even Seneca that it was time for a little purging and purification. "She gets more impossible every day," he said to Burrus as they sat in the steaming atmosphere of the *sudatoria*. They were naked. Vapors rose from the heated floor. A slave stood by with towels to wipe away their perspiration. Lost in the cloudy recesses of the vaulted room were other men, their quiet voices a muffled echo.

"She's a peculiar woman," said Burrus. "The more power she gets, the more uneasy she gets."

"Because she's afraid it can't last," said Seneca.

"It would last longer if she would control her temper."

"And if she weren't so insanely ambitious. She's still young. Still beautiful—in a sort of masculine way. She could have a very good life, a very influential life. The first lady of Rome. Widow of one emperor, mother of another. What more could a woman wish for?"

"The one thing that a woman can never have. She wants

to be the ruler, not the emperor's mother. If we're not careful, she'll devour her son. Nero is terrified of her. And I don't blame him."

"The ironic part of it all, Burrus, is that we have aided and abetted her. We have helped to make all this possible."

"Yes, but our duties now are to Nero, not to her."

"And to ourselves!" said Seneca.

His friend looked at him through the steamy mist. "What do you mean?"

"I mean, she's not to be trusted because she trusts no one, not even us. Or maybe especially us. We have too strong a position in the emperor's life. We can move him this way or that, and she knows it."

"But she has a greater hold on him than we do. Surely she knows that. I hate to even suggest it, but she treats him like a husband—like a lover. There's talk. Unhealthy talk. I think you know what I mean."

"I do. And I wouldn't be surprised to discover that she has seduced her own son to keep him under control. For *her* sex is not a passion but a weapon. It worked with Claudius and with her other husbands, not to mention certain lovers: Pallas and Tigellinus and—will you be offended if I include you, my friend?"

Burrus cleared his throat and reached for a towel to wipe the perspiration from his face. "I won't deny that there's been a certain intimacy," he said, "but it's not what you think. There's no love affair. Far from it. An occasional incident, some moments of weakness. But she knows I'm not to be bought that way."

"I'm sorry," said Seneca. "I didn't mean to embarrass you. I understand all too well. But she's ruthless. We must not let her ruin the boy. If she can possess him emotionally, he will be worthless as an emperor. And worthless to us personally."

"What can we do?"

"I've thought about it a good deal, as I'm sure you have. The boy is just seventeen. He is sexually very susceptible. He will respond to almost any influence. She knows this, of course, and it frightens her. If she could manage it, she would turn him into a eunuch. She would castrate him. She

202

married him to Octavia to keep him home, so to speak. And now she may be going to more desperate extremes to keep him at home. She's perfectly capable of it. She's the sort of woman who would kill her mother and marry her father and persuade the Senate that it was for the good of the state. She knows enough about men to know that they can make fools of themselves over women. In other words, they fall in love. Especially when they are young. Surely, you remember."

"I certainly do. At sixteen I was writing love poetry to a twenty-year-old married woman. What ridiculous agonies I suffered. What an idiot I was."

"Ah, but what a delicious experience! And how helpless one feels. There is nothing like it. It is a kind of religion, complete with promises of immortality. We sigh. We swoon. We say such deathless things as 'I can't live without you.' Only to discover that we can. And really quite well, once we've sorted out the sex from the sentiment."

Burrus laughed. "At that age a boy's heart is between his legs."

"Complete with Cupid's arrow. And Nero is no different. He's ready for an adventure. He's ready for a love affair. If only we can wean him from his mother. If we don't, he will lose his mind along with his empire."

"I begin to understand your strategy," said Burrus. "We've got to find him a girl."

"Not just a girl, not any girl. There are enough of those around. We've got to find him somebody with whom he'll fall in love."

"That's not an easy thing to predict."

"To catch a fish, you need the proper bait."

"Do you have anyone in mind?"

"As a matter of fact, I do. There is a certain freedwoman named Acte, whom I have met in the company of our friend Serenus. We have already agreed that she would make a nice addition to the imperial court, in some capacity or other. I'm sure it can be arranged. She is not only beautiful, but she is intelligent, a woman of infinite sensibility and kindness."

"But an ex-slave? He'll be put off by that, won't he?"

"Don't worry, my friend, we'll find a pair of noblemen to swear that she comes of royal stock—the Attalids of Pergamum, or some such thing. Such an exotic background will appeal to Nero. He likes exotic things. And she has that soft, mysterious way about her, like so many Eastern women. But she is a couple of generations removed and thoroughly Romanized, but not spoiled."

"She sounds very attractive. What about Serenus? Does he have a serious interest in her?"

"Not really. He's a sensible sort. I think we can confide in him. In fact, I think he'll be useful in this little scheme. We can let it out that he's the one who is really in love with Acte. And behind that facade we can encourage young Nero to discover himself in the magic of her eyes."

They were as amused as little boys as they rose to leave. The next step in their progress through the baths was a cold swim to tighten up the skin. After which, they would dress and rendezvous in the garden.

There, by some good fortune, they came upon Serenus, to whom they described their unusual political scheme. He was remarkably generous with his little infatuation and more than happy to be a part of the amorous conspiracy. He was almost as old as they, and a man of considerable learning and good sense. "She will be coming to court in a day or two," he said. "And I can almost guarantee that she will be receptive to the idea."

As the three men ambled along the winding paths, nodding to friends and acquaintances, Seneca lectured them on still another point. "As you know," he said, "I have been encouraging Nero to believe that he is, indeed, a direct descendant of Apollo, a kind of living god on earth. I know we all find this a ridiculous notion, but at the moment I think it is important. You see, if he comes to believe that he is a god, that he can do no wrong, that he can do whatever he pleases, it will strengthen his belief in himself and make it easier for him to assert himself against his mother. What's more, I am also encouraging him to be generous, charitable, and forgiving to his people, using the same argument, namely that he is divine, the source of all justice and goodness. The notion appeals to him. It flatters him.

204

And the result is enormous goodwill on the part of the people. We will have them kissing his feet in a matter of months. And that, too, should drive a wedge between him and his mother. We've recommended leniency in certain prosecutions and a few tax reductions. And this damned business in Parthia ought to give us an occasion for declaring him a hero and savior of the nation. I'm sure we can get a public thanksgiving out of it and a few statues."

"For a man of the mind, you have a marvelous instinct for the jugular," said Serenus.

"As you know," said Seneca, "I believe that the end sometimes justifies the means. Which is not to say that one must abandon his morality. What he must do is fit it to the necessities of his time."

Burrus laughed. "What a grand old hypocrite you are. You could persuade a blind beggar that he was a king with the eyes of a hawk."

# XXVIII

Burrus and Seneca were not the only ones who were concerned about the extremes of intimacy between Agrippina and her son. Pallas, too, found them disturbing. He was a man of remarkable composure, but, taunted by her boast that she could handle any man alive, he stooped to inquire about how exactly she was handling her son. "I daresay he qualifies now as a man, in all the usual ways. If he is as fond of women as he is of horses, then he's a man, indeed."

"He is at least a man in *deed*," she said. "You can take my word for it."

"And what is that supposed to mean?"

"Construe it how you will," she said, fussing with her jewelry in front of a mirror in her dressing room. They had just made love in a perfunctory way, which had left him disgruntled, but her rather amused.

"You should be more careful about the impressions you give people. They are liable to be misleading."

"I have no idea what you mean. What impressions?"

"About you and your son."

"My son and I are very close," she said without turning around. She seemed preoccuppied with one of her earrings. "How close?"

His accusative tone forced her to turn away from the mirror to confront him. Her thin eyebrows were raised. She looked confident and defiant. "Why, we love each other, of course. Didn't you know?"

"There are many kinds of love," he said. "Not all are suitable between a mother and her son."

"And who is to say what is suitable or not suitable where an emperor is concerned? Isn't he descended from gods and, therefore, a kind of god himself?" There was a clever glint in her eye. She was toying with him, and he hated her for it.

"Shall I speak plainly?"

"You often do. You have no special gift for oratory like our beloved Seneca."

"But he and I share a common concern, no matter how we phrase it. Are you going to force me to say what it is?"

"Yes!" she said. "Say it. I want to hear you say it. I dare you to say it. And to suffer the consequences of embarrassing me."

He backed off. "I can't believe that anything could embarrass you. But let's stop this bantering. Let's be sensible. I am genuinely concerned for both of you."

"And for yourself."

"Yes, and for myself. What's wrong with that?"

"Nothing! It's only natural. But I was hoping you'd put the destiny of Rome a notch above self-interest."

He looked puzzled. "The destiny of Rome?"

"Yes, you fool! It's my turn to be serious. Don't you see how important it is for all of us to keep Nero from becoming emotionally involved with another woman? He's young. He's vulnerable. He could be taken advantage of. What's the difference what goes on between us? That's a private matter. Besides, I can assure you that we have done nothing immoral. These rumors of incest that you allude to are grossly exaggerated. You know how the Romans love to gossip. Let them amuse themselves with their filthy talk. For five generations they have been chattering like toothless old women about incest in the Julian-Claudian family. It's almost a tradition by now. I feel I should oblige them."

"And haven't you?"

She put her hands on her hips. "You are incredibly arrogant," she said. "Even assuming that I have enjoyed an occasional scandal, what makes you think I would confide in you? You are yourself one of my scandals. Isn't that enough for you? You're neither my father nor my husband. I owe you nothing."

"I wasn't attacking you, nor was I being moralistic. I was thinking in purely practical terms. Political terms, if you will. I do not think it is to your advantage or to your son's advantage to be talked of in this way."

She allowed the comment to sink in. Her nervous eyes moved rapidly from him to the window to several objects in the room. And then in a subdued voice she said, "How serious is the talk?"

The argument was over. All the cruelty and excitement was gone from her voice.

"Serious enough to be turned into a marketplace joke, along with the deification of Claudius. You know how the public reacted to that piece of ridiculous hypocrisy. Seneca himself satirized it at the Feast of the Saturnalia."

"For a man who spent nine years in exile, he's being awfully outspoken."

"It was Messalina who sent him into exile."

"And it was I who brought him back. You needn't remind me."

"I thought you were fond of him."

"I am. But I don't entirely trust him. I hear he's getting rich."

"He's a good businessman. I admire him more for that than for his philosophy. In any case, he's devoted to you and to Nero. I wouldn't worry about him. He's a good minister."

She paused. "Have you and he talked about this—this gossip?"

"Yes! And we agree that it's potentially damaging."

"And what do you advise?" she said, her haughtiness returning.

"My personal feeling is that you should give Nero a little more freedom. If you hold him too close, he will eventually rebel."

Her temper flared. "And if I don't hold him close, he will eventually escape altogether." She pounded the arm of her chair with her fist, over and over again. "What to do! What to do!" And then she stood up and strode across the room toward the door.

"What are you going to do?" he asked.

"I don't know!" she shouted. She went out the door and slammed it hard behind her, leaving Pallas standing there in a gray pool of uncertainty.

# XXIX

A few weeks later Nero announced to his mother that he and a few friends were going to Antium. "They've put up a statue of me there. Near my birthplace."

"Yes, I know," she said coldly.

"We thought we'd go and have a look at it. A little holiday from Rome. We thought we might stay at your villa, or that one I've recently acquired but never seen."

"I see," she said. "And whose idea was this?"

"It was mine!" he said, but when he tried to look her in the eye he had to turn away. "Actually, it was Burrus who suggested that I might want to see the statue. He says it's excellent. And he will, of course, provide the transportation and the members of the guard."

"And who will be going with you?" she said.

"Just a few friends. Petronius, Senecia and Otho."

"And Octavia?"

"I haven't asked her."

"No women at all?"

"Yes. But I've left that part of it up to Otho. He's much more interested in women than I am."

"And me? Am I invited too?"

He blushed. "We had in mind a youngish party. I hope you don't mind. But, of course, if you'd like to come—"

"No, no, I understand. I keep forgetting that I'm forty years old, no longer a young girl."

"Eternally young!" he said with calculated flattery.

She smiled as though she found it difficult to breathe and then forced herself to say, "Have a wonderful time!" Her recent conversation with Pallas was fresh in her mind.

And then they were off, the men on horseback, the women in a coach, giggling about their heroes and screeching at the bumps in the road. Before them and behind them pranced half a dozen members of the Praetorian Guard, all on white horses, all in immaculate uniforms with plumed helmets. "Freedom!" shouted Otho, who had had wine on wine for breakfast. He sported a wiry fringe of a beard that gave him a slightly barbaric look.

"Freedom!" echoed Nero with a wild expression on his face, as though he were, indeed, an escaped prisoner. He galloped up beside Otho on his handsome black horse, a gift from Tigellinus. Their horses snorted and kicked up dust. They laughed aloud. Otho passed him a skin of wine, from which he drank recklessly, allowing some of the wine to run down his chin and onto his tunic. The breeze tossed his blond curls and his pale eyes blazed with excitement. "Race you to the next milestone!" he shouted. And they were off, bay and black animals reflecting the joy of their young riders. They passed the coach, whooping and hollering, and then galloped past the formation of guardsmen, whose startled horses reared or broke stride. The centurion in charge called out after them, but they were not listening. He shouted an order to his men and they followed in a thundering cloud of dust. But Nero and Otho were too fast for them. They reached the milestone, the black horse three lengths in front. Standing together, their mounts glistening, their faces streaked, they passed the wineskin once again and waited for the contingent of guardsmen and the rest of the party.

"It's going to be a great holiday," said Nero.

"It's about time you did something on your own," said Otho.

"Don't be mean. You know it's not my fault. Ah, here comes our bodyguard. We led them a merry chase, didn't we."

"If anything happens to you, that centurion will have a lot of explaining to do."

Eventually the carriage caught up with them, four female heads protruding from its windows. "Which one is mine?" asked Nero.

"You're the emperor, take your pick," said Otho. "But I think Acte is the best of the lot. You'll like her."

"Yes, I've seen her around recently. She's new, isn't she?"

"New to your household perhaps, but not new to us. Not to the Roman Mohocks."

"What are the Roman Mohocks?"

"Good heavens! You've really been locked up in your mother's closet. The Mohocks are the most famous and most aristocratic of all the street gangs that ever stole a kiss or bashed a beggar. We're all members. Suitably disguised, of course. My nighttime name is Dionysus, and when the moon is full, I bellow like a madman."

"Marvelous! I want to join. How can I join?"

"Well, being an emperor and all, it's a little awkward, isn't it? Besides, I don't think your mother would approve."

Nero's whip flashed out in Otho's direction but missed. Otho laughed and apologized. "All right! All right! You can be our Apollo, and I'll keep your secret to the death. Now give me back my wineskin and let's make time for Antium. The ladies are growing restless with all that delicious jostling."

Word raced ahead to Antium more swiftly than any horse could carry it. The mysterious lightning of rumor and gossip. Though the emperor's pleasure trip was not to be made public, the people of his birthplace somehow knew that he was about to pay them a visit. As they neared the seaside town the crowds that lined the road grew larger.

212

They cheered and waved, anticipating his route to the newly erected statue, which had been duly acknowledged by proxy and a ceremony earlier that week. Nero waved back, his heart warmed by the reception. "You should have been an actor," said Otho. "You're a glutton for applause."

"These are my people and they love me," said Nero, his ebullience partly the effect of the wine. The crowd called out his name. Some children tossed flowers in his path. His black horse snorted and bobbed his head.

The statue was at an intersection that formed a square in the center of the town. Additional troops were on hand to clear the way and hold back the people who hoped for a first glimpse of the new emperor. They had grown weary of poor old Claudius and rarely displayed this sort of enthusiasm when he had come to Antium.

Pennants flew from the corners of the wide stone base. Ten steps led to the pedestal. And twice as large as life itself, the full-length statue stood, tall and regal in a stone toga as real as wool. The sculptor had done his work with astounding skill. And the face that blessed the square was idealized and godlike. Nero was impressed, not only with the statue, but with himself for being able to inspire such work.

He got off his horse, mounted the steps two at a time, and raised both hands to greet his subjects. When the cheering stopped, he said, "I came to Antium to bathe in ordinary sunshine. I did not expect the greater sunshine of your love and affection. I can see by this magnificient piece of work that you are full of faith in your new emperor. I will try to be worthy of that faith. And as a token of my appreciation I am going to give to the people of Antium a new theater. And when it is built, I will come and speak the first words from its stage. I may even sing you a song." The crowd's applause was mixed with laughter.

"The lad's all right," said the local coppersmith.

"And quite a horseman," said the baker.

"I like his generosity."

"I like his manly manner, no matter what they say about his mother."

213

Antium was a busy harbor town some thirty-five miles south of Rome. Its basin was filled with fishing craft and merchantmen, their sails and masts a holiday of colors. To the north of the town, the long sandy shore and low cliffs were punctuated with villas, and beyond them sheep grazed in the grassy hollows. Agrippina's villa, originally built by her brother Caligula, was luxuriously situated on a bluff that overlooked the sea. Stairways descended to the beaches and docks. Gardens extended laterally, enclosed by walls. Also enclosed were the clusters of slave quarters, the baths, and other buildings of the commodious estate. "It's not a villa, it's a palace," said Otho, who had never seen it before.

"Of course!" said Nero, afloat on his newfound sense of importance. "Only the best for the emperor's friends."

They were greeted at the villa by Tiro, the caretaker, and Mestor, the freedman who was Agrippina's private secretary. "I thought you were in Rome," said Nero.

"I was," said Mestor, "but I've come down to take care of some business here for your mother." He was a round-faced, soft-spoken man with tightly curled almost fuzzy hair. His small eyes were set in small bulbs of gray flesh and his benign smile was disarming. He looked like a middle-aged, overweight cherub. "She asked me to be sure that you had everything you needed during your visit here. I trust you will find everything in order and to your liking."

"When you return to Rome, tell my mother that we deeply appreciate her concern. I'm sure that Tiro will be able to provide us with everything we need."

Tiro smiled and bowed and glanced at Mestor. Otho sidled up to Nero and whispered out of the side of his mouth: "Get rid of him; he's a spy." But the others came up and nothing further happened. Nero felt his chest tighten and his breathing grow more shallow. It was a moment of panic. He wanted to blind Mestor with hot pokers because through his pig's eyes his mother was watching him. And that was paralyzing.

They were attended to by a small army of slaves. Everything was carried in, the horses were seen to, the fires were

214

started in the baths, and they were shown to their rooms. It was late in the afternoon, and they were tired from the journey. "You will be bathing, sir?" asked Tiro.

"Of course," said Nero.

"All of you?"

Nero looked at Otho, who answered for him. "Yes," he said, "all of us."

Half an hour later the four men of the party were cavorting in the heated pool under the low dome of the *caldarium*. Steam rose from the water. Torches lighted the darkness. The fractured flames danced on the surface. Attendants waited in the next chamber to massage them with oil. "Where are the women?" asked Petronius, who was struggling gracefully to float on his back.

"They are shy," said Senecia. "They're waiting there in the dressing rooms until we've had our turn."

"Nonsense!" said Otho. "They've all bathed in the public baths with men before. And that's not all—"

They all laughed and called out. "Livia! Portia! Marcella! Acte! Come and join us. Come on. The water is warm and marvelous." Their voices sang in the vaulted room like the chanting of priests.

In the dark mouth of an arched doorway a woman's face appeared. Then a second face. Their white skin reflected the torchlight. "Ahh, there they are," said the chorus of men. "Neptune's virgins, ready for the plunge," said Petronius. Nero drew apart, his boldness challenged by the nudity of the women. He looked over his shoulder as though he were being watched.

The women proved to be somewhat less than shy after all. Livia came out first, a slim girl of eighteen or so with shiny black hair and a slim waist and breasts like magnified raindrops, small and perfectly formed. She paused before the ruby red mosaic on the wall and then descended into the water. "Bravo!" shouted Senecia. And the others applauded.

Portia, who had light brown hair, was no taller, but a bit sturdier, a bit thick in the legs, and with those generous hips and buttocks that some men believe to be the true definition of feminity.

215

Marcella was taller and rounder, big-bosomed and blonde with a wide, full mouth that invited visions of oral delight. Otho, who had already made private excursions into this nothern beauty, dove like a dolphin to greet her as she slipped into the water.

Acte was the last to appear. And when she did, all the others stood so still in the pool that all one could hear for a moment was the slapping of water. She was dazzling in the dancing light of the torches. Her dark hair was drawn back away from her white skin. Her large eyes were gently shadowed. Her lips were parted. All of the symmetries of the female form were hers—a Greek philosopher's vision of perfection. But it was in the subtlety and sureness of her movements that one could see her true beauty. And it was not merely the beauty of a human body, but something higher, something deeper, something that stirred the artist and lover in Nero, not the lecher. She was, in short, a presence, and for a moment she presided over this naked audience of young Romans, holding them entranced with her silent oratory. Then she walked along the side of the pool to where Nero had withdrawn himself and quietly joined him in the water, as if it were the most natural thing in the world.

Shoulder-deep in water they faced one another. "How beautiful you are," he said.

"I'm glad you approve," she said with a warm smile.

He could see her intelligence in her eyes. It both excited him and inhibited him. She was obviously no meaningless toy like the others. She was someone to contend with, and the contending itself would be a pleasure. The noise of the splashing couples at the other end of the pool covered a moment of awkwardness between them. He wanted to sound more manly and imperial when he spoke, but his question was boyish: "How old are you?" he said.

"Does it matter?" she asked.

"Well, I suppose nothing matters really—unless it does." He thought it was a very witty remark, stolen from Chaeremon, but she only raised an eyebrow as if to chide him for trying too hard.

216

"Do you want me to wash you?" she asked, a hint of mockery in her expression.

"That's slave's work," he said. "You don't want to do that."

"I was born a slave," she said.

"Were you?"

"Yes, but I was given my freedom along with my parents when I was very young."

"And are your parents still alive?"

"Oh yes! And doing nicely. My father has orchards at Suana. He's fond of nature."

"And you? Are you fond of nature?"

She shrugged. "I love flowers, but I would hate to be devoured by a wild beast. What I truly love is the happy cooperation between the hand of nature and the hand of man."

The remark left him staring into her face, almost unaware of her nakedness. She confused him and impressed him. She made him feel younger and older all at once. Before he could say anything else, the other six playful youths were upon them. Livia hid behind Acte, gasping and laughing. "He's an absolute monster, a sea monster. He says he's going to eat me."

"Not all of you," said Senecia. "Just a nibble here and there."

"What are you two doing?" asked Otho. "Talking philosophy?"

"We'll have none of that," said Petronius. "We've got more important things to do. We need a judge, for instance, to settle a little debate. We can't decide which of Marcella's breasts is larger. Otho says the left. I say the right. What do you say?"

Marcella lifted herself out of the water brazenly and thrust her bosom toward Nero. "I say they are a perfect pair," she spluttered, her blonde hair dripping across her face.

"One can sometimes tell by the weight," said Otho, and gently hefted one of Marcella's large glistening breasts. Her nipples were erect, her flesh firm.

Nero glanced at Acte. She shrugged permissively, and

217

Nero joined the little game. "Let me see," he said, and held the girl by her broad shoulders. "My, she's a big one, isn't she?"

"Almost as tall as your mother," said Otho.

"Shut up," Nero said, "I'm trying to concentrate." He looked. Then he touched, exploring the white flesh to the delight of the others and feeling himself growing erect under the water.

"Ooh! That feels good," said Marcella, who had been primed with honey wine before the bath.

"I call it a draw," said Nero, "and award a kiss to each contestant." He leaned forward and kissed each nipple. The others applauded. He felt Acte standing close behind him and turned to her. She slipped her arm around his shoulders and kissed him on the mouth. In a tight embrace they let themselves sink slowly to the bottom of the shallow pool. In a moment they came to the surface again in a burst of laughter.

"I don't understand all this fuss about mixed bathing," said Petronius. "It is practically impossible to make love in the water."

"Nonsense!" said Otho. "It's done all the time. Here, let me give you a demonstration." He took Marcella by the arm and pulled her toward him. She pretended to resist. "I love shy women, don't you?" he said to his companions. She splashed water in his face. He pursued her. She retreated, screaming, to a corner of the pool. There he trapped her. She draped her arms on the edges of the corner and kicked water at him. He fought with her legs and parted them.

"You wouldn't dare!" she exclaimed.

"Oh, wouldn't I," he replied.

"Of course he would," said Petronius, who was a confessed voyeur. The six of them, pleasantly paired off, formed a semicircle around the barbarian Otho and the tall blonde. Nero let his hand slide down the slender back of Acte and over the soft flesh of her hips.

Otho forced himself between Marcella's long legs. Her struggling subsided. He held her by the buttocks and touched her nipples with his tongue, first one, then the

218

other. The water washed over her buoyant body, over the roundness of her belly. She clung to the marble edge of the pool and watched him through half-closed eyes. His bronze muscular body was beautifully defined against her fleshy whiteness. Nero had never seen two people make love before, and the spectacle excited him more than he would have imagined. He felt his heart race, and his hungry eyes devoured every motion. He drew Acte to him and her thighs were parted against his thigh. He could feel the softness of her pubic hair and the firmness of her breasts against his. A tightening of her legs and buttocks betrayed her own excitement as they watched.

Marcella reclined on the water. Otho stood between her legs in water only as deep as his waist. His stiffness was clearly visible. It lingered at the gates of her yearning. With one hand he held her hips, with the other he guided himself skillfully into her. At the first thrust she tossed her head back and gasped. Her legs closed around him and sealed the embrace. And in the minutes that followed they seemed to be alone in a world of their own, unaware of the naked audience that followed each stroke, each sigh, as though it all were happening in a theater. They had left reality back in Rome and were free to dream.

Lost in his animal passions, Otho moved with the slow, then quicker, rhythms of a panther. His muscles tensed, his shoulders rounded, his thighs hardened as he thrust himself deeper into her to stab her into a cry of pleasure that made her whole body contract and writhe. And in that instant, his head thrashing from side to side, he emptied himself in her. And then he quickly released her, spun away, and dove into the water to swim the length of the pool.

Marcella sank to the bottom, as if she were dead and drowned. But in a moment she drifted again to the surface. The embracing couples came closer. She blew away the water and said, "He killed me. I'm dead." But there was no pain on her face, only dreamy satisfaction. And no embarrassment. In that instant Nero had an impulse to take her—just as Otho had. To take her while she was still in the trance of lovemaking, still hot with him in her. But he didn't. An urging from Acte drew him away. They faced each other and kissed for a long time, their bodies rubbing together. "Later!" she whispered in his ear. "When we're alone!"

At dinner no reference at all was made of the little scene in the bath. It was as if it had never happened or was only an insignificant appetizer for the real feast of their holiday. They were all gorgeously dressed, Nero in a fantastically embroidered toga that would have been frowned upon in Rome, and Acte in blue clinging silk that gave her the look of an Eastern princess. In her dark hair she wore two jeweled combs, a recent gift, she said, from a friend of Seneca's. Nero would not rest until he forced the name of the admirer from her. It was Annaeus Serenus. "A harmless gesture from an older man," she said. "You mustn't think I love him."

"I'm not jealous," he said, his pouting lips giving him the lie. "I don't believe in jealousy. It's childish."

Petronius played the master of the revels, leading them artfully through conversational acrobatics, for which he had acquired a reputation. He provoked them to semi-serious comments on the nature of the soul, the poems of Catullus, the decline of the theater, the proliferation of Eastern cults, art, sex, and suicide. "The real secret of the universe," he said, "is that there is no secret. Things are exactly as they seem."

"Good!" said Otho. "I was afraid I was being decieved."

"Who would want to deceive you?" asked Acte.

"The gods, I suppose."

"Don't be ridiculous," said Petronius.

"Don't you believe in the gods?" asked Nero.

And the wine carried them into pleasant digressions, anecdotes about their youth, memories of the dead. Down, down, down, they went from the heights of philosophy to the depths of gossip. "Seneca, they say, is getting rich on usury and the proceeds of the wills of childless men."

"Junia Silana, they say, is in love with Sextius Africanus, who is young enough to be her son."

"Pomponia Graecina, they say, has become a Christian Jew, and goes about in nothing but mourning clothes."

There was more food and more wine. There was music and a troupe of nubile dancing girls. "Don't you love their boyish hips, their little breasts?"

"Scaevinius, they say, has taken up boys and has fallen in love with a young actor."

"Speaking of which," said Petronius, "your man Tiro tells me that he has arranged a special little entertainment for us, a pair of girls who are actually boys. Lucipor and Marcipor. I have no idea what they plan to do."

"Well, have them brought in, by all means," said the unimperious emperor.

Two teenage transvestites came into the room and danced with all the agility of a pair of nymphs. There were little bulges in their tunics, and their lips were painted cherry-red. "I don't believe they're boys," said Nero, fascinated by this particular entertainment.

"But they are," said Petronius, and the little ballet that followed proved his point. It was a comic routine done in dance and mime, in which a prince disguised as a nymph falls in love with another nymph, who forestalls his advances by revealing that he is really a boy. When both are revealed as boys, they look about the mythical forest with comic disappointment and, then, finding themselves alone, shrug their shoulders and hurl themselves into a hot embrace. They tear away their female clothes and kiss.

"Naughty boys!" said Petronius aloud.

The actors went on as if they were alone. Stripped naked of their clothes, they played with one another in the amorous Greek way. Sprawled on a green carpet and flanked by potted plants, they mouthed each other and fenced with their hot weapons. In their imaginary sylvan paradise the pretty boys made love, as free as animals and as convincing as dogs, one behind the other, with his hand reached around to satisfy his mate. They collapsed into one another's arms and pretended to sleep in the wake of their pleasure.

Roused by the applause of their appreciative audience, the two lads sprang to life, gathered up their garments, bowed hastily, and fled.

"Did you like that?" said Acte, aware of the riot of feelings that gripped young Nero.

He reached for his wine cup and took a long swallow.

"Do you think being watched excites the little buggers?" asked Otho.

"Of course," said Petronius, the confessed voyeur. "Half of all human pleasure is gathered from the eyes of those who see us enjoy ourselves. We are all exhibitionists. It's a fact of life. Nothing to be ashamed of."

"That's right!" said Nero, instead of answering Acte. "We are all performers. Life is art. Art is life!" His face was flushed. His voice had a nervous quiver.

"Then sing for us," said Otho. "We hear you have a lovely voice."

He looked around and gathered up his confidence. "All right, then, have them play 'My Shepherd Fair.' "

He got up uncertainly and went to the green carpet that represented the stage. The four young musicians consulted and then began to play the old song. Emboldened by wine, but with surprising talent, he sang: "My shepherd fair has golden hair and lives beside the sea . . ."

Acte smiled from within the secret of her conspiracy with Seneca and Burrus. But she was also genuinely moved by this desperate boy, this lad of seventeen. There was an innocence and quickness about him that she liked, in spite of his enslavement to his mother. It was a kind of muscular frailty. Fear and courage vibrating in the high pitch of his voice. Passion and despair! Hope and hopelessness. A wrecked and beautiful ship of a child. She was twenty-two. If he asked her again, she would tell him.

When Nero woke up the following morning Acte was in his arms. So accustomed was he to sleeping alone (he never slept with his wife) that he was startled to find her there. The winter birds first woke him, chirping in the slanting light. Still dazed with wine, he slipped his numb arm from under the woman beside him. He looked at her closely to make sure that it was, indeed, Acte. She was breathing easily, a look of serenity on her face. Under the thin blanket her form was clearly outlined, her thin waist, her rounded hip. He drew back the blanket to look at her. She was naked. So was he. He could only assume that they had made love; he couldn't remember for sure.

He got up and walked about the room. His mouth was musty, his eyes puffy. He had no idea what time it was, but all he could hear was the distant sounds of slaves going about their business. He assumed it was early and was seized with a restless feeling that bordered on distraction. He wanted to do something—anything. But he did not want to wake Acte or anyone else. He dressed quickly and went outside to find Tiro. Somewhere in the back of his mind was the vague notion that he should pay a visit to his newly acquired villa in Antium, which was, he was told, less than half a mile from his mother's. It had come into his hands after the tragic murder of its owner Lucius Camillus. The case was still as fresh as undried blood. One of the slaves had killed him in his sleep. And the law required that when the master of a house was killed by a slave, all the slaves of that household should be executed. Knowing this, the sixty or so slaves fled from the estate and were in the process of being rounded up. Half of them were still at large.

He found Tiro in the dining room, where he was supervising the slaves who were putting the place in order. Even before Nero asked, he said, "They're all asleep. Is there something I can do for you?"

"Where's Mestor?"

"He's in the library looking over the accounts, sir."

"Oh," said Nero, rubbing his eyes and then his chin. Through the window he could see the Praetorian Guard assembling on the lower terrace, the white plumes and metal helmets alive in the morning sun. "Why did he come here anyway?"

"I beg your pardon, sir?"

"I want to know why Mestor is here."

"I'm sure I don't know, sir," said Tiro. "I assume your mother sent him. He comes from time to time."

"Yes, but why this time? Why just now when my friends and I are here?"

223

He shrugged. "Perhaps it has something to do with the estate of Lucius Camillus."

"But that's my estate now. And I have people of my own to deal with these things." He paced up and down, glancing from time to time out the window and then back at Tiro. "Where is this damned villa. I want to see it."

"I'm afraid it's in a terrible state right now. I'm sure you understand. There was a certain amount of violence there."

"Yes, I know. They killed the old man."

"And went on a sort of rampage afterwards, before fleeing into the hills. The place is in the hands of the local tribune."

"Nevertheless, I want to see it. I'm not going to wait around here doing nothing."

"You might have some breakfast, sir."

"I don't want breakfast. Find me some wine and warm water. I'll be in the garden or down on the beach."

He went outside, through the portico into the quad and then out again along a path that led to the stairs that descended to the wharf and the beach. Mestor was still on his mind. He must get rid of him somehow. He would talk to Otho about it later. Otho would think of something.

On the beach he looked out on the cool, serene sea. It soothed the fever in him. He took off his clothes and sat down naked on the sand. He played fitfully with the pebbles, tossing them aimlessly into the gentle surf. The events of the previous evening were an undigested lump in his mind. What was he doing here? And he heard his mother's voice calling to him across the blue-green water. She was going to be angry. He knew it. Mestor would tell her everything. She always knew everything. She would be there in Rome, lurking, waiting, full of sweet vengeance.

Suddenly he leaped up and ran into the water. It was cold. His momentum carried him forward until he had to dive. He went under and swept himself forward with a strong stroke. He felt good. He felt suddenly cold and free. When he broke the surface, he was in deep water. He looked back and saw two guardsmen on the shore looking toward him anxiously. And beyond them, up the low cliff, he saw Acte leaning against a stone balustrade. The breeze played in her loose hair. She was waving to him as if from a dream. And then she was calling to him, but her voice was lost in the air of the distance between them.

When he came back up to the garden, she was waiting for him, as fresh as the morning, her face clear of cosmetics, her body a benign vision in a long white gown. "Come," he said, "we're going to visit my new villa." He took her nervously by the hand and half dragged her into the house where he ordered Tiro to take them to the scene of the recent crime.

They went on foot, accompanied by Tiro and a centurion. They followed the main road for a quarter of a mile and then turned into a narrower path that was lined with poplars. They were almost upon the place before it became visible. And then it confronted them, a silent, sprawling house with red tiles on the roof and a terrace of fig trees that had lost their leaves. Two soldiers stood guard at the main entrance. The shutterless windows gaped like blind eyes on the upper floor. Clouds tumbled in the uncertain sky, threatening the sunlight.

Tiro and the centurion led the way into the large atrium. The furniture had been tossed about. Their footsteps echoed on the marble floors. It was all rather ghostly. "I told you, sir, that there had been some damage."

"I want to see where Lucius Camillus was killed," said Nero. He held Acte's hand so tightly that she winced.

"But, sir—" protested Tiro.

Nero cut him short, shouting suddenly in a high-pitched, almost hysterical voice. "I told you I want to see where Lucius Camillus was killed!"

Tiro was startled by the young emperor's outburst. He looked at the centurion, who acknowledged the indirect order by standing sharply at attention and then leading the way to the former owner's bedroom.

"This is the room," said the centurion, pushing open the wooden door. Nero looked in before entering. He could see a bed with mangled sheets and a fallen chair. He went in, still holding Acte's hand. He stood in the middle of the room and looked around. The open shutters swung lazily in the breeze, expanding and diminishing the light, as though

225

the room were breathing. "How did it happen?" he asked.

"Camillus was asleep," said Tiro. "Someone must have come in through the window. The guards had been lured away by a barking dog. There was a struggle. You can see by the condition of the bedclothes. And there—there's the blood."

Nero felt his pulse throbbing in his throat. He imagined the old man, the intruder, the struggle, the slashing dagger, the panic in the household, screaming slaves, confused guards. And then the realization that one of their number had doomed them all. The looting, the violence, the flight. "I want them all captured," said Nero in his dream. "I want every slave of this house executed by the most horrible means imaginable. Do you understand?"

"Yes sir," said the centurion. "We understand the law. As soon as we have them all in hand—"

"Let them choose between being strangled and being thrown to the beasts."

"The case will come before the Senate," said the centurion.

"The Senate will do what I say," shouted Nero.

"Yes sir!" said the centurion.

"Yes sir!" echoed Tiro.

"Now leave us alone," said Nero. "We have some private business to discuss.

"Here, sir?" asked Tiro.

"Yes, here," said Nero, glaring at him until he motioned to the centurion and they both left the room. Nero slammed the door, bolted it and then walked around from the bed to the window to the fallen chair. He looked at Acte. She was composed. She was reading him.

"I suppose you want to make love," she said.

"Yes," he said.

She nodded toward the mangled bed with its brown stains and torn sheets. "There?" she asked.

"Yes!"

She looked at him for a long moment and then shrugged. "All right," she said.

And he went to the bed and waited for her to disrobe.

226

The next day he ordered a ship and insisted that he and Acte sail down the coast to visit a secluded shrine that he was once taken to as a child. The boat put at his disposal was a Liburnian galley, luxuriously fitted out by Caligula for the adventures with Lollia Paulina and her sister. They would cruise along the coast, raiding the shore for entertainment wherever the wealthy gathered to indulge themselves. Nero, however, had in mind no such adventures. He was on a freedom binge, a real and symbolic flight from his mother, except for the spying eyes of Mestor and the chains that rattled in his heart and head. He felt muddled. He wanted some quiet time, and he wanted to be alone with Acte. The sea lured him like a whispering woman. After another orgiastic night the others were sleeping late. He did not disturb them to tell them he was going.

In the brilliant clarity of the morning, the pleasure ship waited for them at the wharf. It was manned by a crew of Ligurians from Genua under the command of a seasoned veteran of the sea who had served three emperors, and who understood thoroughly the nature of his special duty.

When Nero and Acte came down they were raising the brilliant red sails. The decorated hull with its searching eyes and long, graceful bowsprit was an exotic vision against the gray-white stones and the expanse of blue. The wind was gentle but sufficient, and the captain assured them that they would have an easy and pleasant journey.

The main cabin was palatial by nautical standards. It was divided into three compartments. Oak beams arched over the low ceiling, and the spaces in between were painted with erotic scenes. The bedroom was lined with deep-green drapes and the skins of wild animals, rugs provided by bears and and enormous bedcover provided by tigers, involuntary donations to Caligula's insatiable appetite for pleasure.

Acte was her usual composed self, gorgeous in a blue cloak, her hair sensibly arranged against the wind. Nero was costumed in a elegant version of a sea captain's uniform, complete with cape and sword. From a distance one could not tell how young they were, and they were a splendid sight as they stood on the deck of the departing ship.

227

The hawsers were slipped from the pilings, the oars dipped in unison, and the tight wood spoke to the wind as it billowed out the sails. They were off! The men on the wharf waved. And farther up the cliff on the highest terrace a single figure watched silently. Though he could not see him distinctly, Nero was sure it was Mestor.

They stayed on deck for over an hour as the ship moved seaward and then down the coast. When they retired to the cabin it was to a greater sense of privacy than they had yet had together. Everything had been prepared for them in advance, including wine and food.

Nero stretched out on the tiger-skin bed and looked up at the suggestive paintings between the beams. A man stood by a fountain in a blue tunic and offered his naked sex to a blushing maiden, her expression all innocence. Her face turned half away but her hand reached out. In another panel a satyr took a fleshy woman from behind while several other women looked on, appreciation in their eyes.

"Do you like those paintings?" asked Acte, sitting down on the end of the wide bed.

"Yes," he said. "They show some skill and imagination. I wonder who painted them."

"Some anonymous Greek, no doubt. Nobody cares about art or the artist anymore—only decoration."

He smiled at her, his hand clasped behind his head. "How did you get so wise? I was thinking the very same thing. But art *is* important, isn't it?"

"Of course it's important," she said.

"But why?"

"Because it participates in and expresses the harmonies and symmetries of nature."

"You sound like Seneca. He talks that way. But you're a woman."

"Does that mean I can't read or think or feel?"

"Women are not usually interested in ideas."

"Neither are most men. They are interested in fame and fortune and physical comfort."

"And power!"

228

"Yes, and power. Just like women. And pleasure and love."

"Do you think women are more interested in love than men?"

"No, I don't think so. But few people are truly capable of it, whether they are men or women."

"How can you say that? My friends are always falling in love."

She laughed with that light of secret intelligence in her eyes. "That, divine emperor, is not what I mean by love. That's a little game they play. A game of conquest and self-laceration. It's fashionable. And theatrical. It gives one the opportunity to view himself in a variety of passionate moods: the infatuation, the quest, the triumph or rejection. Such people are forever looking at themselves and rarely see the person they claim to love. When they are rejected, they imagine they've lost the world, but when they triumph they lose interest."

"In that case, I hope I never fall in love," he said.

"You will. And more than once."

"What makes you so sure?"

She shrugged. "I can tell."

"And what about you? Have you ever been in love?"

She hesitated. "Yes," she said.

"More than once, I hope."

"Why do you hope that?"

"Because a woman who has only loved once is liable to remain faithful to that person for the rest of her life, even long after her lover is dead."

"That's part of the romantic nonsense. Love is not exclusive. We can love many people in many ways in our lifetime. It is a certain spiritual connection, a certain sharing of soul."

"You put it very poetically. No wonder Seneca and Serenus are so fond of you. You are very attractive. And very beautiful. If I am not careful, I may fall in love with you myself."

"Would that be so awful?"

He raised himself up on one elbow and stared at her. "No," he said. "But—"

229

"But it would not do for an emperor to fall in love with an ex-slave girl, a mere freedwoman. Is that it?"

"No. Yes. I don't know."

"Would it change anything if I told you I was descended from royalty? Would it make me any different? I would still be here. I would still offer you my affection."

"You like me then?"

She smiled. "No, I hate you."

"Do you?"

"Of course not. But I hadn't expected to like you quite so much as I do. It's distracting."

He reached for her hand. She let him take it in his and then let him draw her down beside him on the bed. "Do you love me, then?"

"I'm a woman; I don't have to answer questions like that."

He kissed her. Her lips were salty. Their mouths parted. Their tongues caressed—another kind of language. She put her arms around him and started to undo his clothes. They kissed some more to punctuate their disrobing. When they were naked on the tiger skin, they lay in a long embrace, absorbing the union of their bodies and their privacy. They felt the motion of the ship, which rocked them half to sleep.

"Do you love me?" he said lazily.

"Is that an order, divine emperor?"

"Yes," he whispered into her hair.

"Why, then I must obey, mustn't I, lest you toss me to the lions."

"The lions don't deserve you," he said. "You're much too great a delicacy." And he playfully sank his teeth into her arm until she drew closer still to his muscular body.

"Where did you learn to make love? You're too young to have had much experience."

"I'm a man," he said. "I don't have to answer questions like that."

They laughed and kissed and explored each other. Her hands traveled down his arms and across his chest. She touched his small nipples and the smoothness of his chest and stomach. And very delicately she cupped his sex and with her fingers made out the form of it. He was hard and

230

pulsating. She rubbed him against her soft thigh, slowly, rhythmically, her eyelids growing limp. He kissed her hair, her cheek, her lips and neck. And together they sank into a kind of dream with the sound of the sea breathing against the sides of the boat.

Eventually they made love, as if for the first time. And it was not that nervous love, that panic of pleasure that they had experienced before. It was slow and long and penetrating. And when it was over he no longer heard in his head or his heart the rattling of chains, only the sighing of the sea and Acte's whispered confession: "I love you."

# XXX

On a warm night some months later a poor freedman named Pittacus lingered late in a tavern in the back streets of the Subura. With him was his mistress Hestia, an attractive enough widow of thirty or so with bad teeth but a generous bosom. Pittacus had lost what was, for him, a large sum of money at the chariot races that afternoon, and he found his consolation in a prolonged drinking bout with his friends that left him reasonably numb to the harsh realities of his life. They included not only impending bankruptcy but a sick wife and an unruly son, who preferred lechery to carpentry, his father's trade.

It was a raucous crowd that gathered at the tavern to rehash the races at the Circus Maximus. The emperor's favorite faction had virtually swept the day, and those who had bet against him had nothing but complaints. "He's got this bloody Sicilian, Tigellinus, breeding horses for the green. Not to mention drivers like Scorpus and Fuscus. How can the other factions compete with the likes of that talent? I don't give a damn what odds they offer. It ain't fair. It just ain't fair!" And Pittacus brooded and drained his cup. His woman followed suit, loathe to return to her dreary widowhood in the tenements, surrounded by four screaming brats. "Oh, he's all right, the boy is," said one of the winners. "As generous as his granddad, old Germanicus. Remember him, eh? Finest general that ever drew breath." And they argued four cups worth over the accident at the final turn of the fifth race.

It was past midnight when the owner, himself a bit gone in drink, announced that the tavern was closed and almost precipitated a small riot among his customers, who sometimes drank until dawn. But Pittacus had had it, and Hestia was beginning to fall asleep against his shoulder. Supporting each other, they made their way into the dark street. Cursing and staggering, Pittacus felt his way toward Hestia's house. "The bastards have got it all figured out. The blasted races are fixed. The white went under for a price in the seventh. You could see him reining in those pigs. Sons of bitches. An honest man don't stand a chance these days."

At the end of a long, narrow street they saw an odd light. "Torches," said Hestia, squinting her eyes.

"What are they doing now?" asked Pittacus, sagging against a wall for support.

"Must have been some trouble," she said. "There are some men up there at the corner."

Through the veil of his drunkenness he was suddenly afraid. "Not a damn gang, I hope. Not the Mohocks."

The silhouetted group of men came toward them. There was nowhere to hide, no alley or side street. They waited, panting with drink, the cobblestones swimming in their heads, the torchlight bobbing, as if the whole night were a sea and they were all afloat in it.

Suddenly they were surrounded by half a dozen youths dressed as slaves and armed with clubs. They were laughing viciously, drunkenly. "Ho, ho, ho, what's this? A bit of dirty fornication in the sweet streets of Rome. We'll learn him a thing or two about civic pride." One of the youths took Pittacus by the front of his tunic and slammed him against the brick wall. "Where are you going at this hour, you rat-faced assassin you? Anyone can see that you're up to no good. Look at him, boys. Did you ever see such a

233

rat-face in all your life? Don't you know, old man, that it is against the law to have a face that looks like a rat's?" And they banged him against the wall again.

He slumped in their hands and tried to fall to his knees to beg for mercy, but they were not listening, and his tongue was thick with wine, so that all that came out was a moaning slur of noises. "Leave him alone," screamed Hestia. But another youth grabbed her from behind and held his hand over her mouth. She bit him instinctively, and in a rage, he punched her and knocked her down. "Filthy little bitch. Bite a Mohock, will you!"

"All right, give us your money," said the youth who was hanging on to Pittacus.

"I ain't got no money," he said. "Lost it all at the r-r-races. Let us be. Let us be. We ain't done no harm to no one."

"A man with no money doesn't deserve to live," said another youth. "Bash him one just for the hell of it. Teach him to be poor."

The youth who was holding him was joined by another. They held him against the wall and started to punch him. They hit him repeatedly in the face and the body, until he moaned and sank to the ground. Then they kicked him and stomped him, until he was a broken, bloody, silent mess.

"Have you killed him?" came a hoarse whisper, a high-pitched nervous voice.

"It doesn't matter. He'll die tonight or another night. Take the woman. Hold the torch closer. See what she looks like." They put the torch virtually in her terrified face. "Not bad for a drunken whore. Shall we have a go at her? Who wants a go at the bitch?"

A broad-shouldered man lurched up to her and ripped the front of her tunic. "Scream and I'll kill you," he said. She froze, her eyes wide with panic in the torchlight.

And then they huddled around her while the broad-shouldered man raped her, urging him on, touching him, touching her, tugging at her hair to hold her head still. When he was done, somebody passed him a wineskin and he took a long drink. "There!" he said. "That'll teach the bitch to be on the streets at such an indecent hour."

234

She curled into a fetal position in her torn rags and cried. They backed off and then were gone at a run, as if they had been discovered.

Breathing hard and laughing like animals, they collected in a square where five streets met and a fountain gurgled endlessly into the night. "What do we do now?" asked Senecia, who was holding the torch.

"Ask Appollo," said Otho, from behind his slave's disquise.

"Where are the gladiators?" said Nero. In his brown rags and black wig he would have been difficult to recognize, even in daylight.

"They are following at a discreet distance with orders to intervene only in the case of serious trouble," said Otho. "Shall we call it a night? Or shall we go back to the Mulvian Bridge to see what the others are up to?"

"No," said Nero. "There's a little visit we've got to pay to a certain cousin of mine, who needs a lesson in humility. She thinks her husband is fit to be the emperor of Rome."

"Not Sulla and Antonia," said Otho. "We can't do that. It's bound to get out."

"We can do anything we want," said Nero. "We're the Mohocks, aren't we? We can be as arbitrary as we want. And I say we pay a social visit to my cousin Antonia."

There were no further arguments. They locked arms and sang their way toward the Palatine Hill. "They'll have guards," said Scaevinius.

"That's all right," said Nero. "Send the boys ahead to have them dismissed—one way or another."

When they arrived at the house, there was no one to bar their way. The windows were dark. The night breeze played in the trees of the garden. Nero himself went unsteadily up to the door and pounded on it. "Wake up, wake up!" he shouted. "There's a fire in your house. The ambassadors of death are here to put it out."

Slaves came to the door and tried to ask who was there, but the Mohocks only pounded more fiercely and shouted, "Fire! Fire!"

The door opened. They rushed in, carrying torches into the atrium and lighting the lamps. Senecia kicked an old

235

slave and said, "Go fetch your masters and tell them they have guests."

"And bring us some wine," said Scaevinius.

The slaves scurried away, white with terror. The hoodlums pranced about the room, mocking the furniture and the paintings and the archaic taste. "I should have this place redone," said Nero. "I should take it away and tear it down." He was very drunk.

Otho tried to steady him. "Why don't you give it to your mother?" he whispered. "She's got impeccable taste."

In a few moments Sulla and Antonia burst into the room. "What's going on here?" demanded Sulla. He wore a simple white tunic but carried a dagger in his hand. "Who are you? What do you want?"

Antonia was standing beside him. "What's this all about?" she said, as defiant as her husband. The slaves cowered in the doorway.

"Ah, here they are," said Nero. "The future emperor and empress of Rome. I hope we didn't interrupt your imperial pleasure of the imperial flesh."

Sulla rushed forward. "You vulgar bastards!" he shouted. "Get out of my house." He hurled himself at Nero, knocking him into a table and then against the wall. His dagger was raised, but he did not use it. With his free hand he grabbed the front of Nero's tunic and shoved him repeatedly against the wall. "Tell your mob to get out or I'll cut your throat."

Antonia had never seen her husband so angry. Nero's friends advanced and then retreated. "Wait!" cried Otho. And in that instant the wig came loose from Nero's head.

"It's Nero," gasped Antonia.

Sulla looked more closely. "Is it you?" He released him and stepped back.

Nero laughed hysterically to overcome his fear. "Yes, it's me—your cousin and the divine emperor of Rome. Come to pay you a visit. Now put away your knife and bring out the wine. Where's the wine?"

Two slaves hurried out from the alcove, one with an amphora of wine, the other with a tray of cups.

"What do you want?" asked Antonia. "What are you

doing with this band of ruffians? You should be home in bed."

"Are you going to tell me, cousin, when I should go to bed?" said Nero, trying to strut imperially, but only succeeding in staggering toward them and then sagging a step or two backward. "I'm the emperor. I can do whatever I please."

"You're a disgrace," said Antonia. "Why don't you go home and sober up. Such childish nonsense."

"Childish nonsense, eh? I'll show you how childish I am. I've a good mind to lay claim to this house. Part of the heritage, you know. More mine than yours, as your father's heir. I've got a good mind to give it to one of my friends. Or one of your slaves. Or, better yet, to my mother. Hah! How would you like that? I know how fond you are of her."

"You're too drunk to talk to. Go home. Leave us alone. We'll forget the whole incident," said Sulla. "You've had your fun. Now put an end to it."

"You'll tell my mother," he said, sinking deeper into his drunkenness. "I know you will. You hate me, don't you? You think I'm a child and a fool. You think my mother owns me. Well, I'll show you. I'll show you all, and her. I'll do what I damn please."

He took the offer of a cup of wine and downed it with one long gulp. He wiped his mouth with the back of his hand. His lips quivered. His sticky eyes blinked slowly. He threw the empty cup across the room. "All right, then!" he said. "All right!" He swayed in front of them and tried to clear his blurred vision. "Just remember. I can take all this away. So don't you tell my mother. Do you understand?"

Otho came up to him and led him away by the arm. He nodded a silent apology to Sulla and Antonia. "Sorry for the intrusion," he said. "Just a bit of fun, that's all. Just a bit of fun."

"All right," said Antonia. "Just go!"

They gathered up their fuddled leader and made their way out of the house without another word. The frightened slaves emerged to clean up the place and lock the doors.

237

"Now, what do you suppose this was all about?" said Sulla.

"I don't know," said Antonia. "Mere youthful rebellion, perhaps. Unless his mother has stirred him up against us. Anything is believable at this point."

# XXXI

"I've had enough!" shouted Agrippina.

Pallas calmly scratched the side of his nose with the tip of his forefinger. It was a habit of his that seemed to help him keep his composure. "Be patient! Nero is only sewing some wild oats. He'll come around. If you press him too hard, you'll lose him."

"But don't you understond? I *am* losing him. And I'm losing him to an ex-slave girl and a bunch of young degenerates."

"An emperor is not likely to marry an ex-slave girl," he observed pedantically. "And some of those young men have rather aristocratic blood. They'll be heard from eventually, especially Otho."

"Do you think he's in love with her?"

"Do I think who is in love with whom?" He was annoyed with the question, clearly a frantic woman's question.

"With Acte, you fool. Who do you think I'm talking about?"

"You needn't shout. And you needn't be so concerned

239

about Acte. A young man will have affairs. And a young man will fall in love. Better this low-born girl in his own household than a high-born lady with political ambitions."

"But if he loves her, if he really loves her—"

"What then, madam?"

"Why then he won't love me."

He frowned. "You seem to forget that you're his mother, not his wife."

"And you seem to forget that we dreamed of a permanent regency in which you and I were the true rulers of Rome. It doesn't seem to be working out that way."

"We're not doing badly."

"But he's getting away from us. Something or someone is driving a wedge between him and me. And I don't believe it's mere accident that he's taken up with this woman."

"Love is rarely calculated," said Pallas. "It is like stepping off a high place."

"Yes, but something could have been arranged for him. Someone could have encouraged him."

"Who?"

"I don't know. Burrus? Seneca?"

"It's possible. But it's also possible that the encouragement was quite innocent. They might feel that it is good for his maturity to have a little more experience of the world. And perhaps they were a little uncomfortable with the degree of intimacy between you and him."

"Did they ever say so?"

He hesitated. "I don't think they had to say it."

"Was I being too obvious, then?"

"I've told you, there has been a certain amount of gossip."

Agrippina wanted to believe Pallas. She wanted to be able to smile and reassure her son that all was well, that she did not resent his friends or his way of life, but when she was actually face to face with him, the boiling cauldron of rage inside her could not be contained. "You lied to me!" she shouted. "You told me that Acte's admirer was Serenus. You told me those were *his* gifts, not yours."

"I was trying to spare your feelings," said Nero. He was

240

still an easy victim of her emotional brutality. He felt his hands beginning to sweat, and his chest grew tight so that it was difficult for him to breathe.

"If you really wanted to spare my feelings, you should have stayed away from that whore altogether."

"She's not a whore."

"A slave, then."

"She's not a slave either."

"All right, then, an ex-slave."

"She comes from royal stock, from the Attalids of Pergamum. It's been sworn to me by reliable men."

"You gullible child, you fool!" She paced back and forth across the room, her face flushed, her body animated. She seemed on the brink of physical violence. "Don't you understand what's going on? Somebody is trying to stir up trouble between us. And they are succeeding."

"Who would do such a thing?"

"I'd rather not say."

"Tell me. I want to know."

"You are being given some unsound advice by your beloved Seneca and his colleague Burrus."

He looked appalled. "Mother, I trust these men absolutely. They love me. They would never harm me. You musn't even suggest—"

"I am only suggesting that they are jealous of your relationship with me."

He shook his head helplessly. "Mother, what in the world are you talking about? How can they be jealous of *you*?"

She threw up her hands in frustration. "Oh, I don't know! I don't know. It's too complicated. I just want you to stop all this stupid running about. All these nocturnal adventures. Stay away from the Roman Mohocks. Stay away from the Mulvian Bridge. And stay away from Acte. Do you understand? I'm ordering you. I'm begging you. Do these things for me." She clutched her bosom in a pathetic pleading gesture.

He walked away from her, sensing a new strength in himself. He looked at her for a long time from across the room. She was beginning to dissolve into tears. "No!" he

241

said at last. "No! I will not do those things. I will not give up my friends. I will not give up Acte."

"You ungrateful beast! You unnatural child! Deny your weeping mother's simplest wish! And for your own good! For your reputation. Not for me!" And once again she pounded her chest.

He looked at her, fear and pity mingling in his guts. And when he could stand it no longer, he simply turned and walked out of the room, leaving her there on the stage of her own drama without an audience. As his boots echoed down the long corridor, he could hear her wailing after him.

# XXXII

Months went by and nothing was resolved. The brick
and mortar of silence and rage made a wall between them.
Nero continued to see his friends, including Acte, and
Agrippina continued to protest, though conversation between them was growing more and more impossible. Pallas
tried to warn her repeatedly that what he had predicted
was now actually happening, but she seemed unable to
control her outbursts. She complained to Nero about everything. "I knew what Seneca was up to," she said, "when he
had you escort me from the reception room. He didn't
want me to take my seat beside you to greet the Armenian
ambassadors. But I always sat beside Claudius there on
such occasions. I don't see why I shouldn't now."

And all he could say, a bit weary of the running battle,
was, "I am not Claudius!"

"I sometimes wish you were," she said.

"I can't imagine why," he said. "It seems to me you were
awfully glad to be rid of him when he died."

"Nevertheless, he did some good things. Speaking of
which, I think it's disgraceful the way you handled the re-

scinding of his decree concerning gladiatorial shows for quaestors-elect. Naturally, I have a vested interested in the legislation, but in any case I saw no reason to tamper with that decree. You only gave the Senators inflated notions of their own importance. I mean, you actually encouraged them to toss out the law."

"Quaestor's affairs belong to the Senate. Why shouldn't they act in the matter?"

"But I specifically asked you to leave the question alone. It was a matter of principle with me."

"You mean, you wanted to have it your way."

"I mean, you ignored my opinion and advice."

"I had to make up my own mind."

And so it went through issue after issue. Sometimes she held the field, sometimes she did not. She was persistent and powerful. She had many friends and a great deal of money. But inch by inch she was giving ground. And before long she began to panic because she was not at all sure her defenses would hold. She took stock of her situation, recalling the numerous conversations she had had with Pallas, and settled on an entirely new strategy.

Finding Nero alone in the garden one day, she approached him with all her statements clearly fixed in mind. "I have something important to discuss with you," she said. Her whole attitude was so pleasantly changed that he was forced to listen. She even looked different. Her hair was simply parted and drawn back into a tight chignon, reflecting all the modesty of an earlier age. Her face was carefully made up to look as though it was not made up at all. And her whole aspect was collected and calm and friendly.

"If it's about my appointment of Corbulo to lead the Armenian campaign, I don't want to hear about it," he said. "I know you had someone else in mind, but I had to do what I thought was best."

"Of course you did, my dear. And I must confess he's a capable enough man. But that's not what I wanted to talk to you about."

"What then?" he said.

"Well, I've been thinking about the events of the past few months, and I must confess that I have been a bit un-

244

reasonable. You must forgive me if I have been an over-zealous mother. I meant no harm."

"Of course I forgive you," he said, somewhat suspiciously.

"Whatever I have done I have done for you. You must believe that. From the time that you were born, I knew that one day you would be the emperor of Rome. I have devoted my life to that dream. For your sake, not for mine. And for the sake of the empire. You are doing an excellent job, as I knew you would. And I am sorry that we have had certain disagreements. You see, it's hard for me to realize that you are a grown man now. I was so used to thinking of you as my darling child, my only baby, my boy." Her eyes grew misty. The wall between them began to crumble.

"I never told you this, but years ago I consulted a fortune-teller. I wanted to know if my fondest hope would ever be fulfilled. She was a fraudulent old witch. She told me that you would, indeed, become the emperor, but that if you did you would kill your mother."

"How ridiculous!" he said.

"Of course!" she said. "I know you would never harm me. And I never believed her prophecy. But I want you to know what I answered her. I said that I didn't care, that as long as you became emperor I would gladly sacrifice my life—even at your hands. And that is what I've come to tell you. That your happiness means more to me than my own life. Because, my darling, you *are* my life. Without you I am nothing. And all my rage has been a kind of motherly concern. That's all. I have scolded you the way a mother scolds a child—to protect him. To teach him. And now that you are no longer a child, I have to scold myself to keep from scolding you. I have to get used to the idea that you are not only a man but the emperor of Rome. Do what you will. I will no longer interfere or disapprove. I will respect your judgment and all your new perogatives. Have your friends, your fun, your lovers. Make all your own decisions. And if you need my advice, I'll be glad to give it as impartially and as lovingly as I can."

"Thank you, mother," he said with a troubled smile.

245

"I'm glad to hear you say these things. The friction between us has made me unhappy because I *do* love you and cherish you. But I hope this is not just a momentary mood. I hope you mean what you say."

"If you doubt me, let me put your mind at ease. To prove to you how sincerely and deeply I feel these things I am going to turn over to you half my entire fortune."

"You would do that?"

"Gladly. I want you to trust me. I want our wealth to be mingled in a common cause, which is your future. All I ask is the simple respect due to a loving mother. And I know you will not fail me."

"No, mother, I will not fail you. Your generosity is overwhelming. And I, too, can be generous. What I have is yours. The moment you desire something you shall have it, whatever it is. Just name it."

"Ah, sweet son of mine," she said and drew him to her where they sat near the shimmering pool. "Come, kiss me as you used to do. Let me hold you."

Their embrace was affectionate and some of the old magic returned, but without the fear.

"And now, mother," he said, drawing away from her with a warm smile, "I have something to give *you*. A token of my love. And something you've wanted for a long time."

"Oh?" she said. "What can that be?" She could not entirely conceal a note of suspicion.

"I'm going to give you Antonia's house. Of all the imperial houses I know it's the one you love best. And, therefore, you shall have it, because you are, indeed, the best of mothers."

"Antonia's house? But what shall I do with it?"

"Why live in it, of course," he said.

"But I am perfectly content living here with you."

"Now, mother, you promised you wouldn't argue. And I am determined to show my critics that my mother does not rule my life. Do it for me, so that I can make a show of independence. In the meantime, come here as often as you like."

She looked wounded but tried to smile. "I know you mean well, my love, but what about Antonia and Sulla?"

246

"They can move into his house. And, besides, Antonia is too arrogant for her own good. We owe her nothing but contempt for imagining that her husband is as good as I am."

A quiet look of satisfaction came over her face. "Yes, I like the idea. The more I think about it the more I like it. I'd love to be there when she gets the news. How she's played the emperor's tragic daughter. How she's wept and complained with all that wealth of hers and with one of the finest houses in Rome. We'll teach her her place, won't we?"

And they laughed and embraced again, a pair of devilish children, united for the moment in the deadly game of vengeance.

But when the terms of their separation became clear to her, Agrippina was hardly pleased. For a high price she had bought only a temporary truce, not the kind of permanent settlement she had hoped for. She scolded herself privately for her impulsiveness. And she persuaded Pallas that she had intended the offer only as a gesture, never imagining that Nero would accept it so greedily. "He would have been a fool to turn it down," said Pallas.

"And I was a fool to make the offer," she said.

"That remains to be seen," said Pallas. "He may yet show his appreciation. There is a bond between you that will not be easy for him to break, especially if he is not provoked."

"Yes, but what of all the provocation that I must endure: robbed of half my wealth, cast out of his house."

"Now, now," said Pallas, "you weren't exactly robbed."

"I was forced into an impossible situation, and those who engineered it will be made to pay. And the fee will not be in gold but in blood!"

As she stalked away, Pallas shook his head. He was afraid that she was more than a little mad. She imagined dangers where there were none and ignored others that were more real. She was flirting with disaster, and he wasn't sure how much longer he could go on being her official champion and unofficial lover.

247

# XXXIII

Agrippina withdrew to Antium for a brooding holiday to nurse her wounds and gather her wits for her next attack. She had as guests her old friends Junia Silana, Aemelia, and Cornelia. They had in common widowhood, wealth, and middle-age, though they would have all denied that they were middle-aged. To hear them talk, often simultaneously, there were never four more put upon women in history. They had difficulties with everything from lovers to slaves to bodily functions. Cornelia was suffering an embarrassing loss of hair that she could not explain. "Perhaps someone has put a curse on you," suggested Aemelia. "I've known it to happen. I had a friend, who shall remain nameless, who missed her period for a year because of an incantation."

"It sounds more like an abortion than an incantation," said Junia Silana.

"Speaking of abortions," said Agrippina, "when are you going to put an end to that ridiculous affair of yours with Sextius Africanus? He's much too young for you. And it would be madness for you to put yourself in the hands of another husband. You've got your freedom, your wealth. What more do you want?"

"If my son were the emperor, perhaps I would feel differently about it. But life is precarious and sometimes lonely. I need someone to lean on. I need a husband."

"Being the mother of the emperor is not as wonderful as one would think," said Agrippina.

"So we've heard," said Cornelia.

She frowned. "What exactly have you heard?"

"Oh, a lot of gossip. How true it is only you can say. And we all hope you will because we are deeply concerned." They all nodded to confirm their deep concern and then leaned forward to gather in the truth from Agrippina's own lips. Inside information from high sources was the coin of the realm for these gossiping ladies.

"I suppose you've heard that I've turned half my fortune over to my son."

"Yes," said Cornelia. "I thought it was some sort of joke at first, but I gather it's true."

"Too true, I'm afraid," said Agrippina. "I have done everything for him. I brought him into the world. I provided him with the best tutors. I endured the humiliation of marriage to Claudius for his sake. I insisted on his adoption. I made him emperor by a thousand contrivances and sacrifices. And this is what I get for it."

"What?" said Aemilia.

"Neglect! Disobedience! And—and—I'll show you what." She rushed out of the room, leaving the three of them puzzled and curious. In a few minutes she returned carrying an elaborately jeweled dress. She flung it on the table before them, upsetting a decanter of wine and several cups. "That's what I get."

"Oh, isn't it lovely!" said Aemilia.

"A present from my son!" said Agrippina sarcastically. "The sum total of the return on my investment. I gave him my life and half my fortune and he gave me a dress."

"But, my dear, it's absolutely gorgeous," said Cornelia.

"But it's only a dress. Don't you understand? With what I only recently gave him I could have bought a thousand dresses like this one, jewels and all."

"Nevertheless, it was a nice gesture," said Junia. "Surely it must mean an improvement in your relationship."

"What it means is an improvement in his financial condition. I didn't trade away a fortune for a dress. I expected more. Much more."

"But what exactly did you expect?" asked Cornelia.

"First, I expected him to refuse my offer. But since he had the unflinching nerve to accept it, the least he could do was to join wholeheartedly in a real reconciliation. But no! Instead, he asked me to move out of the palace. And then he sent me this pretty garment as a token of his affection. And it's all lies. He doesn't care about me anymore. He takes his orders from his ministers, from Seneca and Burrus, who have him convinced that he's some kind of god. Divine Nero who can do no wrong. Arbiter of life and death and the fortunes of all the people of all the cities and nations of the world. What incredible nonsense! He's my son. I gave him suck. I grew him in my womb. If he's a god, then I'm a goddess. They've poisoned his mind. They've turned him into a monster. They've encouraged him in his lechery and violence. If I had it in my power I would wipe them all off the earth, including him, the ungrateful, unscrupulous, selfish, egotistical little degenerate. He's no better than those effeminate perverts and whores he calls his friends. I have a good mind to renounce him altogether. It was only because of my skillful intervention that he became emperor at all. Britannicus was the true heir. He was the one my husband had chosen. His own son. His blood son, not his adopted son. I should have put aside my motherly affections. I should have put that poor boy on the throne instead. He would have appreciated my efforts. He would have respected me. And thank God he's still alive. I may yet ally myself with those who gave him support. With those tribunes and senators who were too cowardly to speak up. I could have provided them with the courage they needed. I could have inspired them to come forth. And perhaps even now I can. For what other future do I have? My own son! My very own son has cast me aside like an old dog. He has kicked me. He has robbed me. And he thinks he can pay me off with this damned dress. I'll show him what I think of this stinking gift." In a rage she rushed to the wall and removed a decorative dagger. And with it she tore the garment to shreds, while her friends gasped in horror and fear.

Later, when they were alone, Aemelia said to Cornelia, "I hate to think what her son will do when he hears about this latest outburst of hers."

"He'll never hear about it if none of us mentions it," said Cornelia.

# XXXIV

But as swift as the tongue of a Roman matron the news tumbled back to Rome: Agrippina is angry with her son. Agrippina will join the cause of her neglected stepson. Agrippina has surrounded Britannicus with a hand-picked guard to protect his life. Agrippina may marry Rubellius Plautus, the great-grandson of Tiberius.

"You mustn't believe everything you hear," said Seneca. "You know what gossips Romans are."

Nero was in a state of agitation. "Yes, but there must be a core of truth in it. Something is happening. I know it. I feel it." He walked back and forth in the library on the Palatine, rubbing his hands together. His eyes darted here and there, as though he were a startled bird.

"You must admit," said Burrus to Seneca, "that she is presenting the world with a speculative picture of the new royal family, complete with a son. There's a lot of rich blood in that threesome: Augustus, Tiberius, Claudius!"

"I think she's bluffing," said Seneca. "I think she has allowed these rumors to reach us so that we will make concessions to her in an attempt to win her away from such a plan."

"But suppose she means it?" asked Nero. "Suppose she's really angry with me? She's liable to kill me. She's perfectly capable of it."

"Now, now," said Seneca, "it's not that simple. Your mother is a complicated woman. She needs to feel important."

"Then let's give her something," Nero said. "Let's make her feel important."

Burrus stood up, his face bright with an idea. "Or better yet," he said, "why don't we take something away from her?"

"What do you mean?" asked Nero.

"I mean that when a person threatens you, you can either stand up to them and threaten them back or you can try to pacify them. But appeasement might be construed as a sign of weakness. If we give in once, we may be asked to give in again and again."

"What do you suggest we take away from her?" asked Seneca. He tugged at the loose skin on his thick neck and seemed to know already what the answer would be.

"Her chief asset at the moment," said Burrus, "is her friends in high places. Her influence is extensive. And there is one in particular who hardly needs naming."

"Pallas?" said Nero.

"Yes," said Burrus.

"You think I should remove him from office?"

"As financial secretary he has enormous power," said Seneca.

"And as my mother's lover a certain immunity."

"He's not your mother's secretary, but yours."

"She'll be furious!"

"Let her be furious," said Seneca. "Let her embrace the cause of Britannicus. Let her crawl farther and farther out on that limb of hers. There is no place for her to go. You are solidly in power and beloved by the people. You are thoroughly protected from conspiracy."

"I don't know. I don't know," moand Nero, still pacing back and forth. "I certainly can't stand the man."

253

"None of us can," said Burrus.

"He's arrogant and insulting. He really doesn't respect me, does he?"

Seneca shrugged. "He respects money." His glance slid across the room to Burrus. They could tell that Nero was giving ground.

"But that's good, that's good," said Nero. "He's rich enough to be honest."

"How do you think he got all his money?" said Burrus.

Nero stopped pacing. His eyes were wide. "Do you think he's been cheating us? That would be grounds, wouldn't it? We could accuse him of —"

Seneca cut him short. "You don't have to accuse him of anything. He is your secretary of finance. You can simply dismiss him. You don't even need an explanation. And the less fuss the better. I personally think that he will accept his dismissal with considerable relief."

Nero searched himself for courage. Inspired by the cool determination of his chief ministers, he squared his shoulders and marched to the large chair behind the desk. "All right, then, bring him in. If we're going to do it, we might as well do it immediately and get it over with. I can't stand to think about it."

The messenger knew where to find Pallas. He spent long and regular hours in his office. He was a man of great energy and competence. No one questioned his ability, but almost everyone questioned his politics.

The moment he stepped into the library, Pallas seemed to know what was happening. But he was too proud and contemptuous to reveal more than intelligent awareness.

"You wanted to see me?" he inquired of Nero, with only a cold glance at the other two men.

Nero cleared his throat and made his little speech. The first words were too high-pitched. He started again. "I have asked to see you because I am planning certain changes in my staff." Under the table his knees were shaking. "I hope you will not find anything personal in these changes. You have been a good secretary, and it has been our good fortune to have your services."

"Am I to understand that you are removing me from office?" said Pallas, still unmoved.

"Well, uh, yes. I mean, I would appreciate it if you would resign, and if we could remain on good terms. That is—" He looked to Seneca and Burrus for support. He felt himself weakening. No one mentioned his mother, but she was vividly in his mind.

"All right, then," said Pallas, cutting him short and making his task easier. "I will resign from office on one condition: that my books be considered balanced and that there be no audits."

Nero leaped at the offer. "Of course! Of course!" he said. "Let them be considered balanced."

"All right, then," said Pallas, "you shall have my resignation in writing as soon as I can have it drawn up." He made no further statement. He did not bow. He did not acknowledge the presence of the other men. He revealed no anger or disappointment. He was coldly businesslike—so typical of the man who would not stoop to showing the world his feelings. He walked out of the library as arrogantly composed as he was when he had entered.

Nero leaned back in his chair with a sigh, as though he were exhausted by the effort.

"One must admit," said Seneca, "the man has an impressive style."

They all looked at one another rather sadly, almost as if they regretted the very thing they had just accomplished.

# XXXV

Distracted by love on the one hand and fear on the other, Nero spent the next few weeks in a highly nervous state. To Acte he wrote love poems. To Agrippina he sent secret apologies and expressions of loyalty and affection. She returned to Rome in the wake of all the disturbing rumors with smiling denials that somehow sounded like veiled threats. "I have never placed the interests of Britannicus above your own," she said, "though he still has supporters who feel he has a legitimate claim, especially now that he's come of age. He's fourteen years old and quite a handsome lad. Oh, not half so handsome as you, of course. But nevertheless—"

In the soothing arms of Acte he confessed his concern: "I cannot tell for sure what she has in mind. And now that she has moved into Antonia's house, it's hard for me to keep track of her movements. She is all smiles when she visits me, but I hear she has a steady stream of consultations with a wide variety of people. Senators and tribunes. Old friends of Claudius. Even friends of Messalina. She encourages compassion for Britannicus who she hints has

256

been robbed of his inheritance and is virtually a prisoner in the palace."

"Poor unhappy boy!" said Acte.

"I can't afford to sympathize with him!" said Nero. "Circumstances have made him my enemy. There are people who would use him to get at me. He is a sword hanging over my head."

"He is an innocent victim," said Acte. "And maybe you exaggerate his support and Agrippina's ability to use him. After all, what can she do. Her options are growing slim. If she had any sense, she would retire to ritual and idle pleasure."

"She wouldn't be happy like that. I know her. Even when she smiles at me she frightens me."

"Your fear of her is an old habit. You will have to find a way to conquer it."

And then, in a growing panic, he confided to Seneca that he could no longer live with the implied threat. "There is only one way out of this dilemma: I want Britannicus killed!"

Taken aback at first, Seneca called in Burrus and had all the doors locked and guarded, and systematically the three reviewed the difficult situation.

"Do you remember," said Nero, "how at the Feast of Saturn he was called upon to sing a song?"

"Yes," said Seneca, "that was a cruel taunt on your part, you must admit. I mean, the boy is not accusomed to singing and does not have much of a voice. Besides, he's painfully shy."

"But it was only a game," said Nero. "I was selected king by a roll of the dice. And I could demand a forfeit of each of the players. It was all in fun. We were feeling merry. All that wine and food and music!"

"Neverthless, you meant to embarrass him," said Seneca.

"I meant to have him forfeit something. That's the point of the game. I did not expect him to be so bold. And now I suspect that he had some help, some advice. He could not have dreamed up that performance of his all by himself. Imagine choosing a song like that: all about a boy deprived of his position and wealth, expelled from his father's house, stripped of his father's goods."

"It's an old song."

"He knew it by heart. He sang it without hesitation. And he had everybody on the brink of tears."

"There's no doubt about it," said Burrus. "The boy has stirred the hearts of quite a few people."

"But if he were murdered, wouldn't that sympathy grow?" said Seneca.

"Perhaps it would for the moment," said Burrus, "but then nothing much could be done on his behalf, could it? What claims has a corpse?"

"And it would certainly put an end to this stupid game that Agrippina is playing," said Seneca.

"Without Britannicus to stand between us, perhaps we could have a genuine reconciliation," said Nero.

"Do you really think that's possible?" said Seneca.

Nero hesitated. "Yes," he said, as though it was a confession of guilt.

"You still have some feeling for her, then?"

"Of course I do. You know I do." He played restlessly with a pair of gold coins on which appeared in profile the likenesses of both him and his mother. "But I want her disarmed. It's not my fault that she's using Britannicus as a weapon."

"It's not his fault, either," said Seneca.

A cold shadow settled over the face of the commander of the Praetorian Guard. "Perhaps we can't afford such sentimental considerations. There are much more important things at stake."

The conversation grew grim. With weary resignation Seneca asked, "How can it be done?"

# XXXVI

On the morning of February 14th, Locusta, the notorious poisoner, was brought secretly to the palace and installed in a small room adjacent to Nero's bedroom. She was still in the custody of the Praetorian tribune Julius Pollio. This wiry, dark-haired woman looked like death itself. She was shrouded in a black cloak against the dampness. It had been raining steadily all night, and the sky was heavy with clouds. The smoke that poured from the chimneys of the city hung in horizontal wisps and refused to dissipate. A low rumble of thunder like seething anger haunted the air.

In the small room there was only a narrow bed, a table, and a chair. The room was rarely used now. When Claudius was alive, he sometimes had an intimate slave sleep there to aid him through his insomnia.

Locusta removed her black cloak to reveal a skeleton in dark brown wool. She smiled behind her hands and said, "May I ask who the unfortunate victim of this visit is?"

"No," said Nero angrily. "You may get to work and mix us a poison that will dissolve in water without being detected."

"Well, then, may I ask my fee?"

"Your fee is your life, you wretched witch."

"Fair enough! Fair enough!" she said and removed from her basket a large collection of small bottles and jars. She arranged them on the table and asked for an amphora of water and one of wine.

"Stay with her, Julius," said Nero, "and let me know personally when the potion is done."

In his library he conferred in whispers with his ministers Seneca and Burrus. "It must not be bungled," said Seneca. "We cannot afford suspicions."

"Britannicus takes a light meal at noon," said Burrus. "And tends to be lax about the tasting of his food."

"But Agrippina has given him two new attendants," said Nero. "Can they be bought?"

"It doesn't matter," said Seneca. "We'll visit him in his private rooms on some trivial piece of business. And while you distract him in conversation, I'll drop the poison in his drink. It will already have been tasted. By the time it works we'll all be gone. If Xenophon is called, I'm sure he'll be discreet."

The hasty plan was soon carried out. The poison was prepared. The emperor paid his visit, accompanied by his ministers. Britannicus was consulted about his role in a forthcoming festival. And then the three withdrew to the library to await the news and prepare expressions of shock and dismay.

They waited a long time. Nero was on the brink of panic. "What's taking him so long? Have we been discovered? Did he look suspicious?" He ran his hands through his hair and over his face. He chewed at his fingers. He sat down and got up and sat down again.

What seemed like an endless wait was actually less than an hour. The suspense was ended by the appearance of Xenophon. His aging face was gray, his eyes as dark and sad as history. He had lent himself to this conspiracy with private reservations. Actually, he had a special affection for young Britannicus. But the realities of the situation made it impossible for him to do anything but cooperate. "I'm sorry to report," he said, "that your brother Britannicus has suffered an indisposition."

Nero and his ministers looked at one another and frowned. "What do you mean?" screamed Nero hysterically. "An indisposition?"

"Keep calm!" said Seneca.

"I mean that he seems to have had a brief attack of some sort, for which I have given him the usual prescription, a purging of the bowels."

"And?" said Nero, as though there must be more to report.

"And nothing, sir," said Xenophon. "He's resting and hopes to join you all at dinner."

"I don't understand," said Nero.

Seneca touched his arm to calm him. "All right, Xenophon, you may go," he said.

"But what went wrong? What could have happened?"

"I don't know," said Seneca. "Perhaps the potion was too weak. Perhaps he didn't take enough of it."

"Well, what shall we do?"

"I suggest we try again at dinner time," said Burrus.

"But we've got a lot of guests," said Nero.

"Does it matter?"

"It may be to our advantage," said Seneca.

"But my mother will be there," said Nero. "She'll see what's going on."

"She won't see anything until it's too late," said Burrus.

"There's an ancient strategy I came across in a Greek play," said Seneca. "We'll pass him a cup of hot wine. It will already have been tasted, but it will be too hot to drink. He'll ask for water to cool it down. The poison will be in the water."

"Ingenious," said Burrrus.

"Unless that witch fails us again," said Nero. His voice was loud. His hands shook. "I could kill her. She's done this on purpose. I know it, I feel it. She's mocking me. She's laughing. But I'll fix her. Burrus, get me a whip. I'll see she does her job right this time."

Together they went to the room where Locusta was lying half asleep on the bed. Julius was sitting at the table, examining with curiosity some of her wares. Nero stormed in, hissing incoherently. "You whore! You bitch! You vile,

261

stinking cadaver!" He raised the whip and lashed her across the face before anyone could stop him. And then again and again he hit her, on the shoulders, the breasts, the legs. "I should kill you. You incompetent corpse."

Locusta shrieked and tried to protect herself with her arms. Julius leaped up but then hesitated to restrain the emperor. "What is it?" he pleaded. "What's wrong?"

"I'll tell you what's wrong. This rotten, scheming, ruthless bag of bones has placed us all in jeopardy. She's ruined our scheme. She's given us a harmless poison."

"It didn't work?"

"Yes, the boy's alive. And well, but for a bellyache. What kind of poison do we need for a bellyache?"

"Please, sir, it was an accident. He must not have consumed enough of it. Please, let me try again, I'll give you something so potent it will work with a drop in a second or less. Just a touch. I promise you! I promise!"

Nero backed off. "We've got no choice; we've got to try again," said Seneca. "Keep your temper. See what she can do."

Nero stared at her, the whip still in his hand. "If what you give us this time doesn't work, you can say good-bye to life. We'll strangle you by slow degrees or give you some of your own poisons to drink. Make haste! Mix us something swift. Burrus! Send for some small animals, some cats or dogs. We'll want to try it out this time."

Seneca observed his protégé, impressed and disturbed. He saw in him in that moment all the madness of the Julian-Claudian family, the hysteria, the cowardice, the nervous courage, and, above all, the utter willfulness. Was he wrong, he wondered, to feed this trait and tell the boy that he was a living god on earth. But there was no time for further speculation. There were poisons to prepare and things to accomplish in the name of expediency.

The guests invited for dinner that night were a curious mixture of the respectable and the disreputable. The emperor's wife Octavia was there as a matter of form. She would say nothing and she would hardly be noticed. His mother was there by invitation. She was a frequent guest,

262

in spite of their recent alienation. His personal friends included Otho and Poppaea, about whom there were matrimonial rumors. Seneca and Burrus and Beryllus could almost be taken for granted. His ministers were with him constantly. But Tigellinus had only recently insinuated himself into this sort of gathering. His flattery and his horsemanship were beginning to reap rewards, in spite of the persistent rumors that he was still one of Agrippina's lovers. Among the more respectable guests were Antistius and Suilius. They were accompanied by their young sons Caius and Marcus, who shared a separate table with Britannicus and Titus, the son of Vespasian.

The weather had gone from bad to worse, and there was considerable conversation about the rain and floods and the lightning that had struck the obelisk in the Campus Martius. "I can't remember when I've seen a more miserable night," said Antistius.

"There's talk of omens and signs," said Suilius.

"Nonsense!" said Nero. "It's only a storm. It'll pass." He held out his cup for more wine, and Seneca could see that he was getting drunk. He could see also that Agrippina was deep in conversation with Poppaea, and he could tell by the tone of Agrippina's voice that she did not like the woman at all. Perhaps Poppaea was too beautiful, or too sarcastic. Perhaps she was too predatory. She wore her bad reputation like a badge of honor. "I was sorry to hear about your divorce," Agrippina remarked.

"I'd prefer congratulations," said Poppaea. "I've been celebrating my liberation all week. With a little help, of course." She flashed her large eyes seductively at Otho, and Agrippina made a little grimace of a smile.

Acte was conspiciously absent, in deference to Agrippina. The two women were not on speaking terms. Acte accepted the awkwardness as gracefully as possible, but Nero seemed oddly annoyed by her capacity for complete understanding. He might have preferred an occasional display of temper. Something more familiar.

Surreptitious eyes kept returning to Britannicus. And eyes that followed eyes wound up on him also, until he was, for no apparent reason, the secret center of attention. But he himself seemed unaware of this. He was in surprisingly good spirits after his brief "indisposition." He joked with Titus, of whom he was fond. And Caius and Marcus were a willing audience for their humor.

The appointment of Corbulo and the Armenian question absorbed the more political guests. "A very good choice, indeed," said Antistius.

"Yes, but how will he get on with Quadratus Ummidius, the governor of Syria?" asked Suilius. "I understand there's something of a rivalry developing there, what with our eastern armies divided between them and Corbulo's gift for flamboyance."

"I hear he's quite popular," said Beryllus. "Isn't that so, Nero?"

The emperor looked at him with glazed eyes and had to be rescued by Seneca. "He's popular because he's a good general. It's as simple as that," he said.

Nero looked from one man to the other and then his eyes drifted back to Britannicus. He was puzzled by his good humor. Was something going on that he didn't understand? Had he purchased some kind of immunity? Was anything at all going to happen? His impatience was a knot in his chest that he tried to loosen with wine. His mother could tell that something was wrong. But her comprehension came too late.

Those privy to the scheme watched tensely as the heated wine was passed to the taster who attended Britannicus. He was a solemn man with obedient eyes. He took a gulp and winced. "A bit hot," he whispered to his young master as he handed it on to him, Britannicus took the cup, held it to his lips and then quickly withdrew it. He gave it back to the taster, confirming the fact that it was, indeed, too hot. Another attendant suddenly appeared with a pitcher of cold water. He was an inconspicious young man, rarely used for dinner service. He poured water into the hot mug and Britannicus smiled at him as he accepted it once more. He was listening to an involved story being told by Titus and did not drink immediately.

The suspense was almost too much for Nero. He put

aside his own drink and listened to his heart race. He could feel the throbbing in his neck. The voices around him faded as if they were all suddenly under the sea. And the face of his mother went in and out of focus, her eyes trying to read his peculiar mood. She knows, he thought. She knows! She knows!

But she didn't know, not until, at last, Britannicus put the cup to his lips and took a healthy swallow. Almost instantly he went rigid and wide-eyed, as if he had been shot in the heart by an arrow. He fell forward. The cup clattered on the table and the wine streaked across it to the other side. Titus and the other boys were too startled to do anything. They looked toward the emperor for an explanation.

Octavia went pale as ashes but kept her silence and composure. Tigellinus sprang to his feet, as did Antistius, but they were halted in their tracks by Nero, who, still reclining, said, "It's all right. An epileptic seizure. He has them often. Let him be. We'll have him removed. He'll be all right in a little while." And then he caught his mother's eye. She seemed stricken with terror, but she did not move, and she did not say anything. Perhaps she expected to be included in the assassination, for certainly that was what it was. There was no doubt in her mind, no matter what lies her son was telling his guests.

Xenophon and some attendants came in and carried the boy out. Nero gave a superb performance and ordered the festivities to continue, though inside he suffered hurricanes of fear,

"Are you sure he's all right?" asked Beryllus.

"What a horrible expression on his face," said Antistius.

"It's in the nature of the disorder," said Seneca calmly. "One has to be careful that he doesn't swallow his own tongue. But Xenophon will see to that."

A sudden blast of thunder shook the room, and the heavens opened up to weep. Lightning cracked in the near vicinity, and some of the guests jumped at the sound. "My god, that was close," said Suilius, who was completely unaware of what had happened before his very eyes.

On the muddy, rain-swept parade ground of the Campus Martius the funeral was held. With difficulty a fire was kept going. And a small crowd had been gathered. A brief eulogy was mumbled into the darkness, and the body of the boy who might have been the emperor of Rome was delivered into the suffocating flames. Back at the palace Nero and his guests feasted on peacock and pheasant and talked about the ultimate destruction of the Parthian Empire. Those who knew what had happened kept the secret to themselves. Those who did not complained about the vileness of the weather.

# XXXVII

It was very late at night. Only a handful of people still lingered in the dining room. The rest had fallen victim to fatigue or boredom or drunkenness. Nero was deep in his cups. He had been drunk every night since the death of Britannicus. Acte was by his side, more worried than amused. He was fighting sleep and demanding new entertainments. "I'm sick of singers and jugglers," he shouted, slapping his sandal against the table and then flinging it in the direction of one of the slaves. "Bring me somebody with a sense of humor. Bring me Paris. Where is that bloody clown? He's suppose to be here, not dicing and drinking in some stinking tavern, wasting his talents on the wretched mob, the illiterate dregs. What do they know about art—or anything else?"

Otho and Poppaea, recently married, dared not leave him in this reckless mood. Having helped to educate him in his debauchery, they stayed close when he wallowed in it. What's more, they themselves were considerably less than sober, and they imagined it was all rather amusing. Petronius, too, liked these violations of decorum and logic. "It gives one such a sense of freedom," he said. But Seneca remained sober and unconvinced. He guarded his protégé with a practical and censorious eye. Having encouraged him to explore himself in these directions, he was now having misgivings. Nero's abuses of his body were unhealthy, and his company was unwholesome. But Seneca played along with a polite applause and even contributed a half-hearted witticism from time to time.

"There's a man in Neapolis who can eat fire, I understand," said Petronius. He had the gift of looking thoroughly sober when he was really thoroughly drunk. His pronunciation was never slurred. His eyes never crossed. When he went beyond his final limits, he merely passed out, but very politely.

"If he can eat fire, why is he in Neapolis and not here, where we need him?" asked Nero. "We do need a man who can eat fire, don't we, Seneca?"

"If he can really eat fire," said Seneca, "I hate to think what's liable to come out the other end."

"Thunder and lightning," said Otho.

He and Poppaea reclined amorously. Her breasts were almost revealed in a low-cut gown. Her slender form was clearly outlined as she lifted her hips or bent her legs in that slow, erotic way she had about her. Nero watched, and Acte watched Nero. He was aroused, and no one really seemed to mind.

"If you were not so recently married," said Nero, "I'd steal that lovely thing away from you. But I'll wait until she grows weary of you, which should be in a week or so."

"Don't count on it, old boy," said Otho. "I have ways to amuse women that women haven't even heard of yet."

"Now there's a boast worth holding him to," said Petronius. "I'd like to be hiding behind a curtain when he makes it good. Something Oriental, no doubt."

"Come, Otho, give us a preview," said Nero. "Or, better yet, let us guess. Is it something you do with your tongue? Or perhaps your little finger? Or maybe that other little digit of yours. Is it true you call it your dwarf?"

"By the smile on Poppaea's face," said Petronius, "I'd say you missed the mark by half a yard or so."

268

"Did you hear what he said, Poppaea?"

"No, I never listen to Petronius. He never spoke a word of truth in his life. He only talks to hear the sound of his own voice. He really has nothing to say."

"Oh, ho, the lady's got a tongue," said Nero.

"She does, indeed," said Poppaea, "and she knows what to do with it." She turned aggressively to Otho, flung him back on his couch and kissed him passionately.

"That's the most sensible thing I've seen all night," said Nero. He moved unsteadily on his elbow, and his speech was indistinct.

Otho recovered from the assault and wrestled his bride to the couch for double revenge. As she fought playfully back, her long legs were revealed and a breast became briefly uncovered. Nero laughed and applauded. "Finish her off," he shouted.

Acte touched his arm and drew him closer. "Shall we go to bed?" she whispered. She and Seneca exchanged a glance. He wanted the evening to come to an end. There was something in the teasing flirtatiousness of the scene that bothered him. Poppaea had a reputation for causing trouble between men, and he did not want to see a falling out between Nero and Otho. Acte understood all this as swiftly as she seemed to understand most things. She put on her mask of gaiety and kissed her lover so hotly that he was seduced away from Poppaea—at least for the moment.

# XXXVIII

The marriage of Otho and Poppaea lasted more than the
week predicted by Nero. It threatened, in fact, to last indefinitely. And, what's more, it threatened to come between
the emperor and his most intimate friend. So enamoured
was Otho of his beautiful wife that he spent less and less
time with the emperor and more and more time with Poppaea. Nero teased him about his enslavement, but he
could not hide his bitterness forever.

Poppaea Sabina was a beauty but she was more than
beautiful. She also had a disarming seductiveness that filled
a man with the illusion of heroism and the promise of profound pleasure. Under a surface of apparent innocence, she
was capable of fantastic adventures of the heart and flesh.
But it was power more than pleasure that drove her. And
this she had in common with Agrippina, who hated her
from their first meeting. Poppaea was now twenty-six, the
same age as her husband. Nero had just turned twenty.

In the early days of the marriage they became a sophisticated threesome, the center of wildness and clever conver-

sation. Otho boasted of his wife's beauty, and Nero allowed himself to be tantalized and amused. But intimacies of one sort threatened to become intimacies of another sort, and the newlyweds retreated into their domesticity, leaving Nero to brood about the erotic possibilities that had been aroused.

Despite sound advice from friends like Petronius, Nero could not leave well enough alone. He missed the company of Otho. But, even more, he missed the presence of Poppaea, her wit, her intelligence, her playfulness, her silly superstitions, and her amber-colored hair. He invited her to the palace without her husband. At first he called it amorous mischief, but later he called it love.

It came as no surprise to Otho to hear, eventually, from the emperor's own lips, that he was in love with Poppaea. Otho maintained his poise. Even his sense of humor. "Well, I can hardly blame you, old boy," he said. "She's a remarkable woman. I'm rather fond of her myself."

"Well, aren't you jealous?" said Nero.

"Jealousy, they say, is a form of madness."

"And so is love. My wits are turned around. I cannot help myself."

"We have all loved each other and been a little mad. Perhaps that's why I stayed away. Where can such madness lead?"

"Does everything have to lead somewhere? We had a great deal of fun. You hurt me by your absence."

"Is this your revenge, then?"

"No, I never intended this."

"Ah, Nero, Nero, which of us knows what we really intend? Our heads rarely know what's in our hearts. And in your soul there is more confusion than either one of us can find language to describe."

"I am not confused!" he shouted. "Don't tell me I'm confused. I love Poppaea, and that's a simple fact."

"You make it sound like an imperial decree."

"Are you mocking me? I may be your friend, but I am also the emperor."

"Be careful, old boy, you'll turn into a statue of yourself."

"Are you trying to provoke me? You mustn't talk to me that way."

"I'm sorry! But haven't you grown a little pompous in these past few months? Whatever happened to the carefree lad who romped with me at the Mulvian Bridge?"

"That lad's become a man."

"And that man is being childish."

"Don't call me a child!" he screamed. "I'm not a child."

"All right, then, we'll talk this over man-to-man, as they say." His tone was sarcastic. "Or would you prefer emperor to subject?"

"Can't you be serious, damn it?"

"Do you think I find this amusing?" said Otho. His exasperation could no longer be contained. "A young man—who just happens to be emperor of Rome—tells me that he is in love with my wife, this woman whom I love more than life itself. What am I supposed to do? Am I supposed to deliver her into your arms? Am I supposed to cut my throat out of politeness? Damn, I love her too, and, what's more, she's my wife. She says she loves me. Should I call her a liar?"

"She does love you. When she's with me she talks about you all the time."

"Do you want me to divorce her?"

"She never said anything about divorce. Besides, I'm married."

"Yes, your mother will never let you forget Octavia. She guards that girl like the last survivor of a slaughtered litter. She made her your wife. And she'll make sure she stays your wife."

"My mother doesn't tell me what to do."

Otho laughed. "And the mouse chased the cat around the moon."

"I'll divorce Octavia anytime I want. For the moment I find the marriage expedient."

"I thought you hated her."

"Love and hate have nothing to do with marriage. I didn't say I wanted to marry Poppaea."

272

"I'm sure the feeling is mutual. So what would you have me do? Play the cuckold for the barbershop wits? Turn my back to let this romance run its course?"

"No!" said Nero.

"What then?"

"I want you to go away for a while. Far away."

"You'd banish me?" asked Otho, his eyebrows raised in disbelief.

"Don't be ridiculous. I'd give you a good overseas appointment. Governor of a province or something like that."

"If I refused?"

"I could insist."

"And if Poppaea refuses to stay behind?"

"She won't."

"How do you know?"

"Because I've already asked her and she's agreed to stay in Rome."

Otho shook his head. "My God, you are incredible—both of you. I can see that it's all but settled in your mind. I suppose you've even selected the province."

"As a matter of fact, I have."

"Do I dare ask which one?"

"Lusitania. A very pretty place, they say."

"And conveniently remote. The far side of Spain."

"Would you prefer an Eastern desert?"

"No, thank you. I've had my fill of barbarism. And since I seem to have no choice, I might as well borrow a leaf from Seneca's book of Stoicism and accept my destiny with dignity. But I warn you, O mighty Apollo, you won't find her an easy wench. She's rich and pampered and far too ambitious for her own good. She bathes in milk and has a passion for luxury. What's more, she has a restless mind. She talks of dying at the height of her beauty. She confesses to a fascination with the Jews and certain Eastern superstitions. Like a cat, she will love herself on you and persuade you it's affection. She will insinuate herself between your ribs, and if you are not careful, she will garrote your heart." There was a tremor in his voice and a sudden note of sadness, as if he were already a thousand miles

273

away and looking back toward Italy across mountains of longing and seas of loneliness.

"I will give her the world," said Nero.

"She'll want more," said Otho, and turned quickly away to leave before his sadness turned to tears.

# XXXIX

Now in her early forties, Agrippina was just beginning to lose her looks. Her tall, elegant frame was starting to fill out in a matronly way. And her face was becoming the outer record of her inner desperation. The lines at the corners of her mouth drew it into an expression of grim determination. She had none of the fatalism and quietude of the Stoics. She had no philosophy at all, only the driving force of her own irresistible will. What she could not accomplish by force she would accomplish by cunning.

Nero did not often visit his mother after she moved into Antonia's house, and when he did, he made the visit brief, bestowing on her, in the presence of witnesses, the filial kiss and exchanging certain civilities. "One must keep up appearances," said Seneca.

Once, however, he lingered longer than usual. There was clearly something on his mind. "Why don't we go into the garden?" said Agrippina. "I'd like you to see the changes."

They walked together in the sunlight, along the newly laid paths. She held his arm and explained the pattern of fountains. "They had a difficult time getting the water to work properly. The place was a shambles for months."

She insisted that they sit for a while in a small circular arrangement of benches and columns.

She looked at him with more than motherly understanding. "You seem to have something on your mind. You look distracted."

"I am."

"Do you want to tell me about it?"

He looked at her. She took his hand to encourage him. He started to pull away, but then gave in. "I was wondering about Octavia," he said.

"What about her?"

"Well, do you think she'll ever have a child?"

She smiled. "Darling, I'm not a fortune-teller. But the girl is still young. And a bit of a late bloomer. She may yet bear fruit. If you give her enough attention."

"I want a son. Or even a daughter. Death is a terrible thing, and I want to perpetuate myself."

"Why are you talking about death at your age?"

"Because one can die at any age. And what if I die without a child? Who will succeed me? I want to know whether or not Octavia is barren."

"And if she is, what would you do?"

"I'd divorce her and marry a woman who could give me a son."

Agrippina released his hand and stood up. "Poppaea Sabina has a son. I suppose she's the woman you have in mind."

"I didn't say anything about Poppaea Sabina."

"You don't have to. All of Rome has been talking about you two for some time."

"And what are they saying?"

"They say you sent her husband to Lusitania to have her all to yourself. And they say that eventually you hope to marry her."

"Do you think that would be such an awful idea? She comes from a good family."

"She's older than you."

"Only a few years."

"Six years, to be precise."

"She's proven she can have children. She had a son by Rufius Crispinus."

"A son whom she ignores almost completely."

"He's well looked after."

"Yes, by a bunch of slaves. A mother's duty is deeper than that. I should know. It takes true dedication. But that's neither here nor there. I don't even know why we are discussing the possibility. You can't divorce Octavia."

"Why not?"

"For the same reason you married her in the first place. It would be political suicide. She's popular. You may not like her, but she has a certain charm. By divorcing her you might drive her into the hands of some ruthless pretender to the principate."

"Such as?"

"Your imagination is as good as mine."

A cloud of anger crossed his face. "The only ruthless pretender to the principate I can think of is Rubellius Plautus. But he seems to have taken vows of disappearance."

"Forget Rubellius and forget about divorcing Octavia."

"Why?"

"Because I said so!" she shouted. "I am not going to allow you to make a fool of yourself. You've already damaged your reputation enough. First by taking up with Acte, an ex-slave. And then by stealing another's man wife, a woman known to be spoiled and unstable."

He stood up also and also raised his voice. "But I love her," he wailed, and his voice floated off through the hedges of the garden.

"Of course you do. And not long ago you loved Acte. And a few months from now you will love somebody else. And each time that love will be undying and forever, and you will write a poem about it. All right, suffer these romantic agonies—if they give you any pleasure, but don't let them ruin your life."

She softened and sat down beside him. She tried to touch him, but he drew away. "Don't you see what I am trying to tell you? The world is full of women. And it is a mistake to worship them as if they were goddesses. You are making much too much of this little fling with Poppaea."

His anger returned. "It's not a little fling! Don't try to belittle it. I told you I love her."

"I wish you would stop saying that. I heard you before. Your feelings are your personal concern. But how you act is another matter. It affects us all. Your private life is limited by your public function as emperor."

"I can do what I damn please," he said, his mouth gathered into an infantile expression that made him seem still unweaned.

"Yes," she said, "until somebody stops you."

"What do you mean?"

"I mean that it is a mistake to antagonize too many people. If you have enemies and if they are sufficiently provoked, they may try to harm you. You can't always do what you damn please, as you put it. You must consider the political repercussions. You must be diplomatic."

"What enemies are you talking about?"

"I don't want to bring any official charges, but may I speak freely, as a mother to her son?"

"Yes, yes, of course," he said impatiently.

"The other day your freedman Graptus came to me, deeply concerned about an incident on the Flaminian Road. I gather that you had been out at the Mulvian Bridge with some of your friends. Oh yes, I know all about that. Don't bother to explain. On your way back you decided to take a different route to Sallust's gardens. The gods must have whispered in your ear. Along the Flaminian Road a nasty gang was waiting to ambush you. And the leader of that gang was Cornelius Sulla."

"Sulla!"

"Yes, shy and innocent Sulla."

"Are you sure about that?"

"Ask your freedman Graptus. Certainly you trust him. He's been with the imperial family since the days of Tiberius."

"Why didn't he tell me about this? Why did he tell you?"

"He came to ask my advice. He did not want to upset

278

you unnecessarily. He asked me whether or not this sounded like a serious incident. After all, the streets are full of gangs. Some of their pranks are harmless enough. But his personal impression was that, in the guise of a gang clash, Sulla hoped to seek you out and kill you. It would have all been explained as an unfortunate accident, since everyone was in disguise and it was dark. I must say, it's not a bad plan for assassination." She wagged her finger at him. "You see what you let yourself open for? What chances you take?"

He was, by this time, walking back and forth and rubbing his hands. "I never liked that man," he muttered. "I never trusted him. Or his wife, either."

"They're not your most affectionate supporters," said Agrippina.

"But I never took him for the violent type. I mean, he's so full of principles and righteousness. All he can do is talk."

"Apparently you were wrong. He has been urged and urged by would-be supporters to make a bold move."

"He has the name and the lineage."

"He has an emperor's daughter as his wife."

"He has money and property."

"And a motive."

He looked at her and frowned.

"Britannicus! Need I say more?"

He stopped pacing. "What do you think? Do you think I should banish him? Get him out of the way?"

"I think it might be a wise precaution. But keep Antonia here in Rome. We don't want to implicate her, and we don't want her out of our sight. We'll deal with her another time."

"All right," he said, staring into a fountain.

# XL

Once the news was out that Cornelius Sulla was to be confined to the city of Massilia in Gaul, both he and his wife were shunned as though they had a contagious disease. "Where are the friends we thought we could count on?" he asked, unable to conceal his anger and disappointment. "When they thought we were close to the center of power they flocked around us like smiling hyenas. But now— now!" He slammed his fist against the white wall of their bedroom, leaving behind a smudge of blood from his bruised knuckles.

"They are afraid of being implicated."

"But there is nothing in which to be implicated!" he shouted. "There is no conspiracy. Surely, they know that."

"Still, they're afraid. And fear is that woman's best weapon."

"I should give her something to be afraid of," he said, pacing the floor with long strides. "And how many times I could have killed that son of hers on the road at night, while he was cavorting with his drunken gang. When he forced his way into our house that time I should have driven my dagger into his fat throat."

"No," she pleaded. "Put such thoughts out of your mind. There may yet be something we can do, if you don't make matters worse. There's no knowing where violence would lead. And, in any case, it would be wrong. We may be victims, but we are not murderers. Besides, we still have our property. And some of our friends may yet find the courage to intercede for us. I will try to get to Seneca through Antistius and Suilius. I don't suppose there's any point in trying to see Nero personally, but I hear that Vespasian is returning any day now from Britain. He and my father were close. He's like an uncle to me. I'm sure we can count on his support."

But one by one their efforts failed, and gloom settled over the household. Antonia expressed her grief secretly, clutching her son to her bosom as though he were her husband and she could, with her own loving arms, somehow prevent their imminent separation. "Why are you crying?" young Claudius would ask her. He was all innocence and beauty. His hair was blond, and his eyes were blue like his grandfather's. A perfect child. But his mother's sadness was contagious, and one day he burst into tears for no apparent reason. Antonia took him into the garden and tried to explain to him what was going on, but he didn't understand. "Why?" he kept saying. "Why does my father have to leave?"

"Because the emperor is sending him far away."

"Oh!" he said, and then "Why?" He didn't know who or what the emperor was or what was meant by *far away*.

Antonia kissed him on the cheek and wiped away his tears. She rocked him back and forth in that ancient rhythm of consolation that worked as well for her as it did for him. Sitting there in the garden, she sang him an old song that her mother sang to her when she was a little girl. He fell asleep in her arms and she held him for a long time, wondering whether or not they had done the right thing to bring such innocence into this den of monsters that called itself the ruling class of Rome. Nothing good could come of it. They would break his little heart or turn him into one of

281

them. Either way, she thought in her despair, he was better off dead.

Their hopes were raised temporarily by a visit from Vespasian. He was a sturdy, sensible man of about fifty, universally admired, even in sophisticated Roman circles, in spite of his country manners. He promised to raise the matter with Nero, and did, in that blunt way of his, and was just as bluntly turned down. "Nero says I've been in Britain too long to know exactly what's going on in Rome," he reported to his friends. "And that, in any case, it's none of my business. He ordered me not to raise the question again. But I will, of course. He's very emotional. Hysterical. He's still very much under the influence of his mother. Until he breaks that bond, I'm afraid there's not much I can do. But I'll keep trying. Bide your time in Massilia, Sulla, and we shall see what happens here."

When Antonia and her husband were alone together for the last time, they lay in one another's arms late into the night. Their sadness and love mingled in the darkness. Sulla ran his fingers repeatedly through her long, unbraided hair and over the fine features of her face. He touched her slender neck, her naked shoulders, her breasts, as if he were committing her to memory. Her palm rested on his chest and felt the beating of his heart. It was slow and rhythmic. "Things will change. She can't have her way forever," she said.

He traced the shape of her lips with his finger and then drew her close to kiss her. "I'll miss you," he whispered. "I'll miss you every day, every night."

Her hand moved across his smooth chest from nipple to nipple. "Will you need a woman?" she asked.

He hesitated. "I don't know," he said. "I will try to be faithful."

"It's all right," she said. "If you need a woman, have one. But pick an ugly one."

She could feel his brief smile. He placed his cheek against the fullness of her breast. She held him there, thinking of their son. And then, as if the thought was shared, Cornelius said, "Don't let young Claudius forget me."

He could feel a sudden gasp of air. Antonia's chest

heaved. She was trying not to cry, but she was. "Come now," he said gently, but it was all he could say.

"I can't help it. I feel like one of those poor victims in the arena. Some beast is tearing out my insides. Oh, what shall I do? What can I do to keep you here?"

"Ssh!" he said and stroked her hair. "Don't talk about it. Lie still with me. You are half my life. Only part of me will be in Massilia."

His hands explored her once again. Their lovers' conversation continued in silence. They slid from satisfaction into sleep, their naked bodies entwined, their minds lost in a dream of eternal life.

And in that sleep their final hours slipped away. When they opened their eyes they could see a hint of light through the shutters. "I must get ready," said Sulla. "The escort will be arriving soon. They will see me to the ship at Ostia."

"May I come that far with you, at least?" implored Antonia.

"No! I don't want you to. I want you to stay here. My friend Sisenna will be with me. And Perseus will see to the loading of my goods."

"All right, then," she said. "I'll try to be a good Roman wife." She stood at attention like a soldier, but the gesture was unconvincing and when she started to smile she almost started to cry again.

When the centurions arrived, Antonia accompanied her husband as far as the door, her son in her arms and her mother holding back a bit to let them say farewell. Antonia turned to her mother and handed her the child. Sulla kissed his son and then took his wife in his arms for the last time. He was unable to speak, but between their kisses she whispered, "We'll be together soon. I promise you."

He said, "I love you," and then was gone.

The horses clattered away. The sounds of the stirring city filled the fragile clarity of the morning air. And Antonia wandered, as if in a dream, back to their bedroom. Moving a small, beautifully carved chest to the bed, she removed its contents piece by piece. There were necklaces and rings and scrolls. Some love letters and poems. But when she came to the very bottom, there was something special. A dagger with a ruby-studded gold handle and a shimmering silver blade. It was given to her by her father Claudius, and she had always treasured it above all other things she owned. And when he had given it to her, he had said, "My darling daughter, if you should ever find yourself a prisoner of pain, let this be your passport to freedom."

She held the dagger lovingly in both hands, cradling it as one might a baby. And then one hand tightened on the golden handle and the point lingered less than an inch from her belly. She turned it upward toward her chest and bosom. And then farther up toward her white neck, as if she were exploring herself for some weakness, some vulnerable place where she might plunge it in. After a long moment she flung herself on the bed and cried herself to sleep.

# *XLI*

Lost in the sweet perfumes of their passion, Nero and Poppaea made love, while obedient Octavia wrestled with her loneliness and humiliation in another part of the palace. She knew what was going on but was helpless to do anything about it. It was almost as if he wanted her to know what was happening, to deepen her pain, and perhaps to heighten his pleasure.

To satisfy the luxurious and exotic tastes of his mistress Nero had a secluded bedroom converted into a special retreat for pleasure. It was decorated with Egyptian tiles and Syrian rugs, with meticulous paintings and Oriental wall hangings. All the windows were sealed off. And it was ventilated through openings in the roof, which could be covered over with giant, gilded seashells. The bed was circular as was the sunken bathing pool. The spouts that fed the pool were golden dolphins, and the rim was a halo of tiny emeralds.

The mere existence of the room was a secret hard to conceal, but what went on in the room was something only the lovers would know. Whatever small part of their pleasure was witnessed by slaves was kept contained by imperial threats of instant death to those who dared to utter a word.

In this private place they brought to life their fantasies and satisfied their desires, whatever they were. Their bodies were oiled and pampered by a Nubian eunuch. They sipped strange wines and aphrodisiacs. Naked nymphs danced for them and were sometimes used by them in playful ways. And, occasionally, lured into their spider web of a dream, there was a handsome stud, an obedient slave, drugged into absolute subservience to please them with his muscular passion, only to be swiftly poisoned afterward to guarantee his silence. These twilight adventures in sensuality excited Nero to excesses from which it often took him a full day or more to recover.

In Poppaea he had found his match, not only sexually, but also intellectually. The many hours between their bouts of lovemaking were spent in idle or serious conversation, in which it soon became apparent that this woman possessed one of the liveliest minds in Rome. She constantly astounded him, intrigued him, amused him, and aroused him.

As their intimacy grew more intense, the angry gap of jealousy widened between him and his mother. And when Agrippina could no longer tolerate this connection as a mere flirtation or amorous indulgence, her temper flared. She put it bluntly to her son. "Poppaea has an appetite for power that will make all her other passions look like whims. She doesn't love you for yourself. She'll use you, then she'll betray you, just as she betrayed Otho. Break it off, Nero. Be done with her. I'll withdraw my objections to Acte. She is pure innocence beside this woman, and just as beautiful. More beautiful, in fact. Take her. Use her. I'll lend you my house if you need a quiet place to meet. These decadent revelries of yours are destroying you."

"I don't care," said Nero. "I don't care about anything. Without her I am nothing."

"But what about me?" shouted Agrippina. "What about me?"

All he could do was to stare at her blindly, as if she no longer existed, as if she were only an annoying voice. Inevitably, she confronted Poppaea directly. And the violent scene between them was a delicious scandal in all the circles of Rome for weeks. During that time Nero refused to see her or talk to his mother. And then, sensing that the conflict might come to a head, and that she might lose, she hastened off to Antium, leaving behind a simple note: "I love you still, no matter what you do."

Poppaea was neither appeased nor fooled by this strategic withdrawal. "I will never forgive her for the things she has said. And," she added, "I don't see how we can go on with her scheming against us. She'll destroy us both rather than lose you to me."

"But what would you have me do?" he asked.

"Get rid of her."

"She's gone to Antium."

"That's not far enough. Send her to an island in the middle of the sea. Send her to the rim of the world and let her conspire with the monsters of the deep."

"I can't do that."

"Why not?"

"I'm afraid she'll find a way to get revenge. She still has friends."

"Then send her to Hell!"

Nero's face went pale. "What are you saying?"

"You heard me. Don't look so frightened and appalled. It won't be the first time that murder has been used to solve a problem in your family. It's virtually a tradition."

"But she's my mother."

"She's also the woman who not so long ago embraced the cause of Britannicus, the woman who, without a shred of conscience, would slaughter you in a moment if she were sure that she could get away with it and place another puppet on the throne."

He was subdued and shaken. "I'll have to think about it," he said.

"And while you're thinking, what do you suppose she'll be doing? She'll be gathering her forces in Antium to do away with you or me or both of us. Which of the slaves and freedmen in your own household are loyal to her? You'll never know until it's too late."

Agonies of uncertainty assailed him. When he spoke

287

again, his voice was a hoarse whisper. "But what if we should try and fail? Such provocation is sure to make her do the desperate thing. As things are, we may still hope that—"

"Hope what?" asked Poppaea. "That she will deceive you into complacency? That she will bide her time until the next reconciliation? Don't you understand? Your differences are irreconcilable. There is only one thing that she wants from you: absolute power. Over you. Over Rome. Over everyone. If you cannot live with that, then you must learn to live without *her*. You must amputate her from your heart or forever be her slave. And there is only one way to do that. Put her feverish soul to rest. You have the wherewithal, certain men that you trust."

"Not Burrus or Seneca. They owe her too much. They do not like her, but they might be reluctant. And, besides, we cannot use the Praetorian Guard. She has too many friends there. They might rebel."

"Who then?"

He thought a while, pushing his trembling hands through his hair. "There's no one in her personal household we can trust. And poison would be too obvious after the death of Britannicus."

"What about the commander of the fleet at Misenum?"

"Of course! Anicetus hates her more than any other man I know. And he was my tutor and friend for many years. He'll do it, I'm sure. And find a way."

"Do you agree to it, then?"

"Yes," he said in his ghostly voice. "I'm agreed to it."

"Good! she said, and took him in her arms.

288

# XLII

Anicetus was called to Rome, where he applied himself with military diligence to the problem. He was a sturdy man, broad-shouldered, levelheaded, and unsentimental. He saw in Agrippina a menace to the old order and the old values. But his distaste for her was personal as well as professional.

"My plan is this," said Anicetus. "If your mother stays in Antium, as she threatens to do, you must go to your villa at Baiae for the Festival of Minerva. From there you should make gestures of friendship and suggest a reconciliation. You should invite her to your villa for a banquet. I don't think she will refuse, even if she is suspicious of your motives. If she stays at Bauli, you can send a boat for her to bring her to Baiae. This boat will have been especially contrived with a heavy lead-lined ceiling in the main cabin that will fall at the move of a lever. And the boat will break apart while at sea. I have consulted the engineers who worked on the project at Lake Fucinus. They agree that it can be done. The weakened hull will split apart from the weight of the collapsing roof and the vessel will sink. It will appear to be an unfortunate accident at sea, for which no one will be able to blame you. When the news of her death reaches you at Baiae, you will, of course, make the necessary demonstrations of grief. You might also consider honoring her with a temple or some shrines to allay suspicions. If this plan meets with your approval, we can put it into effect in plenty of time for the Festival of Minerva."

Nero was so taken with the ingenuity of the scheme that he applauded with childish enthusiasm, until he realized what the infernal machine was for. And then his fears returned. "Are you sure it will work? Are you absolutely sure it will work?" he said.

"It's often a lot easier to sink a ship than to keep it afloat," said Anicetus, whose confidence was reassuring. "Besides, I'll have on board a small band of carefully selected men. They'll know what to do and how and when to abandon ship. Once she's aboard, there's no way she can escape."

Nero gulped his wine and nodded all at once, wetting his chin and staining his toga. His heart raced. His breath was quick. As much as he dreaded the whole adventure, it excited him. He wanted to prove to his mother that he could destroy her, that he could free himself from her. He wanted to kill her, and then, in some insane way, he wanted to run to her like a child, screaming, "You see, you see, mother, I've killed you." And in that nightmare she would smile and praise him and kiss him and say what a wonderful boy he was. There was even in his anticipation a certain sexual frenzy. And as he revealed it all to Poppaea he made desperate love to her, as though he wanted to reach beyond her to the very victim of his daring plot.

# XLIII

It was Antonia's mother who finally persuaded her to
come to Baiae for the Festival of Minerva. "The change
will do you good," said Aelia Paetina. "And, besides,
everyone is there."

"Will *she* be there?" asked Antonia.

"I don't know," said Aelia. "She's at Antium now. But
our friend Vespasian will be visiting with Lusius Geta, who
is also sympathetic to us. It will do us no harm to meet
with both of them. Vespasian, they say, is marked for
greater things. But he will be returning soon to Britain."

And so they went, traveling by road, taking with them a
small entourage of a dozen attendants. They stayed at Aelia's modest house, a villa set back from the beach on a
gentle slope overlooking the sea. It was halfway between
the imperial villa and Agrippina's house by Lake Lucrine.
But the distances were not great in this crowded and luxurious resort. She could easily walk to either house in less
than half an hour.

The atmosphere was lively and the liveliness was contagious. Junius Lupus came by to welcome them to Baiae.

The old outspoken senator had made it clear, officially and unofficially, how he felt about Seneca and his enormous wealth. "The man is a hypocrite and a fraud," he said. He took some wine and continued on his rounds. There was a greater sense of political impunity in Baiae than there was in Rome. Perhaps it was the holiday spirit, the letting go, a kind of joyful irresponsibility.

There was an invitation to dinner on short notice—a cousin of Aelia's who lived only a few houses away—but Antonia pleaded fatigue and went off to bed early.

She spent half the night standing alone by the window of her bedroom, staring out across the sea toward where she imagined Massilia was. Moonlight shimmered on the barely disturbed water, and the waves lapped sadly at the pebbled shore. It was a mournful, faraway sound. It brought back memories of her childhood, that innocent time when whatever the adults did was like things that happened in foreign countries or in books that no one really believed. The true tragedies were the small things: the death of her first kitten, a thunderstorm that startled her from her sleep and made her scream, the sounds of voices arguing in another room. Sometimes a certain sound or even a certain quality of air could send her hurtling back to those magic days when she and her friends played games in the immense house and teased the old slave with the wart on her nose (what was her name?) or begged honey from the cook, hanging on the railings or stairs that descended into the kitchen.

What was he doing now, she wondered, her mind returning to her husband through a veil of childhood. Was he looking toward her across the shimmering water? Was he, too, unable to sleep? Or was he perhaps consoling himself with another woman? She shook her head to drive out the thought. But in a few minutes it returned. And her own jealousy made her angry with herself, so that she slammed the shutters closed and lit the lamp.

# XLIV

The rocky promontory of Misenum jutted into the sea to form the western end of the Bay of Puteoli. It was a jagged finger of stone, an unfriendly cliff that dropped away to a narrow sandy beach. Beyond the strip of sand the promontory narrowed to accommodate the cup of a lagoon that formed a natural harbor for the triremes of the navy that were stationed there. From the tip of the peninsula one could look out to sea or back across the larger bay, beyond Puteoli, to Neapolis, Herculaneum, Vesuvius, Pompeii, Stabiae, Surrentum, and the island of Capreae.

When the news came from Misenum that Agrippina's ship was about to enter the bay, Nero made ready to meet her and to escort her to the villa at Bauli, where she would be staying during the five-day Festival of Minerva. Though the distance between Baiae and Bauli was not great, it was easier to go by sea than by land. Most of the great villas here and along the entire sweep of the bay were built directly on the water and had docking facilities.

"Her ship was sighted about two miles out, approaching the point at Misenum," said Anicetus. "It was moving

293

rather slowly, and one of my men thought it might be listing to the starboard."

"Wouldn't it be amusing if her ship sank before she even got here?" said Nero, laughing nervously. There were deep shadows under his eyes. He had been unable to sleep for days. He had insisted on supervising every detail in the arrangements made for Agrippina. He personally inspected the villa at Bauli. And when the "death ship" was brought into its dock, he went over it a hundred times, asking Anicetus each time whether or not it would really work. He examined the mechanism that would allow the roof to fall. He was shown the weakened sections of the deck and hull. He personally selected the decor for the cabin and asked that the sails be changed to another color because his mother was not fond of faded pink. When it was finished the vessel was beautiful. It was newly painted, newly rigged, and luxuriously appointed. How could she resist using it?

"Have the local people heard that my mother is coming?" said Nero. A slave adjusted his toga. Another held up a mirror, in which he could look at his face and hair.

"Oh yes," said Anicetus. "They seem to have known for some time."

Nero shook his head. "How do they do it? They *always* seem to know what's going on. Do you think they know about this?" he glanced at the slaves and sent them scurrying away with a wave of his hand.

When they were alone Anicetus said, "There is no way that they can know. Only four men have worked on the actual mechanism, and they are all to be trusted absolutely—but absolutely! And that leaves only you and me."

Nero tugged at his clothes and squirmed, as if here were something crawling on his skin. "I want to know what the people are saying. I want you to send some spies among them."

"All right," said Anicetus, "but her coming here was no secret, and word spreads fast between here and Antium. Ships come in every day. Anyone could have brought the news. What's more, it's to your advantage to have all this talk of a reunion."

"Why?"

"Well, for one thing, the people would applaud it. It would be popular."

"Does that mean my mother is popular?" He was frowning. His eyes shifted suspiciously.

"I mean only that they would like to see the disputes in the imperial household resolved. The people want peace."

He thought about that. "Do you think there will be a large crowd at the dock when she comes in?"

"Yes, I think there will. The whole place is in a festive mood. Everybody is here for the holidays. The shores are crawling with slaves and boats and merchants. You can't get through the narrow streets of Puteoli. I'm sure that even now a thousand eyes are following the ship that brings her in, and the crowd that gathers there at Bauli will expect to see the emperor kiss his mother."

"Yes, yes, of course, I will kiss her!"

"And the good feeling of the crowd will have a disarming effect on her. You see, she will imagine that your only motive for the reunion is to respond to a popular demand. She can understand that. At the moment I am sure she is highly suspicious of your invitation."

"She'll be on guard, then?"

"She may smile and kiss you, sir, but she will certainly be on guard."

They went down to the landing to board the small vessel used by the emperor for short trips along the shore. Waiting on the dock for them were Burrus and Seneca. They seemed to be having a heated discussion, but by the time Nero and Anicetus came up they were smiling and polite. "We understand your mother's arriving," said Burrus.

"Yes," said Nero. "She'll be staying in the villa at Bauli for the Festival of Minerva. I thought it might be wise to greet her and perhaps to invite her to dinner tonight."

Seneca's penetrating gaze made Nero look in every direction but directly at his old tutor. "Is everything all right?" he said.

"Oh yes, yes, everything is fine," said Nero, his voice suddenly high-pitched.

295

"You should have warned us about this," said Burrus. "I'll send a contingent down to the shore. There's bound to be a crowd."

Nero looked at Anicetus, who answered for him. "I've already taken care of it," said the commander of the fleet. "My men will be patrolling the coast from Misenum to Puteoli."

"I had the imperial guard in mind," said Burrus. There was a disturbing firmness in his tone.

"It's all right," said Nero. "His men are already there. Keep a heavy guard on duty here." He cut short the discussion and marched aboard the boat. His movements were a bit stiff and unsteady.

"Do you suppose he's been drinking already?" asked Burrus. "It's not even noon."

"I don't know," said Seneca, rubbing his hand meditatively over his bald head. "He's in a peculiar state. Not the sort of thing induced by wine."

"What do you suppose he's up to?"

"I don't know, but whatever it is we're not included."

"Do you suppose that's why he didn't want my men sent down to Bauli?"

"He's been thick with Anicetus lately," said Seneca. "And though he has a certain intimacy with the man, there must be more to it than just friendship. This business with his mother puzzles me. They parted on hostile terms. She's determined to wreck his affair with Poppaea and to keep him from divorcing Octavia."

"Perhaps he hopes to work something out with her," said Burrus.

"Yes, but what can he afford to give her in exchange for her cooperation? And, what's more important, why didn't he consult us? Is it possible that he no longer trusts us?"

"I can't imagine why, unless his mother has managed somehow to turn him against us."

Seneca tugged at the skin on his thick neck. "I don't like it, Burrus. I don't like it at all. Send your spies among the people. They may be able to discover what's going on. Tell them to be very discreet and to report directly to us."

Nero came ashore at Bauli a full half hour before his mother's ship was due to land, according to the latest estimates given to them by the messengers who were watching the progress of Agrippina's Liburnian galley. The curious holiday crowd had gathered along the beaches, right up to the gates that guarded the private dock. They let out a great cheer when the emperor appeared. And he acknowledged their loud greeting by raising both arms, first in one direction, then in the other. He saw their faces pressed against the iron railings. They were, in his distracted sight, a blur of rags and flesh. And their noise shattered his concentration and sent a bolt of fear through his chest. "God, they're a scabby, filthy lot," he muttered to Anicetus. "Don't let them through the gate, whatever you do."

Anicetus frowned. "They're ordinary people," he said. "Slaves and citizens, fishermen and shopkeepers. Most of them have probably never seen an emperor before. But my men are stationed all along the railings from the water's edge to the road. There's no way they can enter the grounds of the villa."

Nero looked out to sea. His mother's galley was inside the promontory now, and they could see that it was definitely listing to the starboard. "They've taken on water," said Anicetus. "There must be some damage below the water line. A piece of floating debris, perhaps."

"Is it in any danger?" said Nero, standing close to the broad-shouldered commander, as if for protection.

"No, no, it's moving all right. A bit slow, but then the wind's been mild. And I see now they're putting out oars."

"There are people on deck. Can you tell if my mother is among them?"

"Not yet!" said Anicetus, and then he took Nero firmly by the arm. "Collect yourself. Your face is flushed. Put on an ordinary look with which to greet her." He said this quickly and confidentially and then moved away to make arrangements for the landing.

Agrippina drifted toward her son like a dream moving across the surface of the water. From the moment she became visible he saw only her. All the other people aboard and the ship itself might as well have been invisible. He

297

saw her golden hair, parted in the middle, tinted and braided. The sun caught it and in his troubled mind she was rising from the sea, an immense vision filling the sky. Her cloak was draped from her shoulders. It was the color of wine. In front it was parted to reveal a white gown. A sudden breeze caught her garments and her hair and woke him from his reverie.

The ship came in on oars. The sails had already been dropped, and now the crew was tying them down. The galley groaned as it eased into the dock. The slaves grunted in unison, until the first mate shouted, "Oars up!" The men on shore fended off the listing vessel with padded poles and then caught the lines to make it secure. The captain shouted orders. Agrippina waved to the cheering crowd and threw kisses into the air.

She came down the gangplank boldly. The crowds shifted from the shores to become ten deep outside the iron railings. Where the rocks sloped up, they found a vantage point from which to watch this piece of history.

At first Nero could not move. He was fascinated by this apparition in purple and white and gold. He didn't actually recognize her until she was ten feet away from him. Yet he knew it was she, he could feel her presence while she had still been far out at sea. Someone nudged him from behind. He was startled. He turned to see the face of Anicetus. He moved forward. His knees were shaking, and there was a cold chill in his groin. He could feel his face assume a smile, but he was terribly afraid he was going to be sick.

But then she was actually upon him and he was in her arms. "Ah, my darling son. How good it is to see you." And then the kiss, with all the people watching, waiting, and then breaking into a louder cheer as their mouths touched and the wounds of the empire were healed. Her lips felt hot on his, and his nervousness did not escape her. "Let me look at you. How have you been?" She held him by the shoulders and at arm's length. He was a boy again and she was calling him her little soldier, her little emperor.

"I've been just fine," he said, "except that I've missed you. And how do you find life in Antium these days?"

298

"I find it somewhat boring," she said, "and much prefer to be here."

His eyes were fixed hypnotically on her lips. They were heavily painted and set off the whiteness of her teeth. He could feel her examining him, and he didn't want to look into her eyes. Her voice rang in his ears. It became indistinct. His head began to swim and he was afraid he was going to faint. Then suddenly he flung himself at his mother and embraced her passionately, as if he was going to assault her sexually right there on the dock. He kissed her repeatedly, first on the mouth, then on the cheeks, then the neck, and even on the exposed portion of her breasts, drawing renewed applause from the crowd. "I'm sorry!" he whispered into her hair and ear. "I'm sorry, mother! I'm sorry!" She patted his back to soothe him and he barely kept himself from crying. Then he seemed to pull himself together and let out a ghastly artificial laugh that was supposed to pass for joy.

Anicetus came forward to explain the arrangements. "You know the villa, madam," he said. "I see you have your own slaves and staff. If there is anything you need, do not hesitate to ask. We have provided for your convenience this little vessel, called the *Paralos*, which you may use while you are here. I think you will find it the swiftest form of transportation. And I see your galley has suffered some damage. There is a crew aboard our boat, and the emperor has had the cabin especially decorated with you in mind."

She looked lovingly at her son, but her smile was somewhat pinched by impatience. "Yes, yes, Anicetus," she said. "I can see that it's a lovely boat. But now, if you don't mind, I would like to rest. The ground is still moving under me as though I were still at sea."

"I know the feeling well," said Anicetus, and bowing from the neck, he backed away to allow Nero to escort his mother up the broad stone steps to the entrace of the villa. There he kissed her once more.

When he came down the steps, Anicetus was waitng for him. "She's coming to dinner tonight," said Nero.

"By sea or land?" said Anicetus.

"She would not say. We'll have to wait and see." There

299

were signs of perspiration on his face and his eyes were bulging slightly from his head.

They said nothing further until they were on board and half way back to Baiae. Then Anicetus said, "If she doesn't use the boat coming over, we'll bring it up to Baiae and offer it to her for the return trip after dinner. She may not want to travel by road in the dark."

Nero said nothing. He was staring into the water as if he were trying to see the bottom.

To honor his mother at dinner that night Nero seated her above him. He could have chosen no better sign of his respect and love. She began to feel that his efforts at a reconciliation were genuine. What's more, he was attentive and flattering and affectionate. He had, during the afternoon, found a way to compose himself, and his mood was considerably improved and calmer, though he was clearly not entirely himself. He was talking a bit too much and too loudly, and there was still a slight quiver in his voice. The wine he drank to excess seemed to intoxicate and steady him all at once.

There were three tables of nine—twenty-seven guests, many of them steeped in the holiday mood, all of them brilliantly costumed. The clever and wealthy people of Baiae. The aristocracy and the elite, and ministers and military men like Seneca and Burrus. Lesser creatures like Anicetus were not included.

The conversation was rich with gossip. The festival of Minerva was punctuated with delicious scandals. All the expensive lechery of Italy descended on the place for these five riotious days. Adultery was as common as water, and all the permutations of pleasure were rapidly being exhausted.

There was an abundance of wit and even some talk of literature and of Nero's plan for an Olympics of the arts. The lavish banquet and good company relaxed Agrippina, who had come by land.

It was after midnight when Agrippina announced that she was exhausted with joy and satisfaction and really had to leave. She thanked her son and all the other guests and

300

called for her maid, Acceronia, and for her attendant, Gallus. Nero escorted her to the landing where the pretty ship lay waiting to take her back to Bauli. They were surrounded by friends and well-wishers, most of them illuminated by the gaiety of the banquet.

They embraced again before she boarded the vessel. He said, "I'll love you always, you are the best of mothers." And she said, "You've made me very happy today." They kissed. He felt her bosom against his chest. Then he kissed her there, on each breast. A sudden weakness came over him again. He felt his heart leap and his hands go cold.

He watched her go aboard. And as the ship moved away from the dock and her face faded into the night, he wanted to scream into the darkness for her to return. But, instead, he turned away and walked unsteadily back to the villa, all the noises of the night magnified in his throbbing mind.

It was a magnificent night, full of stars and moonlight over a gentle sea. The sail gathered in the modest breeze, and the ship followed the lights along the shore, moving south toward Bauli. In the deck cabin Agrippina reclined on a couch with elaborate sides in the form of scrolls. Acerronia kneeled beside her on the carpeted floor and listened with girlish delight to her mistress's description of the banquet and her happy reunion with her son. "What a miracle of good sense has visited him," she said. "I think he understands, at last, how much I mean to him."

Gallus stood at the far end of the cabin, staring out the open door at the stern of the boat and the wake it left behind, a path of pale white that smoothed the fractured moonlight. His eyelids were heavy with sleep. It had been a long day.

There was no warning. All of a sudden the ceiling came crashing down on them. The beams splintered. The weights tore through the deck. The walls of the cabin collapsed. The noise was terrifying. And the ship lurched suddenly to starboard, as if it might go under. Gallus was crushed to death instantly. But Agrippina and her maid were protected by the sturdy arms of the couch. They were tossed down the inclined deck and into the water just as the ship began to right itself. Acceronia screamed, but her voice was lost in the general confusion aboard the badly damaged boat. Agrippina knew instantly that there must have been a plot against her life. The night was too calm. This was no accident.

She realized that her shoulder had been injured somehow, but she began to swim silently off into the darkness in the direction of the lights on shore. Behind her she could hear Acceronia calling for help. The crew called "Agrippina! Agrippina!" and the maid answered hysterically, "Here! Here! Save me." But as she splashed her way closer to the ship, the men who would have saved her beat her unconcious with an oar and rammed her chest with a boat hook. "It's the maid," someone yelled, "not Agrippina."

"Where is she? Where is she? She musn't get away."

"Sink the ship! Sink it!"

But not all the crew were in on the scheme and as some men tried to turn the boat on its side, others tried to keep it upright. There was loud chaos and some fighting broke out. It was the captain himself who, wielding an ax, knocked out the weakened planks of the hull. He escaped just in time before the vessel went down. Two members of his crew were not that lucky.

In the water, protected by darkness, Agrippina swam easily. She was strong in the shoulders and an excellent swimmer. The shock of the treachery made her angry, and her anger made her determined to survive. But she was also frightened because she had come so close to death and because now she knew that her son meant to kill her.

She swam for a long time, angling off to the north to come ashore nearer to Lake Lucrine, where her own villa was. She swam on her side and then rested on her back. Her cloak and gown were gone. She wore only a brief undergarment. Her breath was growing short. The salt water stung her shoulder wound. She was beginning to wonder whether or not she would make it. She had a moment of panic. She felt her mouth go dry and her stomach turn to knots. But she talked to herself. She urged herself on and took another stroke and another, until she was swimming again. But her arms grew heavy and her mouth was so dry she wanted to drink the salt water. What a temptation it was just to let go, just to fill her lungs with water and slip down into the sea, down into death forever.

She was startled from this dream by a voice calling to her across the water. She turned her head and saw that it was a fishing boat. It was probably out of Puteoli, the pre-dawn start of a long workday. She called back and saw the silhouetted fishermen scurrying along the deck and talking rapidly to one another.

They were astounded to find out who she was and practically tore off their clothes to cover her. They gave her warm wine and offered to take her immediately to the imperial villa, but she insisted on going ashore near Lake Lucrine. "I have a house there," she said and struggled to get to her feet.

They babbled on in their local accents, reciting the names of friends who lived nearby, friends from whom they might borrow a cart. "It's not far," she said. "I can go on foot. I don't want you to bother. Believe me, it will be all right."

"Shall we send word to the emperor?" asked a leathery old man with white hair.

"No, no, don't mention this to anyone. I have people at my villa. I will send a messenger to him myself. I have my reasons. Do as I say and I will see to it that you are well rewarded."

Within twenty minutes they put her ashore, wearing a rough wool tunic gathered at the waist with an old piece of rope. She made her way along the beach, avoiding the house until she was sure it was safe. She circled around to the lake side and entered by a back door just as the first light of dawn was beginning to melt the darkness in the east.

# XLV

The first message to reach Nero came from one of the crew, a young man who was unaware of the conspiracy. He had suffered a serious gash in his arm and two broken ribs, but he had somehow made his way to shore, where he collasped. He was discovered by two of the men assigned by Anicetus to patrol the coast between Baiae and Bauli. One of the guards stayed with the crewmen; the other ran all the way to the imperial villa to report what the dazed young man had told them.

The messenger was ushered through the gates and taken to the Praetorian officer in charge. Sweating and gasping, he blurted out the news. He, too, was unaware of the plot. "The *Paralos* has gone down. The emperor's mother was aboard and is feared lost."

The startled centurion grabbed him by the arms and questioned him closely. "But that's impossible," he said. "The sea is as calm as glass."

"The cabin collasped. The ship broke up and sank. We picked up a survivor on the beach, but he is badly hurt. We expect others."

"What happened to the empress? Did anyone see her?"

"This crewman saw her go overboard, but in the confusion, he said, no one could get to her. Everything happened too fast. Her maid and attendant were killed. He didn't say how. This lad seems shocked almost out of his senses. Something very strange must have happened."

"We must be careful what we tell the emperor. He will be shattered by this news. He and his mother have just had a festive reunion. Come with me."

He led the still exhausted messenger into the house. There were no signs of life. All the guests had long since left, and the household had gone to bed. The slave on duty in the atrium had fallen asleep. At the end of a long corridor they could see a guardsman looking back at them. He started down the hall. The centurion shook the old slave awake in the chair where he sat. He sprang to his feet and looked around wide-eyed. "What is it? What's happened?" he said, his face pale with fear.

"Where is the emperor?" he asked in a heavy whisper. "We must see the emperor."

"He's in his room," said the slave.

And then the guard appeared. "Take us to the emperor," said the centurion. There was an urgency in his voice and in his every movement.

"Yes sir!" said the guard, and they all followed him back down the corridor.

Alone in his room Nero lay stretched out naked on his bed like a corpse. He was wide awake and trembling from head to toe. His bulging eyes were fixed on the ceiling, where the light from half a dozen lamps danced.

He heard the hard footsteps in the hall and his heart galloped as he anticipated the news. He could feel his veins exploding in his neck. Panic gripped him and almost stopped his breathing. The footsteps stopped. A fist pounded on the door. He pulled a light cover over his body and up to his chin. Clutching it there with both hands, he screamed "Come in!"

He did not get out of bed to hear the news. He was afraid of falling down. "What do you mean they don't know for sure what happened to her?" he shouted. "Bring that man to me instantly! I don't care how badly hurt he is. And send for Anicetus."

The house began to stir. Word spread like fire from room to room, from wing to wing. When Nero was alone with Anicetus, having hysterically ordered everyone else out of the bedroom, he gave full reign to his panic and confusion. "My God, what's happened? Has she gotten away? Is it possible? Oh, hide me, Anicetus. Hide me!"

"Stay calm, sir," he said. "It sounds as though she's dead. She could not have survived long in the water."

"What do you mean? She swims like a shark. If she was still alive when she entered the water, she must have made it to shore."

Anicetus rubbed his chin and began to pace back and forth. "We should have more information soon. My men are guarding the entire beach from here to Bauli. Even if she comes ashore, they'll pick her up and bring her here— or to the other villa. Even if she suspects us, what can she do?"

"I don't know," he cried. "But it will be horrible. She'll find a way to avenge this. She'll kill me. I know she will."

And then Burrus and Seneca burst into the room. "What's this all about?" demanded Burrus. "My centurion tells me that there's been an accident at sea—the *Paralos*! Is it true? Is your mother dead?"

"We don't know yet," said Anicetus, his shifting eyes betraying his secret knowledge.

With great deliberation, Seneca closed the door and threw the bolt. Then he slowly approached the bed where Nero cowered. Burrus and Anicetus became statues where they stood. From the foot of the bed Seneca lifted his arm and pointed directly at Nero's face. "Now, tell me, you impulsive fool. What exactly have you done?"

Nero looked at Anicetus but got no help. His eyes rattled in the room. His mouth moved, but all he could say was "I-I-I-"

"You've killed her. Is that it," said Seneca.

"Yes!" he screamed. "Yes! Yes! Yes! But she won't die. She's swimming across the sea to kill me. Don't you understand. You can't kill her. She's indestructible. She's immor-

306

tal. I want all the troops called out. I want reinforcements from Rome. I want the house surrounded. I want everybody searched."

"Now just pull yourself together," ordered Seneca, "before you bring ruin down on yourself and all of us. What precisely did you try to do?"

"We arranged the cabin of her boat so that it would collapse," said Anicetus coldly. "And we weakened the hull so that the boat would sink and take with it any evidence of foul play."

Seneca threw up his hands. "Of all the idotic schemes! Couldn't you think of something simpler. A dagger or an ax or a vial of poison. Who in the world is going to believe that on a quiet night like this a brand-new ship is going to break up? What's more, you tell me half the crew had no idea what was going on. How are you going to keep them from talking?"

"We'll kill them," said Nero. "We'll kill them all. Burrus—"

But Burrus was staring at him and shaking his head. "No, you can't do that. You can't expect my men to start slaughtering innocent people. You'll have a riot on your hands in no time."

"Then what are we going to do?"

The pounding on the door seemed to answer his question. It was the centurion. He had with him a messenger from Agrippina. When Nero was told this, he leaped out of bed as though he had been attacked by scorpions. The frightened messenger fell to his knees, as though it was going to be necessary for him to plead for his life. "Please, sir," he said. "Your mother urgently wants you to know that she is well and at her house by Lake Lucrine. She says there was a dreadful accident and that her ship was sunk. She was very concerned that you would be worried about her fate. She wants you to know that, but for a minor bruise, she is perfectly safe, having been helped ashore by some local fishermen. She is resting quietly after her ordeal and begs you not to visit her right away. She sends her love and asks that the families of those lost at sea be generously compensated."

"What is he saying?" cried Nero. "Is it possible that she doesn't know?"

Seneca put his finger to his lips and motioned the centurion and the messenger out of the room. He slammed the door and turned back to Nero. "Of course she knows!"

"Then why—"

"Don't you see what she's up to? She wants to give you the impression that she suspects nothing. It's the only thing she can do to protect herself from further violence."

"Oh!" he moaned. "What am I going to do? She'll arm her slaves. She'll rouse the troops with her father's name. She'll lay her cause before the Senate."

"She'll do nothing of the sort," said Seneca. "Not if we finish what you started."

"You mean kill her?" he said in a strangled whisper.

"I don't see any other way out. Do you, Burrus?"

The commander of the guard looked suddenly weary. His shoulders sagged, as if he were carrying a great weight. "No," he said. "There is no other way."

"Would you dare command your men to kill her?" said Seneca.

Nero looked from one man to the other, too stunned to do anything but stand by, holding the cover about his naked body.

"No," said Burrus. "They are too devoted to the house of the Caesars. They would never carry out such an order against the daughter of Germanicus. We would have a revolt on our hands. No, it must be done by Anicetus. He bungled the job to begin with, let him finish it off properly."

Anicetus stared back at Burrus and picked up the challenge. "All right," he said. "I'll go immediately to Lake Lucrine with my own men. They owe nothing to anyone, except to me."

"Good," said Nero. "Go! Go quickly, before any rumors of your coming can scare her off."

Anicetus came to attention. "We will send word back as soon as the deed is done," he said and marched out of the room.

Seneca glanced contemptuously at Nero and followed Anicetus out. Burrus shook his head, as if there were nothing further to say, and also left, closing the door quietly on the trembling, pathetic boy who saw himself as the living god on earth.

When it was too late for anyone to hear him, Nero said to the empty room, "But what will the people think when the deed is done?" He was stirred from his paralysis and stumbled about the room, dragging his cover and mumbling to himself. Suddenly he was struck with an idea. He rushed to the bed and found the dagger he slept with for protection. Holding it out of sight behind him, he went to the door, opened it a bit and spoke to the centurion. "What is the name of my mother's messenger?" he asked.

"Agerinus," said the centurion.

"Bring him to me. I want to have a word in private with him."

"Yes, sir!" he said. And in a few minutes he returned accompanied by the messenger, who looked as frightened as he did earlier.

When they were alone, Nero produced the dagger. He tossed it on the floor in front of the puzzled man. "Pick it up," he ordered.

Agerinus hesitated.

"Go on, pick it up. I command you."

And Agerinus stooped reluctantly to take the weapon in his hand. As soon as he had hold of it, Nero shouted at the top of his voice. "Help! Murder! Help!

Instantly, the centurion burst into the room, two of his men close behind. "He tried to kill me!" screamed Nero.

Agerinus stared in dumb disbelief as the guards seized him and disarmed him. "He was sent by my mother to attack me. He had this dagger hidden in his clothing."

"We'll hold him in custody, sir, until you've decided what you want done with him."

"No, no, I don't want him held. I want him killed. I want him killed right away. Do you understand!"

The guards looked at one another and then at the centurion.

"There is some mistake," said Agerinus, who could barely talk. "I meant no harm. I did nothing."

The centurion could see that the man was harmless, but

he could also see that it was pointless to raise an objection. The scene was too incriminating. And who would take the word of an ordinary man against the word of the emperor himself.

"Take him away," shouted Nero. "Take him away and do as I say. If my orders are not carried out instantly, I'll charge you all with treason and conspiracy."

They dragged the meek, protesting soul away and closed the door. He listened as they made their way clumsily down the corridor. And then a few minutes later he heard through his window, from somewhere in the night, a single shriek of pain, followed by an awful silence. And then he threw himself face down on the bed to await the news that would make him, at last, sole master of the empire and of himself.

# XLVI

The news of the boat's fate spread rapidly. Crowds of people swarmed down to the beaches and milled about the wharves exchanging fragments of information and rumor. They raised their hands to the heavens and cried out for the sea to spare the emperor's mother. They wept and prayed for her deliverance. Some even waded into the water, as if they wanted to reach out for her. They were frightened and confused. What could have happened? What treachery was afoot? Was the daughter of Germanicus really dead?

Among the people who wandered the beaches and the streets of the village was Helios, a loyal slave of Antonia's. He prayed not for the woman's safety but for her destruction. He was too familiar with her treachery and with the grief she had brought to the household of Sulla and Antonia.

In his quest for accurate news, Helios made his way surreptitiously toward the imperial villa. He came upon it from the side away from the sea, along a narrow path that followed a terraced slope above the vast collection of build-

311

ings and gardens. Soon he was within thirty yards of a small meadow just outside the rear gate. There he saw a group of men gathered. Perhaps twenty-five of them. They were being given instructions by a broad-shouldered man, whom he recognized as Anicetus.

He stepped cautiously from the path into a grove of trees and approached even closer, until he could hear what was being said. "When we arrive at the villa by Lake Lucrine, Sextus and Lucius will form a perimeter about the place to prevent any escape. If there are any guards, we will confront them directly and take them into custody. I will go to the door with the rest of you, and we will force our way into the house. There should be no witnesses."

With a pounding heart, Helios escaped into the shadows to carry his news back to Antonia. He guessed immediately they were planning to kill Agrippina. There seemed no way she could escape.

He made his own way down the slope and raced back through the village and around the wailing, milling crowd that cluttered the beaches, harboring his secret, sweating as much from excitement as from physical exertion. Bursting into Aelia's villa, he cried out "Mistress! Mistress!"

Antonia appeared a moment later. She took him into a small library and locked the door. When they were alone and secure and he had caught his breath, he told her what he had overheard from the crowd and from the men gathered by Anicetus. "She was aboard a boat provided for her by her son. It sank in the bay. It broke up without explanation. Some of the crew have survived. And Agrippina has apparently made it safely to her villa by Lake Lucrine. But Anicetus and his men are going there now to kill her."

Antonia was stunned. It should have been satisfying news but now she felt sick and appalled. What kind of a world could permit this sort of brutality? And how much a part of it was she for wanting it to happen? Her mind was a chaos of conflicting thoughts. She should act. She should do nothing. Soon it would all be over. And then perhaps there would be a chance of seeing her husband once again—perhaps! She had the sudden sinking sensation that it would never happen. Sulla was too good. The world was too evil. And it wasn't only Agrippina. It was all of them, all the beastly Julians and Claudians. They were devouring one another, wolves in their desparation, ripping off their limbs, killing their kin. Would her young son be wolf or victim? She wanted him to be neither.

"We've got to warn her!" Antonia said quickly.

"What?" said the astounded Helios. "Warn her? But why? We want her dead!"

"Because if we don't warn her, we are as good as accomplices. And I will not be an accomplice to murder. The killing must cease."

"What shall I do?" he asked.

"Run to her villa. Warn her that Anicetus and his men are coming. Perhaps she can manage to save herself. She has outwitted or outmaneuvered enemies in the past. But tell her she will not find refuge in this house. I have suffered too much from her."

And Helios was off again, rushing through the early dawn along familiar paths and an old shortcut toward the villa where, so many years ago, he had played with the children of the slaves of Germanicus.

# XLVII

"Why hasn't Agerinus returned?" asked Agrippina. She was lying on her bed, her head propped against a bolster. Only old Europa was in the room with her. "I don't understand. He should have brought a message from my son."

"Perhaps he never got there," said Europa. "Perhaps something happened to him on the way. The place is full of strangers, what with the holidays and all. He could have been waylaid and robbed or even killed."

"No," Agrippina said. "I'm sure he got there. Something else has happened. Send another messenger. Find out what is going on, Europa. Oh, what a horrible night. What treacheries I have suffered!" She rolled her head from side to side. "I must know what my son is doing, what he is thinking. I can't believe that he tried to kill me. Perhaps it wasn't he, after all. Perhaps it was Seneca and Burrus."

"Or Poppaea," suggested Europa.

"Yes, yes, that's it. Poppaea seduced him into it. It's easy for a woman to manipulate a man, especially when he loves her. I'll forgive him. He'll make it up to me. Everything will be all right. Go, send another messenger to my son's villa. Give him the same message I gave to Agerinus. And tell him to hurry."

Europa shuffled out of the bedroom, her blue robe gathered about her sagging body. But in a few moments she returned. "There is a messenger here from Antonia," she said.

"From Antonia?" said Agrippina, sitting up in her bed. She looked startled. "I don't understand."

"He insists on seeing you right away. He says he has desperate news."

"Then send him in, quickly!"

Helios was brought in. His breathing was labored and his face was drenched with sweat. Without preliminaries he blurted out Antonia's message.

"What men are they?" Agrippina asked. "The Praetorian Guard?"

"No," said Helios. "An ordinary band. Anicetus's own men, I assume. I saw them assembled near the imperial villa with my own eyes. I heard his instructions with my own ears. They plan to surround the villa, arrest and remove any guards, and break in. He said they should leave no witnesses. It can only mean one thing."

She did not get out of the bed. She stared at him for a long time in silence as the reality of what he was saying seeped in. Then she sighed. And the sigh became a moan. "Would they dare kill me, the daughter of Germanicus, the mother of Nero? Would they dare?"

Europa wrung her hands and walked quickly back and forth with aimless little steps. "Come, madam," she said, "come, you must get out of here. Quickly."

Through the open door they could see a cluster of slaves, several women, then suddenly they were gone. Europa went to the door and shouted. And then she ran down the corridor, still shouting.

Agrippina looked at Helios. They were alone in the room. "Why would Antonia do this?" she asked. "Why would she warn me, after all I've done to her?"

"Because she will not participate in your death, even with her silence," he said.

And Agrippina threw back her head and wailed. "Oh, oh

315

wicked gods and ironies! I should have been blessed with a
son as noble as Antonia. My struggles would have been
worthwhile." She got out of her bed and looked frantically
about. She began to pull the rings from her fingers and the
necklace from her throat. "Here! Here! Take these to your
mistress. Tell her I will pay her for her warning."

Suddenly she was on her hands and knees searching for
something under the bed. It was a beautiful chest, set with
mosaics of ivory. She carried it to Helios. "Here, take these
to Antonia. Jewels. Precious stones. A part, at least, of my
doomed fortune. Now go! Flee quickly before they come.
There is nothing you can do for me."

The frightened slave backed out of the room almost
knocking over Europa, who came in crying, "The slaves
have all gone. All of them. They've heard the news. Not
one of them is anywhere in sight. They are afraid for their
lives. There are to be no witnesses." Agrippina's shoulders
slumped. She sat down on the bed. "Of course. No witnesses for a deed so dark as this. My orders would have
been precisely the same as Nero's. We're very much alike,
you know." She was slipping into a dream.

"But you too can flee, madam. You can get to the hills.
You still have friends."

"No, Europa," she said, resignation thickening in her
voice, "I have no friends, no will to flee. I have only a
son." She crawled back into her bed and drew the covers
about her. "Let them come for me, and if they dare, let
them kill me. Come, Europa, sit by me, hold my hand. Of
all my slaves, you have loved me best."

"You have been good to me," said Europa through her
tears.

"I have not been good to many. But sweet friend. You
mustn't stay. Take your freedom and go. Live out your life
with a little dignity and tell the world I died alone and
bravely."

Europa cried and threw herself into Agrippina's arms.
But Agrippina pushed her gently away, urging her to go.
"Hurry, now! Hurry!" she whispered. "There will be an
end to all this soon."

And in another moment Europa, too, was gone, and

Agrippina was alone in the stillness of her room. From a shelf she took a piece of parchment and a pen. In a simple sentence she declared her intention of granting Europa her freedom. She paused and then wrote: "And to my son, whom I have always loved, all the rest of my possessions."

When she looked up, she saw Anicetus standing in the doorway, broad-shouldered enough to fill it.

Agrippina squared her shoulders. "If my son has sent you to inquire about my health, tell him I am refreshed and well."

Anicetus and several other men stepped into the room. One of them had a club in his hand.

"If you have come to do me harm, you cannot have orders from my son. He would never issue such orders. Never! And if you murder me, he'll have you all destroyed because he loves me! He loves me!"

They closed around her. Her eyes were wide, but she made no move to escape. The man with the club suddenly hit her across the skull. She screamed and fell back, but she still was concious, the blood streaming down her face. Their swords were drawn. With the last of her strength she rose up again to face them and ripped away her gown to reveal the nakedness of her body. "Strike!" she cried. "Strike me here in the womb that bore Nero!" And they fell upon her with their swords, stabbing her in the abdomen and the chest and the throat. She slipped to the floor and there let out a final sigh, and with it her life.

317

Lightning Source UK Ltd.
Milton Keynes UK
UKOW051501010312

188186UK00001B/117/A